Future echoes in the dark

By Robert Turner

Darksight Publishing

Future echoes in the dark
First published in the UK June 2006
By Darksight Publishing
PO Box 171
Saffron Walden
Essex, CB10 9AH
www.darksightpublishing.faithweb.com

A catalogue record for this book is available
From the British library.
ISBN 13 digit: 978-0-9552631-0-1
ISBN 10 Digit: 0-9552631-0-7

1 3 5 7 9 10 8 6 4 2

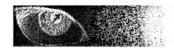

Cast of Characters

Past Memories

Borrador - the spirit
Cat - Novice Master
Celene - High Priestess
Cherish - Training Master
Desidra (Desi)
Edowyn - Security
Grete - Alchemist
Harry - The bowyer
Jho
Penny
Petersen
Rozz
Sanarah - Healer
Sergeant Neville Sharpe
Spike - The swordsman
Stuart - The wimp
Vergoth - Maji

Modern Day

Detective Jane Goody
Detective Inspector Marlow
Detective Wendy Lafley
Jenny the Matron - Troll
Matthew Rider - A student
Mick - The chef
Miranda - M.I.5 agent
Tamzin Scott - A modern priestess

Dedication

To my loving wife, whose encouragement, patience and grammatical awareness I have taxed to the limit, I give my thanks. She has supported me throughout this endeavour and without her words of wisdom this may never have happened. Also thanks go to the rest of my family who have supported my mad bouts of writing and guided me to remove a comma or two.

Note: This text uses some terms which are unfamiliar in these more enlightened times. I will try to elaborate on these here.

Majick – Now written as Magic.

Majickal, majickally – something that is of Majick in nature.

Maji – A person who uses Majick to create effects.

Silves – Like an Elf of popular culture.

Darksight – The ability to see heat emissions as another colour (only visible in the dark).

Different text formats are used in this novel to create a difference in the way people speak. What the character Merith hears, and how she interprets the sounds initially, is un-interpreted and then develops into what looks like bad spelling. This is what she is trying to understand (and therefore deliberate) and is part of the text. Finally *italics* is used exclusively for Thieves' Cant.

Breviarium

Capitulus	Titulus	Folius
Unus	Pullus nocturus	9
Duos	Cogitatoris	25
Tria	Lacative domini	34
Quattuor	Nectar divinia	49
Quinque	Recoperatoris anciles	57
Sex	Nuvos metamorphoses	77
Septem	Exercitium metamorphoses	87
Octem	Sollicitus congressionium	101
Novem	Doni miraculum	117
Decim	Raptus, Necare, Ultionis	136
Undecim	Expiscari depopulor	141
Duodecim	Resipivi	154
Tredecim	Envestigatus bibliotheca	162
Quattuordecim	Ingressus bibliothece	182
Quindecim	Exploro bibliothece	195
Sedecim	Ulterior dimication	205
Septumdecim	Fallux divina	221

Unus - Pullus nocturus

(Radio Cambridgeshire news item)
On the local news this lunchtime, Police are hunting the attacker of a teenage girl who was subjected to a serious sexual assault near a Cambridgeshire village. The 15-year-old victim was attacked and left for dead sometime between 6pm on Monday night and 6am Tuesday morning. Police say her ordeal went on for some time.

Detective Inspector Mike Marlow, who is leading the hunt for the attacker, said; "This was a very nasty assault on a 15-year-old girl who must have been terrified during her ordeal. The man responsible is dangerous and we need to catch him as soon as possible."

Supt Alan Butler, head of operational policing across Cambridgeshire, said; "My officers are determined to catch this man but it is vital that people living in Fulborne help us. I would urge anyone who was out and about in the village between 6pm on Monday night to 6am Tuesday morning to think about anything they might have seen which could help with this inquiry. I want people to come and talk to us, no matter how small or insignificant people think their information may be."

Supt Butler added; "Thankfully, this type of offence doesn't happen very often, but it is understandable that women will be frightened. Our advice would be, 'Don't let it affect what you do but take some sensible precautions. Make sure someone always knows where you are and if possible avoid walking home alone.' "

Anyone with any information is asked to contact Cambridge CID on 0115 4440999 or Crimestoppers on 0800 555 111.

Meanwhile, the victim is said to be in a comfortable state in Addenbrooks hospital. A hospital spokeswoman has reported that she is now stable but has remained unconscious since being admitted. We will update this as soon as we find out more......

(News item ends)

Blue…. Heart beating.

Blue…. Time passing by.

Blue…. Each beat sending another pain through my already overloaded system.

Blue…. I struggle to open my eyes.

Blue…. Through bleary lids I saw brilliant flashes of blue light. I tried to move my arms but the wrenching feeling of pain and a tremendous weight on top of them, dragging them down, stopped me. Noise blaring of a thousand chattering women, sounds of metal grinding against metal and of stone against stone and then, in the middle of it all, a strange sound filtered down through my consciousness. A strange trilling like a bird, repetitive and high pitched. It seemed unbelievably to match my own heartbeat.

The overwhelming pain began to take over all other senses, crowding out all of the noises, smells and feelings. I sought to meditate, to pass into a trance-like state to shut out the outside world. Slowly I started to block out the pain, my breathing deepened and I began to organise my thoughts. The realisation hit suddenly; all of my memories were gone. I had nothing there to remember. I floundered around in my own mind and had to just concentrate on pain management.

(Further Radio Cambridgeshire news item)

In the local news this evening, police are hunting the attacker of a teenage girl who was subjected to a serious sexual assault near a Cambridgeshire village. The 15-year-old victim was attacked and left for dead sometime between 6pm on Monday night and 6am Tuesday morning.

Supt Alan Butler, head of operational policing across Cambridgeshire, said; "My officers are determined to catch this man, but it is vital that people living in Fulborne help us. I would urge anyone who was out and about in the village between 6pm on Monday night to 6am Tuesday morning to think about anything they might have seen which could help with this inquiry."

He later added "We have yet to identify the girl. We are hoping a description of her clothing will aid us in finding out who her family are. She was dressed in hand made clothing, in a black robe, similar to a monk's habit, with a striking emblem of a dagger with lightning sparking off the dagger. The emblem was embroidered in the collar of the robe. This identifying mark must be easily identifiable to the family or friends. She must have had this garment specially made for her, though possibly she may be of foreign origin given the strange clothing and items found at the scene. We believe the assailant or assailants may have been injured in the attack; hospitals in the local area have been alerted to this possibility."

Police feel that this is a vital clue to her identity and are hopeful that they will be able to assist in identifying the victim. Supt. Butler added; "I want people to come and talk to us, however small or insignificant people think their information may be."

A spokeswoman from Addenbrooks has previously reported that the girl is stable, but unconscious, and is responding well to treatment.

Anyone with any information is asked to contact Cambridge CID on 0115 4440999 or Crimestoppers on 0800 555 111.

(News item ends)

The noises continued. I was aware of them now; something had broken my reverie. I felt the pain tighten in my wrist as if something had touched it. Pain lanced through my hand and arm. A voice said something soothing to me and I felt my arm being lowered again. I sensed a numbing flow out from my hand and, as I began to float, a distant voice (the same voice) called to me. I couldn't respond because I had floated away on a beautiful blue stream into the blue sunset.

(Further Radio Essex news item)

In the headlines tonight, Cambridgeshire Police are still appealing for witnesses and relatives regarding the girl found just outside of Fulborn. She has yet to regain consciousness. Relatives are being sought to identify the girl from her clothing.

Anyone with any information is asked to contact Cambridge CID on 0115 4440999 or Crimestoppers on 0800 555 111.

(News item ends)

Pain.... Forced me awake, wracking pain across my chest, arms and legs. Voices called to me to alternately sooth me and shout at me.

The whistling and trilling, confusing echoes which faded then came into focus sharply with a bang. I was aware of many hands on me; was I being tortured again as I had been? The focus slipped from my mind.

(Further Radio Cambridgeshire news item)

In the local news this morning, it is reported that the police are releasing further information to assist in the hunt for the attacker of a teenage girl who was subjected to a serious sexual assault near a Cambridgeshire village. The 15-year-old victim was attacked, and left for dead, sometime between 6pm on Monday night and 6am Tuesday morning.

Detective Inspector Mike Marlow, who is leading the hunt for the attacker, said; "This was a very nasty assault on a 15-year-old girl who must have been terrified during her ordeal. The man or group of men responsible are dangerous and we need to catch them as soon as possible."

A more detailed description has been provided to aid in identifying the victim; she is five foot four inches tall, with long straight brown hair. Her eye colour is blue and she has tanned skin. The girl was dressed in hand-made clothing, in a black robe similar to a monk's habit with a striking emblem of a dagger with lightning sparking off the dagger. The emblem was embroidered in the collar of the robes. This identifying mark must be easily identifiable to the family or friends. She must have had this garment specially made for her, although possibly she may be of foreign origins given the strange clothing and items found at the scene. Police feel that this is a vital clue to her identity and are hopeful that they will be able to assist in identifying the victim.

The assailant or assailants may have been injured in the attack. Hospitals in the local area have been alerted to the possibility.

A spokeswoman from Addenbrooks has reported that the girl has had a difficult night, but seems to have recovered to a stable position and is beginning to respond to treatment.

Anyone with any information is asked to contact Cambridge CID on 0115 4440999 or Crimestoppers on 0800 555 111.

(News item ends)

The searing pain had gone. All I was left with were dull aches. Light filtering in through my closed eyelids had pierced through my fitful sleep. Cautiously, I opened one eye a fraction. The light was blinding and I had to blink several times before I began to focus. The first images and sounds didn't make any sense. Again I could hear the strange trilling I had heard before, but this was accompanied by the sounds of the hustle and bustle of a market place, of people moving around and talking indistinctly. I must have been lying down.

Looking up to the roof I could see flagstones set into it with metal bands, presumably to support them. There were also strange round lanterns set into them, which gave off an odd white glow. I realised they must be lit by a continual light spell, majick. This reassured me, as I realised that I must be in the care of my Temple or at least some healers who employed some great majick. Above my head was an odd white metal cone with a grey ball set into it; it hung off of an arm attached to the wall. Another larger arm (thicker in diameter) held a funny shaped box of white colour, with a black window. This box had what looked like a bone attached to it by means of a piece of rope. Very confusing....

I glanced around and could see wall tapestries draped at the end of the bed and to the side of me. The other two walls were yellow, with white boxes running horizontally across them. The tapestries had woodland figures on them - figures that looked like Silves, dwarves and woodland animals. I couldn't read the story these told (there wasn't a battle or any sort of triumph) and I didn't understand the significance of them. They blocked off the sight of a much larger room, one which must have been maybe four times the size of this little space. I looked around and saw a funny box that was making a trilling sound. There must have been a bird trapped in it, but I couldn't see it. The box was black with many ropes coming off the front of it. Figures flashed on the front with numbers that read "Fifty two" with a red symbol flashing beside them. I realised one of the ropes trailed its way to my finger and ended with a strange box on the end of my finger. This thing seemed to glow pink at its end. I didn't know what it was but it wasn't hurting me, so I left it for now. I turned my hand over and saw there was another odd rope attached to my arm. It was made of a tube-like glass but, as I moved my hand, it moved with it. Very odd....

Behind me there were various odd wooden chests and robes with illustrated drawings on them, which were unlike anything that I had seen before - using strange lettering and symbols. I moved around on the bed and checked myself over. Someone had taken my robes and slip. The only garment I was wearing was a thin sort of dress, which was comfortable but was not something I was used to. I had bruising across my whole chest as if I had been whacked across it with a flat stick. There was bruising across most of the rest of my body, but I didn't know why. There was no reason to anything here, and it disturbed me that I couldn't remember anything. My head felt foggy as if stuffed with rags, and I was generally feeling groggy. The noise of people was all around, so I called out for help!

The tapestries parted and I could see through them a man holding what appeared to be a large parchment. He was dressed in black and wore a flat black hat. The hat had a black and white trim and a crest on the front, although I only managed to get a brief glimpse before I had the shock of my life. A small black troll (a big humanoid with black rock like skin and tufts of curled black moss) stepped in through the gap in the tapestry. I screamed as loud as I could and tried to get out of the bed. However, the bedding stopped me and as I struggled against it the man shot up and rushed to be beside me. The troll also moved over to me and, in a soothing voice, said words to me that I didn't understand. They both held me down as I struggled to move away. The troll called out something and I could see others coming toward me. This time they were humans; were they coming to my rescue?

I knew I was shaking, I was also too weak and hungry to struggle against them and I slowly calmed down. As I relaxed, they let go of my arms and stood around the bed looking at me. There were four women, all dressed in white, but the sole man was dressed in black; was he the Maji? They looked at me, puzzled, the man spoke in a more urgent voice words which sounded meaningless, "Tel uss ur nam sso as oui chan fin ur parints. Cann u rember ennyfing?" The troll (she was a female) spoke softly to me, with words which made little sense; "Dare, dare noe gerlie shoe gest lie shtill an teel us ur nam hay?" She said as if it was a question, but it sounded so odd. I turned to the man in black and asked him; "What is happening? Who are you all? Are you healers using your majick on me?"

I began to feel emotional about all of this. They are speaking but in a foreign language. I didn't know anyone of them, but why can't they understand me? I could feel the tears welling in my eyes, but I didn't want to let them go yet. "What is your name?" I asked the male, almost pleading to be understood. A name popped into my head and, reassured by this, I pointed to myself and said, "Merith."

They all nodded, the man said "Merith ouate?"

I suppose it was my turn to be confused, I pointed to him and said, "Who are you?"

He smiled as if he understood, he pointed to himself and said "Reg."

It settled me to be understood for the first time, if only because I said my name. It was my turn to smile, I pointed to him and said, "Reg," and then back to myself to say, "Merith."

He fished around in a pocket and brought out a small book; using a coloured stick, he began to make squiggles in it. The others seemed to relax and the troll spoke softly to them and ushered them away. She stood as the man sat beside my bed. He said a few words to me, "Ver doo u leve?" and waited for a response. Then he said something that sounded like, "Doo u spek enne Anglish?" 'The term 'Anglish' sounded like the name used for the county I lived in.

"Anglish?" I replied.

Then he said, "Français?"

I stared back at him and shrugged my shoulders, the name meant nothing to me.

"German?"

I said back to him, "I'm sorry but I don't know any of them, but maybe if I could remember something?"

He looked at me blankly, turned and said something to the troll; "Zo, Vat doo u mek ov eet? Et zounded ay bid lik Anglish bud ay verry ode vhay ov speking. Ay koodn't ondershtand enne ov et."

She said something back, "Nno, mestr ay dun't noe, aal ay noe ees, nn de lest tem yers ay been verkin ere ay never sin eenytin lik er!"

The emotions were getting stirred up again and I felt the welling of tears in my eyes. I could hear them talking but couldn't understand. As I watched the discussion, tears flowed down my cheeks and I did nothing to stop them. Everything felt unfamiliar to me; it was all wrong, nothing made sense. I looked at them bewildered.

There was a funny roaring sound and then a tiny voice appeared to come from a small black box that hung from his jacket "Base too zeven too, base too zeven too, enythin too r'port Reg?" He picked it up and started to talk into it, "zevn doo doo bese, ahh yez de gane doe en zee do hs voken an es dalking. Hav sdarted prelimnary cuestons bud kannot mak zence oud ov er anzers. Name givn bud onnly ay furst nam. Vat ish de ee tee aye onn de innvestagashun tem?" I realised at that moment, that indeed he is a Maji. Perhaps he was one of the powerful ones that still existed, maybe he brought me here?

The tiny voice started up again. Maybe this was a captive demon, an evil little gremlin who was bound to this Maji's wishes. "Ee Tee Aye prob aan our ayway Reg Kep aan aye onn er fore nowe, leve et up too dhe teme. Over."

The man (Reg?) spoke into the box for a final time. "Roger, vil doo. Oute."

I looked at him and he looked back at me with sympathetic eyes. He drew breath to speak but, before the sound came out, something behind distracted him. Suddenly a blinding flash of light exploded at me, blinding me temporarily. Shrieking, I dragged the covers over my face and curled up into a ball. There was shouting and the stamping of feet near me. A tussle was going on with the calling of questioning voices and more flashes of light. Above it, all I heard clearly the strong firm voice of the troll shouting orders and commanding attention. The troll was strange. I don't remember what a troll was but I knew that this was what my mind was telling me. This troll was something to be feared, she was probably held under the same thrall as the demon in his box and could probably do all sorts of majick.

The noises subsided, the voices calling slowly moved away and the flashing stopped. I stayed curled up for what seemed like hours until I felt someone sit down on the bed beside me. The voice of the troll, so commanding before now, had a worried soothing tone. "Shey gerl, dont ewe vorry bout dose pressmn, dey teem do ave gottn hold ov ay tory an eell deey vant ish vat dey cn ged. Aye hav tome food foer jeu."

The smell of food hit me, I didn't know what it was but it smelled delicious. I lifted my head over the covers to see a well-built man dressed a bit like a fool. He had all sorts of colours on his hat and hose, but his tunic was white. The man smiled a wide friendly smile and proffered up a white plate filled with steaming goodness.

He said strange words to me in an accent different from the others and I recognised a few words - it was like he was from England but with a difficult accent to follow. In a way, he sounded like my own Petersen from back home in the Temple and perhaps he looked a bit like him too. The food was more important and, as Petersen always used to say, it is too important to waste. Greedily I held out my hands to take the plate, but the troll moved a funny table-like thing in front of me. It was wooden but it had a white and blue patterned top, smooth to the touch and slightly warm. The man placed the food on to the table and offered me a spiked piece of metal and a knife. The knife was obviously blunt and the spike? I didn't know what to make of it.

I smiled at him and moved myself into a more comfortable position, he smiled back and said something to the food. I smelled the food on the plate and grinned back. Picking up the knife, I tried to use it to pick up the tomato sauce. With some success I tucked into the meal, but I began to wish they had a spoon. I realised how hungry I was as I tried to eat.

The man watched me with some amusement. He picked up the spiky thing and said, "Fuk" and mimicked some one putting it into their mouth. Confused, I looked back and then the realisation dawned on me. It must be what they use to eat with. Feeling stupid, I took it from him and began to shovel the tomatoes and funny shell-like things into my mouth. I pointed at them and said, "What are these?" He looked at me strangely as if he understood a little and said, "Pasta schells inn a bolonaise sase ala vegy"

This made absolutely no sense to me but what ever they were called it was gorgeous, but no meat? I repeated back what he said "Pasta schells inn a bolonaise sase ala vegy" to him.

Smiling he said, "Yeass that's goood" he turned to the Troll and asked her a question, "Zao whads er nam?

She replied, "Merith," and moved towards the end of the bed. I looked up at the sound of my name. She began to pull the tapestries across to enclose me again as she did so.

He turned back to me and pointed at me, "Merith?" I nodded vigorously and pointed back.

"Mick aim the sheff arond herr," he replied.

"Mick," I looked at him and pointed - he nodded vigorously in reply.

He turned and stepped out of the enclosure I was in, pulling the tapestries together as he went. I was left with the troll and the food. I quickly set about eating the meal, although I missed the meat it was delicious and very different to the food I had back home.

Once I finished I felt tired again, I tried to remember anything I could about my past to see if I had any memory of how I ended up here. I knew everything was strange but I didn't know why. It was like I had been scooped up into the air and landed in a strange country. The troll moved the wheeled table out of the way and moved to beside me. She said a few soothing words and picked up from the wall a box with a clear lid. From inside it she lifted a box with a pointed end. She came forward to me and tried to place it in my ear.

I moved away from her and said, "No!" She said some soothing words, which sounded like she needed to do this, so I tried to relax. She put something cold into my ear and the box chirped. She seemed pleased with me and put it back up onto the wall. She picked up a board at the end of my bed and wrote something down on it. She then lifted up the plate and began to leave whilst speaking to me. Not a word was understood, but I nodded anyway.

On the bed, I sat cross-legged and unconsciously began to slip into a trance. Inside my memories, there seemed to be thin veils all around as I tried to latch hold of a single event or happening. Memories flowed unbidden as if from an orator or a book of consciousness....

Someone once said to me, "Everything goes silent before the storm," and tonight the silence was unearthly. The night was black as the deepest well, as thick clouds obscured the light of the dance of the night sky. Across the town I could see the heat trails of the multitude of houses as they cooled down in the night, with the swirling vortexes of the air trailing off from the chimneys as the fires burned low. The airspace was still; untroubled by wind or even birds. The heat of the day was now trapped under the blanket of clouds, which promised a welcome rain. The thunderstorms, which would follow this gathering, would throw the fields asunder - but the days that followed would dry the crops that were the lifeblood of the land.

The only sound to be heard was my heart trying to beat its way out of my chest. The pounding of the blood as it pulsed through my body, was loud and distinct whilst it pumped in two distinct phases. The roar of the blood in my ears made me certain that everyone within a mile could hear.

I found myself hanging twenty feet up in the air and dangling from a thin ledge with my fingertips screaming to be released from the pressure. The effort of trying to be as silent as the wind while I bore the pain was excruciating. The wall, rough against my ear, was sheer, almost un-climbable for most people.

It wasn't that I had stopped to have second thoughts about what I was doing. The merchant I had targeted was, as I had discovered, far richer than he should have been. Since he was out of town for a while I thought that I might lighten his worries of keeping all of his ill-gotten gains. He wasn't using this wealth and I believed that I could help him find a better use for it - at the very least, it would be a good sacrifice.

On my part I didn't need the money; I was rich already. No, it was the challenge that I was after. Indeed, I suppose that this was ingrained within me and that I was required to do this every so often to keep up my skills and to please my Goddess. There was also the chance, here, of finding the prize I was after.

No, it was not second thoughts that halted me, it was the Chipping Walden watch. This town was big enough to employ some old buggers who, instead of guarding the town gates, wandered the streets at night. They weren't a physical threat - at least, not to any capable thief. You had to be pretty useless at virtually everything else to become one. The pay was terrible and the hours were long. Many a watchman has been found curled up on the street due to violence or the harsh elements. They were, however, good at running away and blaring a whistle or shouting. One alarm and the whole town were upon you, after you, chasing your heels.

The watchman was standing with his lantern on the doorstep, sorting a pipe out. In the darkness his lantern lit a wide space in which he could see. He stood, almost hunched over, peering down at it. Taking an age over it while knocking it against the doorframe.....

The stench of him wafted up to me, stale tobacco, dried sweat, cheap alcohol, and the worst of all crimes! - Bad breath. He took out a small folding knife and scraped out the pipe bowl. Knocked it out again.... Blowing down the pipe.... Knocking it out again....

AHHHHHHHHHGH get on with it!

I almost screamed with the agony of hanging on. My muscles were beginning to rebel against me so I began to gently flex the muscles to keep the blood flowing. This was something my climbing instructor Cherish had taught me to do. In training, I could keep this up for hours holding onto a ledge smaller than this and have done so loads of times, but not for a while. There always seemed something else to do.

The watchman began to push his tobacco into the pipe. It was a harsh smelling cheap tobacco, probably with several cheap blends (and a bit of hemp within it, no doubt). I never really did get into pipe smoking as it hurt my lungs, and I have only ever done it for show. It was a thoroughly disgusting habit that was obviously doing this man no good. He paused to look around him, seeming to think for a while, and then slowly sat down.

I could have killed him right there. I was so annoyed with him. Killing can be a part of my life. I have been trained to defend myself and move with sharp reflexes; I could easily have taken down a less experienced fighter. In this position, I could have dropped a throwing knife straight into his neck. This would certainly kill him, but not immediately. Besides, if he moved suddenly it could just injure him. I toyed with the idea for some time and, although it would be interesting to watch, I certainly wouldn't want to have it on my conscience. Nor would I like to give up my interrupted opportunity so easily.

Finally, he lit the pipe from the lantern! Son of a AHHHHHgh!!

The smell of the pipe, sweet, cloying smoke curled up from below. How dare he! How dare he light up on duty! How dare he do it whilst sitting on this rich merchant's step? He should be going around protecting the town's property from the thieves and vagabonds – well, other thieves and vagabonds at least! At that moment I hated him for being a lazy old git. He should be getting on with his job, and if I were employing him I'd fire him and fine him his final wages.

Thankfully he stood up. I thought a silent prayer up to Ichmarr for this little task. He stretched his arms out wide, gave a yawn, picked up his lantern and mumbled off into the night taking his light with him. When he was out of sight, I continued to hang tight until his footsteps were only a memory.

Finally the darkness enveloped me; I had chosen this night well. My muscles needed to be flexible for the next movement, so I released one arm and shook it out and did the same with the other. There was a ledge for my feet somewhere and my feet began to feel around. Eventually, they found it and I continued my climb up to the window ledge I had been aiming for. All of the other openings in the building were shuttered firmly shut; some with bars to stop intrusion into the building. This window, crafted out of the finest ash-wood, was small too small for most people to get through and, at this height with an almost sheer face to climb, was practically impossible for most thieves to get to. With a thin blade I checked around the window to find the way to open it. There was a small catch and I pushed it across to release the window. When released, I swung the window open and struggled through the tiny hole. This man was so rich he was able to glaze some of his windows - what luxury! I carefully pulled myself through and placed my feet on to the floor.

No noises, no-one in the room.... I strained my ears to hear if there was any noise in the whole building. Where would he keep it?

Carefully, I moved around the room carefully placing my feet, tensed against the pressure. Time and time again I had practised moving across the ground in specially prepared rooms that had boards set to creak at the slightest pressure. It was in moments like these that this training paid off. I automatically tensed each footfall, sensing whether the board would move and countering such movement. Moving, I continued waiting until the watchman's steps were a distance memory and relaxed. Then, noiselessly in case of others in the house, I concentrated on my search of this room.

I had been in this room before. I had heard from a contact that a merchant, a nobleman, had acquired a special and remarkable hat. This hat, she assured me, would make the wearer appear to be someone else - indeed, whomsoever they wanted to look like. This would be useful to someone wanted in five counties for theft and conspiracy to theft. Not that I had anything to do with it!

The easiest part was to get this merchant's attention. I was blessed with a slim build and a remarkable figure, long brown hair and with some chemical help, sparkling eyes. For me it was easy to lead him astray. We laughed and joked about the other merchants and their woes and, as the evening wore on, he invited me back to his house where he continued to ply me with fine wines. His manners were impeccable and it took real determination for him to forget his wife for the evening. He even showed me the hat. To entertain me, he used it to impersonate important men from the town. It was remarkable, the hat could even change the voice of the individual! The merchant was such a kind man, such a stupid man, and such a short experience.

His servants kicked me out in the morning. He had awakened with a start and had risen quickly from the bed. Without a word, he left the room and I was barely able to open my eyes from my meditative state before his exit. While the servants were locking up the place, they slated me for every evil under the sun, I was a slut, a whore, and a harlot! He deserved this and more, the coward!

Ahh! There it is; a crevice behind a picture of himself. It was so vain of the man to hide his most valuable possessions behind a visage of himself. Was this so that he would still be looking after them, when he was not there?

Only a Silvesi could have found this crevice so easily. Darksight is a wonderful ability to possess and, it is said, that when the gods made the earth they hadn't remembered to light the sky – and only heated the stones. When the Silves arrived, being the first, they had to adapt to their surroundings and they developed this ability to see the heat from their surroundings. Some fish and snakes have kept this ability and the creatures that developed from them. But, by the time the humans arrived, the gods had remembered to light the world with the sun for the day and the moon for the night.

The picture was fixed to the wall somehow, obviously having a hidden hinge with a catch. Where would he have hidden it? Would it be in plain sight, right in front of me? But where?

His signet ring – he was wearing it when he left me to go into this room, but not when he came back?

On the mantle below the painting, a mason had carved an ornate archway out of marble with a large keystone. This had a large and clumsy brass plate, which seemed out of keeping with the grandness. The brass plate had a depression in it similar in shape to the signet ring. There was a round crack around the depression. In the manner in which I was looking at it, the plate was more pronounced that it otherwise would be. This was meant to be turned, but how, without the ring?

There are a few tools of the trade, which we are not allowed to divulge otherwise the Crown and its representatives would get a little more alerted to us than we would wish. Hard putty is one of these. If they could find out how to make it themselves, they might ban the materials it is made from. An alchemist, many years ago, had first made it, but had stuck her hand to the bench with the first compounded material. Luckily for her, a priestess had been going about her devotions in the bedroom above the workroom and had heard her cries. The alchemist was so grateful for her help that, with a little persuasion, she agreed to join the Temple and work for us making the substance.

The putty came in two different sticks which, when mixed together in equal quantities, made the substance ROCK hard! Mixing it in my hands I placed it into the cavity carefully ensuring that the putty would only stick to the depression and not the rest of the plate. I sculpted it into a small mound and set a chain link into it to form a perfect key. The mixture hardens and turns grey - all I now had to do was to wait!

It is in moments like these that my mind tends to wander off and do a bit of 'window-shopping'. It is a wonder that I ever get anything done! Around me, the room had luscious red walls finished with dark oak panelling. It was furnished with opulent furniture to make the kind of office a merchant doesn't really need, but wants to show off to his friends. He had obviously had a penchant for metal trinkets as I could see that the desk was littered with the gold plated equipment of a lord's office.

From the trinkets' heat patterns, I could tell that they were not real gold. The patterns of how the metals released their heat in the dark allowed me to distinguish which metal they were and, with my Darksight, I could see that the majority looked like lead with a hint of gold. Often, during the long nights of the Temple, I would heat up different materials just to see what they looked like as they cooled. I loved to watch the flow of heat off the metals, noticing the eddies and vortices as the heat rose off from the surfaces. I remember sitting in the dark for hours watching the shifting forms that only a Silvesi could see or comprehend.

Jewels have always interested me in the way that they can look so similar to one another in normal light, but look strikingly different in this lack of light. In daylight, only through careful and patient analysis can they be discerned from cheap paste and glass imitations. For this reason, I avoid taking jewels unless I have a useful heat source to shine through them. In this way, all of the differences become apparent as they do scatter the heat differently.

I left off my reverie to check for traps around the mantle and the picture. This was a necessary precaution as many merchants, nobles and rich people are generally very distrusting of those around them. Once during a particularly easy devotion I opened up an innocent looking chest with a simple ward lock on it, only to be thrown back by the searing pain and force of a blow. A crossbow trap with an incredibly obvious latch, if I'd bothered to look for it, was set on the box. It had hit me in the shoulder. The bolt had luckily passed under my collarbone and gone straight through to hit the ceiling. Merely a flesh wound, a deep one, but at least I didn't black out through the pain. Luck was often made by careful preparation; not found through the roll of the dice. It was, however, unlucky for the owner of that house as it mysteriously burned down while standing empty that night.

Finding nothing on or around the mantelpiece to impede me I decided to go ahead, but cautiously. This was a worry, with such a valuable cargo and with such an elaborate way of hiding each part of the crevice and lock it would seem stupid to not trap it. So in turning the 'key' I strained every sense to give me a chance to react to.... whatever?

Sensing, rather than hearing, a click! I spun out of the way in time to see three spinning metal discs spring out between the cracks in the archway. From their starting point I could see that these were meant for the chest of the casual thief. Fortunately, they only hit the particularly unpleasant painting of what presumably was the merchant's father.

I searched again for any traps around each of the stones of the mantelpiece, in the floor and all around the painting. Painstakingly, I looked in vain for any other sign of a trap and, finding none, I continued. Grasping the key again I turned it slowly, with all patience - every sense straining to hear any sign of impending doom. Suddenly, there was a 'click' and I dropped to the floor. As I looked up, I saw the picture slowly slide leftwards out of place to reveal the hiding-hole. Greedily I investigated the contents inside it; I found some papers, five bags of metal coins and a small wooden box. Hmm…. Interesting! I felt into the bags of coins, they were probably gold but I'd have to look at them properly. The box had the hat I had seen earlier in the merchant's greedy hands and I took a moment to dance around the room. The box also had a few jewels in it, which could be useful in the future - big ones too….

Carefully, I recovered the discs that had flown out of the mantelpiece. By close examination of the heat trails and the smell, I could tell that they were coated in paralysing-poison number three, no antidote, expensive and rare. Death within four minutes with the owner of the body choking on his own juices…. Nasty! I left the discs strategically placed in drawers of the desk and in the hiding-hole. I also placed two bags of coins back into the crevice; you have to give the mark a chance to live. I didn't want to steal too much from him and you never know. He might get some of his own medicine. Slipping all of the contents into small pockets in my clothing, I reset all of the mechanisms, replaced the picture and pulled off the makeshift key.

Leaving was even easier. Slide myself back out of the window. Close it tight and wiggle the catch back in place. You might never know I'd been there. It would be a delicious mystery to the merchant to find out that he had been burgled, without any sign of ingress or of access. I picked my way down the wall, slid on a night cloak and made my way back to the Temple. As I landed on my feet the patter of rain began to fill the streets, light at first then the heavier drops began, throwing up the dust of the day into the air.

Duos – Cogitatoris

My mind rebelled against the conscious thought and I broke out of my trance. Strangely, I was sweating. Even stranger was the notion that I knew I didn't usually sweat just after meditation. Memories of my life began to flow from my mind without my bidding. The earliest memories of mine were of a woman dressed in finery unmatched by later experiences. She had silvery eyes and a pointed face; all of her features were pointed from her chin to her nose and she moved in such an elegant way. It was just a glimpse of a memory.

Another memory flashed into my mind, that of a farmyard, with chickens and animals running all around and a man shouting, swearing and falling as he tried to chase me. The houses were wattle and daub, essentially mud-built dwellings, thatched with the straw from the fields. When it rained heavily, as it often did, some of the mud was washed away revealing the wattles that held the walls rigid. The village had plenty of mud and even more wood from the forests surrounding it. It was a farming village on the edge of a vast wood, which had a fearsome reputation for people getting lost, or at least not coming back....

Where was home to me? Certainly not where I started my recollections, nor of that village - what a lovely stink-hole that place was! The only reason for the place's existence was as a boundary where civilization ended and trees began. The village probably hadn't changed for a thousand years and it would stay the same for a thousand more unless something forced it to change. It was built in a circle around a crossroad, with a stream running past the ten buildings to one side of the village. While small, it was large enough to have a watermill to grind the flour.

My real life began very simply when a lady approached my family with an offer I wasn't allowed to refuse. The lady, a priestess, paid my parents for my bond, my labour and demanded that I'd have to go that day. My Mum cried when she heard. My Dad was keen for it to happen, he wanted the gold. I was pushed out into the world in the company of strangers.

It was on that day I found out I was adopted. They never told me I was adopted, and I was never allowed to notice that I was different from the rest of the people. I never did get to play with other children; there were always jobs to do for my Mum. Every day, I had to fetch water and wood from the forest and then there were the animals to feed and eggs to collect. I remember always trying to find jobs to do to avoid being around Dad. He was always drunk and abusive to anyone who came near. Worse, he seemed to hold a particular grudge against me and if I had caused him to be angry, he would spank me over his knee. Sometimes I felt he did it even when I hadn't done anything; he just wanted to hurt someone. Late at night I would be woken up by the shouting and screaming of them arguing and fighting. I would wake to find her bruised and crying, still cleaning up the debris from the night before. She always denied anything was wrong and would send me into the forest to fetch more firewood.

The Temple paid good money for me. Children are, after all, an investment for the future - they have to be paid for somehow. I don't believe my adopted parents even knew where the church was that I was being taken away to, or that they even cared. The money - it didn't last long. Money from Ichmarr never does.

I was taken to a stone building in a small town, where my new real life began. In this new life, I was given two meals a day and put to work. The days where long and hard and I had a lot to learn, not only about the priesthood and who my new found goddess was, but also about the peculiar way in which her priestess's worshipped her. I had known about the church and Christ, but my adopted mother had told me about the other gods, the ones we weren't allowed to talk about. It didn't become obvious in the first few years what I was becoming. I did what I was told. You do as a child; you never argue even if it seems odd, it isn't allowed. After a few beatings, I learned not to ask and carried out all of the finger-hand exercises, dancing, stretching and endless tasks that were set. They demanded a constant repetition of a useless task until they found an even more boring one.

They said I had a talent for it and I was moved from one town to the next each town larger than the last. I always had to find my feet with new people, new dangers and new prejudices. There was endless bullying from the older girls and fights I was always being blamed for because I was different. They were right; I did have a talent for it, whatever 'it' was. I found that being nimble with long, light bones and reflexes like a cat; I could do most of the odd tasks they demanded of me. I discovered that I was able to work out why I couldn't do tasks immediately. Doing things with my hands and my body seemed to be second nature; I just did it. It was learning the little squiggles on parchment that took a long time. What those runes, signs and letters meant was difficult. I spent years of impatient study of writing that I didn't have a clue about. However, when I started to understand it, I began to realise what it was all aiming for. I started asking questions about what I was ordered to do and gradually it began to unfold for me. When, eventually, I was told what the training was for, I already knew what it was all about.

They used to say every one has a god or goddess they worship. There are many small gods out there for every skill, task and occupation. Thieves have a goddess they turn to in times of trouble. She is called Ichmarr and she is the goddess of Deception, Trickery and (occasionally) Thievery. We tend not to refer to the latter, otherwise most towns would run us out! We are tolerated but nothing more. Christianity and all that goes along with it have driven most of these gods out of the way. Nonetheless the older gods still have a place and do hang on to the world in out-of-the-way places. The people of the woods and villages that are too small to have a church, still practice the old religions. Ichmarr had managed to slip under the guard of the Catholic authorities through a series of bribes, backhanders and, basically, some very secretive practices.

To be devoted to the Catholic Church meant you had to lead a pure life, to love your fellow man (but not his wife!) and to look after the weak of the community. You also had to purge yourself of all the trappings of life and loved ones, to remain celibate and to flagellate your mind and body of the evils that humans create in your minds.

This all seems quite easy in comparison to my own religion. With Ichmarr, you had to steal to keep in favour with her (and the bigger the theft, the better!); but, as a devotion to her, all of her priestesses and novices had to steal at least something every week. It couldn't be ceremonial it had to be a real theft. This has caught out a few of the high priestesses who diminish in power as they get older and less adventurous. Of course, you could keep what you steal; but, to whom would you give it? As you improved and moved higher up, the goddess would begin to ask more of you. I was good, better than all of my peers, and Ichmarr was a goddess who demanded the preaching of a 'different religion'.

We have priestesses in every thief's gangs in the major towns and cities. We know all of the wrong people. Wherever there is a gang of thieves we will have a shrine. Wherever there is a lone thief in a tight corner we have a believer. Many tyrants and con-artists give us a passing wave as they trick their way through to the score. We have many enemies and as such we are a secret to be kept by all. When you pass into the priesthood you commit yourself to it for life or death. We could and have been accused of witchcraft, maybe this is true, but we exist and continue to flourish under the protection of many powerful friends.

I knew I was different from the others - but I just didn't know how different I was until I met another like me. The forest was always a favoured place of mine. It was for me a place of beauty and mystery - as I grew up it was a place to escape to. It always felt like home as I wandered through it as a child, and it held no fear for me. I was nine when I met my first Silvesi; she looked like me, yet unlike me. We were drawn to each other – this was possibly due to a common heritage, but more likely from the need to be with someone else who was different. Kelestra was older than me by four years and yet she seemed to be the same age. She had been brought up by her parents until a raid by outlaws left her bereft and alone in the world. She knew her heritage and what it meant to be Silves, with the gifts it bestowed and the common curse (which didn't really seem to be that bad). I had always wondered why I could see clearly in the dark unlike others around me. We have a special membrane like cats at the backs of our eyes, which reflect light. It allows us to see it twice. We can also see another colour, which shouldn't be there. The colour is like dark red but, in light, you can't see it. It is sometimes scary that hot things can be seen through your eyelids!

I remember a nightmare when I was a child; I had awakened with something shining in my eyes, even as they were closed. I woke up to find my 'Dad' leaning over me with a wicked grin on his face, stinking of beer. When he saw my eyes open he kissed me on my cheek and said, "Goodnight" It was my only happy memory of him.

Kelestra also told me we were cursed to walk the earth for years long after our friends had died. I said at the time I didn't want to become 'the walking dead'. She laughed a giggly sort of laugh, one that I will miss for a long time. She always said I was silly and needed to think before I said anything. She also told me that, if I didn't die of violence, I would live for a very long time - much longer than human memory could recall. We were linked to the trees. Indeed, there is a certain tree, which keeps our spirit; one which was born with us and which grows with us and dies with us. If it is healthy, we will stay healthy. If we sicken, it withers with us. When it dies we also perish. To be honest, I thought this was all a load of hooey. But, as the years have gone by, I have heard much the same from others that I have come to believe it. We will never know which tree is ours, but I hope mine is far away from civilisation and the axe. One of the most curious things about my kind is we don't really sleep. We get our rest through meditation and mind control. As a child, I never really slept well and never felt rested by sleeping. When I met Kelestra, however, things changed for me. She taught me how to meditate, once she realised I didn't have a clue about how to do it or what it was for. It is a simple matter of "Bringing your mind into focus and controlling the Alpha waves," as she put it. It was like letting my mind drift with the wind and storing away all of the leaves that get shaken off the trees, picking up the acorns the squirrels leave behind and burying the shit the animals decide to leave on the pathways. "It was," she declared, "through this we bring our minds to rest and our bodies are cleansed by it".... or something like that. It works and that's all I know! She spoke about the wild majick of the forest and the forest gods, but at the time I thought that this was a load of mumbo- jumbo....

The memories shook me as I began to realise who I was and where I came from. Then, unbidden, the rest of that night came back to me flooding my conscious mind, shutting out the room in which I had found myself. Indeed, I was barely aware of the four individuals who had entered the room.

It was easy to get back into the Temple at night. It was known in the town as the Guild of Our Lady of Pity. The building was adapted in such a way there would be an amazing (to a non-thief!) number of entrances, hidden boltholes and windows from which to enter and exit. The Temple had been adapted from a large house, which backed onto a warehouse, and was probably owned and built by a rich merchant who had moved on to a larger, grander residence. All of the entrances were guarded, usually by a novice like me or by a trap, which would mark the unwary thief as she entered. These traps were less common and used only for random terrorisation of the novices, like me, who slipped around at night.

I approached the Temple building with caution, keeping to the shadows and trying to stay out of the worst of the rain. It was threatening to downpour and I didn't want to get wet. My heart was pounding again, as if it was trying to drill its way out of my chest. My instructors would be even more annoyed with me if they knew I was scared. I began to calm myself with an old mantra I was taught early in my priesthood to control myself in a crisis. It goes on about fear being like a wind, which you can either fight against or allow it to pass through you to the other side, leaving only you to face the world. Cat (my master) used to say, "Bend like a reed not break like a twig" - about most things actually....

There was sudden movement at the side of the Temple roof. A dark figure, leaping onto the roof of the Temple from the building next door, was slipping and sliding on the now wet roof. From the style of the jump and the inexcusably noisy landing it had to be Rozz. She was a caring (but often careless) friend who had a habit of getting caught. Our Temple twice had to pay exorbitant compensation to merchants to stop her from being taken to the guards and charged with theft and all of the trouble that it causes.

There is a saying that, "Once is a mistake, twice caught is unlucky, but thrice and you are out, often literally." As I myself warned Rozz, "In the first town I was in, I was caught twice – both times for petty thefts. The second time the guards were going to cut my arm off!" Their operating philosophy was "An eye for an eye, a tooth for a tooth, a hand for a sticky hand" (if you understand my meaning!). I was lucky on that first occasion as the guard, being fat and greed was easy to persuade. I convinced him that it would be better if, instead of taking me back to the guard house, I made it worth his while to look the other way. It cost me forty-five pieces of gold (a year's wages for a guard), but I still have two hands and he is fertilising a small plot in a field just outside the town. It may well be that I am still wanted for questioning about his disappearance, but I hate giving my money away!

Luckily, Rozz was drunk when I warned her about this and she has a poor memory when she is drunk. If the news circulated about some of the more colourful aspects of my past, it could get very unpleasant. Not with the Temple; they wouldn't mind as it is within our devotions. Sometimes things go wrong and we cope with them in the best way we know how. This is what we are trained for.

For us, however, it is the guilds or gangs in the town that cause the greatest problems. They hate lone thieves and, although we are de facto part of the same side, they still get vicious if we don't pay dues or tithes or at least a bit of blood money or whatever they call it. For this reason I am always very wary and accommodating with the gangs I associate with. When I have to become involved with them, I am generous with my dues and keep myself to myself. Looking like I do and going in there unprotected could be dangerous, but as several of them have found I don't need much protection. Most of them are little boys in a man-suit, playing at being a man or at least a bully.... My dues are always paid on time and, here, I have had to double them to run solo in the town. It pays to stay away from others in this game - if I make a mistake I will regret it, but if they mess me up I may never get another chance Anyway, it gets in the way of the fun.

Rozz dropped out of sight, going into a much-used entrance in the roof. Her activities would probably have been noticed by half a dozen eyes and logged against religious precepts laid down by Ichmarr. Always, larger sacrifices were demanded if you were noticed and Rozz couldn't help being spotted by others. I, on the other hand, had a few tricks up my sleeve. Sometimes it was not necessary not to be seen but to appear like someone else - it depended on who saw you and how much they asked to turn a blind eye. I didn't need to be concerned about this as I knew I could try out the hat, but how the hell to work it and what would happen if it went wrong? No, I knew of other ways in, some smellier than others. The sewers were a favourite of mine, but the smell lingered and some of the other novices were already suspicious of me. Cat (the novice master) spotted me down there two nights ago and I know it is going to cost me. However, tonight, the sewers would hold even greater dangers if this storm were to really break. Indeed, a sudden flash of lightning confirmed my suspicions that this was not a good idea....

Along the side of the building there were five entrances, one window and the rest hidden from normal view by plaster decorations or pargetting in the plaster. I looked along the wall, but seeing with Darksight was beginning to be a little difficult due to the rain. I could, however, just make out that two of these decorations had a higher temperature around the crack, so I ruled them out. They were obviously manned and I would be spotted. Each novice had to do a spell of duty at these entrances once a week as part of our training. It was an education to us on how to be really sneaky. Sometimes we caught priestesses on outings and once, this year, the high priestess was spotted by Geldut. She didn't report it, but she was hauled over the coals by the old girl because she should have!

The third entrance was at ground level and appeared to be a storm drain, which dropped you into part of the sewer system; again, a problem. The fourth was better concealed and few knew about it. I had only discovered it two months earlier, when I saw another novice disappear there and went to investigate.

Carefully, I made my way over to it while keeping to the shadows as much as I could. As I climbed up the obscured side of the chimney, I looked around to check that no-one was around. Carefully and slowly, I reached the gargoyle on the edge of the second floor, which was already beginning to spout a dribble of rain water. Ugly little things, purposely designed to ward off evil spirits (as if to say this is my building, hands off!). Gargoyles look even more terrifying in this light! In a light-hearted moment I thought, "Why not make him look a bit more jolly?" I therefore reached into my cloak and located the hat, which fitted the gargoyle's head quite snugly. While it didn't improve his looks, he did look amazingly funny!

Just then a breeze caught the hat on its side and threatened to blow it off. I began to be aware the sky was more threatening in colour. Hailstones were beginning to clatter onto the roof of the Temple blown by a stronger wind. I was standing on a ledge half an inch wide, forty feet in the air, with a hat so valuable and rare that people would die for it! Being aware of my predicament, I stuffed it back into my pocket and squeezed my way through the gap in the masonry, which led through to a small tunnel beyond. It is a good thing I am of slight build otherwise I could never fit in this.

There was a network of tunnels throughout the Temple building and warehouse. These were mostly created when the building was converted to our uses, but some were already there. Obviously the merchant didn't trust his wife or his men as there were peepholes riddling the original passages. Most had been blocked up or boarded over at some point in time, but a few useful ones remained. The passageways were like a maze and, in the early days here, I had found myself quite lost amongst them. It had taken weeks of cautious exploration to become familiar with the ways and, indeed, it is quite a thrill even now to discover hidden or concealed doors in the maze. I have met a lot of the other occupants of the Temple here. Sometimes this area almost seems like a meeting place! Often we pass with barely a nod, but sometimes you meet someone you may or may not have wanted to meet, which can get quite explosive. Blood is often shed by those unwary enough not to guard themselves.

In comparison, the rest of the Temple seemed sometimes empty and forbidding. There are the public areas, with the tapestries, masonry and panelling that disguise the real purpose of the building. They always seemed, to me, too exposed and stark with little decoration - apart from religious artefacts and tapestries. These were usually placed to help to conceal or disguise the entrances of the maze. The panelling and other clever tricks with masonry also served to disguise the multitude of entrances and exits.

The building had been converted into a Temple by the high priestess, Celene, who 'got lucky' in her previous city. Through much prayer and planning, she had amassed a fortune and needed to sacrifice it (somehow) in a devout manner. Leaving her affairs in that city in much disarray, she arrived here and set herself up as a rich widower and philanthropist. She founded the Temple with the help of the town elders in the seedier part of town so it could help the down-trodden. They had been sold on the idea that the church was to be a branch of the Catholic Church founded by Saint Ichmarr of the Lance - with the lance being that which the saint uses to heal (nowadays, it is the dagger!).

The Temple was set up with the title of 'Guild of Our Lady of Pity', to look after the sick, injured and those out of luck. Celene had surveyed several likely candidates before she finally settled on this building in Park Lane. It served most of our needs, but she set about modifying it to meet her own. Craftsmen were brought in from other cities where they had worked on earlier Temples and knew what Celene was after. They also were outsiders who wouldn't be around to talk about what was in the Temple or about its secret ways.

This was the most dangerous part of my journey. There were no heat sources to be seen through the door. I stood by it and listened intently with my ear lodged against the door's surface; every sense straining to notice the slightest sign of someone on the other side. Hearing nothing, I lifted the latch so slowly it could not be seen to be moving and gently moved the door. Every fibre of my being was straining and wishing there would be no sound. Finally, the door was open enough to get a view of the passageway beyond. Nothing was around, so I jumped through it, closed the door quietly and moved along through the corridors of the Temple proper to my cell and home. Once through the door, I knew I was safe. It is only when entering the Temple that we can be caught; once inside the perimeter, the game is up and you are untouchable....

Mine had been a major burglary and the guild would be livid if they caught me. The merchant was one of their best clients and paid them well to protect his home. He would spread the word from here to Cantebrigia that there was a bounty on this hat of at least a hundred pieces. The brotherhood, when it found out, might just ignore protocol and come to visit me! I therefore stashed my gear and took out my prayer mat and holy dagger....

Tria – Lacative domini

Reality reasserted itself and I realised that Reg was back. He was touching my shoulder, patting it to wake me up. There were three others with him; two women and a man. The women were dressed in tightly fitted clothing the like of which I hadn't seen before and both had large satchels and spectacles. The blond one seemed to be the most inexperienced one as she kept on glancing around and towards the two other newcomers. The man was dressed in a jacket like Reg's, but this was more charcoal-coloured and didn't have the shiny brass buttons. Like the women, he wasn't wearing a hat. I think that these were Reg's people who were going to heal me up properly so that I could leave this strange place. I decided to do everything I understood to do.

Reg indicated for me to listen to the others, so I turned my attention back to them. The woman with blond hair opened the tapestries to bring chairs for the other two. Reg moved to stand outside as was his habit. I think that Reg must be a wonderful man to be so patient to stand around for all this time.

The lady with the brown hair started talking to me saying, "Halo ay b'leev yore nam iss Merith, doo u hhave ay saycund nam?" She expressed herself earnestly and with an assertive voice, but with little sense.

I looked at her with the mentioning of my name and pointed to myself, saying, "My name is Merith." Then, while pointing towards her with my other hand, I asked, "What is your name?"

She had a moment of confusion and then the realisation dawned on her and she turned to the others and pointed to the man saying, "Thes es detktive inspektor Marlow." To the other lady she said, "Thes es detktive Lafley and my name is Jane Goody."

I pointed to her and said, "Jane Goody." She nodded to this. I turned to the other lady and said, "Detktive Lafley?" She also nodded and smiled at me. I turned to the man and said, "Detktive Marlow, can I call you Marlow?" Having two people with a funny first name could get really confusing.

He looked perplexed at this and said, "Jurst Marlow."

"Jurst Marlow?" I queried.

He nodded at this and seemed pleased. I was a little confused as he had just given me two names, but I settled onto the second one, and this seemed better.

Jane started to speak again, "Zo Merith, doo u hav enne rekollekshun ov wat hppned too yu b fore yu wer brot hear?"

I carried on smiling, but was unable say anything as I couldn't make out what she said. I shrugged my shoulders and stared back.

Jurst said, "Merith, wehre doo u liv?"

He seemed to be asking me something but what? I shrugged my shoulders again and looked down.

Jane took something out of her bag. It was wrapped in a material like thin silk but completely transparent. I realised that she had my dagger in it. This was the only thing I had that I valued, the only thing that I would never let go of. So, upon seeing it, I put my hand out and asked her for it. She uttered a whole string of words to me, but I was intent on the dagger, "Wat iss dis an vere ded yu git it frm? Dere vas blud own de blad, vresh shuman blud. Dide yu urt de maan dat atak'd yu? Ve noe dat eet ish nod ur blud, ve tst'd eet an de boees inn de lab fond dat eet vas kwite diffrent."

I reached out to take it but she pulled it away saying, "Mm sorree bot aye cant let ewe haf it, whe haf to do moar tsts onn et." I leapt for it, grabbing it in mid air and bowled her over in her chair. The other two shouted and Reg appeared at the tapestries. I pulled the dagger out and immediately noticed that its tip was missing. Holding the dagger brought back a memory of how I first received this dagger....

The classic dagger shape is the holy symbol of Ichmarr. It is the favoured weapon of Ichmarr and is a dual action tool, employed as it is to harm and heal. This particular one was eight and a half inches long, with a jewel encrusted in its gold hilt. The blade is a silver/steel mix, giving it strength and holy powers. It cost me a lot of money to have a continual light spell imprinted onto the tip of the blade, but it was worth every penny. The sheath, made out of steel, was fur lined to make it silent and be light-tight. The blade was given to me when I graduated to become a novice. In those first years, my mentor had been hard but fair. The only time I ever saw her with any softness was when she graduated me from apprentice to novice and gave me this dagger. She had it specially made for me from one of the finest craftsmen in the city. A staggering gift from a mentor, but then I had been a very valuable and productive student for her!

I was stunned by this memory and didn't realise that Reg had come running over to me. He crashed into my side and grabbed for the dagger. Screaming, I held onto with all of my might. Didn't he realise how important this was to me? Couldn't he see what this was?

The dagger was pulled from my hands. Then the women used harsh pulls and tugs to pull my hands behind my back and metal shackles were put onto my wrists. I screamed with the pain of them going on and started to cry, wailing at the injustice of it all. I lay there sobbing and screaming on the floor as an incomprehensible conversation went on around me.

Marlow – "What the hell was that all about?"

Reg – "She must have gone berserk. She was all calm and nice as pie before you lot came along and messed her up. What on earth did you say to her?"

Jane – "The look on her face as she grabbed the weapon was that of sheer determination and total elation when she had it from me. Did you see the almost religious zeal about her? Could any of you understand a word she said?"

Marlow – "I don't think she is English, but where does she come from? I don't recognise that accent."

Lafley – "Can I also point out the flash of light onto her eyes, they seemed to be very strange? Did any of you read the report by the medical team that first inspected her?"

Jane – "Yes, I did. But I just dismissed that as pure conjecture on their part. How can anyone have eyes that mirrored the light shining into them? Pure fiction, they made it up!"

Marlow – "I did get an inquiry by MI6 about that report."

Jane – "Did you? You never told me about that!"

Marlow – "Yes, they were also very interested in the sample of blood that was taken from the Jane Doe as it didn't match up to any of the normal blood types. The Lab boys said it might have been contaminated, but sent it off for further tests any way."

Jane – "So what are we going to do with our little wild child then?"

At that moment, the troll burst in through the tapestries and shouted at them all, "What the bloody hell is going on here then?

What is my patient doing on the floor wrapped up in chains like a common criminal?"

Other women rushed in dressed like the troll. Now, for the first time, I could see that Reg and his friends weren't in charge but that the troll was. She controlled this house and she was like the high priestess of this Temple. They pushed the others out of the way and picked me up. They gently put me back on the bed and one of them took a few bundled up sheets of a thin papery material to wipe my eyes. Meanwhile, I was too far gone to pay any attention to what was happening around me – not that I could understand their speech!

Troll – "You boys had better have a good explanation as to why this child has been handcuffed, thrown to the floor and left there while you gossip!"

Marlow – "Matron, your patient is obviously in a dangerous state of mind. She attacked one of my officers with a piece of evidence and put our lives at risk. I demand that you place her immediately in the Psychiatric ward where they can look after her properly!"

Troll – "You demand it! I'll tell you what you can demand! But, until you get two of these lily livered doctors to agree with you, she ain't leaving my ward.... I'll tell you what I demand. You take these bloody handcuffs off my patient who is already in enough distress thank you! And you can take away your stinking filthy hands, which I noticed you didn't wash as you came in, out of my ward. Come back only when you've the authority to put your weight around like that!"

Jane – "Listen, Jenny is it? This girl went for me and I saw what was in her eyes. She is scared and she still thinks she is being attacked. With the type of trauma she received she must have been attacked for hours and subjected to humiliating and painful acts. That sort of trauma has had to have affected her psyche and without some early treatment she could be scarred for life."

Troll – "So, 'Doctor', tell me, where did you get your medical degree? Did it come out of the same box as your warrant card? As you say, she is the victim in all of this, are you trying to make it worse for her. Bloody Police! This isn't a bloody police state yet! Get them bloody cuffs off of her, NOW!"

The conversation rolled on and on around me, but my mind began to wander again as another memory came unbidden to me....

The sun broke the horizon and shone through my window, producing a bright, clear day washed clean from the storm overnight. The morning was cool and inviting, but I knew the day would once again be hot and dry. I came out of my reverie in the moment of the sun cresting the land, as is my custom. I washed and dressed for action with a simple, short slip, which gave maximum movement with minimum weight. Making sure the bolt was secure and the mat was against the bottom of the door so no-one could look in, you never know. I struggled to control my hair as I brushed it. The hairs almost seemed to take a life of their own as I tried to straighten them out of the tangles. I tied it back with a length of ribbon and looked around my home.

The room was little more than seven by five, it had wooden walls that were more like vanity partitions than walls. There was an open, square window that had a single iron bar down the middle of it - as if anyone could squeeze through its tiny dimensions! Finally, the room had a dominating oak door with a gap at the bottom wide enough to roll an apple through. It was furnished with a box-bed to sleep in, a tall cupboard with footlocker and a small chest - my own addition. This was fashioned from iron-bound oak with two of the most complex locks I have ever designed, harder to open than a widow's purse and yet holding no mystery for me. It was built with no traps but several false ones, two hidden compartments, one findable, the other difficult to spot even by the most discerning of thieves. I know chests, I've opened enough of them, and this was a beast!

I opened the smaller of the chest's two compartments and picked out the hat. It looked like a simple cloth hat with a floppy brim. There was no structure to keep the brim up, just thicker cloth. It was plain canvass like you'd get given to you to plough a farmer's fields. It comfortably fitted my head and I cleared my thoughts.

To say the experience was weird would be to understate it. The hat opened up a part of my consciousness. It opened like a concealed door suddenly breached to reveal a treasure behind. It allowed me to feel what I was wearing and how I looked. If I could feel how I looked, what if I changed how I felt...... Oh bugger! The effect was akin to being like the jelly boiled out of bones; once set on a plate, it takes only a gentle push to set the whole plate a quiver - as I felt now. After several abortive tries, I found how to alter the shape of the hat and left it as a flower in my hair. If it was going to look a complete mess, at least this might distract people from looking at it!

It was my habit to go down for breakfast soon and I knew I couldn't change my habits - any change might be noted and queried. So I put my soft boots on and tidied up my room. The corridors were nearly empty and all I received was a few smiles and looks from the other novices and apprentices. There were few in the eating hall, a couple of new faces to investigate later, but no-one I particularly wanted to talk to.

I went into the kitchen to see if I could scrounge something from Petersen. He is the only man in the Temple. He is the only one Celene could stand and, as he is an amazing chef, I don't blame her. He is very prim and proper in a feminine way and is always clean-shaven and well perfumed. We have taken bets on whether he shaves his legs and the rest of his body. Some of the girls have tried to seduce him! However, he acted as if they weren't even there and carried on chatting to the helpers in his singsong high-pitched voice. He is a beautiful barrel of a man and we always have time for a chat in the mornings. He is, like me, early to rise, always cheerful and always wanting to hear the salacious gossip around the Temple - such a scandalmonger!

Petersen shooed me away with a concerned look on his face, saying he would prepare my usual for me and bring it through. I knew he wanted to talk to me on my own so I gave in easily. We would usually have a chat while he prepared my porridge and talk about what is happening in the town. I returned to the eating hall and sat down in one of the corner tables, with my back to the wall.

The kitchens were at one side of the hall with open doorways that let the diners know what was being prepared. The hall, with its stone walls and high ceiling, was an impressive sight and had once been the main store for the merchant's wares. At the back of the hall were the great doors, which led to the yard and stables. These doors were large enough to bring a fully loaded wagon into the hall but had a door hatch which would allow people to exit easily. The walls were decorated with an array of various trophies the thieves of the hall choose to hang there. Various picks and tools hung in bundles, locks out of doors, barrel locks, chain locks and the like. There were a wide variety of traps, going from huge bear traps to the concealed needle traps with their guts opened for all to see. The bits of climbing equipment and odds and sods were strewn with random effect around the room. The general impression of all of this was of a thousand pieces of metal that had been thrown to the walls from a central point.

I closed my eyes and let my senses drift around the room. There was a strange tension in the air and in my mind I could feel the vibrations of it. On opening them, I spied one of the strangers who kept on facing towards me and, as I concentrated on her, I felt there was something wrong with her. She had a bad look around her and she was out of place here. Her comrade also was different, but I could sense she was relaxed and trying to amuse her friend. She kept on touching her arm and whispering to her, almost cooing to relax her.

She stood up and faced toward me and then began to stalk over to me, coming to a stop at the other side of the table. Staring and glaring, she stood there! I smiled and locked eyes with her eyes. At this distance, I could see she had darker skin like a gypsy and she had several scars on her exposed arms. She was pretty, about five foot six with wavy, black hair and eyes to match. Her gypsy eyes flared as she saw me smiling and shouted at me, in a strange accent, "How dare your kind be here in a good place like this? You must be driven from this place and the very ground beneath you cleansed by her goddess to remove the plague you leave."

Tensing my muscles slowly, I prepared myself for anything as she built up her fury. She was dangerous and I could see her temper was going to explode in my direction.

She pulled out her dagger. Her comrade was already running towards her. She had been a bit slow to react and hadn't realised what she was doing until now.

As she skirted the table, I rose from my seat...time slowed.... as it always does in a fight. My hand reached for her dagger arm as I built up the tension in my mind. A selection of spells came quickly up and I selected 'Command' and let it run through its course. As my hand grasped her wrist, I looked into her eyes and said, "Die," quietly and with little emphasis. One of the many blessings we receive from our goddess is the ability to use some of her essence to produce effects, which can be helpful. With a little of her essence and the right training we can cause things to happen. Mostly we use this to heal the sick and injured. This majick, along with herbs, goes a long way to healing others. We can also calm minds and provide sustenance. One of these is 'Command', which is used to calm a person and maybe tell them to go to sleep. The word is the action they are impelled to do and their body will do so for about thirty seconds before the spell wears off. In some cases this can help the person sleep and, after the spell wears off, they will continue to rest and benefit from it. It can also be used in conflict.

Her eyes went cold she flopped over and folded up towards the floor. As I helped her to reach the floor gracefully, I disarmed her. She had stopped breathing and her eyes stared blankly as if there was nothing behind them.

When her friend arrived, she stared into my eyes and demanded to know, "What have you done?" She bent down towards her and touched her face; it was pallid and lifeless. She screamed at the sight of her friend and began to draw her dagger, screaming out, "You have killed her!"

We were drawing a crowd.

Petersen, behind her put his arm on her shoulder and said, "I wouldn't do that missy, look at your friend and ask yourself, do I really need this today."

She stared down to her friend. We all stared at her. The body lay on the ground, lifeless....

The spell broke and, suddenly, her body shuddered into life. She rasped an inward breath and clung to herself. We all took an inward breath as if we had all been holding our breaths waiting for something to happen. She started to sob and looked about her, bewildered, not knowing what had happened. I moved to help her up, but her friend pushed me away and helped her instead. The gypsy looked at me, her face screwed up and she said, "You will regret all that your race has done to us. You will pay the price of your kind. I will see to it that you never see another day!"

Then they moved away, the gypsy pushing her friend away, and stalked out of the room. The other girl followed quickly behind her.

I sat down, open-mouthed. I gawped at Petersen and said, "What the hell was that all about?"

He sat down in front of me and joked, "You are good at making friends around here aren't you? The gypsy was called Desidra. She comes from down south near Taunton. Her family were travelling when they were attacked and her caravan burned. There had been trouble between her brother and a Silvesi like you. Apparently, there was a lot of killing on both sides. Her brother and parents had all been killed to avenge what they had done, and it was this revenge that has fuelled her hatred and loathing of your kind. She had been left unhurt out of sympathy for what they had done to her."

He pushed the porridge with a spoon over to me. "A generous helping of honey in that one just the way you like it!" I could see he was trying to sweeten me up, literally, and so I smiled and responded, "I hope that she finds the peace that she needs so badly and that this

revenge killing stops before it hurts others." I knew that he would like
me to say that, but secretly I actually agreed with the sentiment. It is
bad for business to randomly kill others and I knew that she was
harbouring hate for many such killings. I could not believe that she
would be allowed to join us. In fact, because of the way she moved, I
knew that she wasn't one of us. She was too clumsy, too
uncontrolled, she had little training and probably less sense.

I demanded of Petersen, "She is not one of us, so why is she here?
Why is she being allowed access to the Temple like this?"

He looked down when he replied, "You know there are many
things to see on the road south and you may want to visit some of
those one of these days."

"Cut to the chase Petersen!" I shouted. "I know you know
something and that you want to tell me. I can tell by the way you are
sitting and the look on your face. She is the key to something and you
think I'm going to be involved, don't you?"

He looked around and mumbled, "If you are going to be like that,
maybe I was wrong to say something"

My most charming and girlie smile appeared on my face.
Giggling, I said, "If it's important, I know you'd want to help me.
You and I go back a long way." For me, a fifteen year old, a week
seemed like a long time. I had come to this Temple just over three
years ago and that was like a lifetime.

Since graduating to a novice, I had been allowed to develop my
skills as I saw fit. I had mastered seven spells, all of which had double
uses, and I was renowned in the Temple for my healing skills,
although goddess knows why. I had even been called away from
watch duty to help in the healing of the injured several times and
most of the priestesses were agreed my skills were remarkable for
someone so young. I was able to heal with the touch of my holy
symbol and could brew up a poultice to help the wound close.
Besides all this, most types of lock and traps were known to me and
so I don't get caught out by them - well not often! I could scale
nearly-sheer wall with hardly a crack to help me and I am as dextrous
as a cat.

One of my biggest handicaps which has always hampered me is
the way I look. I have always been told that if I wanted to look
innocuous I'd still stand out. They said I'd be noticed in the pitch
black. Which is a little untrue, but I knew that I'd notice any observer.
Apparently, I am just too 'beautiful' not to be noticed by man or
woman - something which I have always found very odd, as I feel so

plain and dull. Looking at myself in the reflections of water, or in the little silver mirror I had stolen from a lady's baggage, all I see is my face. However, I knew that, due to my Silves' heritage, I broadcast beauty and cannot help doing so. Also, I suffer from being an optimistic pessimist! This means that I look forward to things going wrong and is probably why I am always planning to get the edge of every situation.

I knew Petersen well enough and so he started to tell me what had happened, "Merith, I have known you for a long time and, in a funny way, I love you as one of my own. I feel I should tell you that I was told not to interfere with what just happened, but to be at hand to deal with the aftermath. She wanted to find out how you both would react to each other. Obviously, not well! I think she has something in mind for you and I don't think it will be easy. There are others who are coming here to join with you. She is risking much to send someone so young. You are strong and resilient, but can you also be persistent and push others?"

He had uttered quite a mouthful. It was the first time I had heard such a competent and straightforward answer from him. 'She' was the high priestess Celene. Whenever he spoke about anyone he called them by name, except with Celene it was always 'She' – he was her man. He was a gossipmonger. A jolly fat man, you can have a girlie chat with because, at heart, he is a bit of a girlie himself - except without the tits (although his were a lot bigger than my little dumplings!). This was straight talk, man to man. Shit! It scared me down to the core of my being.

It took a few moments to respond to what he had said. I replied, "I don't know. You know me. I go my own way. I follow my own path. I don't like to work with others, it hampers me." I did know that I had itchy feet and wanted to stretch my wings a bit. "I would do any thing for my goddess and if this is what is wanted of me so be it. After that scene, they will probably choose someone else!"

Petersen laughed, "Who else would have your impeccable manners to use fighting talk on their first meeting and steal their dagger from their very own hand." He looked down at the dagger lying on the table. A stiletto dagger, five inches long with a thin blade and small hilt, it was the type of weapon, which would be easy to hide down a boot sheath. I have two on me just like this at all times - after all, you never know!

I exclaimed, "I should return it to her and apologise," but thinking to myself that I'd be buggered if I'd apologise for my race or what someone did to her and her family. "Thanks for the chat, Petersen, it has helped me clear my mind."

Abruptly, he stood up and said rather shrilly, "Don't let it get cold! Food is too important to waste."

Laughing, I replied, "You'd never!"

He walked off chuckling to himself. I was left with my thoughts, which were a bloody mess. What on earth have I entered into now? I'm probably a wanted criminal for miles around. I'll have a price on my head by nightfall. I've insulted and assaulted a guest of the Temple and I've probably really pissed off my Temple's high priestess. I might as well pack and go now before it gets any worse.

As I finished my bowl, I spotted Rozz coming into the hall. She paused at the door, scanning the room, when she spotted me and came running over. She was excited and red-faced. You might say flushed, but this was often her colouring. She was a rounded girl with reddish hear and a ruddy complexion. She was very much a country girl who had been brought up on a farm and had been sent to the Temple to learn how to be a healer. I think her family thought that was all that we did. We had come in together from the Temples we were last at, the wagon that brought me here had stopped at her Temple and she stepped onto the wagon. It was that moment that we struck up a friendship and started to share everything.

She came straight up to me and couldn't help but beam. I crowed, "Saw you last night"

Crestfallen, she replied, "Not you too! How did you see me? You weren't even on duty last night. Everyone around here seems to see my comings and goings. Apparently, I was reported by three novices on duty and our master woke me up, early this morning, to tell me this and she wanted to see you. She didn't say why. What were you up to last night? When I passed by your cell you weren't there?"

Ignoring this, I asked, "What did you get? Anything interesting? You said before that you'd been working on this nobleman's son. Get very far?"

Rozz retorted, "He got as far as the bed and passed out. It wasn't worth it; two rings and I shaved his beard to look like a badger! Funny, but hardly rewarding for all the effort I've put in. He could never replace our times together," she added quietly.

"Where did she say she was going to be?"

"Who?"

"Cat."

She enquired, "Are you going now? I thought we could have breakfast together? I'm sure it can wait for a minute."

Picking up the unnoticed dagger, I replied; "With everything that just happened, I think I'd better go and see her now. Ask Petersen if I don't have time to talk later." I stood up and held the dagger up beside my wrist, not knowing where to stow it.

"Wait a minute," she exclaimed "you can tell me on the way! I'll show you."

Rozz stood up and linked arms with me. While I felt like being a bit stiff, she is very hard to be stiff with as her rosy complexion, married with her friendly personality, made her the perfect company for moments like these. She would understand everything and criticise little.

Rozz makes a great healer and a compassionate listener, but a lousy thief. Her skills at the less salubrious side of our nature were often less that satisfactory and she had constant demands on her to do more. Several times I have helped her by teaming up with her to knock over easy targets. I wouldn't normally team up, but do so for Rozz to meet her targets. I have had to do this, as it is very difficult to say no to someone crying in your face!

I didn't particularly feel now like talking to her, but I needed to share my thoughts with someone and so I poured out what had happened. I exaggerated my fear and the stress of the situation as I have found it pays to exaggerate sometimes when you want sympathy. Rozz was shocked by the attack and could not believe that someone would attack me just for the way I looked. She said it was like the guards picking on women just because they had been spanked by their mummy when they were young. I daresay that sort of thing happens with people a lot in life, but without them being conscious of it. Most people don't actually think about what they are doing. They go through the motions of living and just do what they feel they should do. Notwithstanding that, I can have a tendency to react by instinct. I am trying hard not to and, if I had reacted out of instinct, I feel that Desidra would be lying in a pool of blood rather than wherever she is.

She guided me down to the novice master's room, but I stopped and said, "Thanks, Rozz. I think I'll need to go it alone from here."

"Oh okay, I'll see you later?" She always phrased it as a question. Rozz was so uncertain of us and our friendship.

"Yeah, see you soon." Much later no doubt.

She wandered away and I knocked and entered. Cat was sat at her desk, peering over what looked like a clock which had thrown itself apart. She indicated for me to sit down and carried on looking over the mechanism. I sat cross-legged on the floor and closed my eyes. I have always found it easier to think if I shut out the rest of the world, it also calms me down and allows me to sense more of the world. From the look I had of the mechanism, I could visualise it was probably a lock of some sort. It was a combination of a ward-lock with a barrel. It had several quirks I hadn't seen before, some levers on springs? I resisted the urge to get up, to have another look at it and cleared my mind to wait. The dagger, I realised was still up against my wrist and so I put it into one of my boot sheaths alongside one of mine.

After a minute Cat looked up from her desk and said, "So you have learned patience. This is a good trait for one of Ichmarr. It is a necessary skill to have when things start to go wrong. If I had tested you like this a year ago you would have been over my shoulder and touching what you should not." She looked square into my eyes and asked, "Do you think you have improved as a person since you came here? Do you think you have grown up?"

I studied her face looking for clues. Cat has always been a difficult one to read. She has a poker face and she has a sixth sense for lies. She can smell them coming. I replied, "I suppose that I have developed some self restraint in some ways, I tend to look both ways when I cross the road now and admittedly I still have a long way to go in terms of growing up but things are moving along."

What she was getting at? Is she trying to catch me out? Does she know anything about last night? She waited as if she was looking for more. Venturing a reply, I said, "In terms of growing up, who knows. An old friend of mine said that my kind are not considered adults until they were fifty years old, although, I'm sure that individuals can take responsibilities on much sooner. I would consider myself able to take on responsibilities now."

She snorted. "Like today with the incident in the hall or last night?"

It cut through me like a knife. What did she know about last night? Had I been spotted? How much did she know? Staying calm I replied, "I was attacked. I defended myself and didn't harm the girl. I didn't see any reason for the attack so I didn't see it was necessary to hurt her. I used a spell, as it was the quickest method, which had the fewer risks, to both of us. I hope that I might have a chance in the future to help her with this hatred of hers." Being 'holier than thou' was a risky path but I needed to avoid further questions. She may not know and this may deflect her.

She smiled a knowing smile, nodded and asked, "Where were you last night when I wanted to speak to you? No-one saw you leave or come back. No-one knew where you were... Maybe I shouldn't ask that question, I might get jealous. Rozz was."

There was a long pause in which I looked long into her face. The slightly smug smile that was etched into her face told volumes to me; she was trying to illicit some signs of guilt in me. Her Rozz comment was a goad, but I was not willing to rise to it. Secretly, I realised, she is pleased with me. I smiled and asked her, "So, why, did you need to speak to me? What is this all about?"

Her answer was startling, "There comes a time in all novices' life where you need to make a choice. You can either continue to be on the periphery and continue do as you please and then to gradually drift off into marriage and settling down. Or, you can take the next step, to be one with our Goddess and to take the vows. However, the next step should not be taken lightly and it may not be right for you. As you say, you are young and maybe too young to do this. You may need time to consider the full ramifications of what you are being asked to do. Sometimes we are not given time to make an informed choice. You have to discuss this with Celene at midday."

She continued, "This gives you only a few hours to make a decision, to choose your path. One thing though, when you are given the choice it may not be given to you again. This is an opportunity, which can only be grasped once. If this passes you by, it may never come again. You should go and think on this choice. Do not discuss this with anyone! It has to be from you and you alone! At midday, Celene will be waiting for you in her apartment with a selection of priestesses. You will make your choice plain to her there."

No pressure, right? Sitting there, I reflected on what had just been said and realising something profound, I asked her; "So, how did you know about the incident in the hall? Unless she came to you, there is no way you could have known about it!" I was getting riled and on edge. I hate being pushed into a corner, which is how I felt now.

She smirked and said, "You told me what happened. Look, we had to set up the meeting. We had to know what you would do and what she would do. We know about both of your histories and how they could affect your working relationship. This is too important an opportunity to waste on squabbling youths."

At this, I retorted vehemently, "Again someone is talking about us working together! What is this all about? Why all the mystery? I want to know what is going on!"

She thought for a while and began softly, "You do need to know what is happening, but I cannot tell you. Celene is the only one who can tell you and she will only tell you if you make the right choice. Have faith in our goddess; she will help you make a good choice for you. That is all I can say, please go and meditate on it."

Not knowing what else to do I left. I wandered over to my cell blankly staring ahead. After passing Jho and Beth along the passages, I realised I was now out of it. They had stared at me as if I was a ghost and, when I had passed, they hurriedly whispered to each other and rushed off down the corridor. I arrived at my cell and bolted the door. I was in a daze, too confused to think and too elated to meditate. They were going to make me a full priestess with all of the trimmings. "Bloody Hell!" I said audibly, and looked around my simple cell. I giggled and hugged myself. This means a change in lifestyle. I am going to have to get more serious and have more fun. A Priestess of Ichmarr - now that is something! I picked my prayer mat out of my locker and knelt down to meditate. I took out my holy dagger, its light shining undiminished, pure and unadulterated, I closed my eyes to meditate over what had passed.

There was a knock on the door. A voice called through, "When you want to talk about it I'm here for you!" Rozz, of course! Ignoring her, I decided to carry on in - after all, I was told not to discuss it with anyone and I knew she would understand.

In the meditative state, your senses are dulled not stopped (unlike sleeping) and I was aware of a conversation happening outside of my door. Catching only snatches of it I was aware they were talking about me, but they seemed to be saying that my situation must be really bad. The rumour was that I was going to be thrown out of the order. They continued to say there was a special meeting to decide on my fate. These, and other thoughts of my own, were gently coaxed into order. As I drifted along on the wind, calmness washed over me and I felt I belonged, not in this place, but in this philosophy, in this religion. I felt a proximity to my Goddess and knew what I had to do. I would accept the priesthood and all that it entails. I would devote my life and my heart to this order and take whatever comes.

Quattuor – Nectar divinia

I became aware of a sharp pain in my finger and the scene altered back to the tapestry room. A tall thin woman stood over me with my hand in her's. She held my finger in one hand and, with the other, was using a piece of glass to cut into my hand. I screamed and dragged my hand away from her. The woman looked startled and backed away to look outside the tapestries. Glancing over, I could see a man dressed like Reg. However, this was a different man. He looked harder and fatter, with a funny jacket over the normal jacket. It had startlingly bright yellow lines on it with white bands that seemed to glow. He stood up to come over to the woman, and said something to her as if in code, "R. U. O. K?" She nodded in response. He came over to me and stood beside my bed. He looked me straight into the eyes and with his hands out in front on him, palms down, saying, "Kam down, kam down de neurse is ownley tryin too doo her job."

"Oww! Hurt me!" I pointed towards the woman.

He stood solidly in front of me, turned his head to the woman and said something else to her, "Ju git de sampl yu wantd?"

She replied to him nodding, "Yess ay managd too git ay sampl, bud ay just kneed too rite up de nots." She approached the bed, but she looked so scared - as if I was going to leap out and attack her. She reached over, grabbed the board and moved back straight away. She nervously smiled at him. I could see him relax and he stepped back away from the bed. The realisation of who he was dawned on me. This was a bloody guard! He looked too capable to be a watchman, so he must be a town guard or one of the King's men. No wonder he was keeping a good watch over me.

I tried to make sense of everything I had remembered. It was clear to me that everything I am seeing now, is different to what I had experienced earlier. Now, I did know who I am. I have obviously trained as a priestess of Ichmarr, but how is this connected to what is happening now? I need to pray to Ichmarr for my spells and perhaps get some sort of divine guidance on all of this. I didn't trust any of these people. They were all wrong and what they were wearing, well, that was all wrong too. Where would I get a dagger or a knife? I needed to get these. Most of all though, I needed to get out of bed to go for a wee! I said to the woman, "I need to go!"

She looked back at me with a questioning look. She turned to the man who shrugged his shoulders.

"I need to go down here!" I pointed, adding, "Swisssss."

She instantly understood me this time, but she also looked concerned and said to the guard, "Wat doo aye doo, shee needs too goo too de loo?"

The guard replied, "Well ure de nurse arond heare ame onle hear too protek u."

She put her finger up and indicated to me, "Won minut, ayl b bak." With this she turned and left the enclosure.

This I took to mean she would be one minute, so I sat up in the bed. The guard backed off and stood beside the tapestry edge. He looked very uncomfortable, the stupid bastard! Somehow, I felt that I had always rebelled against authority. Given the strong feeling I had against this man, I suppose that I never did take kindly to authority figures.

After another few minutes the woman came back, flanked with another two stronger women in darker blue tunics. Both tried to smile sweetly at me but I could see the tension in the air. They helped me to turn in the bed and, in doing so, I realised I was no longer connected to the box with the funny tube. I lifted my hand; the only thing that was on it was a thin green bracelet with squiggles on it and a bandage around where the tube had been. This is maybe how the healing majick comes into me and fixes me up. It cannot be very strong, though, as I didn't feel as if I was healed.

They helped me out of my bed to stand up. I felt a bit weak, like a newborn kitten, and nearly fell over in trying to walk. They helped me over to the edge of the tapestries and I looked out for the first time.

The room was large but only had four beds in it - mine and three others. There were children lying in each; all had bald heads and had various pipes and wires hanging from them. The one in the far corner had a sort of glass box around him, he looked unconscious. The one in the bed beside mine was sitting upright. The child appeared to be aged six, but I couldn't tell whether it was a boy or a girl. The box on the child's arm was swung in front of it and it seemed to be transfixed by this. Wires coming from the box were connected to the child's ears. I think it was a girl as she smiled sweetly at me. I began to wonder if they weren't actually trying to heal people. Was this not a strangely twisted kind of torture?

The women walked me into a long corridor, which ended in a set of double doors. I watched as a couple walked out of those doors and I could see this was an exit. They led me to a door with two little figures on it. They looked like small children, a boy and a girl. They opened the door into a dark cupboard. Suddenly, when one of them touched a little white panel on the wall, a bright light shone down from the ceiling, yet another continual light device. I regretted the moment I lost my dagger; it would come in handy right now. What struck me most of all was the amazing mirror which hung on the wall immediately in front of me. I could see I was so bedraggled with bruises across my neck, face and eyes. I looked a mess. The room also had a ceramic bowl with tiny pumps attached to the wall, and a little ceramic well with blue liquid at the bottom of it. Paper on a roll hung from beside it. I looked at one of the women and said, "So? Where can I go?"

They both looked at each other and looked at the original women. She said something to me, "Dere iss de toi let, ov yu geo, ve vill vait oudside." As she did so, she indicated to me to enter the room.

"What do I do? How does it work?" I asked them looking into the doorway.

They looked away and started looking at their medallions, which hung from their chests.

Entering the room I was struck by the sparseness of it. Now where to go? There was the funny bowl on the floor with blue water in it, it looked a likely place but I think it must be blocked. There was the bowl that was attached to the wall. It had the funny pumps attached and I pressed one. Water came streaming out of it at a terrific rate. I let it go but the water kept on coming. I began to think it would overfill the bowl but the water leaked away down the hole in the middle. Looking underneath it, I could see there was a pipe attached to it which disappeared into the wall. I pulled the pump handle and the water eased until it stopped. I tried the other one, this time the water came out in the same way but it was hot. They must heat this water and hold it in some sort of kettle in the ceiling. Fancy pipe work indeed!

The pain in my bladder was now getting intense. I needed to go soon, particularly as all of the water noises had set me off. I lifted the dress up and squatted down onto the bowl, it seemed to be the only place to go. It was cold but much more comfortable than I thought it would be. Relief tinged with a little bit of guilt passed through me, eventually turning into satisfaction - a job well done. I ran some of the water from both pumps into the bowl and washed my face and down below. To dry myself I snatched some of the paper from the roll. Silly bits of paper! Why, they don't have proper towels here I do not know. There was nowhere to put the wet paper so I dropped it by the bowl. Whoever unblocks it will have to deal with that mess too.

Looking at myself in the mirror I could see the silvery pupils of my eyes, which marked me out as different. That was from the Darksight I inherited from my real parents, and the chiselled features that I shared in common with my mother. I began to recall my first memory of my mother and how I received it....

I left my novice cell and sauntered along to the High Priestess's apartments. Word must have gone around, as there was a small group of acquaintances and friends waiting there. As I approached they patted me on the back and said plenty of, "There, there"s, and "You'll be all right, it's a first offence isn't it?" They didn't really have a clue but, as we are mischievous by nature, I shed a few tears for them and hugged a few as if I may never see them again. I knocked at the door and entered the 'inner sanctum'.

It looked more like a herbal table than a religious gathering. The six ladies had on their finery and were drinking herbal infusions. All of the major priestesses were there. I looked around the faces and nodded to each of them. They all smiled in turn as I changed my glance. I had pleased them all in some respect and really annoyed them in others. There was Cat, the novice master who was directly responsible for the behaviour and conduct of the novice priestesses and apprentice trainers, as well as Grete who was the Alchemist who had been rescued by Celene. She had become one of the more prominent inventers of chemical poisons and tools of our trade. Then, there was Cherish, the physical instructor, who demands such difficult physical tortures. Edowyn the Security Chief whose job it was to supervise the building and the watchers. Last was Sanarah the herbalist and healer. She is a gifted healer who single handily looks after the public side of the Temple. She was also the newest member of the priesthood. She was a novice when I came here, but I never had the chance to know her well. They all politely put down their cups when I entered and greeted me.

Celene was the first to speak, saying, "Merith, so glad you could come to see us. Will you join us in a cup of rosehip and camomile to refresh and calm you? Of course you will, do sit down." A cup was placed in front of me by Sanarah who poured out the reddish liquid. It was slightly steaming and smelling of rosehips and other slightly acrid smells. I politely sipped it, funny taste but soothing.

Celene paused for a few moments to enjoy her drink, and continued, "So, I believe you have been briefed on the decision you have to make? Please tell us your answer, but know that we would be happy with your decision if it goes either way. You have to make a free choice to accept the benefits and the difficulties laid down to us by Ichmarr. You also could continue as you are with the freedom to do as you please. If you want to be a full priestess you need to completely drink that cup as a symbol of your desire to accept in full the restrictions of Priesthood. If you leave it, you show you are happy as you are and that you wish to leave your life uncomplicated."

Again she paused, this time for the effect, warning me, "Please be aware though, the experience may not be a pleasant one. The drink contains a poison. This poison is designed to take near to death. If you do not meet the expectations of Ichmarr and we have made a poor choice, you will die. This has not happened for years but there is always a possibility. If you choose to not drink the rest of it, you will have a stomach-ache for a few hours with the sips you have had. We have never tested a Silvesi before in this Temple, nor in the history of the church, to my knowledge. We do not know what will happen next."

Suspiciously, I looked intently at the liquid. I was beginning to feel different already. I asked, "If I drink this I may die? Could someone not have explained this to me before? Why do people keep on setting me up to do things? Is everything a test?"

Celene replied, "We are here to test you, yes, but as part of it you have to come to this of your own free will. This is the demand of Ichmarr. I believe you will do great things for her, but we cannot tell you what to do. We do not know what will happen. We are in the lap of Ichmarr. You asked about the setting up? You will have to trust me when I say that after the test I will explain all. At the moment the test is the all-important thing that must either be or not be. If you choose not to resolve matters now nothing more will be done, your life will continue as you wish."

"This is the moment of truth!!" She exclaimed, with all of the exclamation marks in place.

I was suspicious, but I did want to do this. So I thought, 'last one to finish is a tonker!' I downed the cup in Merith style, nearly choking on the hot liquid. Holding back the tears from the pain of the hot liquid, I glanced around the room to the approving smiles of the other women. They all stood up and began to walk past me. Each giving me a message of encouragement;

Cat - "Whatever you do, accept the world as it comes and blow a raspberry at the man!"

Sanarah - "Love yourself and love the world, even if you are standing in a cow pat!"

Edowyn - "Enjoy the experience, I did until I was sick!"

Grete - "Don't listen to her dear, just have fun!"

Cherish (whispered) - "Make love with as many men as you can, it's allowed!"

The High Priestess came over and helped me to stand. I was beginning to feel a little dizzy. Celene lead me through to a bedchamber and told me to lie down. She was beginning to go out of focus. Everything around me was losing focus and getting very soft. She told me what was going to happen; I was about to be going into a trance-like state and this would help me to raise my thoughts up on a journey into my mind where I would meet someone. If she liked me, I would be changed forever in ways I could not comprehend. She told me to be relaxed and to trust her. As I slipped from the world, I heard singing, chanting and the jangling of chains.

It was not like dreaming, nor like meditating. It was so different from anything I had experienced. I began to feel a presence. Something rushed into my mind and scoured every part of it. In my mind's eye, I saw all of the memories being examined. Whatever was happening, the something was picking over all of my memories from the present back to memories I didn't even know I had.

My mind opened out to create a room like the place I had stolen the hat from. I looked in wonder at the room. It was like I was actually there. The presence filled out (as if from my memories) to look like a Silves lady with long luxurious brown hair, slim build, rather like me but not so. She spoke in Silves, a beautiful language I had long forgotten. It came back to me the instant she uttered her first words, "Calm, child of the forest, it is long since I have met such as you. You have been a busy girl I see, many trials and adventures. I am pleased with you. For you have kept yourself in balance doing good deeds and bad deeds, this is ideal. Always keep you eyes fixed on the middle way, we do. I have encouraged all through my teachings to stay balanced and in the background. We can do many deeds if no-one notices us – If, that is, no-one realises our true nature. It is a path we walk. We are the causes of mirth and, through deception, we wind our way. To be true to the philosophy, you must encourage and lead by example. You should also lead by example in training the young, healing the sick and injured. By training youths in the way, you must encourage them to trick and cause laughter. The untrained and uninitiated do need laughter to make the world bearable for them."

She then added, "To this end I will give you a gift." She came closer and put her hands upon my shoulders. My own mother would have done this just like this. I began to realise this woman is the vision and memory of my mother.

Celene continued, "Yes, I have used your memory to make this visage as I have no physical presence. I know you cannot remember your mother and now you will. My gift to you is to allow you to transmute your physical shape to that of another creature, like a druid." She leaned forwards and kissed me on the head. She continued, "The druids, however, can change at will to any animal, mammal, reptile and bird. This gift has restrictions until you understand the gift properly. You cannot change when being viewed by a sentient being. This would change the nature of the act and will not be allowed, it just won't happen. Your clothes and anything you have on you will change but you cannot use them while you are in this state. You can maintain the form only once in the time between the sun rising and the sun rising for the next day, and you can only maintain it for that length of time. At the moment of the sun cresting the edge of the planet you are on, you will change back. This could have serious consequences for you unless you are aware of it."

She paused, "You have questions, but you only can ask three."

I suddenly realised I couldn't talk before and now I can. Isn't it funny that you can be in pain but not realise it until you see it? "Why did I get brought up by others instead of my own parents?"

She smiled, "They were the ones that found you wandering through the forest. They had no children and I directed them to you."

My second question was to ask, "What happened to my parents?

"They lost their way in life and they both lost you," she replied.

I thought about this; I knew I wasn't going to get the answer I wanted for the next question in this series. If I dug into my own mind and looked in those places I didn't want to go, I could find out for myself.

She interrupted my thoughts, "Yes, you are right in your thinking and, no, I won't tell you the purpose of life the universe and everything. Everyone knows the answer to that is forty two."

Confused? I am already! A killer question, hmm; "What would you take out of a house that was on fire?"

She was a little taken back by this question, "Is that it? That's your killer question?"

Yes." I replied. "You didn't say it had to be sensible. I could have asked you important questions about how life would go for me, or what Goddesses would have for breakfast, but you would have probably twisted them - so there!"

"The fire," she answered smartly.

She continued, "Gods don't have breakfast, particularly the Christian god, they don't get up early enough for that. You are usually up before most of us. I like to have porridge but sometimes I have fruit. As for your future, that is for you to decide from this moment on."

As she and the room faded, she smiled and said, "That was five questions I know but I could never resist questions that wanted answering. One last thing Merith, don't trust the man in the blue light, he is dangerous and thinks that he can do wondrous things. If he is given help, he may destroy your world or at least change it forever. You need to stop him from reaching it at all costs!"

The world went black. I began to feel uncomfortable - my lungs burned, my stomach churned and my head had pains throughout it. My body struggled to breath and, abruptly, there was light and air. I breathed in gasping and juddering for air, and then I heaved out the contents of my stomach. Light scoured my eyes as I tried to open them and I immediately shut them again to stop the searing light which hit them. My arms felt so heavy as if the weight of the world was on them. Pain exploded across my head and someone shouted as hard as they could, "YOU ARE OVER SENSITIVE TO EVERYTHING. THIS WILL TAKE A WHILE TO PASS. SLEEP, CLOSE YOUR EYES, LET IT PASS. WE WILL TALK SOON!"

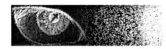

Quinque – Recoperatoris anciles

Lights flashed, strange noises added to the cacophony of sound - shrill, whistling shrieks and the shuddering of stone against stone. White lights blaring into my eyes, which opened for a second. Someone was yelling at me, "Vake up, ish dere eny sines?" Gibberish again!

"Nno polse, nno sines ov breeding."

"R de ayrvays klear?"

"Yss bud che ish stile nod breeding."

"Ged ay krash teem shtat! Kode Blew!" What did they want? I felt my arms being pushed and pulled around, cloth tearing, slapping, pain on my face, voices distant. Is this the memory or is it now?

Flying in the air I landed with a crash. Voices (intense and hurried) spoke nonsense, "Kondishon?"

"Noo vidals, shtart onn modth too modth undil de reesusidador a'rives!" I felt lips on mine, someone blew into my mouth. Then, on my chest, there was a sudden force, pumping a rhythm like a dance. Then, another, blowing into my mouth.

More voices and the scraping of metal against metal, "Ce's gonne indo a'resd, vat de bluddy shell hap'ned!"

"Don'd noe. Ce vas inn de doilet ev'ryding az norml suddnly ve eard aye krash inzide de rum."

"Sav id, Kharg panells, won hundr'd too sdart." The force pulled away and it was suddenly cold on my chest! "Kler!" Pain coursed through my body. Blue flashes turned to red and then blackness....

Seeking to block out the overriding sensations, I began meditating. My usual position for meditation is kneeling on the floor, and my body is used to doing this for hours, but I can do it in any position. During the meditation, I began soothing my feelings and the pain level descended. Time had taken on a different feeling and it seemed that the sensations I was feeling only gradually descended.

My thoughts gradually turned to the encounter. Ichmarr wanted me to feel comfortable, that was evident, and she wanted me to do something for her. To start to preach and train others in the way, I will dedicate my life to doing this. The shape shifting, well, bloody hell! I never dreamed that there could be powers like this. The druid changing, well, I thought it was just the drug hallucinating. Maybe this is all a dream. My life has seemed like a dream sometimes a nightmare without end. A blue light? I was really tripping at this point! What the hell was that all about?

As I ordered my experiences, the pain levels continued to go slowly down. I could feel them descending. Time passed, I could not tell how long I had been meditating. In raising my consciousness, I was only now aware of how deep I had gone into myself. I don't remember ever having reduced my sensory input so low. When I opened my eyes, I could see I was in candlelight. It was still painful, though not as bad, but my chest felt so painful as if someone had knelt upon it. Feeling sick and incredibly thirsty, I needed to have some water. Celene was there beside me on a chair. She was asleep, drooling down one side of her mouth.

Painfully, I moved my arms slowly, feeling pins and needles all over as if I hadn't moved them for hours. I began to flex all of my muscles in sequences used to keep them vital when cramped in a tight space. They were all in a terrible state as if I had been lying here for weeks. I could feel there was no tone left in them and I felt so weak, so thirsty. Croaking, rather than speaking, I tried to ask for water. My mouth felt sandpaper rasping over the word, straining to say it. The noise was enough to wake Celene. She looked at me, delighted but worried. She rushed over to the bed and helped me drink some water. In a whisper, which was loud to my ears, she said, "Thanks, to Ichmarr! You have been saved - we all thought we had lost you. You must to tell me what you need. I will provide for you, as I have done for all those who have passed through."

Croaking again, I attempted to say, "Where am I? What happened? How long?"

"You have been near death for ten days. You stopped breathing for nearly an hour in the first few minutes of going under and then started again. We had thought you were dead and I cried for you. Then when you opened your eyes I was so excited, but knew what I had to whisper to you to settle you. I didn't think you would need this amount of time to get over the experience. When I met Ichmarr, I was up and about after the second day. We knew it would be different for a Silvesi. This was always going to be a painful experience. We have been putting water into your mouth to keep you going for the last few days. We couldn't wake you no matter what we tried. All of the novices have been anxious to her of your progress and the whole Temple feels like it has shut down. Petersen has been pacing that hall for many an hour, waiting for news of your recovery. He even was late in preparing supper yesterday."

I drank slowly, the water feeling like icicles being forced down my throat. The water burned as it hit my stomach, which protested at the effort. I asked her, "What was it like for you?"

"When I met Ichmarr?" she responded.

I nodded.

"I met her in my mother's garden. Beautiful flowers were in bloom all over. Ichmarr took the form of my mother and told me that she was pleased with my efforts, but that I had to spend more time in devotions. She said gold was the key to my future and that I had to hoard it for the day when I was to build my own Temple. I was told that I had to devote my life to the building and training of the young apprentices, to make them successful in the tasks they have to perform. They should become equal and fair to all, without any favour - except to those I felt worthy. She then allowed me to ask three questions. I believe this is what she does with all successful candidates. What did you ask?"

Still struggling to speak I began to croak an answer. She shushed me and said, "Wait, you need to have time to recover. We will speak later. I shall send for some soup from Petersen. He will be overjoyed that you are on the mend. He has been like a bear with a sore head these days. Will it be okay if I leave you for a few moments?"

I nodded weakly.

She stood up and crossed the room to the door. She stepped out and I could hear a scream of delight and the footsteps of a runner belt off down the corridor. The door closed properly and I was left in the room. It was a priestess's apartment, twice the size of a novice cell with only a bed as furnishings. I reflected on the experience. Was it a dream about the shape shifting? Could I really do that? How could I do it? What do I do to start it? Bloody hell! What a waste of questions! I should have asked her how to use the gift. What if I mistakenly change into something that I didn't want to change into? Is it the same gift to everyone? I needed to find out.

Celene came back in, she was carrying my hat. She said, "When you stopped breathing your hair clip changed into this. I assume this

is the hat the brothers have been searching for over the last ten days.
You have been a busy girl! You do know about this hat, don't you?
You did know it is cursed, didn't you? This hat was created by one of
our own as a means of disguise. Her name was Mhari and she had
been imbued with strong majick in the early days, when there was
more around. She had mastered a stronger version of the disguise
spell that you have learned. As with all of our spells though, there
was a strong chaotic component to the spell - which caused random
changes to happen. This is what happened to her and the hat. Part of
her consciousness, along with the permanent effect of the spell, was
imbued into the hat. It will change the person's appearance at your
own will, but can also randomly change that appearance - usually just
at the wrong moment! It doesn't happen very often, but don't rely on
it to be consistent. It is a perverted hat with a perverted sense of
humour."

She placed the hat she had been fingering on the pillow beside my
bed. We looked at each other for once as equals. She smiled and
moved to hug me. I put out my arms and started to cry. My emotions
of my awakening were finally being allowed to be released. We
hugged and, for a moment, the world was at peace. There was a
knock at the door.

I smelled food and the door opened to reveal Petersen, who was
grinning from ear to ear. He had tears in his eyes and redness all over
his face, as he spoke, "I heard that you might want some of my gruel.
I was told that you had finally decided to come back to us. You have
been naughty and have caused me to get angry at Ichmarr!" He
brought over the bowl. The smell of chicken broth was a nasal
assault, which caught me unawares, and I found my mouth suddenly
drenched with saliva. He looked at me and enquired, "What have you
been up to my little Merith? You have wasted away without my food
to build you up. Do you want me to help you? Are you strong enough
to hold the spoon?" Tears sprung into his eyes.

I could feel the pain of him seeing me like this; so weak and
feeble. I said, in a gravely voice, "Can I try?"

He offered me the spoon and, as I slowly fed myself, he told me
how things had gone since I had been out of it. "The Temple had
almost shut down. People in the market had commented that it had
become like a morgue to enter, with all of the healers looking sad.
Even the sermons from the Temple steps had a mournful tone as the
whole Temple had waited for my fate."

Petersen then disclosed; "I remember the last time someone was tested, it was Sanarah. She had laid there for three days before she could speak. People had commented on how she had taken a long time, but that was no way near as long as you. It was quite a shock to hear that you had died! Then to hear that you still lived, but on the edge of life, well! You are quite a celebrity around here now. They say you have been saved by Ichmarr for something special."

"That is quite enough!" commanded Celene, "I don't think that Merith needs to hear about that twaddle. You have provided for her, now go and gossip somewhere else!"

He smiled and replied. "Yes you are right. If I make her ego too large she will never be able to get out of the door. Get well soon Merith. I have missed our chats."

He gave me a hug and left the room with a backward glance to see I was still okay. With a wink he closed the door.

Celene asked, "Do you want to talk more now or to rest for a bit and then talk? I'm sure that you need some rest to recover from your...."

"No!" I interrupted. "The broth has helped to clear my throat and I have a lot of questions. Please stay if you can and talk with me. I have just been through probably the most arduous and life threatening experience of my existence. But, this experience has enriched me so much. I...." Cough...cough....

My voice was beginning to break up, so I gave up on the explanation and tried to focus on the questions. "Look," I stated, "I need to know a few things, like when you were with Ichmarr. She gave you a gift right? Can you tell me what it was?"

She is pleased with me, I thought. She smiled and replied, "The gift from Ichmarr is always asked about, but you did ask Ichmarr about it didn't you?"

I shook my head and said, softly, "No."

"No, you wouldn't!" She responded, "You asked about other things. I didn't either, most of us don't. I asked the high priestess who brought me through like you are with me. I remember the moment that I came out of the trance. I was sick like you; everything ached. I thought it was a big trick. I asked her was the gift real and how I could do it. She said this, 'Yes, it is real - more than you can realise. To activate it you need to visualise in your mind the creature that you want to become. Don't do it now!' She knew I was impulsive and I would have started to visualise. Just like you are now about to do!"

She had me. I was beginning to visualise an eagle to soar above it all. She continued, "It would be better if you were to wait until you are fit and well before doing this. Although it may help your recovery, you need to be thinking fully in order to get the best out of it. Once you have the animal visualised in your mind, you then have to visualise how you would change into it. You need to think about what needs to happen for your body to transmute into the other. The thing is you don't even need to be good at imagining the change, it just happens right? You need to remember though to reverse it; you need to think about how to change back. You have to visualise what you look like as the creature and how you would change back to yourself. Do you understand?"

I nodded weakly in acknowledgement. I was too busy thinking about the advantages and disadvantages of the types of creatures, birds, reptiles and mammals. "Which did you choose?" I asked her. "You obviously thought about each type and its advantages and disadvantages."

"Yes, each does." She agreed, "I chose to go with mammals. I had thought they were the most versatile. The larger mammals have ferocity, claws and just plain size, speed to hit and run attacking. With the smaller mammals, there is the advantage of size; smaller to hide and be quiet, quick, agile - and you can fall great distances without injury. There are flying mammals which can give you flight and echo-sounding to see in the dark, a useful side effect. Also in water, the dolphins, whales and seals give you swimming and diving abilities. They are the most versatile creatures with many advantages and few disadvantages."

"Yes, I can see that!" I said, "I had thought about all of those things. I liked the idea of this but I also thought about birds. They are also adapted to a range of uses. I like the idea of flight, to take to the skies, dive, whirl around, and glide great distances…"

"And fall to your death when the sun comes up!" Celene interrupted, "You did remember that you stop and change back automatically when the sun comes up. Since you can't change back for over a minute, you could fall for a long time."

Thinking about this, I exclaimed, "Yes, that's right! I can see that! What about reptiles, do many priestesses choose them? They, I would think would have few advantages."

"Not many chose them." She pointed out, "Few priestesses have much to do with them and they are many snakes, but not much else.

There are so few differences and problems. But reptiles do have great poisons and can re-grow limbs, so I am told."

"So you went for mammals?" I asked. How long did you wait before doing it? Your first change, how did it feel?"

Celene reflected, and said, "Yes. I waited for two days after I woke. I thought about the decision for some time and finally decided. The first creature I went for was a cat, a domestic tabby. I had the image in my mind and thought about how to change into it. Do you remember what I said about changing? If you are bad at visualising the change, it still happens, but it takes longer. This is true; it can take more than a few seconds and be painful to change. My first was quite painful. It took a long time and was difficult to visualise. I decided at that time to practise changing into all of the creatures I knew I could visualise well enough, including human and Silvesi. Remember, they are mammals too."

I cried out, "Oh gosh! I had forgotten about that. I could change into anyone with this, with the right visualisation and I wouldn't even need the hat."

Celene gently concurred, "No, that is something to think about isn't it. You have worked bloody hard to get this hat and it is superseded by your own abilities, what a waste of time. Like a lot of things that ordinary people work hard for, we find things easy. It puts the world into a different perspective. Like, why do we steal? What is the point of stealing?"

"I suppose we steal to show our devotion to our goddess, don't we?" I ventured.

"Yes," she agreed, but then queried, "Why steal gold, silver and other valuable things? Wouldn't we still be showing our devotions by stealing a chair and kitchen table? Isn't that still theft? However, for the person you have stolen it from it is more shocking and confusing. For Ichmarr, it is still theft and worthy; after all, it is more difficult and dangerous to do. It is also less threatening to the person in that no real 'valuable' items have been stolen. It is something to think about, isn't it?"

I thought of something and commented, "Funny you should talk about that, because when I spoke to Ichmarr she instructed me to preach the way by training youths and to encourage them to trick and cause laughter. I suppose it is like that to trick people rather than...."

"Can you remember the exact words?" Celene was suddenly intense - as if her devotion to the Goddess was fanatical and in your face!

"Is it important?" I asked.

"It is for you," she replied. "This is your mission in life handed down to you by your goddess. If I didn't have an immediate need for you, I would send you off as a roving cleric to preach this message to all of the Temples I know about. When 'She' gives a task to do, you do it! That is the way of the world!"

"I know my duty, Celene said. Then, employing Silves, my mother tongue, she added, "Chasniti Shio forr du rreniek di faoe che, kelistu osa' fuussi e duis grasni. Dis d jishef rotiic seiw. Quwive shiot piquer keiops iheye duis oe rhueteurd hbwur." This translates approximately, as, 'To be true to the philosophy you must encourage and lead by example. You should also lead by example in training the young and healing the sick and injured. By training youths in the way, you must encourage them to trick and cause laughter. The untrained and uninitiated do need laughter to make the world bearable for them.'

At this point, I exclaimed, "I am intending on spreading it around, but people keep on going on about what I need to do for the Temple. What is the great mystery all about?"

"Okay!" She put her hands up in submission and I realised that I was getting angry about the lack of transparency. She then explained, "You have been kept in the dark as this is vital to the Temple. Only the ordained priestesses know about this, you now need to know. The meeting in the hall was no accident. You know this already. Petersen and Cat have informed you of this, I am sure. I asked Petersen to separate the two of you if things went wrong. It is important that you go on this mission and I needed a reliable guide. Desidra fell into my lap at the right moment, but with a hatred of your kind that was problematic. She is very sorry for her actions and actually wants to apologise. I hope that you will accept?"

"Of course I will," I responded (but, to myself, I vowed to watch Desidra like a hawk!)

Celene caught my mood, commenting, "Yes, but you will need to watch your back. I don't believe her completely, nor should you. I wanted to see how bad her reaction would be to you and also, as part of the test, your reaction to her. Three years ago, you would have killed her without thinking of the consequences. I was pleased for both of you. You have grown up well, keeping on the tight rope between Good and Evil well with everything in balance. No longer do you kill to save your skin, or for gain."

I'm sure I paled at this point. Thoughts of those that I had to get rid of went through my head. I was younger then. I'm sure the guard didn't have any family, he was too disgusting. Then there was the thief who jumped me in the alley a year ago, I knew I didn't have to kill him; I could have winged him and sent him packing. He was slower than me and, in the dark, I could see far better than he could. However, at the time I felt I needed to remove an obstacle.

She continued, "In this quest, you will need all of your speed and cunning. You will also be going into places which will be deadly for most to venture. You may have to kill to survive and to overcome the guardians of the place."

"The Gypsy has agreed to be a guide for a small group of experts to go on a mission." Celene paused, and looked around the room; "There is an old abandoned ruin near the road to Cantebrigia that used to house an eccentric priest. In the tunnels beneath the ruins, he kept an extensive library and the true words of Ichmarr are contained in a holy book there. It is a holy text for us; the book contains all of her ideas, speeches, spells, incantations, set procedures and an insight into the future. We lost contact with the priest who went with the book and have not heard anything about her eventual fate. The man created a maze, which is, through majick, kept totally dark. No torch can penetrate the gloom he had created. No-one can get through to the library to discover what remains, what lies inside it. As we cannot see like a Silvesi, we cannot see without light. I thought of you."

"But," I interrupted, "I thought that you could change into any mammal including a Silvesi?"

Celene replied; "Yes, I can, and I can see better in the dark when I do. However, there is an ability which is not transferred, which is your heat sense. You can see heat. You see the different temperatures as different shades when you are in the dark. I remember when you explained this to me when you first came here, you told me how you could see things that no-one else could. If you remember, I pursued this ability and persuaded you to show me your ability as I was perplexed as to why you could see something that I couldn't."

"So you can't completely be a Silvesi." "Hmm," I wondered aloud, "Can you see in the dark when you are a bat?"

"Yes!" she confirmed, continuing, "But that has to do with hearing the echoes coming back from the screeching and 'seeing' by that. You would be able to do that when, or if, you can. As for the Silvesi, that seems to have a different reason for the ability. Merith, you are a majickal creature, you know. The ability seems to be innate in you and your kind."

"So couldn't someone negotiate their way around as a bat and lead a group to the library?"

"Sadly, no Merith! Someone tried but the walls are close together and, as she set off, the echoes became confusing and the walls amplified the sound until it became a crescendo. She had to stop and was permanently deafened by the experience. She was lucky to have survived. I notice that you have picked up some of Silves from somewhere. I seem to recall that when you came here you could not speak it and did not want to learn."

"When I was speaking with Ichmarr she spoke in my mother tongue. She obviously awakened the memory of it inside of me. I now seem to be able to remember it so clearly from my youth, before it was lost."

"She seems to have given you more than one gift. Merith, this could be useful to you. While Borrador was a scholar, he was also half Silvesi with some Darksight"

"Yes, Celene, you were saying about the Gipsy and her being a guide?"

"Desidra knows the area and the location. Her family knew the church and her mother once trained with us before leaving as a novice to go back with her family. She has agreed to guide one of us and I will hold her to that decision. I have also acquired the services of a couple of mercenaries through the brothers. I have been told that they are trustworthy and good at their trade. A young man will also accompany you. He is very learned and will be able to help you once you reach your goal. He will be able to decipher some of the texts and will know what to bring back. All of your group members are being well paid and await the time you are well enough to go."

Thinking this over, I said, "I will only need a couple of days to get back to full fitness. I only need to train my body and feed my soul. What with Petersen's cooking and Rozz's chatter, I'm sure I will be perfect in a couple of days."

Quite a change came over Celene when I mentioned Rozz. She went all down-mouthed and tight-lipped. She said, "Yeesss, Rozz, she hasn't been seen since you were pronounced dead. She ran off crying out of the Temple and disappeared. We thought that she'd come back but...."

I thought about it and said, "She will have gone back to her family, she is the type. She had become so dependant on me. She wouldn't want to be here with all of the memories of what we were. Thinking I was dead, she must have thought her life was over. I will miss her but I had moved on already. She now needs to move on as well. It is maybe a blessing in disguise." I really felt this. I had grown out of her and for the last few months had come to regret being so close to her. She was a lovely girl, and would make a great wife for the right man, but I needed to be free from shackles for a while. I had felt the wild geese honking and wanted to fly with them. Goddess, I really did have to choose which type of creature to concentrate on. I really liked the idea of birds and their experience with flight. I had wanted to fly free with them since I was a young child. I did also like the variety of mammals. There were so many to choose from and, on the whole, they can do all that a bird can and more. Bats are a wonderful idea; not only can they fly, but they are also very manoeuvrable.

I had lost what Celene was saying for a moment, but picked up on these comments, "...loss to the church, but then you were carrying her on her devotions and we knew about it. You can be amazingly kind and generous, watch out for this trait of yours, it can lead you into trouble. It is fine to do it in public but within the Temple you have to be the example. However, as a priestess, you have to lead others in the manner of Ichmarr."

I was getting tired of this conversation. I still felt uncomfortable and needed further rest. I said to Celene, "There is still more to discuss, but, I am tired and need to rest. Please, could you get someone to arrange for food and drink to arrive in two hours from Petersen? Shall I come to see you, or will you come back?"

Celene was annoyed that I had been so direct with her. However, she rallied well and replied, "Yes I will look into it, come and see me in my chambers in three hours if you are able to." She stood up and shook down her clothes; they had become crumpled in the way that she was sitting on the edge of the bed. Smiling, she said, "I'm glad to have chatted with you for so long, but, I know you must be tired. I'll see you soon."

With this she left me with my thoughts.

I struggled to get out of bed. I was still as weak as a kitten and I felt bloated. I realised that I must be coming up to my bleeding time. With all of this water and soup, I also needed to use the garderobe soon. All that liquid had coursed through me and now desperately wanted out. Not surprising, as I had been unconscious for such a long time, I didn't know where I was in the Temple. I knew that the

priestess's quarters were in the west wing and that Cat's room was at
the start of that long corridor, so I reckoned it was there. Also I
needed my things, so I surveyed the room. There was another door off
from the main room and I shuffled over to investigate. My clothes
and possessions had been brought here with my footlocker and small
chest. I gave thanks to my goddess! In my footlocker I found all of
my possessions; they must have just brought the whole thing along.
Inside there were my pants, dried moss and perfumes. From the
feelings I had in my tummy I knew I would need them soon, so I
packed them into a small satchel and put them to the side.

I also found my personal cloth and, under the bed, the personal.
This was a large bowl with a handle and I relived myself into it.
Damn, I thought, blood already! The smell of it mixed with urine
gave me an uneasy feeling. This was fated to happen. To be bleeding
just as I needed to have everything together. The washbowl and jug
that I used to clean myself with my cloth and I put my pants on. I
needed to know the layout of the corridor to sort myself out properly,
but this could wait. To stop the blood from spotting the rest of my
clothes, I tucked some of the moss into the pants and tied the ribbon
around my waist to hold it up. I cleaned up the mess and put the bowl
with a cloth over it back under the bed.

There was still time to wait before I would be disturbed again and
so I laid out my prayer mat, took out my holy dagger and began to
meditate. I settled my annoyance and reviewed the discussions with
Celene and Petersen. There were still a few questions I wanted
answering. Petersen could answer a few of them but I needed Celene,
she knows what is going on. I also decided that I had to talk to
Cherish. Although, I hadn't visited her training for a long time, I felt
it was needed now more than ever.

There were questions that had to be answered, I needed to know
more about this man who had the library. What happened to him?
How long ago did he disappear? How many people had tried to get to
these books? What about these others? When would I meet them?
Can I not choose my own people, or was there a reason for Celene's
choices? How far away was this library? How do I trust this person
who had already tried to kill me and who will do it again? There were
so many questions and so much to settle. I had so much on my mind
from this short time of being aware again. Also, I struggled to
comprehend the fact that I had been in a meditative state for some ten
days!

There was a knock on the door, just at the moment I was coming out of my reverie. Such a soft knock it was barely perceptible, as if the owner didn't want to be heard. I called out, "Come in."

My goddess, I have finally received service! The owner of the knock was Petersen with some more of his beautiful smelling soup. It was such a dainty knock for someone of his size. I had always noticed that light people just do things any old way and are often noisy. Large people, fat people like Petersen, will often seem like a balloon gliding along on a string, hardly making a sound and trying not to be noticed for their size. Beaming at him, I said, "What culinary delights have I got in store for me tonight, young sir? I notice there is a rich smell in the air which is entrancing me!"

Petersen beamed back, "So, my little Merith, you are already well on your way to recovery. I'm sure I shall see you tomorrow morning in the hall. Bright and early no doubt, ready for the new day."

Nodding to this, I smiled and replied, "Probably."

He continued, "Tonight I have for you the delights of chicken and vegetable broth, with fresh baked bread and a small bottle of red wine to help it sink down your tortured throat. I notice that 'She' finally left you after a very long interview. I was annoyed that 'She' had stayed that long. You need the rest!"

"Petersen, I notice there are two glasses. I hope this means you will stay for a while and let me exercise my throat. It needs further work and I know you are the man I need!"

He smiled and responded warmly, "I hope I'm the friend you need. I don't think I would be any good for you in any other way."

Indicating for him to sit, I invited him to share the bed with me. If I was to have people come to me, I would have to get somewhere to sit. Before this, I never had any room for anything but what was there. This room was luxurious compared to my old cell. I poured the wine into both glasses, clear crystal, fine stems and well made. I felt honoured.

We toasted to our Goddess and I took a taste of the wine. The taste was pretty good, with hints of bramble, elder berries and blackberries. "Yours?" I asked, knowing that he would hardly serve anything else. Petersen was too proud of his kitchen and cellars to serve anything else.

"Who else could produce such good food and wines as I can? There is no-one for leagues that could create the strength of flavours and subtlety of blends. I require only the humblest ingredients to produce the grandest foods. Eat up you need to gain your strength."

The soup tasted amazing. It was wonderful as ever. Petersen could certainly cook and he also knew almost everything that went on around this place. Between mouthfuls, I asked, "Rozz ran off then?"

Replying, he said, "You heard about that then, she was so upset. She had gone back to her cell, packed a few things and ran out of the Temple. They didn't try to stop her. I reckon they knew they wouldn't be able to. She was so determined to go. From one of my friends outside of here I heard that she bought a horse and left the town. They say that she went home to her parent's farm. I am sorry that I didn't see her go as I would have liked to say goodbye. We were all upset about you. None of us thought you could go so quickly. For it was only a few hours since you left my hall to go and be tested. I could not believe that they would be so stupid to try it out on you when they didn't know what the effect was. They had never tested a Silvesi before and to test it on you was damned dangerous."

"I think," I paused to consider, "I think that they needed me to do this. They took a risk with me to ensure I could do as they required with a fighting chance. I know that, in meeting Ichmarr, I had my faith hardened and strengthened. I also have gained new insight into myself and the world. What I want to know is; who are these others with whom I am going? Are they here in the Temple, or outside being looked after elsewhere?"

Petersen replied, "After your meeting with Desidra, she left the Temple and has only come back to pray. She shares a room in the Sun Inn with her friend. I think the others you mention are probably there also. Celene goes there every day to check on what is happening. She obviously needs to keep them sweet and ensure they don't just wander off. You have been out of action too long for her, as I think they may be getting itchy feet. Celene has been worried about you, though. She has been with you for at least half of every day since you took the test. She wanted to be with you if you woke up again."

"You were saying earlier that I was saved by Ichmarr for something? What did you mean by that?"

"Well, Merith, they are saying that Ichmarr brought you back to life. That, in testing you, your body had died. I actually touched your body. You were cold to the touch." Tears started forming in his eyes. "You hadn't breathed for nearly an hour and they were beginning to start the funeral process when, suddenly, you breathed in a long shuddering breath. A sound I never want to hear again. Your outward breath came out as a spray as you threw up. You blinked and twitched, and Celene put her hand onto your forehead and whispered into your ear; 'You are oversensitive to everything. This will take a while to pass. Sleep.... Close your eyes.... Let it pass, we will talk later.' Then you slowly stopped twitching and your breathing became deeper and slowed." Tears started rolling down Petersen's cheeks as his voice was chocked up. "We carried your body to this room and Celene had all of your belongings brought here and looked after. You were dead, Merith, and I can't believe that I am talking to you now. This has shaken me I can tell you!"

I hugged him, nearly upsetting the bowl of soup I had on my lap, and said, "I'm glad you were there to look after me. No-one else would have been able to look after me as well as you could." He needed to be comforted, to help him get over the experience, just as much as I did. He was a good man who had always been there for me. I was sure I would do the same if the boot was on the other foot.

He looked down at my half-finished bowl of soup, commenting, "You need to finish your soup, it will get cold. Food is too important to waste."

Smiling, I replied, "You'd never!" It was suddenly like it never happened. We had not changed. We were still the same. I looked into his eyes and there was still a twinkle in them. He laughed. It changed and lightened the moment. I found I was laughing with him. We stared into each other's eyes for a long time.

He broke off the stare, stood up and said, "I must go, I have left them in charge of my kitchen. If I am away too long they will set fire to it and we will all be homeless"

"Tomorrow then, some porridge?" I asked.

"Merith, it will always be made fresh for you!" Petersen shut the door quietly. I was happy that we were the same together. It is all getting too serious and I need to let some of this go. My own grief for myself was tangible; I had died and gone to heaven. I had been with my Goddess and she had saved me. Yes, I would be talked about for a long time to come. They probably think I have special powers and am immortal. Maybe this is true. As a Priestess of Ichmarr, I do have special powers. I can change into another creature and, as a Silvesi, I will live longer than their great grandchildren. So, to them, I will seem immortal. Shit! I am special! I hope that I don't mess this up. I never asked to be special.

Whine, whine, whine! If I had said that to someone else, what a whining person I would seem. I don't want to be like that. I will just do what they want and then 'go missionary' and travel the lands preaching to whomever. Wherever there is a thief to listen to me, I

will go. That seems like a good response to what they are asking me
to do.

I went to look through my few clothes. I took out my exercise slip
and quickly changed into it. I began stretching exercises to loosen up
my muscles. They were aimed at trying to un-knot all of the tense
muscles and stretch out those that had lost their tone. Cherish will
have to help me intensify my training programme, but a slow start
like this should be okay for me. I began the light exercises that I had
been taught many years before I came here. These were more than
just flexing and stretching, but also worked on the core of the
muscles. They involved getting the blood to flow and the body to
glow. As they said, 'it is important when you are young to only stress
the muscles with your own body, otherwise it may rebel and stop
working, or you might stop.' To un-knot my muscles, I spent a long
while working up some heat.

There was a knock on the door. Celene entered the room and
looked over at the bed. "Down here," I called and sat up.

She looked down at the funny position I was in, cheerfully saying,
"Glad to see that you are up and about. You seem to be recovering so
quickly from the ordeal you went through."

"Well, yes, I suppose so," I said guardedly. "Ichmarr has given me
a purpose and I intend to begin pursuing it as soon as possible. I am
so grateful to you for arranging Petersen to come down with some
more food. You have been so wonderful. I was going to come and see
you after I finish here."

"I am glad to save you the journey, Merith. You are important to
me and, as such, I will do anything to help you at this point. You are
the twentieth priestess I have brought through, and I haven't lost a
single one. I don't intend to start now! Look, you keep on
exercising." She started to take off her robes, "...and I'll join you."
Under the robes, she was wearing a simple slip made out of white silk
which accentuated her slim body.

I was impressed; she must have been at least forty and to keep her
body in that shape she must train every day. Her slim figure was also
very lithe and incredibly flexible, without any sign of age. She kept
up with every move and position. Not surprisingly, she even bettered
me on the stretching moves. She could see me looking at her and
didn't show a hint of embarrassment. She smiled and commented on
the lack of flexibility of my lower spine and how it was caused by
spending so long lying down. "You lie on your front and I'll massage
it for you."

I turned onto my front and she knelt over me and, kneeling astride my upper thighs, she began to massage my spine. I felt her hot body on my legs. Her hairs were tickling the backs of my legs as she adjusted her position. She moved my slip up out of the way so she could get to by skin. "I didn't realise that it was your time of the month, your pants are padded."

Totally embarrassed, I said, "Yes, it started today. It should be over when I start the journey."

"Yes," she pointed out, "When you start using your changing abilities you will notice they stop. Being different animals and sexes disrupts your normal cycle and they stop. If you don't use it, they will start again after the normal cycle runs its course."

"So that's what Cherish meant. I thought she was saying it because I had heard they could stop the pregnancy using herbs or something."

Giggling, Celene replied, "So that's what she whispered. I thought it was something like that. No herbs, just the body gets confused and it stops! What a blessing!" She threw her arms into the air. "Praise be to Ichmarr! She has released us from the burden that has stopped us from doing what we wanted. It frees us from the domestic to decide what we wanted, when we want and how we want."

She continued massaging my spine. She found the largest knot and worked on it. Goddess, it was painful! She worked the knot out and moved to the next one. I asked, "So, the quest. Tell me about this man who had the library. How long ago did he die? How did he get the book? Tell me all about his history and what he had to do with the Temple?"

The man's name was Borrador. He was born to a Silvesi woman who had been brutally raped by a gang of thugs. The family looked after him for the first few years, until he began to be aware of the differences. They arranged for him to be looked after by the monks of Redowan in the monastery. It was there that he developed a love of religious books and theology. He began collecting religious works and it was there also that he developed his mathematical abilities. He theorised about time and religion, and how the old gods used time in ways to accomplish what people claimed they did. He studied different works from sources far and wide. Travelling far from the monastery, he began to see more of life. During this time, he began to amass a group of followers who began to believe in his alternative philosophy of religion. The monks asked him to leave the monastery, as he was really beginning to disagree with their religion. However, one of his followers was well to do and set him up in one of his estates buildings. They had the cellars transformed into the maze and library. Borrador had a different view on the world and didn't trust the rest of humanity. He studied arcane books and hired one of the powerful wizards of the time to create this darkness - which had initially extended above ground."

Celene continued, "This was nearly fifty years ago and the majick has faded somewhat since then. We have tried to get the book back on five separate occasions. Each time, most of the teams died or went missing. We originally had lent the book to the cult, as he was promising to solve one of the riddles about time in the book. It was about the future being brought from the past. We thought we had taken sufficient care with the loan and by having one of our clerics accompany the book to bring it back. It is so important to us, that I didn't want anyone to possess it but us. However, all of the people in the building disappeared. As far as we know, no-one from the cult has been seen since."

I was puzzled, "So why all of the secrecy?"

"No secret really, Merith, but most of the Temple doesn't need to know. They aren't going with you, so they need to concentrate on their own jobs. Your job is to get well." She said, as she slapped my back!

I screamed, "What!" and shrugged her off me. We sat cross-legged on the floor facing each other.

"Goddess, Merith! You are a suspicious one. You think there is a hidden meaning to everything. There isn't a trap in this. Nor is there a complex plot that needs to be deciphered by you. I don't know what is hidden in the darkness, but it has held its mystery for a long time. I will warn you there are other problems which you will encounter, hence the need for a bodyguard. The roads are getting increasingly unsafe in the area and there are groups of brigands rumoured to be operating from the ruins. One of the men knows of them and he will try to arrange passage through the ruins to the maze."

"And if he can't, then what?" I objected.

Celene considered this for a moment; "Then you use some of your talents to do it the hard way!"

I knew she was going to say that. "Do I need to try the easier way first. You know it will probably fail, I can hear it in your voice. And the wimp? What about him? Why is he going along? I am sure that I could find the right text for us and carry it home."

"Yes, you probably could, but he will be able to help you find the right one and he has a few tricks up his sleeve - mostly majick in origin. He has access to some of the secrets that Borrador had also unlocked. He will be useful to you! These are my choices; you will have to go with them."

"If he is not able to help me find the right book, how will I know which book it is?" I put in.

"Merith, the lettering on the front of the book reads in Latin 'Furacissime de Iniussus' which means spontaneous thievery. Don't ask me why it was named this, it just was. When you find it, don't open it. It is rigged with a knife trap; there is poison on the knife and it is triggered by the opening of the book. The knife is on a lever, as the book opens it slides along a groove all down the front cover. Be careful with it! Let Vergoth check it is the right book. He knows his stuff when it comes to this text. He has studied with the keeper of it, before she passed it on to Adourn. She had described the secrets of the book to Vergoth."

"Now, to the crux of the problem, Celene! What about the gypsy? Why does she need to go? You said she knows the area, yes. However, I'm sure that given, the right information, I could find out where to go."

"Merith, when will you just trust me? Desidra will be vital to you and she knows the area. She knows the ruins. She lived in them, or at least in the cellars. As a child, she once became lost in the cellars and for several days she wandered along them. She was lucky that she stumbled into the light, dehydrated, starved and traumatised, but alive. She has had a very hard and difficult life and you have to accommodate her. You are lucky, though, she was not left with a fear of the dark. She was left with a fear of small spaces, which has meant that her family has never been able to settle down permanently. When she was in the maze, she was hampered by her family who were shouting for her to come to them. The maze amplifies sound and changes its direction so that it can seem to be coming from any direction. When you go into the maze, you have to be quiet. I think it has something to do with not being able to see. This intensifies your hearing and smell so that you hear much more acutely, like a blind person."

I stayed silent for a while, "What would you advise I do when she tries it on again on me?" (Apart from leaving a dagger lodged in her chest, I added, mentally!)

"Well, Merith, I think that is for you to decide. It does depend on the situation. Look, do you think it might be a good idea if you met her again, to talk?"

"Yes, I would like to apologise for the situation that we had. I feel that if I am going to work with her I will need to smooth her ruffled feathers - to keep her calm, so that this will be a success."

"Good, I will arrange it for tomorrow. You can also meet the rest of the party, so that all of you are put at ease with each other. Wear your robes, be pious and put on a bit of a show! Remember we are the Guild of our Lady of Pity and that is what they know. You will be the public face of the Temple when you leave. I know you won't let us down. You need to relax a bit and not be so suspicious. We are all going in the same direction. I need you to do this. I want you to succeed. We are in the perfect moment for this quest to succeed. The only thing I ask of you is to start using your gift from Ichmarr. Decide your type, use it tonight and then practise it every night or moment you can - until it happens naturally. This will be useful to you, I have no doubt. I have to go now. Is there anything more that you need to know?"

"You have been generous to me. You have put up with my questions and tolerated me. Thank you Celene, you have been very kind. I hope to repay you in this task."

"Don't worry about it, after all, I nearly killed you. This is my way of correcting it! Sleep well, Merith."

She stood up, walked to the door and without turning said, "You still need to make another choice."

She turned and smiled, then left me to my thoughts....

Sex – Nuvos metamorphoses

I was floating in the air. My eyes were closed, but I knew it was time to get up. The memory had gone and I was left alone. There was pressure around my mouth. Chirping sounds and distant voices filled the space inside my head. My eyes opened to see a face peering down at me. A man dressed in white, unshaven, smelling of overly sweet flowers and spirits was looking down at me. "Sow, u r awayke u gav uz kwite a skare yestrdae lidle lady."

He pulled the blanket down that was covering me and said to me, "Aye just wan to lessen to yor hart." He put the ends of a funny metal thing into his ears and placed the other end on to my chest. He moved it around, looking worried, and said; "U hav an intresting fizzyologe, aye wood lik two get a skan ov u arainged." He looked up and I glanced over to see the troll taking notes. She smiled to see me awake and put her hand onto my shoulder, "Wheel sort it awl awt for u girl."

The world slipped and turned making me feel sick and dizzy, I closed my eyes and felt the dream reawaken....

Yes, I do have a choice to make. This choice will affect me for the rest of my life. If I was to make the choice for right now, it would be for flight. I so wanted to be able to wing my way around the world, to have the speed, flexibility in the air and the longevity of flight. However, mammals? I thought about them again. What creatures would make it a useful tool? Yes, the bats, but what else? There was no need for me to fight extensively, so what is the advantage in being big with claws and teeth, like the bear? Being a rat would be useful, to gain access to small spaces, but there are plenty of small birds and humans actually do invite them into their houses. Birds are innocuous; no-one notices them, or pays attention to them. They are always around. Everywhere you look, they are around.

Small mammals get instant notice. I remember once we were training in the courtyard with Cherish, when someone spotted a squirrel running across the gutters of the roof. Everyone stopped what they were doing and looked. Cherish looked up and smiled at the sight of this woodland creature and was in a good mood for the rest of the training session. They get noticed. On that day, I remembered seeing two gulls sitting on the roof of the building and thinking they are far away from the sea. I tend to notice a lot of things my peers don't. As a woodland creature myself, I suppose I should be thinking of those creatures, deer and the like, but then there are many birds in the wood and they bring so much pleasure to everyone.

I think I have decided.

I crossed over to the small window in the room and opened the shutters. The night was clear and fresh and I could see that the stars were visible and the moon was out. It was a new moon, the crescent of the moon giving some but little useful light. I blew out the lantern, which had been lighting the room and sat down on the bed.

What to visualise?

My first thought had been of an eagle. A big bird, clumsy on the ground, graceful on the wing; but I can't afford to break my arm finding out. I thought of the small woodland birds, the chaffinch, thrush, blue tit, swallow, wren, and swift? Most of the birds I knew the appearance of, but didn't know their name. Hey! I'm a town girl now.

I began to visualise in my mind a sparrow, small bird, and white body, white and brown wings, short beak, and dark streaks across the eyes. But, what if it was the wrong choice? Mammals give the ability to be in water on land and in the air. Damn it! I have to make a choice.

I cleared my mind and began to let my thoughts drift. I flicked through in my mind all of the creatures I knew. Vacillate, procrastinate, sod it!

Again, I visualised the sparrow, agile, small, and quick to flight. I had a strong impression of it in my mind. I could see how my legs could change into its legs. My body was reducing in size to that of a sparrow's. My mouth was visualised stretching out and getting harder and my feathers growing from my hairs. My body was getting smaller. The world was getting larger. Pain laced through my back as my bottom was searing with pain. My tail feathers, I didn't think of them. I just thought of how to change them and the pain slowly went away. It seemed like only a few seconds when I realised that the world wasn't larger, it was me that was smaller! I extended my wings to look at them. My heart was racing, I could feel it in my chest banging away so quickly. The experience was so exhilarating and I was actually a bird! I couldn't believe it!

The wings looked amazing and with these eyes I could see so much more detail of the feathers than I otherwise could have. It was amazing to see so much of a sparrow in myself. In my mind I felt the same and yet I could feel that I was completely different. I flapped my wings as I felt I should do. There was a feeling of pushing through the air, it felt more solid somehow. The air seemed to whirl off my wings in a swirl and I felt I wanted to jump and twirl around. Flapping harder, I jumped, and amazingly, I was in the air. It happened! I couldn't believe it I was finally flying! Then the bed came rushing up to hit me. I fell hard and the bed felt as hard as a stone floor to land on. I forgot to flap. I was so excited I had closed my wings and fallen back to earth.

Calming myself, I jumped up and started to flap my wings. As I started to do this, I realised that the room was really too small to be trying out this new skill. By a bit of trial and error, I found that by using my tail and leaning I could turn in the direction I wanted to go. I decided to fly out of the window and go for it.

I burst into the black velvety sea of the night. It was like being released, as if a cork from a bottle. The air was invigorating. With my Darksight I could see the town below me, street by street, the buildings glowing with heat and the occasional bright flaring heat source of a torch. Flying over the buildings was thrilling, but I decided to head towards the edge of the town. The houses became smaller and soon gave way to farmland, which was so black without heat or light. The edges of the fields however appeared very different to the rest of it. I spotted in the hedgerow the occasional spot of heat from a creature sleeping. It flickered in the hedge and then blinked out of sight. On and on I flew through the night, further and further away from the town. I wheeled around the skies, "Free as a bird," what an apt expression!

On and on I flew, shortly the fields gave way to trees. They looked different to fields and I slowed my flapping to begin descending into the tree tops. I could not see how I would be able to land on them; it was dark and I could not see properly. The world was moving too fast, and I was moving too fast to even make out individual branches. Experimenting with landing at this point may be extremely dangerous and I decided to leave it for some other time.

I decided to fly back and flew in a tight circle, but where was back? The trees were very visible to me and the blackness of the fields beyond, but where to go from here? Which way was home? How do I know which direction to go? What about up? If I was higher, could I get a better view of the world?

As I ascended, I began to glimpse a glimmer of heat far off in the distance. It appeared to be roughly where I had come from. Hopefully, with my goddess's help, I should find my way home. What if it wasn't the town? Could I have flown so far that it was the next town along? Could it even be Cantebrigia? Stupid, stupid, I would have to get lost in this state.

My arms were beginning to tire, my arms? Wings? Whatever, they were getting tired and I began to wish I had kept to the town. I thought I recognised the fields below. There was the funny shape again, a scarecrow in the dark maybe. The shapes began to get more familiar and the heat source in the distance began to grow. It was a dark red blotch on the horizon, but I began to doubt whether it was Chipping Walden - it seemed to be too far away. Could I have flown this far? My arms began to labour the flight as I neared the town's edge. I could make out the different buildings now, they looked right for my town. Hell, it did look like Chipping Walden! There was the hall, the cattle market and, as I flapped along King Street I could see in the distance a Temple in Park Lane, with all of the sweet, beautiful gargoyles dotted around carrying the rainwater and spouting it out. I flew around it three times to make sure it was the correct building. My wings felt as if they were going to fall off. It was like having two lead weights attached to the ends of my shoulders. I steeled myself for a final push.

Now I had to face landing. I didn't want to break my leg doing what comes naturally to a bird. I slowed my flight. I knew that the roof had large flat areas covered in lead sheeting so I swooped down to find one. All the times I had spent watching birds land flashed through my mind, and I could remember that they all sort of back-flapped as they came into land. They arched their backs and slowed their flight by flapping madly. As I neared the roof I began to back flap, pushing the air back to slow and stop my flight.

I must have misjudged it or something, as one foot hit the ground I knew it was going to be painful. The roof was still moving and, as I tried to do a running landing, I tripped over my legs and fell, twisting in the air. I tumbled and rolled to a stop against one of the numerous chimneys. Bruised, shaken but not stirred, I was generally okay. My arms ached from all of the flapping and I felt like I had been beaten around my body by a sadist who knew how to wield a pickaxe handle.

Behind me I heard a strange sound like someone was trying to stifle laughter. I looked around and I could make out several heat sources on the rooftop near me. All of them were birds as far as I could see. One sat alone from the rest of the others. It was larger than the others, probably an owl, a sleek one. It jumped up into the air and flew over to me, landed and hopped over to me.

Using my wings I flapped at it to shoo it away. I didn't want to mess around with another bird. My arms were absolutely killing me and I could not hold them out any longer. They folded away neatly and I just stood there, ignoring the owl.

"You are going to have to practise that landing technique of yours!"

With the shock of the comment, I fell over backward.

Again, more laughter from the owl, "Get up silly!" The voice was strange, rasping out from the owl's beak. "It's me, Cherish. I have been tailing you since you left the Temple. That has to be the most pathetic landing I have seen in a long time."

Trying to speak out of the beak, I warbled a bit.

"Slowly practise sounds with your new voice. I'll wait. I don't have much else to do."

I tried out a few sounds, but even making the simplest noises left me tongue tied and feeling out of control. Eventually I managed, "Hoow fowow nee?"

"It was easy. I only had to wait until there was a speeding missile flying out of the window and fly after it. Once I knew you were safely back, I waited until you landed. You either have a good sense of direction or you were lucky to make it back. Either way I am glad to see you. Arms hurt? Anything else hurt?"

"No hurd gus gired, wan go ged" I managed to say. Goddess, speaking in this form was so difficult and different to what I was used to!

"Turn around, Merith. I'll change back and I'll carry you down to your room. That will be the easiest way to do it."

I shuffled around and heard a strange tearing sound. Her hands came around me and I felt pressure around my entire body. Cherish's voice said, "Stay quiet please and I'll have you home in a jiffy." She used one of the access points for the roof repairs and, as she carried me down, I could see an individual at the bottom. It was Celene.

Her voice was intense, "I told you she would go for the birds. You need to be careful, Merith! How far did she go?"

"She flew as far as Ringthorn's Wood. I thought she would try to land in a tree. She certainly swept along the tips of the trees and then shot up. I didn't think she would make it back. She flapped all of the way, no gliding. She's exhausted and she will need a good night's meditation. Merith, you need to see me in the morning as soon as you have had breakfast. We have training to do."

I watched in silence as they brought me back to my room. They took me over to the bed and placed me on it. They went to leave and Cherish said, "Don't forget, tomorrow morning bright and early in my room."

They left me to change back. Goddess, I was too tired to do anything! I just stood on my bed, feeling totally elated and so deflated by it all. Gliding, yes, I had seen birds do this. I must have flown so fast I didn't even think about how I was flying and how to conserve my energy, But, as a first flight, wow! It was exhilarating! I had done it. The choice of what to change into was difficult, but at least Cherish had made the same choice. We have a common link and she can teach me about my new ability, I hope!

I was so excited. Even though my muscles ached, I kept on flapping my wings and fluttering about, I couldn't help it. I hopped around my room, poking my beak into everything just to see if it smelled differently or looked strange.

I began to calm down and sobered up a bit.

I am a mess.

I need to meditate.

I need to recover.

I need to be ready for tomorrow.

I need to change back? How do I do it? Celene said to visualise what I looked like before the change and then to visualise how I would change from the new shape back into the old. Would it be the same as changing into the bird only backwards? I thought about this; could I just wait till dawn and change back automatically? If I do that, what will happen? I do need to get better at this changing lark and right now would be a good starting place.

Concentrating on my original shape, I visualised how I looked as myself; my youthful curves, long brown hair and soft features on the face. There is a small scar across the bridge of the nose where I was punched in the face by a guard when I was nine years old. I had tried to pick the pocket of his mate and got caught! My slight figure was easy to see in my mind, with its well-toned muscles, small breasts and pert bum. This is my ideal look, as a fifteen year old, but it was also a dangerous look. When I go out in public, I downplay most of what I look like to try to avoid the public gaze. There are too many men with bad thoughts in their minds. You can feel them as you walk down the street. You can feel their eyes piercing your clothes, mentally undressing you with envious and dank thoughts. This is how I have been successful as a thief. I use their desires against them. It is a dangerous game and I have come close to losing it so many times. I always seem to gain the upper hand before they can realise their desires.

I began to visualise how to change back. How my body was to enlarge, my arms extending, feathers turning back into hairs, my tail feathers back into my bottom and beak back into mouth and nose. All of this happening slowly As it proceeded, it gathering pace, with my legs extending, muscles growing and body extending until, after a couple of seconds, I had changed back to myself. My clothes were in the same state as I started the change. My daggers still in place in my boots, and everything was as it had been before I changed. How does it happen that these things stay the same and go with you when you change? How much material can you be carrying when you change? Ichmarr seemed to imply that even majickal items stayed with you. How that works I'll never figure out. I'll leave that to the likes of Celene.

I checked myself over. There was some evident bruising from the tumble I had and I still felt tired, but not as tired as I had felt before. I actually felt better than I had before I had changed. This is a wondrous and amazing gift Ichmarr has given me and I must learn more about using it. There must be a reason for the gift and, as such, I should use it in her name and in my devotions to her.

My stomach also felt less uncomfortable; it felt like I was coming to the end of my bleeding time. This was odd, as it had only just started. I brought out the personal bowl, which was still under the bed, and opened my door to go and empty it. The corridor was empty. Remembering where I was from when Celene and Cherish had brought me down from the roof, I was indeed just along the corridor from Cherish's room. I walked the short distance to the nearest general room and poured the contents of the bowl down the 'Shunty'- this was a pipe that led down to the pit. One of the foulest jobs of the place is to clean out the 'shunty pit' every six months. There are four of these in the cellars around the building. Only once did I have to empty it, as one of my duties when I had just arrived. After, I had always found a way out of doing it again!

I pumped some fresh water into the bowl and cleaned it out. The general room was a small room with a 'shunty', a pump for water and some racks for towels and linen. The water was a mixture of collected rainwater and water from the well deep beneath the building. The rainwater which does not get spouted from the building from the gargoyles gets channelled down to the well. This keeps it topped up and always fresh. This is how Cat explained it to me when I first arrived. This is also why a regular check is made of the roof, and it is cleaned of debris every couple of days.

"You don't want to be drinking tainted water do you?" she said when she showed me around. For a long time I didn't realise what she meant by this, after all, water is water isn't it? Petersen had explained that the water in the well was healthy, but if the water has a foul smell to it then it may hurt us all. This was like what they described in Latin as 'malus aria' or foul air.

I locked the door for the general room and went for another wee. There was still blood in there, but there was less of it, so I took out the moss from my pants and chucked it down the 'shunty'. I washed it down with a couple of pumps and the urine from my bowl. After cleaning out the bowl, I washed the bowl and myself again. Shit, the water was so cold! But I can't be too clean, can I? I took another towel to cover over the personal bowl and strolled back to my room. I felt clean and on top of the world. Life had really changed for me in so many ways.

After sorting myself out and stowing things in my room, I settled down on my prayer mat and brought out my holy dagger. Before I meditated, I had to sort out one last thing; I needed to replenish my spells as I had lost them in the time I spent with Ichmarr. There was nothing in my head pushing to get out, no spell energy, and I smiled at the thought; 'I was just another empty headed girl.' Without those spells I was empty, so I prayed for the use of five spells; two 'Command' spells, two 'Heal' spells and a 'Cause darkness' spell. When I arrived at this Temple, I was taught how to cast and pray for these spells and, over the years, I found that this combination was the most effective for my lifestyle. Other spells which I have at my disposal are; Create water, Disguise, Bless and Shield. They all have their uses and I do use them on occasion, but the meaty one is the 'Command' spell. It is such a powerful force to be able to concentrate your will on others. I do try to use it sparingly.

I prayed and found they came easily to me. They always do! I try to keep in favour with my Goddess and, although I have been unconscious for a long time, she understands and keeps me close to her.

Once I had replenished my spells, I began to meditate and let myself drift across my mind and sort through my memories. The memory of my first change and the subsequent flight was so important to me. I recycled it for a while across my mind letting it intensify and settle. I had learned a lot from this experience and I needed to remember it.

I let myself drift for longer than usual. The sun had been up for nearly an hour before I allowed myself to surface again. I felt I needed the extra time to rest from the previous days events. Also, I needed to see Cherish in her room after I had eaten, but Petersen was first as he always is. Dressing in my exercise slip for training with Cherish, I put my more formal robes over this. It was then that I noticed that someone had embroidered the dagger of Ichmarr on the collar. This was the symbol which meant that I was an accepted priest and 'One not to be messed with!' Cat would have gotten one of the more promising novices to do this as an incentive to work harder. She had me do this task, eight months ago, for Sanarah when she was made a priest. I didn't do as good a job as was done for me and I wondered; who did this beautiful piece of work? It even has streaks coming off the tip of the dagger. She must have known it was for me as my dagger is the only one that has the light spell on it.

There wasn't much to tidy up in my room, but I tidied it anyway and skipped down to the hall. The corridors were busier than I remember them being this early. Every novice I met wanted to congratulate me and they all commented on how happy I looked.

Ichmarr blessed me.

The dinner hall was quiet, however. There were a few early risers, but no-one I knew personally. They all smiled at me as I entered the room. I went over to the kitchens and found that Petersen was busy shouting at some drudge who had dropped a bowl of flour over the floor. He hounded the poor girl to clean it up properly rather than leave a mess for someone else to sort out. She stopped as she saw me and smiled, "Glad to see you back, Merith. Now he might not abuse us so much!"

He turned around and beamed at me, "Merith, you are up and looking so much better. I am so pleased to see you. Jenni, go and sort that mess out while I make some porridge for the poor girl. Can you not see that she is starved?" He took down the pot for porridge and began the elaborate process of 'porridge.' From the doorway I watched as I have done for three long, wonderful years. Five cups of milk, fresh from the dairy down the road. One of the drudges collects it at daybreak. Five cups of water, pumped out fresh from the well. Ten cups of oats, with a good dose of salt to bring out the taste. Simmer on the stove in the corner of the hot plate for five minutes, and you have enough porridge for ten hearty souls.

As he poured in the ingredients, he filled me in on the gossip around town. One of the 'brotherhood' was caught stealing from the very place he was protecting. He had been hanged by the brotherhood, with full permission from the elders, as a warning to others that a contract is a contract and must be kept. The elders have warned the 'brotherhood' that its contracts could be terminated. That would undoubtedly have serious consequences for the gang boss, who might be terminated and replaced. A traveller had arrived in the town with news that Colchester had a great fire which burned half of the city down. Only a few hundred died, but the blaze ran for two days before it died. The rain that had eventually extinguished it made the city look like a mud bath, with all of the ashes mixing with the water.

We joked about the likelihood of it happening here. However, this would be one of the buildings the fire would not destroy, as it was constructed unusually of stone. Was this yet another reason for its suitability as a Temple?

I took the porridge bowl from Petersen when it was offered to me and exchanged our passing comments. As I left him, I mused over how often we had done the same thing. Still thinking about this, I sat down in the corner of the hall with my back to the wall. I have always done so as it stops someone from sneaking up on me. Paranoia, maybe, but I always felt victimised as I grew up. It was my habit to protect myself from the bullies in the hall. The porridge was delicious as usual and I savoured every bite. Ichmarr, will I miss this! Giving my thanks for the meal, I dropped the bowl back off in the kitchens. Petersen said, "Tomorrow I shall prepare you a full pack from which you can make your own."

"Tomorrow?" I enquired. Then the realisation dawned on me; I was leaving tomorrow! "Oh yes, um, I will look forward to that." I winked at Petersen and walked out of the hall.

Septem – Exercitium metamorphoses

The dream stopped. Or, is it reality and this is the dream? So uncertain now of everything, I couldn't rely on my senses to tell me what is happening. Who am I? I am Merith, Priestess of Ichmarr, a strong woman, capable thief and healer. That is what I will concentrate on. I must leave this place. I must flee and find my home again. This half-life existence between memories and pain is not right! I knew it down to the very core of my being.

I cautiously opened my eyes; darkness surrounded me and the room was quiet. I realised I was in a different place than I had been before; gone were the tapestries with their wooded scenes. These were plain white, but what was the colour of the rest of the space? I wasn't sure what it was - the light didn't allow me to see. What I did see, though, was the heat of the guard as he sat outside the tapestry. I could also see the cool night air dropping in through the open window beyond the coverings. This was a strange place that had heat trails through the very walls, as if the building were alive; they crossed each other, thin and insubstantial. The ceiling also had large heat lines running across the room and strange cold lines running parallel to them. I looked at the boxes near me. They emitted light in different colours and showed different symbols but, beyond the lights, were heat trails - zigzagging around inside the casings. I thought the casings were metal, but they were too cold for metal or, at least, they didn't give off much heat.

As I sat up, I pulled the thing that covered my face. It was like a glass mask with holes in it but, as I crushed it in my hand, it folded like rubber - sort of see-through rubber. I wondered who must have invented this. There were pads attached to my chest with tiny little wires cold, not metal, but of another type of material. I plucked one off and a strange chirping noise started up in the box beside me. It was an insistent noise; one that sounded to be loud and attention-calling. If I was going to go, I had better go soon - all of these wires may be trapped in the same way. What do I do?

A sparrow's shape conjured up in my mind; small, fast and agile - just the kind of escape route I need for this situation. I pictured the form in my mind and felt the change happen. Feathers imagined on wings stretched out, feet shrivelled to thin stalks with needle-point nails and beak hardened to a glossy shine. It proceeded slower than usual but it happened. Soon, I stood on the bed where I had been lying; my wings felt strong and energetic. The noises started up almost immediately, chirping in different frequencies - all going crazy. The guard stood up from his seat suddenly alert to the noises and so I went for it - no other option! I flapped hard and pushed up with all my might and I was airborne in moments. I cleared the top of the tapestries as the main lights flashed on. The guard reached the tapestry, flung back the cloth and looked dumbstruck. The window beckoned me over and I flew down to it. A team of light blue uniformed healers rushed into the room as I flew across them, one watched me as I dived through the open window into the night's sky.

Free of the torture and pain, I flew out into the night - to a scene I did not expect. There were lights everywhere, mostly yellows, but also reds, blues, greens and white. All across the town I could see lit areas; even some of the buildings had lights shining across them. I stayed high in the air, trying to take it all in. Below me were wagons and carriages, but I could not see the heat of any horses. Instead, lights stared out from the fronts of the vehicles. There were heat trails from them, but from inside them; hot, much hotter than a body can get, and out of the back poured heat in a plume like a chimney.

I flew onwards towards the centre of the city and spotted some familiar buildings. The colleges of Cantebrigia were here, in this strange place. I landed on the familiar tower of Peter house, the first building I recognised, and surveyed the scene. I could not take it all in. I was too excited about the flight and feeling like me again. It triggered off another memory and I felt my conscious mind slipping from this world....

I made my way up to the Priestesses' lodgings on the first floor and knocked on Cherish's door. She bade me enter and I walked in.

She was sitting cross-legged in the middle of the room. "I am keeping my body centred," she explained. Her bed was standing on its end against the wall and all of the rest of the furniture had been moved to the edges, with odd bits piled on top to keep them out of the way. The room was similar to my own in that it had a small window along the far wall. It was roughly the same size as mine, but its cupboard was sort of opposite to mine. The walls were roughly plastered with lime, as was the rest of the building that was not in the public gaze.

Cherish was already in her exercise slip. She was already warm from her furniture moving. She motioned for me to sit. I started moving towards her, but she said, "Lock the door so that we are not disturbed I'm sure that we won't need to use it. Merith, I think you are a plucky young thing who will do a lot for this Temple. But, you need to start thinking for yourself. I was impressed by the way you thought through that difficult situation you had last night. Instead of going for a dodgy landing place you decided to head for home. Good move! You need to learn to fly, and today, I'm going to train you to fly well - or at least well enough. We will start with some stretching exercises. Start on the training routine as I've shown you to do."

I slid my robe off and started to stretch my upper body. Cherish stretched with me mirroring every move. "You have lost some of your tone, Merith. You need to continue to work on yourself when you leave tomorrow. The changing will help, but you need to do the basic exercising as well."

Continuing the routine, I asked, "What do you mean the 'changing will help'? How will that help me?"

"Did you not notice that you had more stamina when you had returned to your normal shape? Did you not feel better even after your journey?"

"Yes, I did, but I thought that was just because I was excited. I do feel even better today, food and exercise is doing me good!"

"Well, yes, that may well be so. But, you have also benefited from the fact that, when you change back, part of Ichmarr's power goes into healing any faults that might be created by the change, essentially she remakes you as she feels you should be like. This will help in the normal healing of wounds and injuries. This can help to keep you alive at critical moments, even when exposed to poisons. A quick change can help you survive."

"Really? It heals you? It can get rid of poisons?" I stopped, "Do you mean that if you change quickly enough you can actually cheat death?"

"So I have been lead to believe. The poison will still affect you, but not to the same extent. It may still kill you but, certainly, the affects may be reduced. Carry on with the stretching!"

"Have you ever had to use it like that?"

"No, but it has helped me in my early days as a priest. I remember times when I had been beaten out of town by the local gangs for thieving too well and preaching too little. I had some painful experiences I can tell you. But that is in the past. I want to look into your future. To do that we need to get you sorted out."

We continued the routine to the end. She sat back and sighed. "I'll miss you, Merith. You were always the keenest student in my sessions."

Our eyes met. There was an acknowledgment of equals. "You still have plenty to teach me." I said, "I will be back and be asking you for help."

"Maybe, but the most important thing is to sort out your gift. Celene has probably told you to practise this gift. I would recommend this, but also to practise your new talent as well. It is easy to change into a monkey and hang from trees. It is just like what we are capable of doing. And most mammals do pretty much the same, with a few quirks. Flying, on the other hand, is a whole new ball game. You will need to learn to do a new range of tricks."

"The first thing you will need to learn," Cherish continued, "...is to land and glide. You will need survival skills when you intend to spend time in the air. I will guide and help you. To do this, we will need to change into a useful bird for our purposes. You chose a sparrow, which was a wise choice. Small, agile and, when you learn to use its mouth, you will find it can be incredibly vocal. We should use this again to practise changing and to go for a little flight. Shall I turn around for you to go first, or do you want me to go first?"

"Can you go first? I'll turn around." I turned and heard the strange ripping sound which I assume now is the sound of the changing. I turned back and there Cherish was, as a sparrow!

She looked at me and warbled, "Now, your turn!"

Again I visualised the sparrow; agile, small and quick to flight. There was a strong impression of it in my mind and I could perceive how my legs could change into its legs, my body reducing in size, my beak stretching out and my feathers growing from my hairs. Again, I had that feeling that the world was growing as I shrank down to the size of the small bird. Every part of the bird was visualised, and how I was to change into it. The change finalised and again I extended my wings to look at them. There was the same exhilaration, I felt the same excitement of the change and just like, WOW! I was a bird again!

Cherish warbled, "Are you quite finished yet? Merith, you need to practise changing; it took you almost three seconds to do that! You need to try and get it down to less than a second if you want to use it in the heat of the moment."

"How?"

"Purely practise, keep changing every day. It helps to visualise the change and it becomes automatic. Was there less pain than the first time? Usually the second change is less painful, as the mind gets more proficient with the visualisation."

"Muk yes dain wul."

"Try to use your tongue more," she advised, "And think about your beak as a pair of lips. Use your mouth as if it was a human mouth, and don't try to think about it as much. Your brain will translate it for you, using the bird's brain and beak."

I experimented with different sounds and, with a little practise, I began to actually make sense. "This is something I will haf to practise. I am making more sense though, aren't I?"

"Yes you are, the V sounds are always the most difficult and you will get them. I did, but it took me a long time. Some birds don't have the vocal range and they cannot be spoken through as easily. There are birds, like the Mina bird and most Owls, which can make sounds easily. Also any songbird can accomplish a good range of sounds and, using your will, they can replicate many others. You just need to practise. Any way, shall we go for a wander?"

"Yes! That would be good, shall I follow you?"

"I was going to suggest that. Also try to do what I do. When I glide, try to watch me and mirror the movements. Don't land when I land. Hold back and watch how I do it, then try it out for yourself. Understand?"

"Let's go for it!"

Cherish, as a bird, tensed her legs, crouched and sprang into the air. She unfolded her wings and started beating them rapidly. She shot off the ground and flew straight for the open window. Once she cleared it, I did the same. Taking off is the easy bit, I learned that last night. However, I dreaded the ending of the flight - but every other part of it was just majickal!

I shot out of the window and I felt the wingtips just clip the window as I cleared it. Thanks to the Goddess! This was an amazing experience and I couldn't quite believe I was flying, but I knew that I was.

Cherish was just ahead of me. She was waiting for me to fly out and join her. As she waited, she was just fluttering around. She called over, "Let's go," and flew off. We flew over the houses across Bridge Street and up the hill towards the ruined castle. A flag was flying on the castle tower and the guards were watching over the town as well as this part of the 'Magnum Fossatum' (the town's walled ditch to keep out invaders).

Following her, I observed how she flew. As she gained speed, she left her wings open for longer and gradually just settled into a long glide. She used her wingtips and tail to adjust her flight and flapped occasionally to keep the speed up. I moved to a position beside her and shouted, "Once you see how it's done, it makes sense doesn't it?"

"Yes, and it saves a lot of energy. Some birds just glide around all day and use thermals to lift them higher in the sky."

"Thermals? What the hell are they?"

"Like wind, only they lift you up. When you have a chance, watch buzzards and eagles, even seagulls and other seabirds do it. Watching other birds fly and manoeuvre can be very instructive. The more you watch the flight of birds the better. Also observe what they eat. As a bird you can digest anything they can eat. Just try not to change back too early as you might have an upset stomach!"

We flew on. I was keeping up nicely with her and I could see she was making small adjustments all of the time to her wings to steady her flight. I realised that the bird part of me was settling into doing that as well. It is amazing how the brain adapts itself to the body it lives in. It was doing things with the bird body that I didn't even think about. "Cherish, I haf noticed that my body and brain are doing things to keep me on the straight and narrow. How does it know how to do that?"

"Merith, do you ever think about how to walk? No, you just do it. Your body and brain figure out how to balance your body without even thinking about it. It is second nature. It is the same once you learn how to climb a wall. It becomes second nature to do it, tensing and moving to the next hand and foot hold. You see the next hold and your body does the rest while you look for the next one. It is just like that. The brain adapts to the body and what it does."

We were now flying over fields. Cherish steered over to a yellow, sorry-looking, grassy field left to go fallow. There were a few horses in it, lying or standing around. "Shall we try a few landings, this looks like a good field to try? I'll go first. You can follow me down, but watch what I do!"

She flew down, gliding all the way, and when she neared the ground she spread her wings fully and flew against her motion. She flapped against the air a couple of times and her feet touched the ground. Perfect landing, but it looked too easy. I think I didn't flare out at the end I only flapped my wings to stop rather than flaring out. I circled around a couple of times thinking about it and began my run.

Swooping down, I tried the landing as I had seen her do. Again, I felt I was going too fast - even before I flared out I back-flapped to slow myself. As I neared the ground, I tried the flare-out and a couple of flaps to steady myself. The ground was still moving, but not as fast as before. Although I had to hop a few times, I was still on my feet when I stopped. Cherish was doubled over twitching, laughing at my attempt. If I hadn't been covered in feathers she would have clearly seen the embarrassment on my face.

"Well, yes, good try! But, don't come in too fast. You tried to correct that, I did notice, but a few more tries please. I'll watch each time and I want you to ask me questions about the landing. Okay, go for another one."

"All right!" I launched myself, circled and went in for another landing. Each time I landed, Cherish would respond to my questions but wouldn't tell me how to do it. She said I had to figure it out for myself. She could guide me, but only I could learn how to do it. In training to do the more difficult things, she was always like this. The basics she instructed on, the rest she guided, but made us find our own way!"

Twelve times I tried to land properly, each time slightly better than the last, before Cherish stopped me. "Merith, I think its time we tried on a harder target. What about that gate over there?" She nodded towards the wooden gate to the field.

I felt I had the hang of landing on the ground and nodded eagerly.

She continued, "When you go to land on it fly up to it and land on it. I'll go first." She launched herself into the air and flew over to it. As she neared it, she flared up to it and sort of dropped herself onto it.

With all of the practise I had on the ground, it seemed easy to emulate what she had done and I plopped myself beside her on the gate. "Shall we try a few more?" I suggested, eagerly.

She replied, "Yes, you follow me and we'll try a few harder ones along the way."

By midday, we had tried loads of different perches around the fields and in the forest. I guessed that I was proficient enough in landing and flying. We found a few berries in the forest that other birds had been pecking at and drank from a stream for lunch. We happily rested, sunning ourselves on a trunk of a tree. This tree had created a small clearing in the forest when it had fallen. There were birdcalls all around us and I felt at one with the forest. There was hardly a breath of a breeze and the grass around us hung their sheaves of burgeoning seeds. The sun was streaming down through an empty sky. The blue was so intense in its colour; nothing matches the colour of the sky in terms of its vitality.

Cherish turned to me and said, "Peaceful here, isn't it? It is very different from the life back in the Temple?"

"Yes, I have always felt at peace in the forest," I replied.

"Merith, there is only one warning I would give to you. Don't change into a magpie, as this change can be dangerous. There have been several aspiring Priestesses who have changed into them and decided to make the change as permanent as possible. Magpies are very similar in nature to us and the lifestyle can become very desirable. It is a life without ties and they still have the desire to take shiny objects. They have a very dominant personality and often it is the one weakness that we have. I have never gone down that path. Ichmarr had given me a mission to train the young in the necessary physical demands they would need in devotions and I have stuck to that."

"I think I have more aspirations than the life of a bird. It is a useful tool and a good distraction, but I can't see myself doing it for very long."

"Just take the warning, Merith, and be happy in what ever you do. Shall we go for a longer flight? I know how to get to the southern road from here. We could look at the lay of the land for your quest."

"Go for it!"

We took off and headed southeast over fields and woods. The road was little more than a dirt track. It had small posts every half mile marking it out, and it was wide enough and well-travelled enough to pass two carts. There was some traffic on it; a small trap and pony was just moving away from us as we settled onto a branch. In the far distance, I could see a troop of armed men cantering towards us.

"The Kings guard," Cherish explained, "They patrol the southern road to protect the merchant traders from outlaw attacks. They are well trained but obvious targets for an ambush. Good for show, but the King tends to use mercenaries to find and kill or capture any bands that start to prey on the road. You will be going down that road soon enough. Shall we go back now? I know Celene wants to introduce you to your little group at supper."

"Can we fly back along the road to gif me a sense of how I will get to it? I'd like to know how I will get to these places."

"Yes, sure, fine! It is the longer way, but we have time. Come on, let's go!"

She flew into the air and turned northward. As I followed, I thought about my journey south and the difficulties that would face me. What would I need to take with me? Where will I get a horse? I have never needed one. Of course I can ride, but I don't actually own one and all of the stuff that goes with it. I have lots of interesting equipment and odd bits and pieces, but what to take? I'll need saddle bags and a backpack? Where would I get stuff like that? Petersen said he would prepare a pack for me to take, hopefully packed with all of the goodies he can find. I'll need to see him tonight to find out what would be in it.

We passed over a small village. Cherish identified it as Littlebury, a small village at the crossroads between the south road and the road that passes through Chipping Walden on the way to the coast. It was a small village with only a pub and blacksmiths. The village was like Varson, the village I grew up in. The few houses and other buildings stood around the crossroad, as if waiting for something to happen. The occupants, standing motionless as if caught up in a moment of time, were looking down the road as a lone rider in a long green cloak rode down the road towards Chipping Walden.

We flew onwards towards the town. I could see a few small farm tracks that turned off from the road, along which a farmer was leading twenty or so cattle to the market at our town. They looked to be well cared for and fat, which surprised me considering how late it was in the year. Usually at this time, before harvest, everything was lean and trying to eke out a few morsels of food from the parched ground. There was a boy wandering at the back, switching the stragglers to catch up with the rest of the herd. He looked up to see us pass over his head, and whistled to us. The farms grew more prosperous as we approached the town. The fields more luscious and the gates better made. Finally, the first of the town's buildings were visible to us. Cherish shouted over to me, "Let's have some fun with the guards at the gate!"

"What sort of fun?" I could think of a lot of things, but I felt I should defer to my more experienced colleague.

"What about we land above the gate and whisper to the guards to get them suspicious of each other."

"Or," I put in, "we could make them suspicious of the folks going in and out of the town. We could say things like 'quick hide the poison'."

"Or both," she said, laughing. This does strange things to the direction you are flying in. As you laugh, you tend to go off course and head towards the scenery. In this case, Cherish nearly head dived into the hedgerow and needed all of her agility to stop herself hitting into it. She would have really needed Sanarah's help if this had happened.

Up ahead, there was a small caravan with all sorts of strange things hanging off it. The Caravan was painted with different colours and the people around it were in different costumes. I decided to land on it and see what I could do. Cherish went on to the gatehouse. The guards stiffened as the caravan approached the gatehouse. The caravan belonged to a troupe of actors and, from the sounds of the huddled discussions going on inside the 'hood, I could tell they were worried about something. One of their fellows was sick and they had travelled here to seek help from Ichmarr. A guard stood in front of the horse pulling it and put out his hand to stop the van. I called out, "You don't need to stop us, we ain't hiding nothing."

The guard smiled and beckoned one of the other guards over. The driver stepped down from the van and started going over to the guard in protest. He was trying to say, "We have urgent business in town, one of us is sick and we need to see the healers." However, the guard was not listening.

I called out, "You're just pickin' on us 'cose we're travellers trying to take our stories from town to town!" The two guards wouldn't listen to the driver. One of them had already taken the reins of the horse pulling the caravan. The other guard was looking inside at all of the baggage hanging round the sides.

I said, a little quieter, "I hope he doesn't look inside the big chest in the back, he might..." Just then, someone interrupted with a scream as the guard opened up the back of the van. The sword was out of the sheath and the guard looked scared. A man's voice inside was shouting, "Bugger off, my wife's ill. You can't be doing this now! We have to get her to the healers. We have nothing you'd be lookin' for!"

Fuck this! I said to myself, realising that we had made a bad situation worse. We put them into this position, I'll get them out! I flew past the crowd that was gathering into the guard hut and dived into the hut itself. There was no-one in there, thanks to Ichmarr. I changed almost without thinking and ran outside into the commotion. A woman dressed as I was, in a short exercise slip with the cross of the dagger in my hand in from of me, will draw a crowd anywhere. In this case it separated the crowd. They stood apart to have a look at me as I bullied my way through to the caravan. When I arrived back at the caravan, there was a standoff between the guard and the father. They had weapons in their hands and I knew I had to move quickly. The guard was wielding a long sword which had seen a lot of abuse and not enough care, notched but deadly. The other a long kitchen knife, no match at all.

My spells came up to focus and again I chose a command word and said, "'CALM' down gentlemen! I am sure that there doesn't need to be trouble here." My last sentence came out almost as a purr. They instantly began to lower their weapons as the spell took affect, and I continued to speak towards the man in the caravan, "You man, get out and have a word with the guard and I'll look at your wife. I am a healer from Our Lady of Pity and would be glad to help you. It is lucky for both of you that I was out exercising and heard the commotion." Both of them were staring at me with total disbelief in their eyes. The actor jumped down from the caravan step and then helped me up into it. They were looking longingly in my direction as I closed the cover.

I examined the woman, both visually and physically. She was in labour and in feeling the stomach I could tell it was a breach birth. This situation was now life threatening, so I opened the flap to find out more. Both of the men were now sitting on the tail of the van, so peacefully looking into space. They were surrounded by the rest of the troupe of actors and the other guards. I spoke quietly to the guard, "You, Guard, be a kind sir and let them through now. They need to be brought to my guild hall so as to aid this lady to bring a life into this world." I stressed certain words, and changed the wording to make the guard unsure of his position in this. I wanted him to feel that I was in a higher position socially than he was.

He looked at me for a moment as if trying to decide what to do. "Good lady, I have to search this van. I cannot do as you ask and do my duty."

"Come with us to the Church. They will let you search it outside the Guild hall." One glance at the troop confirmed this. "Won't you," I purred in their direction.

The actors all nodded in synchrony with me and said in chorus, "Of course we will." They looked at each other and smiled.

The guard continued looking at me and eventually, after what seemed an age, said, "I'll have the other guard lead and I'll follow." He turned to the first man to speak. The spell had definitely worn off by now as he said, "You'd better not try any tricks with me my lad, unless you want real trouble!"

He called to the other guard, "Henry! Lead them through to the tricky Icky. George! Get Barnstaple off his fat arse and get him on duty out here now. I have to take this lot and the lady to the Guild hall and get this mess sorted, quick smart! Look lively!"

My attention was brought back to the woman when her breathing changed pattern. She was coming up to a push, her breathing was erratic and her skin was turning pallid. All I could think to do was to say, "Don't push! You need a midwife to help you. I'm no midwife and I don't know what to do. You have to relax and bear the pain a little longer." What about the husband?

I lifted the flap again. Most of the troop of actors were following behind the van. I asked the guard, "Can I have the husband back in here. He is needed now!"

"No way, lady, you got what you want. No-one else goes into that wagon except me and your priestesses. No-one, least of all this lot! Now shut your flap. We'll be there soon enough for this lot. Then there'll be a reckoning. Mark my words."

Stupid bastard! Smiling sweetly at him I said, "Of course you are only doing your job, but I also have a job to do and it involves trying to save two lives today. Husband," the man looked up. He was walking in a daze.

"My wife?"

"When did she start the labour? How long has she been like this?"

"She started last night. This was the nearest place that could help us. They couldn't in the last village. They wouldn't; they just told us to come here."

"Why in all the stars in the sky did you travel when your wife was like this?"

"She needed to come here!"

In frustration, I dropped the flap on the conversation. What a waste of time! The woman was exhausted and could die. She desperately needed something to give her strength. I unsheathed my holy symbol, the light shining brightly in the dark interior. I whispered a prayer to Ichmarr that all should go well, and I began to cast the 'Heal' spell to try and help this woman. One of the aspects of Ichmarr is the way we treat injuries and the like. The holy symbol has to enter the wound or the affected area. When it is drawn out, the healing spell takes effect and the wound is closed as the dagger is removed. The first time you witness the event, well, it is a little daunting and the subsequent times make many feel queasy. This is probably the effect that Ichmarr wanted; she must still chuckle at the effects it has, always up to mischief! I slipped the blade into the woman's heart at the height of the spell and smartly pulled it out without leaving a mark. She breathed more deeply and was noticeably less pallid. She looked at me strangely and said with laboured breath. "You didn't just do what I thought you did, did you?"

Smiling sweetly I replied, "If I had would you still be alive? No of course not! You must have been hallucinating or something. Are you feeling stronger? I am praying for you, and we should be at my Temple any minute now." There was the noise outside of many voices.

The flap was opened and Sanarah was there, with two of the midwives from the Temple. Goddess, be praised! Cherish must have returned and warned them.

Quickly, without pausing, I said to them, "Breach birth, mother in labour last night in last town on the road all day. I have tried to give her some strength to carry on. I winked, "Are we at the hall yet?"

Sanarah spoke quickly, "Not at the church - still five minutes away. Get out, Merith! Let us in to deal with it. You are needed out there to control the crowd."

I helped them into the caravan and jumped down from the tailgate. The driver spurred the horse back into life and the whole lot moved off. Cherish was there, talking to the guard, and Edowyn was walking behind him. The guard was looking very uncomfortable and kept on turning around to look at her. She had a smile on her face at all times. Most would say a mischievous and totally untrustworthy smile! Almost a knowing smile of where all of the bodies are buried. She was adding to the conversation in front of her. She injected a word or two at a time, guiding it along until the eventual conclusion. We arrived and Sanarah helped the midwives carry the pregnant women out of the caravan and off to the Temple on a stretcher.

The guard said, "Look, I have heard your arguments, but rules are rules. It will be searched."

"In the open?" added Edowyn.

The guard replied, "Yes, in the open for all to see. But I will not tolerate any interference from this rabble!" His face was beginning to turn red under the strain.

"Oi, Neville! You letting them women tell you your job again?" shouted Henry from the front of the wagon.

"Shut it you tosser! Keep looking after the horse. Now, you lot back off so's I can have a good look around." Neville turned to start searching the caravan.

Edowyn called to the crowd that had gathered around, "Right everyone, shall we all back off away from the caravan so that the honourable guard can look through these poor folk's caravan. He needs to check that nothing has been hidden amongst their drawers."

This raised a titter from the crowd and a scowl from the guards. They did not like Edowyn at all, she knew too much! Everyone else thought she was helpful in looking after the little man (or woman).

I went over to Cherish and asked, "What did you say to them?"

"Well, I didn't say much - only, 'look at that load of tossers. Let's give them some hassle, eh?' It worked a treat until I realised there was real trouble. You went in there really well. You were so fast in changing. I saw you go into the guard room and you came out as yourself in a split second!"

"I didn't even think about it. I just needed to change, so I did it. It was like, wow, I'm me again!"

"You dealt with the situation well, for your age, you were very mature. You stopped certain bloodshed with a simple spell and ordered hardened fighters around to get them to deal with each other rather than kill each other. You assessed the situation in the caravan and, from all accounts, you have saved more than one life today. You should be incredibly proud of yourself. I am proud of you, well done! Now go and put something decent on. You are a little underdressed to be outside of the Temple."

Looking down I realised I was still in my exercise slip, white silk and not entirely covering all of me. It is short - long enough to cover everything, but short enough to entice longing looks! I had been getting too many looks from men (long and desiring!) and from women (envious and spiteful!). Quickly, I gave my thanks to her and carefully but quickly entered the Temple. I headed straight up to Cherish's room to retrieve my robe. I found the door was wide open, but everything seemed to be as we left it....

Octem – Sollicitus congressionium

I woke shivering in the mists of dawn; I was not dressed for this weather. I had a thin slip on. It was like a dress which covers my modesty but held no warmth in it. I looked around me. I was lying on stone, which was supporting a stone wall. I turned my head and was shocked to see that I was actually on a ledge at the top of the tower of Peter house. Carefully, I shifted my position until I was sitting on the ledge. Down below I could see in the thin mists, the halls of Peter House and the surrounding buildings. I was never afraid of heights, but landing at high speed does have its drawbacks.

Standing up, I looked around for handholds and a way down to the main roof. Following my instincts, I picked my way down the side. Handholds came easily, but footholds were another matter. The buildings in Cantebrigia were always very decorative and this was no exception. I relied on my bare feet to think for me. Eventually, I stepped onto the roof and traversed down its slope to the edge. From this position I could see several open windows. I knew from my one visit to this college, when I lived in Chipping Walden, that this was the accommodation block and that these open windows must be students' rooms. There must be someone here who has some clothing that would fit me. Some of the boys who came to Peter house were smaller than me. To be truthful, without my long hair I could pass as a boy in the dark. I climbed down to the first line of windows and made my way to the first open one.

Inside, I could see a big man lying face down almost naked on the bed - with only a loincloth to cover his modesty. Bottles littered the room and it stank like brewery slops mixed with the vilest bodily fluids! There was no way I could even enter this room, let alone gain something out of it.

I shimmied along to the next open window, popped my head inside and saw that the bed was occupied by two people. I was a bit surprised at first; women were only allowed in Colleges as cleaners and cooks, and certainly not after dark. This girl must have been smuggled in. Well, he will have a job of sneaking her out. I lifted myself over the frame and stepped into the room. The faint buzzing of a box on the desk distracted me. It was strangely shaped, with a large glass front and sides tapering into a much smaller shape at the back. It had an odd set of coloured lines on it, which changed colour and wriggled around the glass front until they occupied the whole of the screen. In a blink of an eye, they disappeared and new lines started to snake around. This was a bizarre and strangely majickal device, although I could not believe that a maji would waste his energies on this nonsense.

On the floor there were clothes of several descriptions; strange hose (like the things that Reg wore back at the healers' rooms), jerkins, short skirts, thin hose, shirts, button tops, etc. I rummaged a bit and realised that this girl must have stayed here for some time to have accumulated all of these clothes. Moving silently, I picked up a few likely things, short skirt, hose and shirt top, and made my way over to the door. The handle moved soundlessly, but the door didn't want to open. I pushed, then pulled it, but to no avail - until I saw a smaller handle below the main one. I turned this and the door moved. Stepping out into the corridor was dangerous, but I didn't have time to check it properly. I boldly went for it and stared down the hall, looking both ways.

No one around, I stopped and pulled my thin dress off, it looked too conspicuous if someone was looking for me. I pulled the skirt on. The girl must have been a bit bigger than me as it felt loose, but not so that it would fall down. I sat down to pull the hose on and as I sat there, I was aware of footsteps coming down the corridor from behind me. I pulled the top on to cover my modesty and stood up. Without looking, I made my way to the end of the corridor walking at about the same pace. I rounded the corner and sprinted down it. Stairs at the bottom were taken three at a time as I whirled around the corners.

Finally, I reached the bottom - to be confronted by a double set of doors. I continued my pace and hit them hard but nothing moved. No visible locks, handles or anything to open them, I was trapped. I turned around to see another set of doors made of glass, behind the stairs. I rushed over to them and tried to go through these. Again, there was nothing to open them with! I could see a small hole, like a lock, but much smaller than anything I had encountered before. There was nothing I could do, I sat down on the floor and started to cry. Again, I was trapped. Meanwhile, the footsteps were coming down the stairs now, getting closer and closer and then stopping above me. I looked up to see a man, I think, with long blond hair and a face full of growth. He had a white shirt on, which was painted to have a yellow face with black features.

He leaned over the banister and shouted, "Hay, beutiful! Watcha upset bout? Hadd aan r'gument wif yor bloke?"

I stared at him, trying to calm myself down. I stood up to wait for him to come to me. If he was going to take me to the guards, I would put up a fight.

"U hungrey? Want som brekkie?" he said, while coming down the stairs slowly.

I looked up at him and said, "Don't you try to grab me boy, I've handled much bigger than you before!"

He looked confused and put his hands out, palms towards me, "Lok, aye waz only off'rn. U don't hafe too tak et up. Bud, ifnn u r hungry, aim byin." He put his hands to his mouth and looked like he was eating.

I looked at him and put out a hand, and said, "Pasta schells inn a bolonaise sase ala vegy?"

He smiled and said, "U Italian? No Pasta, bud I wz gonna haf a Makie D OK? As he said it, he turned his hand into a circle with his thumb and pointer with the other three fingers in the air.

I repeated the gesture and nodded. I was hungry, and anything he had I would gladly take. He took my hand smiling and walked towards the door. He hit a button on the side of the door and it swung open to reveal the morning light.

"Sow, u noe mush English."

"English?" I repeated back as he walked along. He seemed to be in a good mood and wanted to chat. I thanked Ichmarr for the good fortune and smiled at him.

"OK, Ill tak that as a now. Howe r we going two get two noe ech odder if u don't speaka da English? I noe speaka da Italia."

I didn't know what the hell he was on about, but I carried on smiling and shrugged my shoulders.

He stopped and looked at me, "Me Matt," he said pointing to himself.

I knew this routine, "Merith."

"Ohh! Nise nam, doesn't sond forin two me, bud whad doo I noe? Iss itali wear u cum frum?"

I stared at him, hoping he would give me a clue about what he was saying. "What did you say?" I asked.

"Rite well, enywho, led's ged som food." He took my hand again and led me on out toward Trumpington Street. I didn't recognise any of the buildings on the way. As we left the alleyway, a carriage zoomed past, all noise and frighteningly fast. It terrified me! I jumped back into the alley and clung to the wall. Matt looked at me and started to laugh a real belly laugh; he doubled up uncontrollably laughing. Another carriage flashed past the alleyway, wheeling its majickal way along the road.

I slowly let go of the wall, Matt looked up. A look of concern crossed his face and he approached me. "U R relly friddened, rnt u? R U a bit agrofobik? Aye get lik dat somedimes, cum here." He held his arms open for me to hug him.

I approached him with caution; he was a stranger, but the only person I knew here. I held onto him and started to cry, sobbing uncontrollably. He said some soothing noises, "Hay, hay! Ive bin dere gerl. Hay dond vorry, id wil B O K."

I looked into his eyes, they looked gentle and sweet.

"Leds ged sum food," he suggested, pulling me towards the road which was paved in stone - black with grey gravel on the surface. As I stepped out into the street another carriage flashed past going the other way. The carriages had a surface all of their own, which was stepped down from the street we were on. I could see up the street, several carriages coming our way - they travelled so quickly, faster than a galloping horse. Near the end was an absolutely massive carriage, as big as a house with windows set on two levels. I watched with some terror as it made its way towards us. Mat began to pull me along the street. He said to me, "Dond vorry! Dey cant hurd u."

We approached a corner of the street where the mill used to be. The street was empty and we hurried across it. I could see ahead that there was a round white mark in the middle of the street, which the carriages were using to go round the corner. Some carriages waited, while others went around it. I supposed it must have some majick on it which controlled the vehicles. I began to hope that it would work for us, as we were fast approaching it.

The fear of the moving vehicles began to subside. After all, it was only majick that was driving them. I imagine that they would be very safe, they must be there were so many of them. I still clung to Matt as we walked along. He seemed a stable and helpful man, plus he was going to feed me. He chattered away to me, saying things that made little sense, but I realised I was catching the odd word or two as we went along. The shorter words began to piece together as he talked, but I lost him in all of the longer sounding words. Could it be that he spoke a language that was related in some way to my own language?

We walked along, past what I realised were shops with all of their wares displayed. In some of them, I recognised a lot of what was being sold - foodstuffs mainly. What really caught my eye, however, were all of the colours being used and the abundance of food everywhere! It seemed to be spilling out of the shops wherever I looked. Matt seemed to be more interested in the funny little metal and glass boxes in other shops. I didn't understand the fascination until we came to a displays that had moving pictures on them (like the coloured tube), but these showed people moving. On one of them, they seemed to be playing a game in colourful tops. I pointed this out, but Mat just shook his head and said, "Wat a wast of time!" The next had pictures of strange creatures, which looked to be painted or drawn rather than real things. Matt said about this one, "It's ai, good fhilm but I've seen it, apparntly shrik too is cuming aut soon."

He pulled me along, saying, "Cum on Merith! We whil never get dere." I let myself be pulled along, but in the distance, I could see two guards dressed in black like Reg. The thinner of the two looked straight at me and carried on walking. He looked again and a sort of recognition crossed his face. He nudged his mate and said something to him. The second looked at me as they approached and nodded very slightly. We were now about ten feet away and I could see Matt getting a little nervous too. I couldn't put my finger on why, but he seemed to tense up.

The thinner guard moved to the front of us and stopped. He said, "Xcuse mee zir, but can aye assk how U noe this yong lade? The second one started to say something into his little black box, whilst looking me up and down.

Matt looked him square in the eye and said, "Wat bizness is it ov urs?"

"Well, zir, wee have rezon too beleev that this yong lady could B an escaped azilem seeker ho brok out nite."

Matt smiled whilst saying, "Sorree gov, but this is my gerl frend. She wazz with mee yezterdy and the day B fore. She cant B ho U R aftr."

The guard took out a little book and a coloured stick, "Rite zir, can I hav UR nam and adres?"

"Y?" Matt stood looking at him with his hands on his hips. He looked so defiant I almost laughed!

"Sew wee can rul U out off hour enkuires."

A look of understanding crossed Matt's face, "Ohh, rite! R wee under arrest ofiser, or R wee free too go?"

"U R not under arrest, but with that additude, sunny jim, U mite B!"

He turned to me, winked and said, "Thank U zir, cum on Janet."

I picked up on his que and repeated his first phrase, "Thank U zir," to the guard.

I hoped that I was right to do so. The response from the guard seemed to be fit with it being the correct thing to say. He put his finger up to his hat and said to us, "Off U go."

We carried on walking. As soon as we turned the next corner, Matt stopped and breathed a long sigh of relief. He looked at me and laughed, "Hoo R U?"

I realised that he was like someone I met back in Chipping Walden. As I realised this, reality began slipping away again....

I thought about what to do while I returned to my lodgings. If I went over to the Sun Inn, I bet I could spot the others and maybe even have a chance to talk to them outside of my normal self. If I changed my appearance to someone else, then they might talk to me and reveal their true natures. When Edowyn is in a room, she doesn't call attention to herself. So, I decided to appear to be like her but with a few distinguishing features - like slightly heavier eyebrows and a small beauty spot. I visualised how I wanted to look as a human and how I was to change into the different shape. The transformation happened slowly and was painful (which I didn't remember when I last used the hat). It was such a different change, so I checked my appearance using it and realised that the hat hadn't changed anything - I had!

I collapsed out of shock onto the bed. Goddess, I had morphed into a mammal, but this wasn't supposed to happen! Celene said I had to choose a type and I would be stuck with it. Ichmarr had implied this, hadn't she? She said I would have restrictions and that I could change my form, like that of a druid, but only once in a day.

What does this mean? Have I chosen twice and now I'm stuck with mammals? Was I supposed to be a mammal and not a bird? Was Ichmarr pushing my decision? Did she do this, and now I'm caught?

Shocked and stunned, I sat for a long time trying to figure out what happened. I didn't know what to think, so I took the hat off, just in case; but there was no difference to my appearance. What happened? I couldn't understand what this meant.

Sod it! There was a mission to do and this can wait. For the mission, I needed to find out what these other people were like. I found my common robes and a cloak to disguise my origins and left my room. Fortunately, I did not meet anyone as I left and turned towards the way out. As I proceeded down the corridor, I passed by two novices I vaguely knew - but they hardly gave me a glance. Cherish turned the corner on her way to her room; as she walked past me, she glanced my way.

"Hello, who are you? Are you new?"

I stopped. I knew I looked like no-one in the Temple. "I only arrived yesterday, I'm a bit lost," I replied and turned around to face her. She looked a little concerned, so I went on; "I was looking for a priest's room and I think she was called...." I smiled, trying to look uncomfortable. I remembered that, when I arrived, someone told me to report to a priest called Dog, instead of Cat, and I had a difficult start because of this.

"Called what, Girl?"

"I'm sorry. I was told she was called Dog. I don't think it's her real name, but she is the master of novices."

"Oh, her name is actually Cat and she would be livid if she heard you say that. I'd get it right if I were you! My name is Cherish and I am the training Master. Let this be the first lesson for you. She is at the start of the corridor on the right; you have just missed her room."

"Thank you, Cherish, I will remember!" I gushed with open embarrassment and relief. The funny thing was that this was actually how I felt.

Turning to carry on along the corridor, I heard a door open and close. Looking back I saw that she had already gone, so I hurried down the corridor and, at the junction, I went through a sliding panel into the tunnels. No-one gives you a second look in the tunnels. If you are in there, you are meant to be there. I rushed down the tunnels towards the nearest exit. I chose a way out, which was not an obvious one as it had a window. It was partly boarded up, allowing me to see who was around. So I waited until there was no-one around and slipped out of the window.

It felt quite different, not having my face and hair covered to avoid people looking constantly at me. It felt good being able to stroll around through the town as a new fresh-faced young woman who was looking to explore new places - so free and unnoticed!

I was so happy.

I was so happy, that I didn't notice a young man detach himself from the shadows of a building and come up behind me. My unconscious mind sensed him, instinct took over, and I managed to twist out of his grasp as he tried to grab hold of me. Incensed, I spun around and, as I did so, I pulled out one of my daggers. His expression changed as he saw this - from the confident youth to the frightened little child. I snarled at him, "Run along little man, unless you want to take on a real heap of troubles! I don't have time to play nicely with you!"

"Bloody hell, you are fast! You must be new in town and yet you carry yourself well. Are you from that church of whores?" He was a dishy young man, probably seventeen, with charming features and long dirty blond hair. He wasn't smart, obviously, nor was he muscular, but he looked strong enough to hold me down.

"Ichmarr! Yes, just arrived this week," I replied. "They warned me to be careful of the little thieves in this town."

He laughed, "Look I think we have started off on the wrong foot and I'd like to buy you a drink to welcome you to your new home. Shall we forget what I was going to do and maybe discuss a business idea?"

Lowering my dagger, I still felt a bit wary so I kept it in my hand. As innocently as I could, I suggested, "I heard that the Sun Inn was a nice place to drink." That was where I ultimately wanted to end up, so I might as well have an escort.

On the way, he chattered on about the history of the town and its relationship with the Temple. It was interesting to hear the story from the other side of the wall, so to speak! Apparently, the Temple was founded by the 'Brotherhood' and owes its allegiance to them. We were the female part of the brotherhood, looking after its sick and injured; they were the male part, who had formed the brotherhood long before the Temple founded. They had found Celene in another town, penniless and destitute. He also claimed that it was the brotherhood that helped her to set up the Temple and controlled its activities.

In return for his chatter, I gave him a lot of "oh really" and "that is interesting." Finally, I resorted to, "Gosh!" This, I know was a little gushy, but I wanted him to impress me.

The Sun Inn was visible now, in the distance, and he asked me, "So, what is your name then? Mine is Stuart."

"Alyss," I responded. It was the first name that I thought of! It was the name of my first master.

"So, Alyss, what will your poison be? I believe they serve a nice barrel of mead here." We entered the building and my eyes instantly reacted to the gloom. As I looked around the bar, of the fifteen individuals here I discounted ten immediately - the barman, a few locals and two merchants in a corner quietly discussing business. I recognised Desidra immediately and her friend. They were seated with two burly men in leather armour trying to look the part of a guard. The last was a skinny but tall man, with things over his eyes that were like lenses which made his eyes look tiny. He was seated at the bar with a simple meal of boiled vegetables in front of him.

We went over to the bar and I said to Stuart. "I'll have half a pint of mead. Bring it over to the table and we'll talk about what you are proposing! But, if it has anything to do with sex, I'll walk out!"

This caught the barman's eye. My attention however, was absorbed by the group that I could see, as I walked over to the table next to the one Desidra was sitting at. They were discussing the length of time they had waited and they were all unhappy about it. The two men were both in fairly new leather armour, which was sculpted to look like muscles on the surface. The larger one was blond, with very much a Nordic look about him, and he had blue eyes that seemed to be so white it was like he didn't have any colour in his eyes at all. They were very creepy. The other man was less well-built, with curly brown hair, and would have been very attractive but for the fact that his chin looked almost non-existent and he had the strangest way of grinning. He placed his top teeth on top of his lip, which made him look clown-like and quite odd.

While they were talking, the two mercenaries were playing with the drops of ale they had spilt. In their movements, I recognised that they were signing Thieves' Cant. One of them had spotted the thief at the bar and the other had his eye on me. "*Little tart,*" he called me, and he said I was "*too small*" and, if they had me, "*I would break!*" Both of them chuckled at this signed remark.

Stuart sat down in front of me, spoiling my view. "Thanks for the drink Stu', I hope there is only mead in this and nothing else."

"What else could there be?" he asked innocently.

"Scrumble, or some such liquor," I replied. "I was told not to trust young men in this area."

"Yes, but you can trust me, I'm an honest lad. My hands are on the table, now let's talk business."

"Did you recognise those two men seated behind you, when you sat down?"

"Mercs, with new armour. Probably in the employ of the two women – guards, maybe? What has that to do with us?"

"Nothing, what were you going to propose?"

"Well, I've been doing a little thinking and planning and I need someone to help me get into a place."

In Thieves' Cant on the table, I asked him, *"What sort of place? Is it guarded by you lot or hired help?"*

"Well? Don't just play with the table."

"Ok! How long have you been with the brotherhood?"

He was indignant at such a question, exclaiming, "Long enough!"

I went on, "Maybe not long enough to really learn anything. You have recently begun training, I would guess. Otherwise, you would not have been so clumsy outside. Have you checked whether the place is guarded by the brotherhood or by hired help?"

"You caught me off guard!"

"If I wasn't in such a good mood you'd be dead and, remember, it was you who was trying to catch me off guard. You are a little boy trying to play at a man's game, by the look of you. You ran away from your pappy's farm and you are trying you hand at this game. Go home, farm boy!"

Just then, Celene walked in accompanied by Cat. They looked around the room and went over to the table with the group of four.

Stuart smiled, "Not a farm! My folks run a business in the next town and that's the place I want to knock over."

Celene sat down with the group and said. "Merith will be along soon. One of our novices is bringing her along but, before she arrives, let's settle a few things."

Stuart continued, "I thought it would be easy, training to be a thief, but I'm running out of money. I need a big score, or at least a few small ones to keep my place."

At the other table, Celene continued, "Desidra, you must stay calm! Merith is not your enemy. She only wants what I want. I want this to succeed and you have promised me to help my messenger."

Desidra looked her in the eye and replied, "I will help her, but there must be a price to pay."

Stuart interrupted, telling me; "You are not really listening to me, are you, Alyss?"

"No," I replied. "Not really! I don't see much point as you need money you want revenge for whatever your pappy did to you. That's your business, not mine!" I then stood up, "Thanks for the drink." I downed it in one and leaned over to him, "you want some advice?"

He was quiet. I looked him straight in the eyes and said quietly, "Go home to your pappy and apologise! You'll never make it in this game. You will be dead inside a month!"

I turned away and started to walk out.

He said, "But...."

I ignored his plea.

I walked out the back way. As I did so, I checked the area around me. There was no-one about, so I visualised an image of myself and how to change back; my normal shape slid back, with the minimum of discomfort. I then re-entered the pub.

Stuart was still sitting at the table, looking down at his drink. Cat saw me enter and moved over to me, saying, "You received our message then?"

"No, but I guessed that you'd come here. When I saw that Celene's room was empty, I thought she might have come here to have supper with the rest of the team. So I thought I would join her."

"Come over and join us! Celene was going to introduce you to everyone."

We moved over to the table. I sat down opposite Desidra, and beside Celene. Celene greeted me warmly and said, "The maid of honour has arrived! Everyone, this is Merith, she will be accompanying you all on this holy mission."

She stood up and indicated over to the barman. Then she turned to face the whole group, saying, "Merith, this is Spike. He is an expert swordsman and protector." Her hand swept over to indicate the larger of the two Mercenaries.

I nodded towards him and smiled a knowing smile.

Pointing to the smaller of the two, she added, "And this is Harry, a fine archer and one to trust in a close quarter's fight."

I nodded towards him and signed a brief warning, *"Watch yourself!"* I saw him stiffen slightly, but make no attempt to reply.

"Of course, you have met Desidra and Dulce. Dulce is not actually going on the holy mission, but will stay here with us and await your return."

Smiling at Desidra, I said, "I am so pleased that we can work together after the trouble we had. It made me so angry with myself that I had to restrain you in the manner that I did. However, I didn't want any harm to come to either of us, and I acted too quickly. You will forgive me, won't you?"

"Yess!" she spat out. It was obvious that she loathed saying it but, in front of Celene, I daresay, she had to keep up appearances.

Celene cut in; "Ah, the wine to seal the group! And, of course, here is Vergoth the Sorcerer!"

The wimp with the lenses followed the wine while it was brought over. As the barman distributed the glasses, he sat down next to me. I cringed as I could feel him looking, scanning me over - taking in every fold of cloth and every hair and millimetre of skin that was exposed. I said to him, "I, uhm, will only have a small glass if you please."

The barman poured the wine in generous quantities. However, when he came to Vergoth, he gave only a few drops to the 'Sorcerer'- pouring out these with obvious dislike. As he moved to leave us, Celene pulled at his arm and asked, "Is the meal prepared?"

"Yes, my lady! When you are ready, we are ready. If you wish to move your guests to the back room, we can start to serve."

This was the most polite I had ever seen Rufus! He is never this polite to anyone.

Celene spoke to all of us. "I have a meal prepared for us all to enjoy when we are through here, to start the holy mission off well. Now, let's toast to success! Not just to this mission, but to you all! Peace and prosperity for all"

We all toasted. Vergoth touched the wine to his lips, but drew away as if he had been poisoned. I turned to him, "Don't you like the wine?"

He grimaced, "I don't like any sort of alcohol, and I deeply disapprove of everything to do with it."

I thought to myself, "Ichmarr, why on earth have you mixed me up with this little lot - a lecherous weevil, a psychotic gypsy, a probable rapist swordsman and misogynist archer? What fun I'm going to have!"

Celene stood up, "Shall we go and eat? 'The Sun Inn' has prepared its speciality for us all."

As we all stood, I grabbed Cat's arm and walked along with her. I whispered into her ear, "This is going to be a disaster. These people are dysfunctional and will…"

"Merith, you need to be less judgemental and more trusting!" she interrupted. They will be paid handsomely for the completed mission and will be of great help to you! We will talk later!"

The table was laid for us all and Celene directed us to our seats. As I was the honoured guest, I was sat at one head of the table - with Celene at the other. The rest were seated around us; to one side of me was Desidra and, to the other, was Spike. I said to him, "So, you are an expert swordsman, do tell me of some of your exploits."

He chuckled, "You are too fine a lady to hear of the battles I have fought. In dark times like these, deeds must be done and I have met many challenges." He looked over to his friend, who signalled to him; *She is a thief! She can read this! Give her a real story, one of the gory ones.*' Spike considered this, and continued; "Maybe, though, you might want to hear of the time we slaughtered a band of Silvesi thieves who had stolen a baby."

"Maybe you should leave that till after we eat."

"No, I'd like to hear it!" said Desidra, "It sounds heroic!"

He started telling the story of how he and Harry had been engaged to hunt down a group of Silvesi, who were accused of stealing a baby from its cot as the family slept. It was a classic tale of how people accuse, and then go on to murder, innocent Silvesi. Silvesi, who had done nothing except being in the area – wandering, as they do. I tuned out of the story, not wanting to hear it, and listened to the rest of the table.

The main dish began to be served. As the roasted boar was brought through, the gorgeous smell of the sweet pork hit me, my mouth watered and suddenly I felt really hungry. The whole animal was spit-roasted and had an apple in its mouth to hide the spit-hole. Rufus started to carve it like an expert. As he sliced the best meats off it, the serving maid served it out on to white plates and carried them around to each of the guests. Vergoth, who was at that end of the table, refused to have any of the meat and hotly declared; "I will not eat dead flesh, it is abhorrent! My lady, I have already eaten at my specified time, May I be excused from this funeral?"

"No, Vergoth!" Celene responded firmly. "You are part of this group, are you not? You will go where they go; this is our deal!"

He sat cross-armed and defiant and I could see that, for all of his learning, he was still a child. He was as a child who would be petulant, obsessive and sulking. He turned his face away from the meal and I chuckled to myself and zoned back in on the conversation around me.

"Wow, what a feast! These priestesses really know how to treat us don't they?" Spike shouted over to Rufus. "Oi! Chuck us over a whole leg would ya!" He laughed a deep-bellied laugh - one that is often used when the man is trying to be deliberately obtrusive. "Veggies are for wimps like him. Meat. Real meat is what a man really needs. In't that right, Harry?!"

"Yeah!" Harry grabs the arm of the girl who was trying to serve his plate. "No, stupid! I want a whole leg - something I can really get my teeth into." He pushed her back to the meat with a spank on her bottom and grinned. "Now that's a rump I can really get into."

"Can you really?" I asked innocently. "I suppose now she will really want you to get 'into her rump', won't she?"

They laughed. Harry came back to me, querying; "What's it to do with you? Are you, jealous little girl? You want a bit of me instead? You want to play a while, little girl?"

"To be honest, little boy, I wouldn't play with you if Ichmarr herself demanded it! I'd rather play with cow dung."

"You're only playing hard to get!" he replied. "Just wait till we are on the road, Spike, then there will be a different story. When she gets cold, she'll be whimpering for it. I'm looking forward to lying with you, Merith, and playing with your pussy lips!"

I laughed and I felt I had to defuse the moment. If I were to carry on with this line of conversation, they will become more and more intent on doing something I will regret later. To ensure the mission's success, I have to try and get along with these cretins until I have finished with them. "Maybe, later," I replied. "But, now, let's just enjoy the meal! It may be the last hot meal we get for a while. So, Harry, how good are you at the bow? Is it a longbow or a short one?"

"Long bow, of course! What man would go with a short one?"

"But, I thought you had... well...Spike here was indicating...." *'A short, titchy one'*, I finished saying the sentence in Thieves' Cant. He was not at all impressed! He then looked at Spike, who was laughing so hard he nearly fell off his chair.

"She's got the hots for me, Harry! No use you trying your hardest with her, she's already mine! Aren't you, darling? I saw it the first time you looked at me."

"Or, I could have just farted!" I commented.

They both laughed at this. "She's got a sense of humour, Harry! Even you've got to admit that! She's okay - leave it at that!"

"Thanks for that! I thought he was going to get rough" I said to Spike, thinking that it would be easy to align to him. He was the older man and, probably, the more dangerous. There may come a time when I might have to get rid of one of these men if they don't improve. Desidra had been quiet throughout the entire interplay, and I could see that she was intent on Spike. She seemed to prefer him as well and I sensed that she was beginning to sympathise with me. She may have been violated by someone like this, or in a situation like this. So, I used this opportunity to speak with her, "Desidra?"

"What?"

"I just remembered I have something for you." I took out the dagger that I had put into my boot sheath and handed it to her, hilt first. "You left this behind the other day and I picked it up for you. Again, I needed to say that I'm sorry for what my kind did to you. I do hope that I can help you get over it and move on from it."

"Thanks for the knife back, but I have others." She put it into her belt. "We will see about the rest. What happens in the future is uncertain and may be influenced by the circumstances. Remember this; life is so ironic in its ways, but it is perfectly circular. It keeps on coming back to the same point time and time again and, as this is true, in the future we will get to the same point again. Then we will see what happens."

"You have said a mouthful there, girl, and I believe that could be true. But, when we come around again, I hope we don't have as much baggage. Today, I was responsible for saving a baby's life and I'm glad that I was there to save her rather than no-one being there for her. It's funny, you know, she was named after me – something which made me feel that, at least, the name will continue and I will always be around in the world."

"Good for you," said Spike, as he rudely broke into the conversation. "And I was probably her father, what with all of the women I've sired!"

"Yes! And I helped to deliver her into this world," said Cat (the first time she had spoken all evening), continuing; "She was a darling little girl with black hair and brown eyes. The father took one look at her and just melted. He went from being a concerned husband to a doting father in a split second. The family are in a troupe of actors who travel around the countryside, and fortunately they have been given permission to perform tomorrow night for a week in the market square. It is a shame you will all miss them as they tell me they are very good."

"My family were actors," Dulce said, "They were excellent. They used to travel from town to village and tell the news from far and wide. Sometimes, the town's people would open their bars to everyone and there would be music, dancing and singing. Everyone liked the actors because we amused them and lifted their lives above the drudgery of life. That's what my mummy used to say."

This was the most I had ever heard Dulce say. She is the quiet secretive type that surprises you just when you least expect it, and she is the one that sits at the back of a group being shown how to read a sign and, then, is the first to be able to do it. She would do well in our Temple, although she is probably too old to start. Who knows, they might try her out.

Desidra joined her friend in saying, "Yes, I remember, when I first met you, our families had a great time together. Before…" Her face crumpled and she buried herself in her hands. Dulce moved to be behind her, holding her, cuddling her and trying to sooth her.

It was like a poison that kept on coming back. The flashbacks were strong in Desidra. She would hold onto those memories for a long time, and I knew there was not much I could do to help her. She, first of all needed to take out the fetid, putrid mess that resides and then close the open wound. Then, to try to hold together what is left, until the healing process can begin. I may have to be her punching bag for a while.

I concentrated on my food for a while. The boar was beautifully cooked; tender and sweet. Rufus certainly was a good host and he picked out some of the best meat. Spike and Harry were really going for the leg meat. This comprised the less tender parts of the boar and, good luck to them, they asked for it. Meanwhile, Celene was in close discussion with Vergoth again. They were discussing a theological situation and were beginning to disagree….

Novem – Doni miraculum

Noise surrounded me; not the same as before, but with more sound and music to it. I feared opening my eyes, but I felt that I had to eventually. I smelled food - bacon – frying; the sounds added to the general maelstrom. I opened one eye just a crack and, then, both to take in the strange sights. The ceiling was painted with amazing pictures of women, some nudes and others scantily clad in various laces and silks. I compared myself to those paintings and felt that I was a bit inadequate, I realised my top must have rolled up while I was asleep. It felt a bit uncomfortable, so I pulled it back down - finding that my skirt had also ridden up a bit as well. It must have happened when I was unconscious.

I looked around and there were more paintings; so many I believed I was in an artist's room. The bed was so comfortable and had a lovely manly smell to it; everything smelled so clean and lived in. There was a piece of cloth across one side of the bed which separated it from the rest of the room. I drew it back at the corner and saw Matt standing over a table. I imagined he was cooking, but there was no fire to cook with - nor did I see a chimney. Whatever he was doing, it smelled delicious!

I pulled back the cloth, revealing the rest of the room. It was a mess of stray clothing, paper packets shoes and (?) bits of metal. There was a black box on the floor beside the bed, which had a tube coming out from one side of it. I swung my legs over the side of the bed and sat up. My head felt as if I was in a boat, my mind swimming awash with uncertainties. Who is this man and why is he helping me?

He turned to glance at me, and gave me a second look, saying, "Ah, Merith, aye hav somthig for u all cooked bye myself U didn't lok wel enof two go two Maky D." He picked some bits of slightly charred bacon and placed them onto some bread. He brought two plates over to the bed and placed one on my lap. "Hear ewe go, bakon and egs on tost, well roll really." He put his meal down on the bed beside me and picked up the funny black box. Looking a bit flushed, he said, "Sometimes aye doo a bit off fotografy." He placed it carefully under the bed and sat down beside me.

I opened the roll and picked up a charred piece of bacon, "Bakon?"

"Yes, well it is supposed too B."

"Eggs?" I said pointing to the almost unrecognisable yellow and white things lurking under the bacon.

"Yes," he said, nodding, "Well, it wood hav bin an eg but it kinda got a bit mashed."

From all of the clues, and the occasional word that I picked up, I realised that what he was saying was actually in English. However, he had a very strange accent - so different from anything I was used to. In a way, I felt really stupid for not spotting it before, but I had never been party to a long conversation with the same person before I met Matt. I tried to match the accent, "Can ewe understad mee?"

"Hay u doo spek English!" he said, while he was pouring a red liquid on to his roll.

"Yus a littl bit but aye find it hard two catch it." I picked up the roll.

He stopped me and said, "Hay stop, u cant et that!"

I stopped and took it away from my mouth, "What?"

"Yew hav to put som sase on it, lik pasta shells in a red sase ala vegy." Grinning, he indicated the bottle of red sauce and passed it to me.

I looked at it as if it was a bottle of poison. It looked really odd and rather unlike congealed blood - more like a red paint. I sniffed at the open top; sweet, vinegary, with a strong undertone of tomato. To be polite, I tried to pour some out. However, the stuff was so thick and congealed that it struggled to get out. I waited - as I have always been told, the best things come to those that wait. Eventually, a small amount plopped onto my plate and so I put the bottle onto the floor. I politely dipped the edge of the roll into it and took a bite. To be honest I would have eaten anything, but it actually tasted amazingly good! The fulsome taste, rich and strangely meaty, was fully savoured as I chewed the roll. The bacon was salty, but tasted unlike any that I had ever had before, and the sweet sauce complimented it by covering some of the salt with the sweetness. I turned to Matt and, with a full mouth, put my fingers out in the sign he had used before and nodded vigorously.

"So, tell me about your faighnting. Does it happen often?"

"Faighnting?" I replied. "Oh when I fell, it must have been the sight of all of that majick."

"Magic? I have never heard of kars being talked about like that."

"Kars?" I queried. I must have looked confused.

"Yeah, you know, kars, modors, vroom, vroom!" He pointed to a painting on the wall, which had one of the carriages that I had seen before.

"Oh, yes! That's what I mean - a kar! I haven't seen them go so fast before."

"Where have you been all of your life?" Matt asked. "Africa?"

"No, mostly in Temples around the countryside."

"Oh, so you were brought up by nuns? Are you an orphan?"

"Yes." I answered. "But I don't like to talk about my past, it hurts."

He finished his meal quickly and watched me for a while. I then said, "What are you staring at?"

"Oh, sorry!" he exclaimed, "but it isn't everyday that I have a gorgeous girl in my room. Can I ask how old are you?"

"Fifteen, I think. But I could be fourteen, I dunno. Why?"

"Oh, nothing, you don't know where any of your family are?" He put his arm on my shoulder. "It's just that you are so beautiful, I was, well...."

"Well, what?"

"Just thinking." He then leaned over to say something and ended up kissing me on the cheek.

I pushed him away, but he said, "You are so sexy, can I just have a kiss." This sent shivers through me and sparked off a memory of something that happened. I tried to remain with this world, but the images were too strong....

I excused myself from the table and went to find the 'garderobe'. I knew from experience that they had an outside one, like most buildings in this town. They would dig a hole in the ground and erect a wooden shack over it. You would be provided with a board to sit on, and a copy of the Almanac from last year to use when you had finished. I preferred to do it in the way of our Temple, but I will have to get used to roughing it. So, when needs must, I braved the shack. The smell hit me like a hammer as I opened the door. Shit, literally! The smell was bad; they really needed to fill this over and start again. However, I had not gone since I had woken up yesterday and I was beginning to really need to go now. Being unconscious for a while makes you constipated. Moreover, with all of the moving around today (plus the berries!), I had to go now.

Five minutes must have passed before I had finished. The, errr umm – well, it had come out like sling bullets being fired in rapid succession. As I cleaned myself up, I could hear someone outside. Spike was standing there, right in front of me when I opened the door.

"Hello sexy, give us a feel of you!" He said.

"Sod off, Spike! Put yourself on hold and get out of my way!" He grabbed me and tried to kiss me. I sunk my head down and, in a neat movement, hit his jaw with my head and simultaneously kneed him in the nuts. His lower jaw bounced and chattered off his upper jaw, and he gave a satisfying "Awwwughhh" - as he collapsed slowly to the ground.

"Thank you so much for being a gentleman, Spike! I didn't know you were such a lovely, kind man."

He continued groaning on the ground as I stepped over him. I stopped, bent down to him and said, as sweetly as I could; "Oh Spike, I don't like people cornering me like that! Please don't do that to me again! You might find you will have difficulty breathing."

Leaving him in the back yard groaning away, I returned to the table. Most of the diners had finished their meal and were now sitting back, smoking their pipes. Harry seemed a little surprised to see me so quickly. He looked me over and looked very confused. I smiled at him and said. "You seem a little confused, is something wrong?"

"No, nothing! Did you see Spike in your travels?"

"Oh, him! Yes, I left him in the back yard. He had issues that he had to resolve and so I left him to it. But I dare say that, if you wanted to see him, he would be tending to his laurels."

I sat back and tried to catch the eye of the waitress. She came over and I asked for a glass of Scrumble. I knew the barman had some Scrumble tucked away somewhere and that he would get some for me. Scrumble is a liqueur that is made from apples. Once the cider is brewed to a dry drink, it is distilled to a much stronger liquor. The liquid tasted of apples and was really strong, strong enough to strip varnish off to bare wood. It was only good for one thing, therefore; getting seriously drunk! It was usually only men who drank it; the occasional naive female was given it to drink or, more usually, to get herself drunk.

Cat was chatting with Desidra and Dulce. They looked like they were plotting the downfall of the world. They were animated and giggled occasionally. Cat was more involved in the conversation than she normally would be and she seemed drunk. She was acting and, from the way she was deliberately slurring her words, I could see clearly that she wanted to look drunk. However, she was occasionally steering the conversation in different directions. I think she was trying to figure out which buttons could be pressed in Desidra. Cat always tries to figure out people and I could see she was confident about Dulce, but was still figuring out Desidra.

My drink was brought over to me, and I asked the waitress to also bring a pint of whatever the gentlemen were drinking for them. She asked "Which gentlemen?" and laughed.

"Yes," I replied. "It is hard to tell, the two idiots in baked leather is who I meant."

She laughed again, "I'll bring them straight over."

She walked off chuckling to herself. I sipped my Scrumble and felt the burning sensation of alcohol burn down my throat. This was strong - stronger than usual. A couple of glasses of this and most women would even find Spike attractive! But, I suppose I was fortunate that Silves are not affected in the same way with alcohol. It is processed by us far quicker than in humans and it doesn't affect our brains as much. While I do feel some affect of the alcohol, I find that, to get drunk, I need to drink strong spirits really quickly. I have been challenged to drinking contests before and won every single one! People - men! think they are so clever and have the stamina of an ox when it comes to alcohol. Unfortunately for them, my own body keeps me on the straight and narrow.

Spike came back into the room. He looked daggers at me and walked over to Celene. He whispered something in her ear - a few words, nothing more. She nodded her head and obviously agreed to what he had said. She stood up and said, "I have had some wise counsel from Spike. He has asked that we all get an early night and clear our heads. An early start in the morning is important and he wants the group to be ready for just after daybreak. I wish you all a pleasant journey, a successful mission and a speedy return! I only ask that I be able to thank you all for undertaking this holy quest. The book that was lost to us is precious to our Temple for the knowledge it holds. It was taken from us unfairly and unjustly, and you will be the privileged ones that may return it. You will be able to complete the works of our Goddess and give us guidance in the trials to come. She wanted us to have the guidance and she will help you in bringing it back to us."

Celene then turned to me, saying, "Merith, come with me and talk a while. I will miss your counselling and questioning."

I walked over to her and she took my hand. Meanwhile, Vergoth had already left the room and the rest of the diners were beginning to stand up and look around.

The three of us left; Cat, Celene and I. Celene lead us out into the night and stopped in the road outside of the pub. "Merith, tell me what happened outside? I can guess, but please tell me."

I looked down to the ground, "Celene I know you have chosen these men and that you have been told that you can trust them." I looked up to her, into her eyes and said, "But I don't. They know Thieves' Cant and outside, by the shack, Spike tried it on with me. I could see in his eyes that, no matter what I did, he was going to have me and sod the consequences. He was going to force me there and then and cover up what he had done. I have seen it before. Stories I have heard. He would have used the need for this holy mission as a reason why I should keep silent. I am surprised that he did not suggest that we all stay in the inn tonight so that he could keep an eye on me!"

"He did suggest it, which is why you are here now." She began walking towards the Temple and continued, "Merith. I need you to go on this mission, I need Vergoth to help you when you get there and I need Desidra to guide you there." Her voice getting stronger, "But what I do not need is two FUCKING, RAPISTS, FUCKING IT UP FOR ME!!!" She was very angry. There were a few other people on the street, and they were looking our way. Swiftly calming down, Celene smiled at them and said to the world in general; "Sorry! Rehearsing the play for tomorrow. Have you heard that we are the players in town for this week?"

She continued to us, more quietly, "I had suspected that this was going to be the case, but I needed to see it for myself. Cat, I want you to quietly get Desidra and Vergoth to the Temple tonight. Do not alert these two bastards. I also want you to find me Edowyn; we have plans to make and I need to speak with her. She will have to find someone else to replace them fast. And I want her to ensure these two bastards do not spoil our party tomorrow. As for you, Merith, you need a good night's 'rest' and you need to replenish yourself. Before you do so, go speak to Petersen. He has, on my orders, sorted out a collection of gear for you to select the things you require. You need to be packed and ready by dawn. Now, go!"

I had never before seen Celene as angry as this. She wasn't angry with me, I knew that, but I also knew that when people are in a mood like this they get the job done - not in a pretty way, but the fastest way possible. I picked up my pace and left them behind. They had plans to discuss. I found my way back to the Temple. It is only five hundred yards from the pub, but it is through a busy part of town and not one of the main thoroughfares.

The main eating hall was quiet after the supper had finished. There was only the daily table still laid out, with bread rolls, dried fruit and the like. The daily table is laid like this as the occupants of the Temple do not always lead a day and night existence. Because of this, they are often around at odd times and need sustenance. This is such a necessity and Petersen has always kept it thus. There were noises coming from the kitchens, which were normally empty of food and people at this time. Petersen was in there, fussing over a frame pack, stowing wrapped parcels into it and taking them back out again. "How now, Petersen," I enquired. "Celene said for me to come and see you tonight."

Petersen joked, "It is so late, how do you think I will get enough sleep to be up fresh and early in the morning to serve breakfast? I'm not young and fit like you, Merith. I need my beauty sleep."

"Lots of it, Petersen!"

"Very funny, Merith! I have slaved over your pack. In the bottom, I have wrapped ten days dried biscuits; they are dry and bland, but will keep you alive. You should have only one biscuit a day; break into three portions and eat it dry, or mix it into water and have it as a soup. I have included some small bags - each of salt, rice and herbs." He placed every item into the bag as he spoke; "Round of cheese, my favourite flavour, don't give it away! Two round sausages; if you slice them thinly with the cheese - lovely meal. Three loaves of hard bread; eat it in small amounts - it is trail bread and will keep for over a week. Three water skins - I bought them new a week ago and have tested them. Good quality bags, they hardly leak. I have tied them on the outside to save space. I have also tied onto it a tin mug and billy-can, but they are in leather bags to stop them from sounding."

Petersen then turned to the table behind him, which was laid out with a range of tools, devices and general equipment. "Celene asked me to get this little lot, Merith, just in case you needed something else. Oh, and flint, steel and tinder are in a box in this pocket, along with ten candles! I thought they might be useful." He indicated a bulging pocket on the pack.

Looking over the items, I picked out a couple that might be useful, and put them down again. I stood over them, thoughtfully, and looked into Petersen's eyes, "You have done yourself proud. I can see a use for all of these things and, yet, I think I have them all already in my room. Thank you for preparing all of this, but I don't want to keep you up much longer. Celene mentioned a horse?"

"Oh, yes, the horse! She was brought in a couple of hours ago and I asked one of the novices who grew up on a farm to tend to her. Let's go down and see her." We walked the short distance to the stable in silence. Petersen was carrying my pack He was quiet, and I think he is really going to miss me. I knew that I would certainly miss him.

"Her name is Limerick," he said, as we entered the stable yard. He went over to one of the occupied stalls where a lovely white horse was standing patiently. "Saddle and bags are here. I was told you knew how to ride, so I thought to leave it to you to sort it all out in the morning."

"Thanks, Petersen, you have been wonderful!" I picked up the saddlebags and the frame pack from where he had put it down. He yawned and so I told him, "You go off to sleep. I'll introduce myself to her, and sort myself out." I watched as the tired man left the room, then I checked the contents of the saddlebags; one side contained a bag of grain for the horse, with a nosebag; the other was empty. I transferred most of the food (except for the trail rations and the wineskins) into the empty side. The horse can carry them. I went up to the horse and looked her over. She was fourteen hands, with new shoes and was well used to the bit. From the look of her teeth, she was young but fit and full of life. She will do. I blew up her nose to show I was happy with her and she returned my gesture with a gentle nuzzle against my arm. She blew that funny sound that horses make when they are content.

I left her to go back to my room, carrying the bags.

Most of my own gear, I loaded into the frame-pack along with my good robes and an extra blanket. I was already carrying seven daggers, one in each boot, one up each wrist, two at my waist and the seventh, my holy symbol, hung from a shoulder sling to be over my heart at all times. I had my two hand crossbows; they were small, but can be deadly in the right situation. These were kept sprung, but unloaded when not in use. I also had a leather strap with twenty short, metal bolts with barbs to stay in the target. They were less effective against armour but, aim for the right spot, and armour shouldn't trouble them! The realisation that I had been trained up in a lot of apparently useless stuff (unless, of course I had a mission like this to go on!) hit me like an arrow. Had they been training me for this mission? Did they have me in mind for this mission, all along, for the last eight years? This seemed an impossible idea. No-one thought that far ahead, did they?

I was alone.

I was a bit bored with packing and there was far too much on my mind to do it properly. My mind is too scatty to think consistently about what I need to do. There had to be a greater challenge out there; this mission was just what I wanted - something that will take me to the edge, to help me find my limit. It would also help me to get out there in the rest of the world, to find out what it is like. This town is too small for me.

I thought about what had happened earlier on with the changing. I definitely changed into a bird, and I probably also changed into a mammal, a human. I wondered, what about a snake? A reptile, can I change into that? Will I be stuck with it, if I did?

Mulling over these questions, I reviewed the conversation I had had with Ichmarr. 'My gift to you is to allow you to transmute your physical shape to that of another creature, like the druid named Jesmend. He, however, can change at will to any animal, mammal, reptile, and bird any number of times. This gift has restrictions until you understand the gift properly. You cannot change when being viewed by a sentient being; this would change the nature of the act and will not be allowed. It just won't happen! Your clothes and anything you have on you will change, but you cannot use them while you are in this state. You can maintain your chosen form only once in the time between the sun rising and the sun rising for the next day, but you can maintain it for that length of time. At the moment of the sun cresting the edge of the planet you are on, you will change back. This could have serious consequences for you, unless you are aware of it.'

This is exactly what she said. She did not say I could only be in one type of form, only that I can do it only once - but does that mean each type for once in a day?

Could it happen with three creatures every day? This is more than I had dreamt. Just being able to change into a bird was amazing, but to be able to do more than that was simply staggering. I wondered if I should try the reptile species? A snake would be the easiest; it is something I know and I have seen them so often in the forest. However, before beginning this change, I thought; 'What if I don't change going down to the floor?' So I laid down on the floor and concentrated on the form of a snake - an adder, which was simple, common and I had seen a lot of them in the forest. I concentrated on the creature and how I would slide my form into its. Morphing was becoming easier to do, and a lot less painful to change. Quickly, I found that I was now a lot shorter and I could smell so acutely. The floor along my new body felt so odd, and it was so strange to be in contact with the floor like this. Was I feeling the roughness of the stone floor through my skin (or, rather, scales)? I turned my head and looked along my body. Wow! It was long, beautifully scaled and smooth to the touch - just as I visualised.

Exploring my room using my new senses, I discovered that, while it was interesting, I couldn't really see a use for this form except in sneaking around crevices. The air smelled - no! - tasted differently, and I could see heat sources as a different taste. These have a sort of metallic taste, in different quantities to the heat that is there. I could feel vibrations across my whole body; there was someone moving past my room. Wriggling over to the door, I found it difficult to describe the movement except as a wriggle - as it seems to be done by moving different sections of my whole body at different times. I realised that the body knows a lot about how to move itself, without the brain needing to input how to do it. The vibrations moved away, but I began to get the feeling of a sort of vibration coming from the next-door occupant. It was rhythmical, almost like breathing, but I couldn't hear the sound. I think I could actually feel the snoring of someone next door. I explored my surroundings further for a few minutes.

Just then I thought to myself, 'This is really getting the job done, isn't it?' What I really needed was to sort out myself and my stuff, so I decided to change back to my normal self. So I visualised the change from snake to thief. As I did so, I chuckled to myself; being like this reminded me of the similarities between the reputations of both! Maybe this is why only a few priestesses chose the 'snake in the grass' as their animal of choice. I completed the change and looked around the room.

The hat would come with me, it was too valuable to leave and I was sure it would come in useful. When I put the hat on, I became so aware of myself and so I concentrated solely on the hat. It looked out of place on me, so I changed the appearance of the hat into a hair braid, with coloured threads around a small bunch of hair with beads to stop it all falling out. I know the hat will be useful, like the rest of my junk. There just has to be the right situation for it. I brushed my hair to neaten it and generally tidied myself up.

I concentrated on packing for the journey. To sort out the crossbows, I cut a four-foot length of rope off the main piece and tied through the end loops of the hand crossbows - one at each end of the rope. This could now be tied to the pommel of the saddle, and I could easily fire them from the saddle without having first to worry about where they were. The rest of the bits and pieces were fitted into the bag, but carefully wrapped all of the metal pieces in small pieces of cloth to stop them from jangling. As a thief, I knew there would be situations in which I would want to be completely silent and move about. It was crucial that the weight of the bag was not too much, so I hefted it onto my back and felt the strain. It was too heavy to carry long distances and I needed to be lighter. Half of the pitons were removed and I also ditched some of the larger picks; the crowbar I definitely could lose as I had the climbing pick and didn't need both. I hefted the bag again, nearly there. Would I need the grapple? Yes, it is small, but heavy. If I put it into one of the saddlebags, it can weigh the horse down, not me. What a brainwave! I could also put the other items I had removed into the saddlebags. They might be useful.

Now, what did Celene say? '…that I needed to replenish myself'. She probably meant for me to sort out my spells. I have the ability to carry five spells in my head and they will stay until used or death. However, we can fizzle spells out if we don't want them any more, so I decided to leave out the 'cause darkness' as this is one spell which is unnecessary.

I prayed for the ability to use the spells and they started to pop into my head; 'gifts from the goddess'. It takes a lot of learning and reading initially to understand how to pray for a spell; this is not a natural thing to do. You need to learn the spell and how the mind remembers it. You have to get the images so clear in your mind that they cannot be forgotten and, once you have the pathway set for the spell, you have to pray to Ichmarr for the energy to do it. Ichmarr is a busy Goddess; she grants spells to the worthy only if you are keeping up with the devotions. The few tricks I played today helped, but I needed to do something to keep it up. I did not want to lose any of the things I am able to do and, besides, it would also be disastrous to not remember how the spell should flow. The brain is a fragile thing and the energy needs to go somewhere. There have been priestesses who have died, or had strokes or fits, whilst casting spells. It can happen and it can kill.

As usual, I was granted the use of five spells. Two healing, two command spells and the fifth I thought to use was the 'Shield' spell which gives the user a limited shield. This will stop blows aimed at the user from an attacker, but can only be used for one attacker and does not do any thing for any other opponent. However, it has the advantage of not requiring the user to concentrate the spell. I am told that, as I get more advanced as a priest, I will have other spells at my disposal. This will take more reading and learning to generate additional pathways that are stable. This is what majis do to use their majick. They, however, seem to get their energy from somewhere else. I wonder where do they get it from? This I must discuss with Vergoth some night, to better understand his majick.

My brain and my body needed to be rested and sorted, so I concentrated on meditating and reordering my memories. Sitting cross-legged on the floor on my prayer mat, I held my holy dagger in my hands and slowly turned all of my senses down. My mind drifted across the events of the day. Spike and Harry would have been a big problem if they were allowed to go. Certainly, I would have had to get rid of them before we actually made it to the ruins. They were a threat to me and to Desidra and, I daresay, in the state of mind that she is in she would have probably rid herself of them fairly quickly. The wimp Vergoth? Well, I think that I would trust the wimp; he looks too ill to do anything serious and I'd just have to breathe in his direction for him to fall over!

I realised, just then, that I still did not know who was going with us to the ruins. Celene must make that decision. I let it drift across my mind.

Dawn was bringing light to the world. My consciousness registered the gradual shift from the blacks of the night to the dark blues and lighter tones, as the day began. Slowly, I let myself lift to full consciousness and looked around my room. It was funny, I had only been in this room for a couple of days but I knew I would miss its comforts. I retrieved the personal from under my bed, deciding to do as I had done the previous day and go to the general room to sort myself out. Again, there was no-one in the room and so I bolted the door - at this time of the morning, there would be few about. All of the humans needed to sleep for hours yet. Petersen, however, would be rising soon to sort out the kitchens and get them prepared for the new day. He has always been one of the early risers.

I had a pee, only a few bloodspots this time. My period was stopping, so quickly. It was surprising that my period would be over so soon. Usually, I could be bleeding for four or five days and sometimes more. I used my personal cloth to wash myself out and thought about whether or not I still needed to prepare for more blood today. After I cleaned out the bowl, I pumped some water around to wash the area and ensure that it would be fresh for the next person. Wishing to be safe rather than sorry, I used some more of the moss to hold back the flood. Evidently, I would need to find some more while we are travelling, just in case. Once I had cleaned up the area, I went back to my room where I checked over the whole space again and tidied up as I did so. It was ingrained into me, that when you left a place, 'no trace of your passing should be left'.

There was a sharp rap on my door. "Yes," I called.

"Merith, are you ready to go? The others are being brought down to the dinner hall now." It was Cat's voice, she sounded so tired.

I grabbed my bags, slung them over my shoulder and went to the door. "No!" I called back. "I will need another couple of hours to sort myself out. Can you come back later?" On the last word, I opened the door with a huge grin on my face.

"Well, at least you had some sleep! Some of us have been up all night, sorting out what to do about protecting the mission."

"I am the mission, and I thank you for all of your help Cat. I know you have been working hard on my behalf. Tell me, what is the situation now?"

"Let's walk and talk." I followed her down to the hall. "Merith, since you went to rest we have all been busy. I went back in the early hours to Vergoth's and Desidra's rooms and helped them pack as quietly as possible to get them out of the Inn. They have had a rough night sleeping in a novice's cell. I sent a novice to wake them as I came up to get you. Edowyn has found you a trusted guard, and, although he isn't exactly who we would want, he is a trustworthy fighter. He is waiting in the hall and Edowyn has also arranged a surprise for the two lads. The town guard have orders from the Elders to grab them as they sleep; well, just about now actually! They will be arrested as suspected thieves and held for a couple of days. Celene will pay to have them released and get rid of them for us."

"Good, I'm pleased that is sorted out and my thanks go to you all. Now, who is this fighter? Why should I trust him and why wouldn't I want him?"

"Well, you have already met him. He has been lent to us by the town to aid us in this holy mission. He is the best fighter in his profession that we could get at this short notice, and he follows the rules to the letter!"

"Yes, and I'm still waiting for the name?" At that moment, we turned the corner into the hall. Neville was the most prominent individual I have ever seen; he stuck out like a sore thumb. He was wearing a suit of scale-mail, with chain links with small, scale-like plates linked into the chain. The armour was much lighter than having large plates of metal and it allowed greater movement, but was not as protective. The mail was ill-fitting, having been made for a man who was broader. On Neville, however, it looked like it was hanging off him! He did have skill with the long sword he had by his side, I knew this – but, would he have the temperament?

As we approached him, Neville stood up and tipped his head in acknowledgement. "Good morning, milady. I see you have managed to find some decent clothes."

"Neville."

"Sergeant Neville Sharpe! At your service, Ma'am. I have volunteered for hazardous duty, as ordered by my superiors. My lord De Morrow has seen fit to put my sword arm to your disposal."

"I hope the rest of your body comes as well, otherwise there is going to be a lot of mess on the carpet!"

"Yes, I suppose there would be." He said in all seriousness, having little in the way of a sense of humour. Goddess, this was going to be an interesting trip!

"You have been promoted?"

"Yes, thank you, Milady. My lord, God bless him, has seen my better qualities. He said to me, 'Sharpe, you do this for me and you'll start tomorrow as a Sergeant, complete with all that entails'."

"Well done to you, are you ready to go? We have a long journey ahead of us."

"Yes, ma'am. Your man has seen fit to pack provisions for me. My own mam couldn't do better in a kitchen than that man. If he were a woman, I'd marry him for his cooking skills!" At this, Cat tried to stifle a laugh, but ended up doubling over and sounding like she was coughing.

"Yes, I dare say he would look forward to that." Cat was shaking uncontrollably. "If," I added, "If she, sorry he, were a woman." Cat was now on one knee, choking with laughter.

"Your lady friend, is she okay? She seems to be chocking on something? Do you think we should pat her on the back or something?"

"No, I think she should be fine. So, where did you get the scale-mail?"

"Now, there's a funny story. About a month ago, a man came through the gates and he said he needed to sell the armour in a hurry. He said he needed the money to marry his sweetheart who lived in this town. I only had twenty gold pieces and he accepted." He chuckled to himself. He looked at me expectantly and, in giving up, he said. "The mail was worth at least one hundred."

"Oh, yes Ha! Ha! You bought it cheap." Turning to Cat who was finally back on her feet, I signed *'Is he for real??'* It is one of the amazing things about Thieves' Cant that there are actually signs for questions and emphasizing words. In addition, there are signs for ten different types of traps without having to name them.

"Thank you, sergeant," Cat said. "Can we get you anything while you wait for the others?"

"No, I'm sure I'll be fine. Are you okay? That coughing fit looked so painful?"

"I'm sure I will be fine. Now, I will have to get Merith some breakfast."

As we left him, I saw Vergoth and Desidra come into the hall. They both looked shattered. They were seated by the novice who had accompanied them, and a bowl of porridge was brought for them. Vergoth looked at him in disgust and asked a question. He looked surprised at the answer and picked up a spoon. I did not think that he would look so animated about food.

As we walked, Cat said, "Once you have eaten, you should make an early start. I don't know if our plans for the boys in the 'Sun Inn' have come to fruition, so you will need to make it snappy."

I went to the kitchens to get a bowl for myself and I saw Petersen there. He was chuckling to himself. "What is all of this mirth about today?

"I have satisfied two men today and I have only just got out of bed! No, don't think about it! That skinny man likes my porridge. I had made it especially for him out of goat's milk because he had turned up his nose to virtually everything else the last time he was here."

"Can I have some with normal milk?" I said in my sweetest voice. Smiling, I knew that he would have prepared it for me any way. It was all part of the game.

"Well, if you put it that way. Merith, tell me what is going on here. Last night you were going with two mercenaries, now Neville is here with a scrawny horse outside and I am packing rations for him? Also, those two were put up in the Sun Inn before and now I hear they stayed the night?"

"Long story, make the porridge and I'll tell you what happened."

Petersen nodded, "Always there is a price with you!" He started to prepare my porridge.

"Well, last night I had a big fall out with one of the men. He tried to attack me and I dropped him to the ground. He tried to keep me at the Inn, but Celene had us all brought here. Celene has changed the arrangements to prevent problems on the road. I think Neville is going with us to protect us if something happens to us. I'm not worried, but I think that the rest of the group need protection."

"So, they stayed here to get them away from those other two?"

"Yes, exactly! Spike would have used them to get to me. Celene saw through him and arranged for us to be here tonight. She must have arranged to have them detained to stop them giving us problems."

"I had heard problems about them. Cat had doubts, and Edowyn certainly would have cautioned against the use of them. What do you think of Neville?"

"He is unimaginative, and quite thick. I see that he is dependable, but I worry that he will get suspicious of me if I let him."

"Don't let him! Just be normal and get the job done." He poured out a bowl of porridge for me and topped it with honey. "Don't let it get cold, food is too important to waste"

Smiling, I replied, "You'd never!" We laughed.

I moved to give him a hug. For a change, he let me and kissed my forehead. "Look after yourself, Merith. I will be thinking of you until you return."

"Keep the food warm and the pan ready, I'll be back soon enough!" I picked up the bowl and left the kitchen, possibly for the last time. I looked back to Petersen and saw that he was crying. He had turned away and had a towel up to his eyes. I would miss him too.

I returned to the table with Neville. I had left my bags there and I hoped that he wouldn't want to chat much. Sitting in a seat which allowed me to see the rest of the room, I had a good look around. The hall seemed to be much busier today than at any time I remember. Neville was deep in thought, but even he occasionally glanced around the room.

"Ear, what is your name, milady?"

"Merith, why?"

"Just wondering what I should call you? Milady and ma'am seem too formal if we are going on a trip together. I never thought I would be doing stuff with the tricky Icky."

"Neville, why do you keep on calling it the tricky Icky? Are we that bad?"

"No, not bad, but I heard you like playing tricks on people and that your saint saved a load of thieves and a bit rubbed off of 'em. Your people are always looking after the thieves in this place. Why do you do that? I mean they are evil, them thieves are. They should be locked up. Stealing stuff from decent honest people, they should be stopped by someone."

"Yes, but someone has to look after them too. Most thieves steal because they have no choice, or they need to feed their family. Would you lock every one of them up? If you do, who looks after their family? Do you?"

"Well, they should go out and get a job, shouldn't they!"

'Maybe they already have', I thought. "Maybe."

I picked up my spoon again and finished off my porridge. I could see that Vergoth and Desidra were nearly finished too.

We should go soon.

Are we waiting for something, or just someone, to make the first move?

Who is in charge of this?

I hope I'm not!

Maybe I am. Cat implied that we should go soon.

We should be going.

I looked up to Neville. "Nev, you ready to go?"

"Been ready for a while now are we going now?" The look he gave me told me that he thought I was in charge.

"Will you get your horse ready and take these to the stables? I'll get the other two. Let's go, Nev!" I left him to it, knowing with that look of mine he would do everything I told him to do. He was used to taking orders and I was just another boss. I walked over to the others' table.

They were beginning to bicker about something. I said to them both, "Guys, we need to go. I have sent Neville to get his horse ready. I would suggest that we go to the stables and get moving. The quicker we leave town the better."

"Why the rush, Merith? It's not like there is a set deadline or anything," said Desidra, "I think we should wait for Celene to see us off."

"I get the feeling that, if she was going to see us off, she would be here now." I saw Cat coming over to us.

"You are getting ready to go, aren't you?" She stressed the last bit. Evidently she wanted us to go as soon as possible.

"We are going now, aren't we guys?"

They stood up and, struggling a bit with their bags, accompanied me down to the stables. One of the novices had tied all of our horses out in the stable yard. Saddles had been put on and my saddlebags were already in place. I walked over to Limerick and said my hellos to her. I checked the tummy belt was secure, but not too tight. I also checked over the rest of the tack. Whoever had made her ready knew horses and checked everything. I was the last to mount. However, before I did so, I ensured my frame pack was secure and comfortable on my shoulders, and that the saddlebags were seated properly.

We were ready to go. The thrill of going somewhere new suddenly hit me. I waved goodbye to Cat and told Neville to lead on. Desidra went next and I had Vergoth in front of me. As I moved off, I gave out a 'whoop' to the world in general. I was so excited! It was all going to be one grand adventure and I had centre stage. We all carried the hopes of the Temple with us, and we were sure to succeed.

The journey through the town was a much quieter one; at this time of the morning, few were up and about. We passed through the gates with little fuss and Harold passed us through with only a sign of good luck. We rode down the road, with Neville now riding next to Desidra discussing with her the roads to take. We needed to get down to the North road and ride it for three days. After that, there was half a day's ride roughly east through treacherous forest and hills; that is really when we would need Desidra.

At Littlebury, we turned on to the main road north. This was the King's highway. The road stretched out before us like a dusty snake winding its way through the countryside, treacherous in the winter and dry and choking in the summer. It went over most of the higher ground, making it harder for footpads, highwaymen, and robbers in general, to rob travellers. There were a few places that could be ideal for ambushes, but they were really few and far between. These places were also frequented by hired mercenaries who disposed of most of the nastier problems. Hit and run outlaws were the main problems;

like those who have apparently taken up residence where we need to go.

The first days travelling went by with few problems. The trees had been cleared to twenty yards from the road. The surface was dressed dirt, which allowed easy passage for most of the year, and we were lucky it had not rained recently as this can turn it into a quagmire over the winter months. Our spirits were high in the group; everyone was chatting and pointing out landmarks to each other. Riding at the back of the group, I occasionally went up and down the line to speak with the rest of them. It was my job to keep moral high and keep everyone going. We ate on the road from our packs, and I told everyone to only satisfy their hunger; no more than that, as these rations may have to last longer than we could dream. However, we did have to stop a couple of times for 'poor Vergoth' whose bottom was giving him problems. I allowed him to walk for a while, which slowed us down, but also tired him out and stopped the whining. He was having problems with his hay fever and was constantly having to blow his nose to keep it clear.

We made the last night's camp in a clearing of trees near to the road. This site had obviously been used before, as there was already the remains of a fire with a ring of stones. From the look of it, Desidra said it had not been used in a few days. I lit the fire, as Desidra and Neville picked up pieces of wood to burn. Neville had a large tarpaulin, which he strung across several trees to keep us all dry. We boiled water for the meal and I put into it some of the special meats that Petersen had given me. We would be approaching our destination tomorrow and I wanted everyone to be ready for it. Everyone at the meal was quiet and thoughtful. Desidra, for once, didn't even shoot any daggers at me. We settled for the night.

Decim – Raptus, Necare, Ultionis

I woke up, feeling someone on top of me. Pain exploded throughout my entire body! Something was inside of me, forcing its way into me. I opened my eyes and screamed; his cruel face was so close to mine, our skin was touching. He laughed in my face and licked my cheek. I tried to get away, but I realised that my hands and feet were tied to something. I was tied spread-eagle on a board in a small stone walled room. This man was absolutely rank, stinking of rancid ale, tobacco and the stench of unwashed bodies. My robes had been ripped open and, each time he thrust into me, I felt pain lancing through my body from cuts in my stomach and just the force of him inside me. There were men all around the board. They were jeering at him to come quickly, because they all wanted a go. So many hands were all over my body, touching me, caressing me, groping me. I couldn't stop them and I hated every one of them. I was being violated and I could do nothing to stop it. I spat into his face and he slapped me across the face with the back of his hand. I must have blacked out again.

I awoke. Someone was struggling with me; I felt him inside me again. Matt's voice called to me, "Little Merith, don't struggle! This is a dream, lie back and enjoy." I opened my eyes to see his black box with its tube facing towards me. A red light flashed at the top of it. I could see Matt's arm holding my arms, and I could feel the painful thrusting into me. I yanked my hand away and tried to reach around on the floor. Stretching around me, groping for something as a weapon, my hand found a thin metal object....

I woke up. Was it me screaming, or someone else? It still felt like there were people touching me and I felt a hard thing inside of me. The sensation of the thrusting was raw inside my belly. There was still the weight of someone on top of me. I opened my eyes and the feelings died. I began to recall what had happened to us. I pieced together the journey from my broken mind. Throughout the whole ride down the highway, I had felt someone following us. I sensed it. I saw it, but dismissed it often as a bad feeling. Repeatedly, I had checked every night to find nothing to worry me. The journey had certainly been without event; each day moving into the next with equal certainty, with the new day being as boring as the last. We had passed a few merchant caravans, travellers and the King's guard – all without comment. It seemed to be so fluid and easy.

On the last night of our camp, I had begun meditating as I had done for the entire journey. I was on duty most of the night, as was the arrangement. Then Neville had taken over to stand guard, as he had done, for the last two hours before dawn. While the others slept and he was on duty, I had begun to meditate. He must have dozed on duty, as the first I knew of the attack was the sudden intake of breath. It was the sound of a sword thrusting through Neville's lungs. In the surreal light of the campfire, I saw blood gushing out of his mouth and this mighty man crash to the floor to be replaced by another man with a cruel face.

I screamed and took out my daggers from my wrist sheaths. The first ended up in his left eye socket. The second, I held, as I saw the ground around us erupt with over twenty men. They came running towards us like a crushing tide. I saw a flash of bright light erupt to the side of me and heard Desidra screaming. The first to reach me came from behind. He hammered my head with what felt like a tree. Twisting, I stabbed at him. As I felt the knife tear through him, I was hit again in the head and everything went black. My last image was that of Vergoth, being hit with a club. They meant to take us alive.

There was screaming; it wasn't me screaming, it came from the wall. I could hear Desidra's voice, screaming away, shouting for them to stop. There was an appalling, jubilant clamour of men jeering and cheering, chanting to go on and on in the beat of a slow march. The hatred sparked me within me; revenge! All I wanted to do was to kill every last one of them. I looked around the room and saw there was little to help me, but nothing to stop me. The image of a snake came to mind; no legs and poisonous bite. I visualised the change and quickly transformed into a viper – deadly, poisonous and totally pissed off.

In the course of the journey, I had managed to practise transforming into many of the creatures I had seen in the forests. I had practised changing into badgers, bats, snakes and the like. I once saw a kingfisher, dipping into a crystal clear pond, with water so clear and crisp that I could see, under the liquid, the fish as it was impaled by the beak. The water rolled off the bird as it surfaced like an avalanche of stones. Each time I had practised, I was aware of the need to change quickly and change back. I was already getting looks from the rest of the group for my long absences. Neville had commented on it once. He said it was as if I had a secret lover following us and had to be with him. They all laughed at me, but I could tell he meant every word. He must have seen the follower and connected him to me. It is a shame I shall never know.

I moved over to the door, and slipped under it. In my haste I had not really assessed the situation so I stopped and looked up and down the corridor. There was one man on duty, and he was watching the door to where I assume they were raping Desidra. I moved silently to his leg and bit hard into it, injecting a full load of poison. He shouted in agony and bent down to look at what happened. I could see from the way he was moving that the poison was already working. His whole skin began to look pallid, and he started slowing as the poison began to paralyse him. He collapsed onto the ground and started with fits as his lungs filled with blood and his heart stopped. Blood spurted out of his lungs as he tried to breathe. Fuck him!

The chanting and raucous shouting continued. I could only hear Desidra's high-pitched yelps every so often now. They were really going for her. Slipping my head under this door, I saw the heat more than I saw the light in this form. There were seven heat signatures in the room, one was larger than the others. I guessed this was the man on top of Desidra. I saw that none of the men were actually carrying any weapons; no swords were evident, but I did see the flash of a couple of daggers. I knew I couldn't take them all without serious help, but there was none at hand.

I had to have a plan. I still had my spells in my head. I didn't know if I could use them as an animal, but anything was worth a go. I thought about how to reduce the odds. Black bears have a ferocious bite and claws that you don't want to meet in a dark alley. It is probably the most dangerous creature I know of, and it has its weapons already attached. If I can, I will cast 'shield' on one of them and 'command' them all to sleep - this is more effective on a group, and will cause a few to actually fall to sleep. 'Die' can only really be used on a one to one basis, as it is a direct command.

The door was slowly rocking on its hinges and the wind, which caused it to move, was sighing through the gap. I paused for a fraction of a second, taking in the ends of the wood that made up the door. I could see that it was oak, with the silt of the years of use imbedded into its grain. The silt had fallen and had been collected by the open pores at the ends of the wood. The curvature of the grain showed it to have come from an ancient tree. An incredibly strong door, if locked. However, it wasn't locked.

I slid under the door and hugged the wall along to the middle, where there were two men drinking and roaring at the scene in front of them. I could hardly look. Desidra was on a wagon wheel. The axel hub was under her bottom holding her hips out. Her hands and feet tied to the rim to hold her as I had been, spread out and unable to stop whatever was happening. Her head was lolling around and there was blood down her breasts and chest. I could also see blood coming out of between her legs, as the bastard was ramming her. I suddenly recognised him. Harry, the bastard! He was grinning from ear to ear and I realised he was shouting at her, "After you, I'm gonna go back to Merith and finish what I started."

At this, I just went ballistic. I changed straight to the bear, without changing back to myself. The first swipe clawed the necks and spines out of the two in front of me. At the one in the corner, holding a dagger, I fired off the 'shield' spell. I could now ignore him for a while. I then shouted 'sleep', and cast the spell on the room in general. One of the two across from me slumped to the ground. Harry on top of Desidra, and Desidra herself, also relaxed their positions.

At this point, the only one that was left, that could harm me, took out my own fucking dagger - as he did so, light bathed the room. He grinned in the light and said, "I don't know where you came from bear, but you are going to hell now!" He lunged for me and, as my claws left his chest, he was still grinning. He fell to his knees on the floor and sighed. Blood from the final pumps of the stricken heart spurted through the four massive furrows across his chest. The last man standing was still trying to stab me, with the dagger he was carrying. Every time he tried to lunge for me, the dagger slipped away from me. I cornered him and bit his throat out.

The carnage only lasted ten seconds, but for me it seemed like a lifetime. I was hurt in a way no man knows how. My butchers lay around me, but I knew they were not all where they deserved to be. I changed back to my normal shape and picked up my holy dagger. I had never used it for death. I was not going to start now. He had the sheath for my dagger with its strap tucked into his belt. I pulled it off him and put the dagger into the sheath. I hugged the dagger to my exposed chest. I felt violated and just wanted to curl up into a ball and cry, but I knew I had to go on. Desidra was still there, tied down with her rapist still on top of her. Harry and this other man were still asleep, under the influence of the spell, but that would not last long. I took the fallen dagger from the ground beneath the cornered man and looked at him, as if for the first time. If I had seen him in the pub, I might have chatted up this youth. Underneath the blood and grime, he looked so young. He could have been no more that fifteen himself. How did he get mixed up with these rapists, these murdering cutthroats? I slit his throat, he deserved no more than this.

Gently, I pulled Harry off Desidra. She was a total mess. There was blood dripping down her face from a head wound, her hair was matted from all of the blood that had seeped through it from the other head gashes across her scalp and there were scores of small abrasions and cuts across her chest and stomach. Her genitals were bleeding, rubbed raw from all the use, and there was massive bruising around the area. Her legs also had multiple cuts and further abrasions. With tears in my eyes, I removed the ropes from her feet and carefully removed her wrist ties. I helped her lie on the floor and made her comfortable. To heal some of the wounding around her labia, I used one of my remaining heal spells and I tried to wipe some of the blood from her face.

With Harry I carefully, without waking him, used the rope from Desidra's bonds to put him into the same position. Desidra should decide what to do with him. I knew I would want to do something evil to him if I was in the same position, but I didn't want to do it myself. I didn't want it on my conscience. My anger had been spent on avenging myself on these bastards, and I didn't want to do more.

Undecim – Expiscari depopulor

I felt sick. I was cold and was uncomfortable. I tried to open my eyes, but something kept them shut. I felt around my eyes and found that they were encrusted with something. I wiped them several times before I could open them. I had to blink several times because of the light and when I could focus I saw the spray of blood.

I tried to piece things together. I was lying naked on a bed; I looked myself down and could see that I had congealed blood down my body, my inner thighs were painful and so was my vagina. I knew from the feelings that I had been attacked again. I looked beside me and the shock of the discovery made me scream and push myself away. I landed on the floor but at least I was away from the corpse. Matt was lying on his side naked on the bed, with a knife stabbed into his heart. I just kept on screaming and crying Even when I heard banging on the door, I couldn't do anything. I just screamed.

This had to be part of the awful dream I was in! Eventually, the door burst in and faces peered around the door. I felt reality slip away again....

I looked around the room. The only clothing was being worn by the deceased and, as we needed it, I pulled off a couple of coats from those that were less covered in blood. Feeling self-conscious, I put one of these on and draped the other over Desidra. She was sleeping so peacefully; I decided to leave her to find help. I carefully picked my way out of the room. The hallway outside was deserted, except of course for the recently deceased. There were four other doors leading off from this room. The door at the end was closed and I gave it a second glance. Wooden, possibly locked from the other side, but the door did have a latch on this side. I would have to deal with that later.

Three other doors each had a small shutter to look through. They all had a large bolt holding them shut. I looked into the first; it was dark as pitch, but with my Darksight I could see a small figure curled up in a corner. It was naked and cooling, and I could see it was still alive but in a terrible state. I called over to it. The figure picked up her head and shouted, "Bugger off you bastards, if you want any more you'll have to kill me to get it!" She stood up shakily and raised her arms to fight the first one to come through the door.

I called to her, "I'm Merith, a priest. I've managed to free myself and kill the guards with my Goddess's help. You won't attack me if I open the door?"

She shook her head. She looked defeated, but still had a bit of fight left in her. "My name is Penny. I am trained as a bodyguard. I was guarding a rich woman. They captured us five days ago, the bastards. They haven't fed me since. The fucking bastards have brutally…"

I interrupted her "To all of us. I'm opening the door now." I slid the bolt back and helped her out. She saw the body on the floor and ran over to it. She kicked it and spat onto the corpse. "This fucker was one of them."

"Keep your voice down, I don't know where the rest are. Look, in there," I said, pointing to the room Desidra was in. "My friend lies on the floor. She is asleep and her attacker is tied up." I opened the door to the scene of carnage. "Don't wake either of them, just grab some clothes and a weapon and come and help me."

She nodded and went in. I heard a lot of kicking as she went among the bodies. She returned after about a minute with an overcoat and two daggers. Indicating the door at the far end, I said to her, "Can you guard that door and give me a shout if someone is coming?"

Nodding, she started towards it. "Merith," she said to me, "Thanks for saving me. I hope I can do the same for you!"

I said, "You are!" I moved to the next door. Looking in through the shutter, I saw Vergoth. He was lying on the floor in a pool of blood. He was still alive but there was fierce heat in his hands; they were larger than they should be. The damage done to his hands had made them swell. I opened the door and went over to him, noting that his clothes were ripped and his hands had been smashed - the bones had been broken by a heavy weight hitting the inside of the palm. He would not be able to use them for a long time to come, if ever! But right now they needed to be stabilised, so I ripped some of the cloth off his shirt and wrapped them around the damaged hands. As I lifted each of them, the blood dripped off in long streams of droplets. He was still out cold and although I tried to wake him I couldn't. I opened up his eyelids; his pupils were like pinpricks, so I dragged him over to the doorway and propped him up in the frame.

"Who's he," Penny whispered.

"A maji, but his hands have been smashed."

"Oh. Bloody useless, like most men!"

I stood up and walked to the other door. Looking into the shutter, I saw our packs, which they had obviously stowed here until after they had their fun. I looked around the room to check if there was anything else here. Seeing nothing, I opened the door and picked up my pack. It was untouched! I opened the top and grabbed my spare robes. Feeling totally unprotected and rather vulnerable in this overcoat, I slipped the robes over my head and felt like I was returning to normality - what ever that was. Looking for some food, I rummaged through the pack and found the pack of trail rations in the bottom. I grabbed two of them, and said a silent thanks to Ichmarr that they were still there. Although our packs were here, untouched, I could see that nothing else had come with them. The saddlebags, weapons, and all of the stuff that was on our horses was gone; nothing was left here.

I picked up my pack and Neville's. He wasn't going to complain that I was giving his stuff away and, anyway, Penny needed whatever was in that pack more than he did.

I carried them over to her and gave her one of the trail biscuits. "Nibble on it slowly," I advised. Don't eat it at once - you will never be able to swallow! This is a friend's pack of stuff, but he won't need it anymore. I think he has a few spare clothes in here, also another pack of trail rations."

There were no wineskins attached to any of the packs and I was bloody thirsty myself. "I need a drink and there is nothing else along this corridor. How do you feel about going for a look around the rest of this place?"

"Can Desidra fight?" Penny enquired, as she opened the pack and found a long shirt, some hose and a tunic. They were long for her, but she started to put them on. I could see that she was cold and didn't blame her. "We would do better if she was able to come with us. I have a spare dagger and can arm myself on the way through. We could use the help!" She rummaged through the rest of the pack and took out a couple more of the trail biscuits. "I am so hungry!" She had a beautiful smile. Penny was dark haired like me, though was taller and more muscular than I was. Her face was a round moon that lit up with the smile she just gave. I would guess that she was probably chubby in her youth, and that had made her have a large frame. She was tanned from a life of being outdoors and had several scars in long cuts across her arms, legs and body.

I remarked on her scars, and she said, "When I was trained for this life, the man who trained me said the only way to learn was to get hurt once and a while. He used blunt swords and daggers, but even these can cut and hurt. I never thought I would survive the training but, here I am, in this fuck hole of a cellar, with a gang of soon to be dead rapists!"

I could see that she was protecting her ribs. "Have you injuries? Can I help you out?"

"I think my ribs are cracked, but there is not much anyone could do about them. I can still fight, but it does hurt a hell of a lot. There is not much point in worrying about it."

"Are you sure? I have healing powers and could help to set them. We need you fit and well. You could be our only hope."

"I doubt that. The way you cleared that room, with whatever weapon you had, you would make a threatening opponent. What weapon did you actually use? Two of them looked like they had been clawed to death, and the third looked like he had his throat bitten out."

"I'll go and wake up Desidra. You are right, she may be needed." I left her, not wanting to answer her questions. Penny was evidently very observant and she had come to a conclusion about the injuries very quickly; she suspects something. I have to be careful with her until we are out of here. I need to get my priorities straight and sort out explanations later. I stopped and looked back to her. "Yes, we do need her, but I think it would be better if we brought her into the room with the bags. She will just freak out otherwise."

"Okay! Let's go - let's do it, now!"

We found Desidra as I had left her. Penny had to help me pick her up by her arms and legs - she weighed more than I thought. I struggled with her weight, but eventually we managed to get her into the room. To keep the noise in, I closed the door, thinking that she might be a little distressed when she awoke. I used a bit of rag and spit to clean her eyes and face a little. Gently, I rocked her back and forth. I said her name. Her eyes opened in a flash and she screamed!

We both backed away from her as she clawed the air. I quietly told her, "Desidra, you are amongst friends. Calm down, you have to listen to us."

"You rapist bastards! Let go of me! STOP! NO, NO...."

"They are all gone now, Desidra. There are just us here!" She crumpled into a ball, sobbing. I bent down and held her in my arms and said, "Don't be frightened, they are gone now and they won't be coming back. You are safe with us. We need you to be here with us. We need you, Desidra." I rocked her back and forth. She began to relax and, after a few minutes, she stopped sobbing and looked up at me.

"What happened to us?"

"The men came, captured us and hurt all of us." I expanded my arms to show Penny. She smiled at Desidra.

Penny spoke to her in a soft way. "Desidra, my name is Penny. The men have hurt me too, but we cannot dwell on this. We need to get out of here before they hurt us again. We all need to stay together and look after each other. Those bastards have to pay for what they have done."

Desidra's eyes looked wild in the dim light, she replied, "Yes, they have to pay. Merith, you have many daggers, give me one now!"

"I have one," said Penny. She gave her a dagger. "You both stay here and I'll see if I can find another." She left us together, Desidra playing with the dagger.

I watched her go, and I realised that we couldn't let Desi kill Harry. She would not be totally sane if we allowed that. It would be bad for her - and for us, too.

As Penny came back in, she looked at me and put her finger to her lips. She had done something, and I knew that she had another dagger. I could guess that she had dispatched Harry, the bastard. Good for her! I was glad that she had seen to that. I said, "Right Penny, you have sorted things out, let's get you dressed Desidra." We opened her pack and found her spare clothes. She couldn't bear to look at herself, so we dressed her.

"Merith, I can't stand the smell of them, I need to wash now!"

"You can't wash until we get out!"

"I have to wash now!"

"Desidra, look at me, we are not safe. Any minute now, someone could come through that door and we could have a serious problem. I don't want that. I don't want to be raped again!"

She crumpled and began sobbing.

"Stop the sobbing!" ordered Penny. "Desidra, we need you to be strong like we are! Both of us have been though it, just like you. Don't be so selfish! You need to think of all of us. We need you to help us kill them all. Think of revenge and steel yourself to kill them. Keep that thought, and you can have revenge yourself!"

In a savage voice Desidra said, "Right, let's find the rest and kill them."

We moved to the end of the hallway. "I'll go first" I said, "I can move much more quietly than you can."

I checked the door over. It had a simple latch keeping the door closed, and so I opened the door slowly and stepped into another corridor with doors similar to this one. There were voices from the far end and I also saw that there was a hint of natural light. I closed the door and shared this with the other two.

"What do you think?" I asked.

Penny said, "We need to get the hell out of here. We don't know how many there are above ground or below it. I say we scout along the corridor and find the light. Once we're there, we deal with whatever the opposition there is and get away as fast as possible."

I asked, "We are going to do that with daggers and no armour to fight in?"

She looked at me and said, "Yes, with whatever we have now."

I looked confused by this, "Even if, behind one of those other doors, there is a store of weapons and armour that can help us? I for one think we should search the rest of the rooms and go out there with crossbows and long-swords - that would even up the contest against the bastards."

Desidra cut in; "That actually makes sense, Penny. Look, I don't know about you, but against armed men I wouldn't have a chance- not with just a dagger, no matter how angry I felt."

Penny persisted, "And, if there are more men behind those doors?"

"Then," I said, "We kill them with these little daggers. They would be unprepared for such an attack. If we do it quickly enough, they wouldn't have time to shout or raise the alarm."

"Okay," Penny agreed. "You've persuaded me, let's go and explore this place."

Desidra spoke up again, "What about him." She pointed to Vergoth, who was propped up against the doorframe.

"How about we lock him in one of the cells until we are ready to go, then drag him out?" I suggested.

"Good idea," replied Penny, "he will be safer there. If we don't succeed, he will be safer in their hands if they don't realise we had brought him out."

Listening intently, I peered around the door and heard the men towards the lighted end. They seemed to be chatting and larking around, just like men eating or gaming. Carefully, I crossed the corridor to the door opposite ours. I listened closely at this door and, hearing nothing human, I turned the handle and slowly opened the door. Inside the room was dark, dank and empty. It looked unused and probably had not been used for a while.

The corridor went in two directions; both directions had doors on each side. The corridor was very symmetrical, like the cellars beneath my own Temple. With six rooms from a central walkway, it was as if there had once been a need to store things separately.

Moving to the next door on this side (nearest the outside), I listened and could hear breathing beyond the door. To separate out the noises inside the room, I had to listen for a long time. Eventually, I singled out the breathing of at least three individuals and, slowly, I pushed the door open to look into the room. Although no torches were lit inside, I could see with my Darksight that there were three sleeping figures in beds. A hooded lantern in the far corner was giving off heat, still lit, so I silently moved to the first one closest to the door. I looked into his face. It was so cruel, with scars and lines about the features. I realised that he was the one who had been on top of me.

He was the one that raped me!

I felt a combination of sheer terror and fear that he would awake, but also the total loathing of the creature. Without any satisfaction or remorse, I held his mouth and slit his throat. He opened his eyes so widely and, in the dim light, saw me and died. I hoped that his soul would carry the burden of what he had done for eternity. With the same detachment, I moved to the other two and repeated the same actions. They were both in the crowd that jostled for position to grope me and, although I hated them for what they had done - to me and uncounted others, I felt some pity for them - that they wouldn't have a chance to reprieve themselves. I was beginning to confine the thoughts of hatred that I had about them. It was unhealthy and I knew it. This was something I would have to think about for a very long time. It would dwell in the lowest parts of my mind, occasionally surfacing to make me cringe with self loathing and disgust.

The rest of the room was empty, so I went back to the door and signalled the other two to come in. I un-hooded the lantern to give them some light and tried to warn them about the sight they would see.

The scene of the three bodies, with their throats cut and blood still dribbling out of their open necks, must have disturbed them. The blood did not show very much on my black robes, but I could feel it on them. The blood was already congealing in pools on the beds and dripping in long dripping streamlets onto the floor.

The room was large enough to bed twenty or so men. It had beds for them with footlockers and shelves above each of the beds. This was a very organised band of outlaws - almost military in their organisation. We began opening the lockers, but found little in them to use. Penny did find a couple of swords, one long and one short, that she said she could use. I also found my hand crossbows, with eight of the bolts I had made for them. I handed one of them to Desidra and showed her how to cock it. We split the bolts and I said to them, "Girls, you need to search the room for anything useful. I will check out the rest of this cellar."

Penny looked at me, as if to say, 'Why check any more, when we could go now? We have weapons that we can use, why stay?' I ignored her look and slipped out of the door.

I crossed the corridor and again listened at the door opposite. There was no sound coming from it and I slowly opened the door. The room was about half full of Merchants' wares, piles of silks, cloths etc. I stopped myself from engaging in a shopping spree. This was not the time for it!

At the next door down, I could hear the sound of one person breathing. The sound was not as if he were asleep, but more like he was awake and alert. I could make out the sounds of scratching and rustling, but I couldn't tell what was going on. I left that room, at the moment it was too dangerous to open.

The last door in the corridor was completely silent, so I opened the door and could see only half the room with the light that entered it. With my Darksight, I could see that there was another door across from this one. It was closed and I guessed that this was the entrance into the maze. This was the whole reason for me being here and I was dammed if I wasn't going to explore it, but not yet! For now, I had to make sure that the others were safe. I closed the door and went back up the corridor. The girls had obviously prepared for someone to come into the room, as they nearly attacked me when I opened the door.

I told them what I found, except for the maze. Desidra explained to us that her family used the last room as a study and that there had been maps and books of the local area shelved within it. These could come in useful, later.

I then told them about the room with the man inside it. I said that it was likely that this was the leader of the outlaws and that he may be planning his next hit. "Why don't we go in there and kill him?" I suggested. That would stop them from hurting others."

Penny quickly replied, "If he is a really good fighter, he would almost certainly kill us. The only way would be for one of us to walk in there and get the first blow in while he wasn't expecting us."

"Yes," I said thoughtfully. Remembering that I still had the hair braid on, I asked, "Penny, how good is your imagination?"

"Why?"

"Watch," I checked my appearance with the hat, and changed it slowly to transform into Desidra's appearance.

"What the fuck!" She pointed her sword at me, "That is evil."

I reached up to my head and lifted the hat off, "No, no, no! It is majick. This hat was made long ago. It is a hat of disguise and it can make you look like someone else, even one of them. You could change your appearance to look like one of them. Do you remember any of them strongly? One of these guys, maybe How about this fucking bastard here?" I pointed to the recently expired and, I hoped in eternal damnation, rapist.

"Yes, I can see him."

I placed the hat on her head. "You will feel a strange sensation, when I put it on your head. You will become acutely aware of your own body and appearance. When you can sense it fully, you should imagine that you look slightly different and the hat will change your outer appearance to the desired features."

"Alright! I can imagine what I look like."

"Think about what you look like with flowers in your hair."

She concentrated and a few flowers began to appear in her hair. "Excellent! Now, think about this man; what would you look like, if you looked like him."

She began to concentrate and her features slowly changed into that of the man lying on the bed. She looked pretty similar to him, but her clothes were still the same.

"And now the clothes, imagine what the clothes looked like. Think about the clothes in the same way as you thought about the flowers."

Her clothes changed to look like that of the man. She was nearly his twin. "I don't feel any different," she said. "But I know that I look different. I could walk out of here without them giving me a second glance. I suppose it is lucky for us that you didn't just go for it and leave us behind."

"To be honest it didn't even cross my mind." I had always thought about everyone else on the mission. They were vital to me and, now that I am inside the cellars, I didn't really need them any more. However, I still felt the need to have others around. I suppose this was because I was scared to be alone right now. "Your voice is still the same," I told Penny. "Don't say anything unless you have to, but, if you do, grate it out."

"Yes, mother superior! I had guessed that. When I go in there, you two stand by the door and, when you hear the struggle, come in and help me out."

"Desidra," I said, "load up the hand crossbow to get it ready. I will do the same and keep your dagger handy. Right?.... Let's go."

We walked out of the room straight into the corridor without checking, we were so familiar to it that it didn't seem to be as frightening. It was empty, as it had been all the time that we had been using it, but I knew our luck will run out soon. I knew my task would be made easier if we cleared out from this rat's nest.

Penny, disguised as the man, opened the door and left it slightly ajar as she walked into the room. I could see there were several lanterns hanging from hooks in the wall. A man was seated with his back to the door. He was well built, muscular with brown hair. From the position I was in, I could see that he was seated at a desk writing something on parchment. He said, as she neared him, "What is it? What do you want?"

She walked up to him and moved to drive the sword through him point first. I instantly winced, as I knew it wouldn't succeed; such a clumsy move, one for the total amateur. Time slowed for me as I watched the scene. He turned in his chair towards us and Penny's sword swept past his stomach. I threw open the door and fired the crossbow, aiming for his body, but it hit him in the thigh and he reached down for it. Desidra fired past me, and I heard the 'twip' of the bolt whip past my head - but it only hit the leg of the desk. He rose from his chair and turned towards Penny. I ran towards him as I saw Penny's sword swing around and, whistling through the air, slice into his midriff, digging into him several inches deep. As I reached him, he fell to his knees with blood pouring from the wound. I grabbed his hair, held his head up and sliced through his throat. Blood spurted out of the open wound. He finally collapsed as Penny wrenched the sword out of the body. I stood over it; the world returned to surround me again, as my attention uncoupled from the fight.

I looked around the room properly. There were several small chests that immediately caught my eye and I made a careful note of them. The walls were lined with shelves. Parchments and scrolls littered the shelves, with a large pile of scroll cases in one corner. There was small cot in the corner, with blankets heaped up at the end, and a large chest at the end, covered by Neville's suit of scale-mail. The floor was littered with parchment and odd bits of wood, metal pieces and bones. Several large paintings hung from pegs on the walls, each from a different era and in different styles, including landscapes, portraits and odd paintings of creatures.

The desk had parchments all over it. The scraps of parchment he was reading from had pictures and marks, which seemed to describe the traffic on the road. These were possibly made by a person who was illiterate, using symbols and marks. Shit, most of the people I knew were illiterate; reading and writing were for the educated few. I wondered who these people actually were, and how they had avoided the King's troops for so long. There were some other papers and I scanned them quickly. One letter that caught my eye was addressed to Count Wincy De Morrow the powerful lord of the county, it made interesting reading. I was just tucking it into my frame pack, when we heard a noise.

We must have made more of a racket than I thought, as we heard a voice calling down the corridor, "What's going on down there?"

I whispered to Penny, "Give me the hat, quick!"

She took it off, her face, body, clothes and everything swept off her as she did so.

I grinned to her, "I want to have some fun!" My real reason was that, while Penny may be good at the hack and slash of real combat, sneaking around and being a complete bastard was actually my forte'. I had, after all, just seen her make a real hash of the attack on this guy who, by the looks of him was a bit of a writer, possibly the leader, but definitely an agent of some description.

I whispered to Desidra, "Don't get angry, but I'm going to look like Harry the bastard, may he rest in hell! Don't get too upset please."

She nodded, and turned away, as I changed my appearance to that of Harry. I knew his voice and was able to adjust my own to sound just like him. My dagger I held up inside my wrist, and swaggered out into the corridor, as if I owned the place.

There were two of them, with swords out already, and they were cautiously stepping down the corridor. They had not reached the middle doors yet, as they paced towards the end rooms. When they saw it was me (Harry), their swords lowered.

"What the fuck was all of the noise down here? It sounded like a fight."

"Nah," I said in Harry's voice. "I heard it too. It's just the lads' havin' a bit of fun with that hard bitch you guys brought in a few days ago. They said they was going to when they left us."

I approached them and they stood relaxing looking at me. One of them asked, "You having an 'interview' with the 'Cont' then?"

"He had words, but I sez it wasn't my fault." I replied.

They both slid their swords back into their sheaths. "I thought he was pleased with yah, bringing them to us like that. He told Brian here, that you done a good job getting away from them and bringing them here."

"That's not what he sez to me. He sez that I was sloppy back in Walden, and that I shouldn't have lost Spike."

I started going up the corridor with them, as the second turned to walk in front of me, I grabbed his mouth and inserted the dagger between the bones of his spine and head. This is a fairly instant method of killing a person, requiring only a good understanding of how the body works and what makes it tick. The insertion of the dagger has to be quick and incisive; it cuts though all of the strings that keep the body upright and the victim cannot make a sound. I was shown this technique by Edowyn, who used another novice to show us where to strike (Obviously not actually killing her!). It is just above the base of the neck, usually you can see a person's spine just there. You aim for between the bones and push hard. There is very little anyone can do to this sort of attack, and it is fast!

I helped the body onto the floor and said, "He also said I should have brought along some more bitches for you lot to play with!" I tried to say it without any tension in my voice, to not let on what was happening. I carried along the corridor and caught up with him.

He chuckled at my last remark and said, "Yes! But I can't wait for that scrawny one to wake soe'z I can have another go at her. She is a fucking 'looker', and I'd love to have her screaming my name as I came!"

I grabbed his mouth. As I slid the dagger home, I whispered in his ear, "In your fucking nightmares, rapist fucker!"

I helped him slip to the ground and spat at him. When I heard a noise like 'twip', I realised that by concentrating so much on him I hadn't taken in anything else. The pain of the crossbow bolt shook me throughout my body. My leg absolutely erupted in pain, as the bolt dug itself deep into it. We had reached the bottom of the stairs by the time I had caught up with the guy. As I went down on one knee and looked up, I could see that it was a single bowman who had fired at me. I watched as he dropped the crossbow and started to run down the stairs; he was pulling his short sword out as he did so.

In the haze of the pain, I reassessed my life.

Ten steps away from me.

It had been good up to now. I have been having a pretty cruel day today, but most of my life has been good.

Eight steps away from me.

I have met a Goddess, in my own mind maybe, but I have met her.

Six steps away from me.

I have been given gifts that most could only dream about.

He started to smile as he approached to within four steps of me.

I am usually an observant, fast little fucker who picks stuff up really quickly, like spells. Shit, spells! I had forgotten about them.

They bubbled up in my mind and, as he jumped the last remaining steps to run me through, I locked eyes with him and shouted "Die, you mother fucker!" As the spell was launched, I felt the energy pass through me and out of me. He collapsed onto me, his blade missing my face by an inch. His body crashed into me, and I fell over with him as his clothes caught the flights of the bolt sticking out of my leg. I screamed in agony and tried to stop the pain. I blacked out with it as the pain overcame me, my last thought was, 'Here we go again....'

Duodecim - Resipivi

The troll's face was the first thing I saw, as I opened my eyes. I wondered if this was safety. She smiled to see me awake again. I said to her, "What happened? Where am I? Did I get him?" I was surprised by how tired and grating my voice was.

"Oh," she replied, "Oh, so you do speak English after all! All of the po'lice tink da you might be foreign. P'arently, you have led them a merry little dance troue Cambridge."

"Cantebrigia?"

"No, dear. Cambridge! You where brawd back here. The po'lice vic'tim support team have given you a turough going over to take all of de evidence they need. My team cleaned you up! but we couldn't find any injuries. The po'lice are outside and want to speak with you when you are awake."

"I know this is going to sound odd, but who are the po'lice?"

"You remember Reg?"

"Yes."

"He is a po'lice man."

"Oh, a guard. Maybe I need to speak to him."

"I'll bring them in, hold on!" She walked out through the tapestries. In a sense, it comforted me to think I would see the three of them again. I remember they were the first sight I saw since coming to this place. The door opened again and I could see it was Jane Goody, Just Marlow and Lafley - the three I had talked to before. Seeing them triggered something in me, and my memories took me once again....

As I opened my eyes, Desidra's face began to come into view. Her face was fuzzy at first, but, as it cleared, I could see that she was blood-spattered but smiling. I looked around and I could see we were in one of the cellars, with stone-lined walls and a curving roof. Torches lined the walls, and there was a sweet smell in the air.

Desidra stopped me from sitting upright, saying, "It's okay, Merith, you killed the last of them! We checked around the rest of the ruins and those three were the only ones on guard. Penny is up there, with four loaded crossbows, keeping an eye on things."

I looked down to my leg, to see that it had been bandaged up with some herbs inside the bandages and, although it still hurt like the blazes, at least it had been dressed. She saw me looking at it, and said, "I did that, the herbs will keep the infections out. You were lucky, the bolt wasn't barbed or poisoned. It had just missed your bone. Penny pulled it out and I stopped the blood."

"How long have I been out for?"

"Only about an hour. While you slept, I have been trying to clear some of the bodies out of the living quarters. I have been dumping them in the damp cellar; it was as good a place as any to let them rot! We will have to sleep here tonight, but we will go back tomorrow when we have rested."

"Where is Vergoth?"

"Over there in the corner," she said, pointing to another bed. "He's still asleep or unconscious maybe, I don't know."

"Desidra, I am a healer, you know that don't you?"

"Yes, Merith, it is part of you. My mum could do a healing spell on the odd occasion too."

"And you know how she did it?"

"Yes, she prayed to Ichmarr and she gave her the power."

"Okay then," I said, bringing out my holy dagger which was still around my chest. I pulled it out of the sheath and leaned forward to heal my leg.

"Bloody hell, Merith, that is bright!"

"Yes," I said almost absent-mindedly, "It glows with the force of Ichmarr." I slid the end into my leg where the pain was most acute, and cast the spell. I didn't often do this to myself, but I felt this was absolutely necessary. The rush of energy through my head was exhilarating and, as I felt it going through to the dagger, my leg was in pain one second and the next second, when the blade withdrew, the pain had disappeared. What a blessing from my goddess!

"I have never seen her do it that way before!" Desidra said, in awe; "That was something to behold!" She slid down on to her heels, with her mouth wide open. "My mum could heal, but I didn't ever see her doing that before!"

"Don't you think of it like that!" I told her. "This was my goddess acting to heal one of her own; she can do the same for others. This is the power and the gift of Ichmarr; she grants us the powers to devote ourselves to her." I felt, at this moment in time, that this was true. I had been given all of these gifts to see this through and I have had to use them to fulfil it. There was still the book to find, but that could wait for a while.

After putting the dagger away, I slid the bandage off my leg. There was a purple scar left by the wound, but it had closed up nicely. I knew that I would be hobbling for a few days, but at least I could get around easily.

"Have you eaten?" she asked me.

"A little." I said thinking of what I needed to do. "Have you?"

"Yes! We had some of the trail rations from the packs, as I have yet to explore the ruins to find their larder. The kitchen is obvious, but they don't store their food where I would expect...."

"Desidra," I interrupted, "I still have my mission to complete. I will need rest and pray for spells. Can you go and keep Penny company up in the ruins? I will be okay down here. I will need about three hours to meditate, to get myself ready for the maze."

"Are you still insisting on going in there, after all that has happened to us? You realise that it is a cursed place, which no-one can dwell in? I survived it for three days and, finally, happened upon the light. My family had given me up for dead and were packing up to leave when I reappeared."

"I know the story, Desidra. Your family called and called for you. This only confused you as to the way to go. I will use something else to help me."

"What?"

"My ingenuity! If I am not back with you by tomorrow morning, don't expect me to come out! Please, leave me now and let me get some rest. I will come up and say'goodbye, when I leave."

I watched her go. She had changed from an angry, spiteful, and dangerous young woman into a caring and rather vulnerable girl. It was as if she had been reborn in the fires of hell. She obviously cared deeply for my well-being, and Penny's. The change in her was miraculous to see. This was not the result of any intervention, but more the result of the circumstances that we found ourselves.

Once she had closed the door, I stood up and checked on Vergoth. He was totally out of it. He seemed to be suffering from the effects of a spell back-wash, rather than a blow to the head. His eyes were like pinpricks when they should be dilated, due to the low light. It will be difficult to rouse him up, and we may have to take him back to the Temple to see what they can do.

I left him and knelt down beside the bed. I took out the dagger from its sheath, and started to pray to Ichmarr for healing spells. When I needed to get fit fast, this was the best way to do it. However, I had used all of my spells today and I decided to pray for four heal spells and one command. This would give me the ability to heal myself, and Vergoth as well, if I made it back. There was the familiar rush of energy entering my body, as I concentrated on replenishing my spells. I gave my thanks to Ichmarr for being generous, and began to think over the day's events.

To prepare for meditation, I began to turn down my senses - once again slipping into that meditative state. There were a lot of ripples and tangles in my mind that needed to be smoothed out. I reviewed the experiences I had just witnessed. The feeling of what happened to me just made me shudder. Reviewing the memories in my head, I felt sick, the pain and humiliation of what I had briefly experienced and witnessed. The utter lack of humanity in those evil men, who had obviously perpetrated this crime on many women, was fully expressed inside my head. The men touching me, and the thought of what they had done, made me nauseous. Did I have the right to kill them for what they had done? No matter how wrong they had been, did I have the right to stand in judgement over them? I was disgusted with myself for the excitement that I had felt, but I also thought that my goddess would forgive me if I balanced this act out with another. While I felt that I had done this in rescuing the others, only time will tell.

The same sensations had run through my mind when I killed the first two men. I had been brutalised and they had suffered for it. But, did they all deserve to die? Could we have just imprisoned them and given them over to the guards as criminals? My memories began to drop into slots, and I commenced the long process of smoothing out the whole day. Memories just kept running through my head. I knew it was an awful thing and brutal. They all just wanted to use me, but it was such a strong sensation that I wanted to keep it. Not for the anger it had caused me, but for the sensations, the feelings, smells, sounds and the pain caused. I felt I would never allow myself to forget this!

Excising my demons was a painful process. Slowly, however, I sorted myself out and I was able, gradually, to lift myself out of the meditative state to full consciousness and check my world. As I stood up and put my dagger away, I lifted my frame pack and took out all of the items I would not need. The rations I kept, just in case, along with the pitons, climbing pick, lock picks, rope and the lead marker. The rest, I ditched. I needed to sort out some water as I had none. Apart from that, I was ready.

I left Vergoth to sleep. He will die before getting to the Temple if I am not there. There was a pang of guilt here, but this is my mission and my only reason for being here. This is what we all have suffered for. I have to go through with it!

Making my way up into the ruins of the building above, I looked for the girls. The entrance to the cellar was from the kitchens, and this is where I found Desidra. Over a fire, she was busily preparing a soup that smelled wonderful! "So, you found their larder then?" I asked.

"Penny found it while looking over the ruins. There is also a wagon and a string of horses, which should make it easier to take our hoard back to town and, then, we can put our feet up as rich women."

"Eh?"

"Oh! Didn't I tell you? In those chests we found, over four thousand silver pieces. With these, along with the easily sellable merchandise, there is a haul of, maybe, five or six thousand silver. That is two thousand each! Merith, we could buy land and live like kings with that sort of money!"

"No," I told her. "I will settle for the book. You can keep my share and maybe give Vergoth some of it. I have no need for money." What I failed to tell her, is, that I already have a fortune in gemstones and jewels back in my chest in the Temple. I just don't need any more money. Instead, I said, "I have my faith and my occupation. That is all I need."

"Oh, Merith, you are being silly! Of course you will have a share; if it wasn't for you, we would not be in this situation now!"

I thought to myself, 'Yes, if it wasn't for me we wouldn't be in this situation now!' I replied to her, "I only need you to wait for me until midday tomorrow. That is all I need."

"Of course we will wait for you. I will wait, even if Penny goes."

"Where is Penny now?" I asked.

"She is up on the top floor of the ruin. There is a stair way that goes up just over there." She pointed to a more substantial mound. "She has the shooting gallery up there, as that is the highest point in the ruins. Go up to see her, and I will bring the soup up to both of you."

From the position of the sun I could see it was late afternoon, which meant there was maybe four or five hours of daylight left. I had planned to be back before nightfall because, if anyone else was out there, it would be then that they would return.

I climbed my way through the ruins and found my way to the stairs. They were built out of heavy stone and had survived for this reason only. The first floor featured a small landing to the stairs that had survived the catastrophe befallen the house. A section, probably in the middle of the house, had been supported by the stairs and this 'tower' had low walls around it, overlooking the whole area. The rest of the building's walls were no more than four or five feet high. This was the highest point, and had obviously served as an observation point many times before. Penny was up in the tower and I could see as I came nearer that, occasionally, she would look around to check all of the approaches.

She was smiling when she saw me, "So, our conquering hero awakes! You are top notch aren't you, the real dog's bollocks! How old did you say you were? Desidra said you were only fifteen?"

"Penny, I am only fifteen and I was lucky! I took too many risks and could have really suffered for it."

"It took a shit-load of nerve and real experience to have done what you did. I have never seen someone take out two great huge fighters and knock a third one out, with only a dagger to work with. You have had more training than just in religion. What sort of history have you had?"

"A long and fruitless one! I was lucky, as I said, but it could have been a lot different if it had turned another direction. The first bloke was the risky part; after that, I didn't anticipate anything else until that third guy jumped me from the top of the stairs."

"Yess…. And, I suppose, they teach you how to defend yourself with weapons you have to hand and stab people in the neck in every religious course?"

"Umm, well, no! I suppose not."

"Merith, if you don't want to talk about it then that's fine, at least you are on my side. However, if you do, I am always willing to listen to you. I am just very curious, and willing to learn from anyone who could do what you just did. That's all!"

She was smiling when she said it. I really liked Penny, she had been through hell and she still smiles at everything. She is happy with the situation. I suppose it could also be that she is now quite rich and only has to be careful to live a long life. She could stop working, buy a tavern or farm and just live the quiet life for a bit. I didn't envy her. I would rather cut my arm off than live a quiet life.

"So, what are you going to do with your share of the loot?"

"Well, first of all I'm going to hire a body guard for myself and get stinking drunk. Then, I might go for a wander around this land. I have no interest in settling down anywhere and, anyway, I have found that I prefer the life of a wanderer. For some time now, I have had this wanderlust and this is one of the reasons why I trained in warfare. I want to take risks and beat the odds."

"And why not?" We both twirled around and there was Desidra, standing at the top of the stairs with the soup pot in her hands and three tin bowls balanced precariously on the top. "Grub's up girls, let's eat!" As she served it up, she continued, "I don't think I want to settle down either. I was thinking of staying on the road. I wanted to get back to Dulce, and do a bit of exploration myself - maybe explore along the Eastern roads, or even go north up to the mountains."

"Well," I said, "I don't think I'm going to get much choice. I will have to visit all of the Temples of the land to spread the new word to all of the novices."

"Do you have to go anywhere in particular?"

"No, just as long as I spread it as far and wide as I can. Why?"

"Mind some company? We, Dulce and I, we could go with you. Dulce can handle herself in a fight and she has some training as a scout."

A scout is a well-known euphemism for a thief, why didn't I spot it? "Really?" I asked.

Penny jumped in and said, "Any chance of my joining you to make it a four-some? I don't have any particular path to follow and we might find something along the way that will keep my arm working? I could also train you both up on a bit of swordsmanship!"

"Swordswomanship, you mean!"

They both chuckled at this.

"Look, this is all fine and well, but I still have to complete the mission we started; if, that is, you are prepared to wait? I don't know how long I'll be, but I don't think it will take me more than a day. Would you both wait for me and...?"

"Yes, Merith!" they chorused together and laughed.

We all went silent. We looked at each other, sizing up the friendships we had forged in those dark cellars. They both looked to me for strength and leadership. On my part, I looked to Desidra for the kindness and vulnerability that I had lost, years before, in the harshness of the regime in the Temple. She reminded me of Rozz in the manner that she could fuss over someone and be there just at the right moment. As for Penny, I looked for her to provide the brutish strength that I didn't have. She had been trained to fight and to use weapons of war, armour, shields and the like. Okay, so she wasn't that good, but she was still young and I'm sure she will improve before she kills us.

"Look, finish your soup, you don't want it to get cold and be wasted!" said Desidra, breaking the silence.

Without thinking, I replied, "You wouldn't!" Goddess, this moment reminded me of the Temple. I did miss Petersen and the rest of them. Tears welled up in my eyes, and I tried to blink them away and be strong about everything.

Penny leaned over to me and hugged me. "Let it out, Merith. You can stop being strong now for a while."

That broke me, and the tears spilled out. I felt the grief of a loss course through my body, so I let go and felt Desidra join us. The pain and horror of the shared experience racked my body. I thought that I had excised my demons in meditating, but I hadn't. They came back with all of the horror of the moment, softened a little by time, but still all there - my lost youth and my lost innocence, or at least what was left of it. I cried it all out. Penny, the mother, the elder, held strong for us now. She soothed both of us and held us tight. The experience drained from me, slowly ebbing away.

I broke from the embrace first. "I can't stand here blubbering all day; I have a mission to accomplish!"

We sat down together and finished the soup in silence. Penny gave encouraging smiles and we both smiled back. I didn't really have much to say. We all had said everything we needed to say.

I finished and stood up, "I have to go now otherwise I will back out. I'll be back for breakfast, and then I'll have a lovely bowl of porridge with some honey on it."

"Get it yourself!" laughed Penny. "You are too lazy, Merith, and you are getting fat!"

"I'll miss you, too." I gave both of them a hug and left. There had been enough emotions for today, and felt I needed to get on with it. In the kitchens, I found a couple of full wineskins which were quite old, but didn't leak too badly, I picked one of them up and took it with me....

Tredecium – Envestigatus bibliothece

"I think she is coming out of it, her pulse is getting stronger." These were the sounds and words I heard, as I regained consciousness.

I looked around me to see that the three police were still here, as well as the troll, who was holding onto my wrist. "Where are Desidra and Penny?" I asked.

"Who?" said the troll, "You never mentioned them before?"

I looked around, confused.

Jane Goody spoke to me, "Merith, we have been told that you can under'stand us and that you speak English. Is this so?"

"Yes! It took me a long time to realise you were speaking in a very different accent, but I under'stand most of it now."

"We have to ask you many questions, some from before, but more about the recent events in Peter House."

"He raped me!"

"Who?"

"Matt."

"Yes, we know he had sex with you. Can you tell us about it?"

"At first, he was kind to me and I thought he was nice. He found me wandering and took me back to his room."

Just said, "From the CCTV pictures, he carried you to his room. Is this correct?"

I looked at him, "C...C...T...V pictures? I don't know anything about them, but I must have fainted and he found me. I awoke in his room, with all of the paintings on the walls and the hanging cloths. He cooked me a 'bacon and eggs' roll. I ate some of it and we talked for a time. He tried to kiss me."

Jane put a small rectangular box on the bed in front of her. "Right, shall we start from the top? Before we do, I have to read you your rights. Do you under'stand that you are under a'rest?"

"What does that mean?"

"We are holding you for your own protekshon, but also as a suspect for murder. You are under arrest for the murder of Matthew

Rider, resident of C31 West Wing, Peter House. You do not have to say anything, but it may harm your defence if you fail to menshon, when questioned, something which you later rely on in court. Anything you do say will be given in evidence. Do you under'stand these rights?"

"I didn't murder any one."

"That remains to be seen, what is your full name?"

"Merith."

"Second name?"

"I have never had one."

"Where do you live?"

"I am a priestess of Ichmarr, in the town of Chipping Walden. We go under the Guild name of 'The Guild of our Lady of Pity'. It is in Park Lane."

"How old are you?"

"I don't really know, but I think I am fourteen or fifteen."

"Do you know your date of birth?"

"I was born in fifteen twenty three, I think, but I can't be sure as I was orphaned when I was young."

"Sorry, I don't understand you. Did you say fifteen twenty three?"

"Yes."

The Troll butted in, "Hey, you heard the girl she say' she is fifteen. You cannot question her wit'out an appropriat' adult present. Nor should you do no more questioning, until she has spok' to a solicitor. I know her rights and so do you. Let's stop all of this nonsense and get the appropriat' people in!"

They looked confused, Jane pressed something on the little box on the bed and said, "Yes, I think before we continue, we will require a social worker to be present. I also think you need to speak to a solicitor, to explain the gravity of the situashon. Please, Merith, we are trying to help you, but you have to give us real answers, not preposturous ones. We will look into the Guild you talk about, and will arrange a solicitor and a social worker to visit you."

I watched them leave; they closed the tapestries and went over to the door. As they walked, Jusrt said, "Right, Jane you need to check the Foster Register and the Adopshon Register, to see if there is a match for her fingerprints or foot prints. Meryl, can you check into this Chipping Walden, and the guild or Temple, she talked about? Jane, have any of the reports come back about the books she carried in her bag?"

The book! I had it on me, 'Furacissime de Iniussus'. They must
have it hidden in their house. I need to find it again; it may hold the
key to why I am here. I focussed my mind on the book, and this
triggered the memories to flood back again....

Returning to the cellars, I found my bag of stuff where I had left
it. Vergoth was still lying on his bed and I knew that he was suffering
internally and that his hands were so damaged I was determined
therefore that, on the way back, I'll have to reset them and sort him
out.

I tied the water skin to my bag and left him alone again. I walked
along to the cellar room with the entrance to the maze. I opened the
door and could see the way the darkness changed from the dim light
to the majickal darkness of the maze. I walked to the entrance and
looked down the corridor. It was not what I expected. The walls were
five feet apart and lined with a smooth rock, possibly granite or
marble. I could see how the sound was amplified and misdirected. It
would echo and echo all around the maze. The only sound I could
hear along the corridor was of water dripping somewhere, loud and
ringing, and the sound of my own body. The corridor curved towards
the left, and I could only see a few feet beyond. In a maze it is
important to have a fixed route, so I took out a piton and tried
hammering it into the floor. It took a lot of effort and noise to get it in
but, eventually, it broke through the surface layer. I attached the silk
line to it and used it to keep myself tied to the outside. If I was going
to get lost in here, I damn well wanted to be able to find my way out!

I set off and began to mark every couple of feet with a scrape of
lead on the wall. The lead showed up as darker red on the stone wall.
It was always better to be safe rather than sorry.

I had been into mazes before. There was one on the common of
Chipping Walden, and another in the lord's manor, both cut out of the
grass. The chalk under the grass showed bright white against the
green of the grass surrounding it. In the one on the common, it was
not so much a maze you could get lost in - it was more of a 'follow a
path'. Sometimes it was used as a punishment for unfaithful
husbands, to teach them the error of their ways. The path was over a
mile long, and the convicted had to crawl the whole mile with the
jeering of the town ringing in their ears. The manor maze was quite a
different matter; it was twisty, but it also had many paths running

through it with lots of dead ends. It wound its way through the orchard and, often, the pathway would lead straight up to an apple tree. At the end of it was a sunken garden, with herbs and scented flowers. I had been told about this maze by one of the guards who patrolled the grounds, and I had to look upon it myself. I had used him, in his drunken state, to get me into the grounds and we spent a happy hour treading on the maze. We were caught by a couple of other guards in the sunken garden, half naked and kissing. I was merely kicked unceremoniously out of the gate, but I think he was dismissed from service. This sort of thing has happened lots of times to me, and I think I could develop a complex about it.

The thing about most mazes is that, when you come to a junction, you turn left and eventually you will come to the middle or the ultimate goal. From the middle, you should turn right and you will eventually come to the exit. So, I walked slowly forward, as the passageway curved round to a corner.

Along one edge of this new passageway were large bundles of cloth, man-sized bundles, and the floor had scratches and scrapes across it. I went down on my haunches to inspect the first bundle; it smelled musty and old, and I discovered that the 'bundle' was actually a corpse! This was very old, probably forty to fifty years old. In the damp environment, it had rotted quickly and there was little left of the original person. He or she? was so close to the outside world when they died. I was surprised that he or she had given up, here of all places. There were no signs of violence, and I could see nothing of consequence that would tell me how this person had died. The skin was covered in dust, so I was careful not to actually touch the corpse or the cloth covering it. I had heard stories of bodies in crypts having this sort of mould covering them, and that when it is disturbed it can be very dangerous. If these were mould spores, it would be a bad idea to disturb them.

Along this corridor I could see that there were six more of these corpses, all lying on the left hand side. Carefully, without touching any of them, I made my way along this corridor. At the end, there was a meeting of this corridor to the next. Turning to the left, I began to make my way along it. As I walked down the passage, I started to feel a slight vibration and heard scraping noises. The noise was coming from all around me. It felt as though the whole earth was moving around. The line I had set behind me became taught, it started to pull me back and then went slack. I pulled it towards me and it moved easily. Something must have interfered with the line.

I turned back to the original corridor, and it now seemed to be blocked at the end. As I rushed over to it, I could feel myself beginning to panic. The end of the corridor now had a solid surface, like one of the walls, but there was some damage on the face from blunt and sharp implements.

The panic, was rising through me.

I sat down, resigned to my fate. Staring at the corpses around me, I thought, 'Was I going to join them in this death trap? Was that the fate of the original priestess, to be lost in this maze to die of thirst or starvation?' Trapped, lost and totally alone, I was still emotional and I just sat there crying. I lay down, with my head in my hands, and sobbed and sobbed.

I couldn't believe that I just walked into this. I felt so confident in coming to this. I thought I knew what to do. I had all of the tricks up my sleeve. I so was full of myself, and now my future will be as long as my food will last.

Oh, Shit!

Oh, bloody shit!

Idiot!

Damn!

What am I going to do now! I cried for a long time. I had to work out what had happened. I had to think it through!

Desidra managed to get out, so I must be able to. She had survived the experience, but she had not mentioned anything like this. She didn't have the advantage I have, of being able to pierce the darkness and see what is happening. With regret, I realised that rope or marks on the wall were going to be little help in this situation. I was going to have to rely on my ingenuity. Glancing around the corridor, I could see that the corpses were still there, but strangely they were now on the other side of the corridor.

I realised that the maze was changing as I was moving through it.

I went back to the end of the corridor. There were two ways I could go from the end, what would happen if I went to the right?

I tried this out and, again, there was the now familiar movement and scraping noises. I stopped until they finished. I returned to the corridor and. as I had suspected, the bodies were back on the right and the corridor now led somewhere. I walked down it and found the rope end where it had been cut. The corridor curved around, and I was back at the piton.

Interesting! Thank Ichmarr, I can get out. I have an escape route! Elated, I was almost giddy because I had worked out the maze and I knew I could escape it.

The maze must move around, depending on which direction you take when you turn. What else will surprise me in this maze? What directed the movements? Probably the floor, it could be sensitive to pressure on it - causing the direction of movement. How would I be able to get around it without moving it around? The walls were smooth, no good for traversing. How do I know this is not part of the maze? How to figure out, not only the location of the 'centre of the labyrinth', but also how to get there? How can I use the maze to get me to the library?

I decided to just explore it, to chart the maze and to look at the movement combinations. If there were any more, I might get stuck but I am sure I'll figure it out. If I could use the lead marker to help me chart my position, I might be able to know where I was; I could make a mark for the first, two for the second and so on. What if I changed into a bird? Could I fly around without changing the maze? Or, maybe do so as a mouse? Would that prevent the movement of the maze, being perhaps too light to alter it? Hopefully, therefore, I would be too light to make a change in the maze.

Goddess, do I vacillate! I seem to spend more time thinking than actually doing, so I decided to change into a mouse. This would be interesting, as I hadn't actually been a mouse before. In beginning the visualisation, I imagined the transformation from myself into the mouse gradually acquiring the tail, the body, the claws, short ears and a twitchy nose. My world suddenly became larger and the floor zoomed towards me, it was happening as such a faster pace than before! I completed the change and looked around me. The walls seemed to be so tall and the floor looked so much rougher. I also found that I could sniff so much more intensely than I had been able to before, but the smells were musty with decay.

Dodging around the corpses, I ran along the side of the walls. The corridor seemed so long now, compared to when I was a human. When eventually I came to the end of the corridor, I turned left as was my original instinct. As I carried on down the curving corridor, I did not hear the rumbling, nor the scraping sound. The maze didn't move, I thought. Just to check this, I ran back and I was so pleased with my ingenuity in thinking out the problem that I squeaked a loud "Yes!"

As I followed it around, the corridor was now curving away to the right and I came to a side junction on the left. From the main corridor, it looked just like the last one and so I followed it down. In this corridor, the floor was clear and, although scraped like the last, was relatively undamaged. It ended on a flat wall; just like the wall that I had seen, when the maze moved, when I was a human-sized creature. From the angle that I looked at it, the wall appeared similar to the other wall. There were marks and gouges out of the wall indicating that people had tried to break through it - a tactic, which had been doomed to failure.

I returned to the main corridor and scampered deeper into the maze. Further on, I came to a corner where the whole corridor changed direction. Turning into it, I found that there was a passageway leading away from the main corridor with the main way leading off continuing in the curve. The main corridor seemed to have a formation like a switchback ahead of a bridge, to slow the carts down before they crossed it. I decided to explore the side passage as I had done previously.

In this corridor, the floor was clear and, although scraped like the last, was relatively undamaged. It split again into a two-way junction, but I could not see the destination of either way due to the curve in the corridor. Accordingly, I turned left. The corridor curved to the left, and I thought somehow it may meet back up with the original corridor, but it ended abruptly at a dead end with a smooth wall uninterrupted with any marks. I went back and tried the other way, but this was the same, so I scampered back up the corridor to the main passageway.

I returned to where the main corridor must be, and I carried on down it. Along this corridor, about the same distance from the last, there was yet another corridor. This one seemed to be different from the last, so I scurried down it to see what was there. Down this passageway, there were two corridors leading off from it. This corridor was longer that the previous ones and I could see that there was a slightly wider gap between the blocks. I passed through the threshold and it led down to a two way junction, with each of the passageways leading off along curving passages.

Deciding on the left passageway, which curved around away from the main maze, I thought as I walked. It seemed to me that the maker of this maze didn't want the junctions to be seen, nor the destinations. As the passageway opened out into a small room, I felt the thrill that this might be the library but the shelves which lined the walls; were empty except for cobwebs and a few ancient scraps of paper. The room had obviously been used as a resting place by several visitors, who had tried to burn papers on the floor. I could smell the burned remains, and could tell that it was tens of years old. I wondered who had tried to light a fire. What had the experience been like for them? They could have felt the heat of the fire, but under this majickal darkness they would have never been able to see the light. I could not see how they would have benefited from the experience; certainly, it would have demoralised me. Fortunately, I am blessed that I can see in the way I can with my Darksight. With this, the walls and other surfaces are viewed as slightly different shades to the other objects. It was a lonely room, without apparent purpose, and a reminder of the empty and desolate nature of the place. Leaving it to its fate, I tried the other way.

The three walls were lined with shelves, long and empty. In this room, however, there was encrusted material across the floor and two bodies lay splayed out amongst it. Each of the bodies had armour, one of which was rusted into a solid crust on the body while the other was still fresh and apparently clean. The armour's chain-mail was of a strange type of metal, quite different to any other metal I had seen before; not steel, nor silver, but somewhere in between. Within it, the body had rotted, but the metal and leather looked as fresh and clean as the day it had been made. I never wore armour as a rule, but I decided to come back to see if I could scavenge the armour for Penny. I didn't want to lose this shape I was in, quite yet; it was too useful. I left the room and scurried back up to the main corridor.

The main way continued on to a two-way junction; another choice! But, which way to go? Turn left to a corridor, or turn right to a switchback which leads back to the main through route? As I had done all the way through the maze, I tried out this side path. It led to yet another two-way junction with its curved walls stretching away from the main maze. Choosing the left-hand side again, I darted along it, hoping to come across the library down this one. After a short distance, I found another side passageway going off to the left. I took it, willing this to be the one, but found myself back in the original corridor. It was circular and met itself! If someone following this was only touching the wall on the right, they would go round and round in a circle for ages before realising their mistake. Whoever built this maze clearly had an evil sense of humour. I ran back up it and joined the main passageway. It was heading clockwise around a central feature, and I was beginning to assume in my mind that this must be a circular maze with a central main passage.

The next side passage was longer than the others, and I ran along it until it came to another two way junction. Turning left again, I entered the largest room so far. This room had, at one time, probably been a study for several individuals; there were wooden tables with holes for inkwells and all the desks had sloping surfaces. These desks and chairs had been thrown around the room, as if there had been a mini wind-devil spinning the room about. I looked around on the floor, but I found little of interest.

The room to the right of the corridor was a long room that was bare and unfurnished. I wondered about the uses for all of these rooms? Did this maze get used for some sort of teaching or learning centre before it was pitched into darkness? This room would make an ideal tutorial room for book learning. There was even a raised dais at one end; to lift the speaker into the air and help her broadcast her voice across the room. The room contained nothing of interest for me, so I returned to the main corridor. By now, I was getting a bit tired of all of this scampering around, so I sat back and looked around my present locality. One thing that I did notice was a slight airflow back down the main corridor from where I had come. The walls seemed to be made of the same material as the others had been, and I suddenly realised that I had seen material like this in one of the break-ins I had done with Rozz, on a town house in Walden.

At that time, Rozz had been fretting about the fact that she could no longer get any energy to cast any spells. Apparently, her standing with Ichmarr was at an all time low, so she persuaded me to help her in this caper. I thought the house was too easy a score for me and I saw no merit in it. Rozz, on the other hand, felt that it was beyond her capabilities to do solo - and she needed a big score. So, we turned up in the dead of night Behind the building, the walled garden loomed over us, providing us with cover and deliciously dark shadows. I scaled the wall, and slung myself low over the top to be able to look around. There were no candles flickering in any of the rooms, so I helped Rozz over the top. Her landing was clumsy in the garden, and she must have twisted her ankle; I could plainly see her checking it and trying it out. I dropped down beside her and landed lightly with little sound. "How do you do that!" she hissed to me.

"I just landed, like I had been shown in training with Cherish. Why? What happened? It sounded like you might have landed badly?" I whispered back to her.

"Nothing! Look, let's get to the back door. I think it is unlocked," she replied, still whispering.

I let her lead the way; this was her score and I took the back seat. I felt that she needed to prove her devotion to Ichmarr. As for me, I had already been on several little jobs that week and had played loads of tricks on people; I was still at the peak of my form. Rozz was definitely injured, but I did not wish to intervene when she needed to concentrate on the task at hand. I could see in this dim light that the back door had a lock in it. If I personally was away for the week, I would definitely lock this place up and I could also see the Brotherhood's marks all over this place. They warned of dire trouble for the unlucky thief who was caught stealing from this place. We arrived at the back door. She turned the handle and, surprise, surprise, it was locked!

"Ohh! Umm, what do you think?" Rozz whispered to me.

"Open it, quickly?" I whispered back, sarcasm was already biting in my voice. It was always like this, but she was not cut out for this business and it still amazed me that she was always surprised how difficult it was.

"Umm, do you have a pick set?"

"Don't you?" I raised my voice just a little too far. I knew she wouldn't have planned for this, only a real novice wouldn't plan for this. Of course, when you are breaking into a house, you have a lock pick set, or at least a few skeletons to try your luck. I just stood there looking at her, annoyed. I could feel her squirming in her shoes. Out of my pocket, I lifted her own lock pick set that I had taken from her room. Rozz had meticulously put together this set of picks using the advice of Edowyn and Cat. However, no matter how many times she went out on jobs like this, she would forget it!

Bashfully, she took the set from me and I could see the heat of her blush hit her cheeks. "At least you plan for problems," she hissed

Yes, I did plan for problems, especially when I go out with you! I didn't say it; it was too harsh a thing to say. She needed to be told this, but I wasn't the one. She was older than me, and had been in the Temple for years longer than me, so obviously she should have the experience to know to plan for eventualities. However, she never learned from all of the times she has not planned ahead.

She turned to the door lock. With my Darksight, I could see her trying to find the lock hole and then hitting the outside of it several times before finally getting the pick into the hole. She struggled with the lock for five minutes, several tools and oil before she finally

managed to click it open. It was such a simple lock! I would have it
open in less than five seconds with a dagger point. The right tool and
a little greasing would open any lock!

The door opened into a dining room. The floor was polished
stone, like the stone in the tunnels, marble, cut and smoothed off. It
was a very expensive commodity, but incredibly difficult to steal! As
far as I know, it was not something likely to be stolen by anyone in
the Temple - even though it would really mystify the owners. This
could be a good idea for the future. I remember looking at the floor
and being distracted by how smooth it was and how the heat was so
even across it. I knelt down to touch the smoothness of the stone. The
feel of the stone was like touching ice; cold, unyielding and so
slippery smooth.

That mess with Rozz probably was the last time I had any respect
for her. She drew me out on a few more jobs, it was difficult to say no
to her, but I never expected her to have anything on a job. However,
outside of our vocation, she was a lot of fun and I miss her. She had a
way of touching me that sent tingles down my spine and passion in
my heart.

Standing up on my four legs I sniffed the air. It was the same as it
had always been; musty, and slightly damp. I scampered along the
corridor and, again, there was a side passage slightly longer than the
centre section. This had a two way junction with doors at the ends of
the passageways. The passages were shorter than before and, in
looking at the doors, I could see that they were stout and firm. So, I
ran up to the left-hand side one and examined the door from my
perspective. It was heavy oak with metal bands all around the joins.
The lock was bulky and inset into the door and, although it looked
old, that didn't necessarily mean it was simple. There was a lock like
this on a safe room in an old town house in Radwinter; it was in good
working order, but was over fifty years old. Twenty minutes I spent
trying to figure out that one. Once I found out the trick it was easy.

What was behind this door? Could it be the library and all of its
contents? An easy entry for me was barred by the door being larger
than the passageway. Worse, the bottom of the door was flush with,
or below, the floor. I ran over to the other door and found the same
situation. Either, I would have to not open the doors, or change back
to myself and open it the hard way. So, I decided to come back to
these after I had explored the rest of the maze.

The main passageway continued to curve around, and I came to another side way, which was blocked by a stone wall at the end. There was no point in checking out this one; I could see that others had, and there were two bundles of cloth and organic matter along this corridor. Both of these looked about the same age as the two fighters that I had earlier seen dead. Perhaps they had gotten lost when their guide had been killed, and they made it to here. They must have given up the search for a way out and just lay down to die.

Ignoring this side way, I left it behind and carried on round the main corridor. I realised that I had been here before, when I turned into the next passageway. This was back at the start of this maze and I realised it was actually very small; the total size of it couldn't be more than three hundred paces wide, maybe four hundred. What really made it difficult was the fact that it turned around as the person inside it moved. I would have to be very careful in the way I made my way through the maze in order to control it to achieve my mission.

The first thing I had to do was find the library, which I thought, was probably back at the locked doors, so I returned to them. I reconstituted back to my original self at the start of the corridor. The world suddenly had a different feel to it. The whole perspective changed, and the doors looked now to be a much tougher prospect.

Although they seemed to be much smaller and less imposing, the doors were heavily barred with iron ribbing and strong ties. In addition, they were made from oak and seemed to be sealed around the edge with something. I checked the doors carefully, and could see no obvious traps or dangers. My instinct was that if this were the library, it would be protected, so I examined one of the locks and could see that it was old and looked a bit corroded. Lubrication for the lock was needed, so I squirted some oil from my lock-pick set into the centre of the lock and moved the levers around with a set of small pushers. The lock was stiff, and did not want to move. I took out the climbing pick hammer, and tapped it a couple of times (sometimes, a bit of brutality is required to get some locks to start working!). I reinserted the picks and found the levers were moving much more freely. I played around with the lock for a few moments, trying to figure out what was inside. It was an old gate and lever lock, of little complexity, but the size of it made it difficult to open it.

I thought of the trick I had used on the lock back at the safe-room, and tried it out. No success! This was beginning to annoy me, so I played around with it for a few more minutes to no avail. Suddenly, it became clear to me! Jiggling the tool I was using, and pushing it harder into the lock, I tried to turn it and then..."Click!" Instinctively, I jumped back away from the door. Nothing happened! Nothing jumped out at me! Still, I felt jittery; I was unsure of the dangers. My senses were now at full alert, and I was aware that there was something happening as the hairs at the back of my neck started rising.

Slowly, the door began to open. The hinges were creaking and protesting from the effort they were being forced to do. I backed off, away from the door. I could see into the room and what I saw scared the bejebus out of me; some movement behind the door, one, maybe two things moving, shuffling around. They were at the same temperature as the rest of the room, but were still moving. The smell coming out of the room was of death, old death, like they had been entombed there for a long time. I could not believe what I was seeing. They looked to be dresses in robes, one featuring the emblem of Ichmarr on the collar. It had long hair and the shape of a woman. Was this the emissary we had sent out with the book?

Terror had me in its grip! I was rooted to the spot, unable to move or do anything. The creatures shuffled closer and closer to me. The stench increased in intensity, while the noise of their feet scraping across the floor as they moved was so unnerving. When they had shuffled to the edge of the portal, I blinked and everything changed; the door was back to being closed as I left it. The shuffling creatures coming towards me had disappeared, like some vision. Was this of the future or the past?

Shit! I was so terrorised by the illusion that my legs gave way and I collapsed onto the floor.

Did I really want to open this door?

Could it be the prison of the long dead emissary, who had been sent out originally?

I am too damn curious to sit and look at a closed door!

Slowly, I summoned up the courage to stand up and approach the door. With the utmost care, I turned the handle and opened it. It was shocking to have the handle pull itself away from me, as if something was pulling on it from the inside. I stepped back quickly, as the sudden intake of air into the room stirred up the dust, which made the whole room look misty in the Darksight I was viewing it by. The smell of death was strong in here; the air was choking and, for a time, I found it difficult to breath. I had to step back to get further aw ay from the room due to the dust, but also out of fear. The room was obscured for a short time, anyway, so I let it clear. As it settled, I could see two bodies lying on the floor; they were the individuals I had seen in the vision. Their clothes and shapes were the same, only lying long dead. The fingernails were broken and scratched, as if both had been desperately trying to get out of the room. It was small; a mere six by six feet, square and ugly. The door had a leather seal around the edge of it, and I guessed it must have been air-proof. The rest of the room was bare stone, like the rest of the maze. This was a horrible place to die in. They must have been so scared, and so desperate, when they realised what was happening.

I took out a piton and hammered it into the stone floor to wedge the door open. I was damned if I was going to let them be shut in again! The floor seemed unyielding and the noise deafening, but eventually my piton broke through to the earth below. It would now hold the door open and would be difficult to remove.

The other door was similar to the previous one. It had the same format as the first one. It had the same lock type, and the door was larger than the frame. Hesitating, I mused; would the same thing happen to me? Was that a warning from this priest from Ichmarr, to stop me opening this door? Is there one of the walking dead behind this door, which would rip me to shreds? The only way for me to find out, I supposed, would be to open it up and take the risk.

Shit, I was scared! I didn't realise how bad I was. My teeth were chattering and I shivered uncontrollably. It was not just the cold, I was plain terrified; the hairs were standing all over my body, and I felt that I had never been so frightened in all of my life. The vision from the other door, the ghosts from the past, had done their job well.

The door lock felt cold, freezing cold! While I could see that it was the same colour as the other lock, it was like a block of ice. I checked to see if the door was locked. It wasn't, but it began to open by itself. The encrusted hinges were grating, screeching almost, as if they were screaming to protest that they were having to move as they were forced to turn.

The inside of the room was bare; empty of dust, cobwebs or any other matter. It looked as if the room had been scrubbed and cleaned just before I had opened the door, sealed as it was against the ravages of time. Everything within me relaxed; all of my muscles that had been tense started to drop, and I felt them all suddenly release. I was so relieved! My thoughts had conjured up all of the most hideous monsters I could have found in here, and all of these images had been running through my mind. The sum of my fears had come to naught, and I began laughing. Chuckling at first, then moving onto a real belly laugh, with tears streamed down my cheeks as I realised I was safe from it all. I had faced up to a great fear and survived.

The maze had given up all of its secrets to me, or had it? I still needed to find the library; I could not accept that the rooms I had been in were the library. They seemed too small, not protected, not hidden. The man who had designed this maze had done so to hide things. Why else had he created a majickally dark maze? Why had he made it change its pattern? The pattern changes and the darkness had to mean something. He was clearly trying to hide things. The emissary must have seen what he was up to, for him to kill her like that. It was not an ordinary way of killing. He must have been fanatical to have built the room in the first place!

I began to search around the two rooms. I examined the walls for concealed entrances or hollow areas, I also checked the floor. These rooms were static, and would not change as the maze moved. This search I repeated in the passageway leading out from the rooms. I found there were only little changes of noise here, but that the noise reverberated around and began to amplify the sounds. After I stood still, the noise levels slowly dropped back to the background noise.

Carefully, I advanced along the passageway - tapping occasionally as I went. I would have to assume that, for his followers, the designer of this maze would want it to be easy to find the library. Thus, he would either have it in a fixed location, or a prominent part within the maze itself. I stopped for a moment. "Well, that's obvious!" I said aloud to myself. However, would he have placed it in one of the corridors, as a side room, or would it be in the centre? What about the movements of the maze? Wouldn't that make it more difficult to get to the library, if it moved the wrong way? If I wanted to check the other rooms I would have to keep the movements neutral. How on earth would I do that? I realised that, earlier, I had already done that very same thing. When I first moved the maze, I moved it back by going down the corridor in the opposite direction; I could do the same thing here! By only going along the corridor as far as it took to move the maze, and then retreating, I could change it by one position.

I began to try this out, walking along the corridor anti-clockwise in a circle. Whilst walking, I tapped the wall as I went along. The maze then moved rumbling and vibrating, as I steadily approached the centre of the corridor. Returning back to the corridor, I made my way down it to find that the rooms had changed to those of the classroom and study I had found earlier. I searched these rooms again to be sure. This classroom, I felt, was a possible location of the library and, if I were designing it, I would seek to have easy access to the library and its collection of books. Indeed, I would want to study in, or just off the library. After all, a shorter distance to carry those expensive tomes of knowledge would make it less likely that they would get damaged or dropped.

In response to my searching, the rooms revealed no peculiar areas. Through experience, I had found that I could discover concealed or hidden areas much more easily than others of my persuasion. Often, walking into a room, evaluating all of the clues (visual and aural) and assessing how the room 'felt' to me, I could come to a conclusion of where concealed panels or doors were. Sometimes, I could do this without even paying much attention to the walls and what was covering them. I was more aware of the world around me than most people.

Using the handle of the climbing pick to try to sound out what was behind the walls, I checked along each of them. Nothing again, so I left these rooms behind and went back up the corridor. The next position along was the circular corridor with the switchback. Perhaps I could miss this out and just go to the next set of rooms? But, what if the library was in the corridor branching off from this? Could I afford to miss that chance?

Decisions, decisions! I had no-one to help me decide – as if I ever needed someone else to tell me what to do. However, there was no sense in missing an opportunity, so I decided I would check out the corridor.

The maze moved forward and I returned to the corridor. As I made my way around it, the corridor seemed solid all around - just as I thought it might be! But, I had to make sure I checked everything.

The next ending to the passageway was the one with the two corpses, and I decided to check them out first. The bodies were not covered in the mould as I had seen in the first passageway. They were better preserved, and had probably been there for only a few years. I looked over the armour that had attracted me back here. This chain mail would do Penny nicely, as it looked to be roughly her size, so I un-strapped it from the body and picked it up. I had thought that this armour would be heavy; armour of this type should weigh about sixty pounds. However, I was surprised that it was so light; less than ten pounds in weight - lighter than leather.

I checked over the body I had removed the armour from, and noticed that it was also slightly different in stature than the other; it was taller, more slender and the bones not as heavy set. If I didn't know any better, I would have thought that it was Silves in origin. I had noted that there was no mould on these bodies, due obviously to a different environment. Indeed, these rooms felt drier and slightly warmer than in the rest of the maze. I looked over the bodies and found they both had purses strapped to their belts. Each of the purses had quite a few coins in them, and so I popped them into my pack? While we did have a fortune in gold and silver up in the ruins, why waste the coinage; a few pieces here and there would be useful!

Inspecting the armour again, I noticed inside there were some Silves runes and realised that it had been made by a Silvesi! It featured five symbols from the written language of the Silves, which was a pictorial language with the pictures meaning words, feelings, moods etc. The runes had been adopted by the Majis, and they used them to express their majick. Most of the majick, I thought, had come from the Silves anyway and that this loss of potency was due to the decline of my own kind. I had not seen one like myself for weeks before all of this started and, before that, the sightings had been few and far between. The runes said approximately Forest, Air, Silver, Essence and a symbol I had not seen before. The meanings I attributed to them had come from seeing them used in different ways. It was now that I wished I had badgered Kelestra for a greater understanding of my kind, my language and my culture!

Considering carefully, I thought that, if I put the armour on over my shoulders, it should make it easier to carry and, hopefully, it wouldn't slow me down too much. I slipped it on and roughly strapped it on over my robes. It felt so light, it didn't encumber me at all; I actually felt lighter for wearing it. I tried a few stretches and found that, far from the movements being harder to do, they were actually easier. What amazing armour this was! It would be such a boon to me to be wearing chain-mail, but not have any of the ill effects of wearing it, so I decided to keep it and wear it under my robes to conceal it.

However, while removing the armour, and then my robes, it occurred to me that, if I put on the armour straight over my skin, it'll chafe and I'll be bleeding in minutes. So, I checked in my pack to see if I had my spare exercise slip, which should cover the worst areas from chafing. Yes, I had packed it! The smooth silk of the slip was luxurious, luscious and beautiful to the touch. When I first put on one of these, I felt like royalty. Silk was such a rare commodity, and was so expensive to buy, that I had to specially commission a tailor in Cantebrigia to have the materials brought up from London to craft the garment. Twelve gold pieces it cost to have it made for me, and the tailor insisted on the money up front because he didn't believe that I could pay for it! I knew the effect this garment had on men and women, so I usually kept it to myself. I strapped the armour on over this. The silk was so fine it gave nothing for the armour to snag on, and I knew that those armoured knights of the King used the same materials to protect their skin. The armour went on like a second skin; I felt so secure in it that I felt nothing could touch me. My robes went on over the armour. Once I had it all fitted back in place, I jumped up and down and, although there were metallic sounds coming from the armour, it was not serious. If I wanted to be completely silent and run at the same time, I would have problems – but, it was the quietest armour I had heard in a long time.

I slung my pack over my shoulder and searched the rest of the room. There was nothing more of interest in the room and the walls tapped to solid. It was the same story in the next room, the smell of the smoke was barely perceptible to this body's nose and I supposed that it also helped to be so near to the ground; without a sensitive nose, I would never have spotted it. The walls and floor checked out again to be solid.

The same methods were used to check out the remaining three ends of the passageways. Finally, I ended up at the entrance again, only there was no entrance, instead I faced a blank wall. There was no way that I could have miscounted the passageways, nor could I have made a mistake in the way I had arrived here. I knew that I could return back to the entrance at the first passageway, so I didn't panic. It was a puzzle; I could get out, but it did worry me. This is perhaps another reason why people couldn't escape easily? Maybe the entry passageway only met one of the passages to it - the first one that I had entered. However, it was odd. If they couldn't leave, how did someone else enter to reset the machinery? Was there some sort of mechanism involved which reset itself?

I quit worrying, but I did sit down and rest. I had been walking around this maze for a couple of hours now, and I was hungry and thirsty. If I have only been down here a couple of hours, then it should only be mid-afternoon up there. There was still plenty of time for me to become completely lost and then find myself.

My wineskin had cool refreshing water in it, and I took out a trail biscuit. I munched my way through a third of it and, as I did so, I thought of Petersen - so far away, he must be preparing dinner for those lucky few who were still in the Temple. He always had time for me to chat and gossip about what was happening around town. The breakfasts that he had always prepared for me were the same, delicious every time. The method I knew off by heart and, until this journey, I had never tried it. Petersen was certainly a prize winner; Celene certainly knew how to pick the right one! I finished the third of the biscuit and popped the rest back into the frame pack. I washed it down with the water and stowed this as well.

Right, I knew my way was not down any of the passageway ends that I had been down. If the first passageway was different from the rest, then could it be the way in to the library? I stood up and packed all of my things. Returning to the first passageway, I used the same method as I had used before to move the maze to access all of the side passageways. Each time I checked the wall out properly. I found that they all had some damage to them. Someone else had tried this out, but the only passageway end that actually did anything was the original one. It was the only end that lined up with it.

Okay, where to look next, the walls? Well, that was a possibility. I would have to search all of the walls in all of the passageways. What about the centre of the maze? I had been tramping around the maze for the whole afternoon; what if I had been circulating around it, without knowing it?

The wall around the central area sounded just as solid as the rest of the maze. I tapped around the surface near where I was and, although I couldn't do both sides of the corridor, at least I could do the central wall first and then each of the passageways. Examining, tapping and feeling the walls, I eventually came to the peculiar switchback. Tapping the wall of the strange bit that stuck out, I heard a slightly different note from that of the rest of the maze; it was muffled, but certainly different. I inspected the stones that made up the wall, and noticed that they had a gap that was different from the rest of the maze. There was a movement of air passing through the wall along this gap and, although I didn't know where the air was going, it was there nonetheless. There was no obvious way of opening this door, so I fully examined the wall, visually with my Darksight and by touching, prodding, and pushing all of the features that I could find that were possible ways of opening it. Okay, so I now studied the ceiling and saw that there might be a ring of material up there that was different. It was too high for me to reach up to it, but I had a brainwave; I found the room with all of the desks, and picked one up that was still in good working order. I stood it upright, making sure it was steady, before jumping up onto it. There was definitely a worn area up here, which was of slightly different stone from the rest of the ceiling. I pressed it upward.

The 'button' moved slowly. I pressed harder and the panels in front of me began to open up. A noise, like the 'Twip' of a crossbow firing, suddenly hit my ears and four bolts flew out at various heights from the door! One bolt passed cleanly between the legs of the desk, the next thudded into the desk top (showering the floor with wood splinters), the third one missed my leg by an inch, however the fourth hit me! Well, it sort of ripped through my robes and glanced off the armour at an acute angle - knocking me clean off the desk. When I picked myself off the floor, I could see that the head of the bolt was mangled and twisted as if it had hit a heavy stone block. I checked my armour and there was no appreciable damage. Astounded by my good fortune, I was so grateful to Ichmarr to have found this marvellous armour. I would have definitely been either dead, or in serious pain, if I hadn't been wearing it. The armour must be enchanted, or made of such a material, if it can take such punishment as this. However, I would, have a long job darning my robes! The bolt, I carefully stowed as a souvenir. As I did so, I could feel a bruise developing where I had been hit....

Quattuordecim – Ingressus bibliothece

My name was being called; the voice was sweet and delicious. It was like a child's voice, but it held the notes with such clarity. I opened my eyes to see a girl of about nineteen or twenty, wearing a yellow tunic over all white clothing. Her long black hair had large curls which she controlled by platting her hair into a long bunch behind her. Her slim frame and boyish bodily features gave her an almost Silvesi look. She stood by my bed, with a tray in her hands, smiled down to me and said, "Hello, Merith! Mick asked me to bring this down to you. He couldn't wake you to ask you what you wanted, so he made you cheese sandwiches. He told me that everyone loves cheese."

She placed the tray on the wheeling table and brought it over to me. She was slim, but very well toned, and the way she moved was graceful - too graceful for one without any training. Her feet were placed in such a way as to spread the load across her whole foot, rather that the ball or the heel that most people use. She had placed the tray down soundlessly, making little impact on the wheeled tray. It was a curious thing, but I strongly suspected she had some training in my own trade.

I asked, "What is your name?"

She looked up, smiled a tight little smile, and said, "Tamzin Scott." She moved the tray into a position for me to be able to eat something and, as she drew her hands away, she (perhaps unconsciously) made the sign of Ichmarr. It might be easy for most people to miss, as it involves putting your thumb to your pointer, then to your pinky and back again, but for me, it was like seeing a ray of sunshine.

The joy in my face must have been clear to see. My fingers did the same gesture and I added, '*Are you one of us?*' in Thieves' Cant.

She smiled again and said, "Shall I sit with you as you eat, to keep you company?" Her fingers said a different thing; '*Who are you?*'

I picked up the corner of the sandwich and let my free hand do the talking. '*My Temple is in Chipping Walden, Park Lane. It is known to*

*the locals as the Guild of our lady of pity. My High Priestess is
Celene. Where are you based?'*

'*Where is Chipping Walden?'*

'*Twenty miles south of Cantebrigia, or Cambridge as I have been
told it is called.'*

*The only towns down there are Saffron Walden, Little Walden and
Littlebury. I do not know a Chipping Walden.*

'*What? Little Walden and Littlebury are right next to it. It's the
Market town, you must know it!'* The feelings of panic were
beginning to rise in my throat and I felt a deep hole opening up
beneath me. What could have happened to Chipping Walden? Maybe
it was renamed?

'*I think you do mean Saffron Walden, Market, Castle and Big
Church of St Mary.'* These things I recognised, I remembered the
church of St Mary and the castle where I had hidden some of my
stash.

What about my Temple? I was going to ask Tamzin, when we
heard through the door the Troll's voice calling; "Hey! Tamzy, you
lazy girl, get your self over here now! I need you."

"I have to go, I'll be back soon to have a proper talk!" She stood
up and signed, '*We will get back in touch, look after yourself.'*

Oh, Ichmarr! I knew you were still out there. I felt finally safe. I
felt I was getting somewhere in this mad world. I relaxed somewhat
giddy; the dream came back to crowd out my consciousness....

At last, I felt I was getting somewhere! Finally, I have found the
entrance to the library! But, I had the feeling that this may not be the
only impediment in my way. I opened the wall and moved the
crossbows out of their slots. They had obviously been triggered by a
string, which looped through all of the firing levers, I removed them
from the door and tossed them across the corridor; they may come in
useful, later.

The passageway, now opened, slightly sloped downwards in steps
cut out of the stone floor. The walls were rough hewn out of the chalk
bedrock and, as I made my way downward, I saw that the passageway
opened out to a large expansive room. The thrill of finally being in
the library was intense, and I took in everything I could about it.
There was a different smell and feel to the rest of the maze. The air
was drier and had a faintly sweet but leathery fragrance to it. The

room was enormous! It must have been a hundred feet in diameter, and occupied the whole middle section of the maze. In the centre, was a massive circular desk made out of metal. I guessed that this might be the pivoting point for the whole maze, and wondered how on earth it worked. The enormous metal construction glowed slightly hotter than the rest of the room, as if it had been in use recently. Around the perimeter of the room were bookshelves, set on the walls, and jutting out from the walls in fourteen neat stacks. These were lined with books from floor to ceiling, books varying in size across the entire library.

The entire floor was covered in a continuous rug from wall to wall, and I could see five bodies lying in various poses around the room. Something bad had happened here. The faces of the corpses were barely recognisable as human, even taking into account possibly fifty years of decay, and they were fixed in a look of pure horror - their hands clawing at their throats as if they couldn't breathe. Closely, I inspected one of these. In this light, I could make out the features of a man; he looked about thirty, with smooth facial skin, a beard and long hair. He had dust in his mouth.

Suddenly, I realised that I had just rushed in without barring the door open. I turned and ran back, in time to see the rock door closing. I arrived at the door as I heard it click closed. Desperately, I crashed into it with all the force I could muster, but it didn't budge. However, the door was only a couple of inches thick, so I reckoned that I could knock my way through it, given time to do so.

Damn! I felt so bloody stupid; of course, I should have found someway of holding the door open! I could be stuck down here for hours trying to get out, and I would have to knock a hole through the door - if I don't find another way to open it. There must be another way to open it from in here. A breeze was still filtering through the gap, so I scanned the ceiling and spotted that there was a cold region up there, possibly a vent. Certainly, it presented a way out of here, if you were small enough, I hoped. But, at the moment, I wasn't. Studying the entranceway, I noticed a small block of stone that had a wider crack than normal. After pressing it, prodding it - nothing I did would budge it. I unsheathed my dagger to see if I could move it with the point and was blinded for a few moments by the light.

The majickal Darkness didn't extend into here, and I gave thanks to Ichmarr. The light from my dagger was so refreshing to see, and I marvelled at it for nearly a minute. It was like I had been blinded and could now see. Viewing with heat only is a funny thing. It is like normal sight but unlike it. It was like feeling the world through a glove, there is no detail and it muffles the senses. After a while, it verges on the painful and you could almost beg to see proper light again. The beautiful white light shone in this grim and silent place; a piercing light to disturb the dead in this mausoleum.

Turning back to the door and, using the dagger point, I prised the stone out of its location. Behind it was a lever attached to a rod. The rod extended towards the door and I thought this must be what is used to unlock the door, but why hide it? Who are they hiding it from? After all, the users of the library would need to enter and exit from the library; scholars and scribes would need full and easy access.

I pulled the lever and the door swung open. The light from my dagger stopped almost immediately; it was like the sea rushing in with the tide. The spell was obviously kept out by the stone walls but, when the walls were breached, it would return into the library. The door swung open and started to swing shut again. However, if I kept the door open, I would not be able to see. Writing cannot be seen with Darksight, it doesn't show up; the paper and the ink are at the same temperature, and there's not enough difference to read it. With this need to see with normal light in my mind, I had to let the door shut. The light on the end of the dagger point shone brightly, illuminating the room once more. I studied the room again. The shelves were full of books and I guessed that there must number over a thousand. They must be priceless! I had heard of the King's library which has over five hundred books, and that was thought to be a large and extensive. This library, however, must be the largest in Angland - let alone this happy isle.

I was privileged to have been allowed to read a few books that Cat or Edowyn had in their quarters. One of them was a manual on the use of arms, 'Libellus militia,' a diary of warfare. Edowyn valued the book, and cherished it above all of her possessions. It had been illustrated and inscribed by a scribe who had worked on it for six months. The book was short, being only a hundred pages long, but it had been painted, inked and gilded with painstaking diagrams of weapons and how to use them. It was a rare tome, copied and inscribed from a Latin text, and the book had a leather cover over what felt like wood. The spine was ridged and beautifully bound.

The books in this library were similar to that book, but were larger. Some had gilding and letters burned into the spine, and I could see some titles on these - but they were mostly blank. I walked up to the first set of shelves and opened the first book I came to. It read,

'Condocefacia relligiosus Cuthberti de Fustis', "The teachings of St Cuthbert of the Cudgel." It was a religious text, I put it back. Suddenly, I realised that I hadn't taken any precautions before opening the book. If it had been the one, I would be a corpse now when the knife trap poisoned me. I had to be more careful when I opened the rest of them. This was going to take a lot of time; I would be searching these stacks for several hours, and I would have to look at every book until I found it. It was going to be probably the most boring task I had undertaken in a long time. It would be repetitive, and the only interest was to see what mysteries the books held. As I opened and replaced the books, I mused over what the most boring task was that I had been asked to do. Once, I was asked to read a passage from a slate and imagine in my head an image of a river. To do this, I had to keep the image of the river in my minds eye as I memorised the passage. Time and time again I had to say the words in my head - until I could not forget them. For over an hour, they had us remember this image with words and, the funny thing was, they didn't even connect! Every time that I see a stream or river now, I think of that passage. We had to then do the same with another passage, with another image, and slowly, over the next few days, we built up a complete spell. This was then memorised as continuous prose with set images that made up the whole sequence.

Some of the spells even required a gesture or movement associated with them. It took me over a month to completely memorise and repeat, without mistake twenty times in a row. I had memorised all of the parts of the spell in half the time of those around me, and I knew when I had it absolutely right. The last spell I learned, I actually enjoyed doing! It had become a challenge to learn it, as quickly as possible, and my tutor Cat had demanded a lot from us. She was secretly pleased by my progress, I think, but I was never sure that she was. She always said that I was 'too impulsive,' that I would 'never have had the patience to make it as a good priestess' and that I 'needed to learn how to control my impulses.' Yes, I still thought I needed to learn this. How could I have walked into this room without thought or planning? If it had been a trap without an exit, I would soon be dead.

Most of the books, so far, were religious texts, but all were beautifully illustrated and written in such intricate neat writing. Each time I opened another book, I was so very careful of its edges. I had remembered what Celene had told me of the knife trap, and so I used my own blade to open the covers. Those books that were not religious seemed to be more mystical in nature and some were even mathematical, but the titles were often unclear as to the nature of the book. I had not found the one I was looking for. It seemed to me that this Borrador character had examined every religious text from all the religions that he could find. Many of the books had used materials other than vellum to write upon. I have been told that vellum lasts for years without yellowing, but several looked to be papyrus bound into a book. Others used different skins to write on (not the usual skins used for writing on, anyway) and rough paper was also quite extensively used. I separated out the non-religious books and piled them up on the floor. I thought that Vergoth, if he wakes, may want to have some of these.

It was surprising how many different languages were used to write these books; not just the usual, Latin, Greek and Norse, but there were a couple written in runic Silves. This was a surprise to me, as I didn't realise that anyone would be interested. I held onto these books, wishing to study them later. There were so many volumes written, or at least copied from, another pictorial language. This had so many creatures and different shapes in it that I began to think it must be from a completely different people. All of the papyrus books were written in this language. I had heard that Majis could cast a spell, which allows them to read and speak (or, at least, understand) any language. This may have been the method by which this man and his followers were able to read so many diverse topics.

After two hours of the most boring task I have ever undertaken, I had gone three quarters of the way around the stacks. The books seemed to be arranged very haphazardly, without seemingly being in any order. I had almost fifty non-religious text separated out for Vergoth, when I stopped looking. I didn't want to look at another book as long as I lived! I appealed to my Goddess, "Why on earth have you given me such a loathsome task?" If she had asked me to do something difficult, like stealing a pair of shoes from a horse while it was running through the forest, I could see the challenge in that. However, this, it was impossible to keep sane mindlessly checking books.

Carefully picking my way back to one of the desks to sit down, I mused over the state of the room. I had made quite a mess. Apart from the corpses I was not willing to disturb, this room was neat and tidy and in good order before I started. If someone could move the bodies out of the maze, this would be quite a centre of learning. There were fifty or so books on the floor, and I would never be able to carry all of them out by myself. I still had not found the book I was looking for. I glanced across the desks and even these had books on them. Mostly, they were lying open on the desk. I turned one to me and, again, this was in Silves. I found it surprising that there would be any books written in this language being held by a human. I closed the book and put it with the other two. The rest of the books were religious texts, but not from my own Temple.

Looking for something to do, I sat back and brought out the biscuit ration I had already started. I munched it for a while, as I scanned around the room. There was, I realised, something wrong with the shape of the room; there was a stair coming down to it from the rest of the maze, but that didn't account for the whole section of the wall that jutted into the maze. My instinct was that there was more to this room than meets the eye. However, before I looked around for anything else, I had to find my book.

The rest of the books sat there on the shelves, staring at me through their bindings, and I hated the thought of looking through them again. This was, probably, the end of my mission and I needed to do it, but, goddess, this is so difficult for me! As I stood up and walked back to the shelves, I sensed the spines of the books seemed to be smiling at me - as if they were sharing a private joke. Books are inanimate objects and can't possibly have any feelings or emotions, but they did, however, seem to be enjoying my internal pain.

I began looking at the books again. I opened and leafed through a couple of them, but the Latin was complex to read and not my most favourite language; I preferred the more common English. Reading was something I had to do, but I never enjoyed it and don't think I ever would. When it suited my purpose, I had to do it. There were uses, I suppose, in recording history and passing on ideas - but nothing more than that. This text seemed to be about a man who was born in humble surroundings, and who preached love and forgiveness. I liked the ideas behind it, because they followed the ideas that my Temple had - though we followed a different path. This man had believed that theft was wrong and a sin. Many people would agree with him, but I didn't understand in what way his followers would show their devotion to their god. How do they empower their god and what do they get from it? I didn't understand how he thought his god would become powerful. After a while, I realised that I was holding an early copy of the Christian bible and, within its pages, I found striking parallels to some of the things that we did - at least in the section that I had read.

The rest of the books beckoned me back. Titles flitted and filtered through my mind, and I knew that I would remember all of them. My memory was a funny thing, and I had to consciously forget something in meditation to get rid of it. Early on in my life, I had organised my memories so that they would be stored neatly. In my mind, I visualised a way of storing memories in boxes on shelves and, every time I meditated, I would have a new room of shelves to store things. All of my experiences had been stored like this and I could, after thinking about things, bring those memories out and re-experience all of the thoughts and feelings. I suppose it was like a library; I hadn't actually thought about it like this before.

It was, for me, a moment of revelation. Could I reorganise my thoughts as books and have a new book for each day? I wouldn't have to worry about having all of these rooms to search through, because I could use the books with their spine writing to tell me what the experiences were. This was certainly a different way of looking at it, 'memory architecture'?

It took me another hour of slogging through the rest of the books. Although I had found a couple of interesting books in Silves runes, that talked about earth majick which would be useful to me later on, I had not found the book.

It was the end of the library, and the last book had given up its secret to me.

There were no more books to check!

I searched around, under desks and between the stacks, to see if there were any others. I checked the piles of books already on the floor, just in case it had been accidentally dumped with the others.

The book, Ichmarr's book, was not here.

What a let down!

My elation had been a little premature. I had thought that, once I found the library, it would be easy - the book would be on a shelf, and I could return into the light, triumphant.

Damn!

As always, that thought was much too easy.

This guy, Borrador, obviously was a twisted maniac who was as paranoid as I was, and probably as fixated.

I scanned around the room, there should be something else near the stairs down here, it was obvious to me, but would it be obvious to most other people? I doubt it. Also, would you expect a secret door to lead off from a secret library? Most people wouldn't. Searching along the wall, I found that there was a crack outline of a possible door and it had a slight movement of air around the outside of it. Now, how to get it open? I hit it as hard as I could with the climbing pick and, although there was not much affect, it felt good!

I carefully searched the area around the door, on the floor, walls and ceiling, but I could find nothing that looked to be an opening mechanism. The door was near the entrance stairway, so I searched carefully around there. At the third step, up there was a loose fitting riser and I found that I could remove it by hand easily. Behind the stone, there was a small bronze handle and my instinct said immediately, 'DON'T TURN IT!' So, I tried anyway. Unfortunately, when you are as impulsive as I am, you don't often listen to your instinct. As I tried the handle, it wouldn't turn, but I discovered that it did slide out easily. It was attached to a square rod, which extended into the stairway and, as I pulled it, I heard a 'clunk' and a faint hissing noise. It was the noise of something blowing or escaping. I glanced back towards the rest of the room and it had a faint green tinge to it. A greenish mist was billowing into the room and it was rising. I could smell a strong choking acrid smell. I realised that this may be the way that all of these people died and was I going to be next!

Turning back to the stairway, I quickly ran up it to escape only to find that the door at the top was closed and, although I tried the unlock mechanism, the lever wouldn't budge. The door was firmly shut. I was trapped in here! When I ran down the stairs and tried to push the lever in, the mist was much thicker and it made me start to choke badly. I pushed the handle back in, but I didn't hear any difference, so I hauled it back out to see if that made any difference. It didn't! I ran back to the door and it was still stuck fast.

I was panicking. I abused myself for pulling the handle. I shouldn't be so bloody impulsive to just, pull the handle! I had felt the danger, I could see the evidence of the possible danger all around, and I was stupid enough to ignore it. The mist was rising up the stairs; it would soon surround me. I could already feel it at the back of my throat, acrid and burning. My eyes were already beginning to burn and I needed to get out! How to get out? The mist was staying fairly near the floor; could I fly out?

The kingfisher was not the smallest bird I knew of, but was very agile and could hang in the air over a target before swooping down. Standing on the topmost step to keep my head above the mist, I started the visualisation. What about the light, would I be able to see in the mist if I didn't have a light? What if the Darksight wouldn't see through the mist? I threw my dagger down to the bottom of the stairs and it illuminated the mist as a bright green. I began the visualisation again and transformed my body; it was quick and painless, as they had all become. Choking in the fumes, I flexed my new wings. The smoke seemed even more dangerous, I was almost breathing it, and I knew I would be dead soon if I didn't get myself out of it. I jumped into the air, closed my eyes and swooped through it - aiming to pass through the middle of the room and rise above it there. I thought about heading for that vent that I saw in the ceiling.

Once I felt that I had passed through most of it, I opened my eyes and I could see that the ceiling was coming closer - very quickly, so I altered my course. From this distance, it was obvious that the vent was blocked, some wire criss-crossed over it and, in this form, there was no way that I could remove it. I looked around for a suitable perch and found an uncluttered beam in amongst the trusses. After I landed, I sat on the beam looking down at the room. I wondered how long the mist would stay. It glowed green and menacing around the bottom of the stairs and still hung around the dagger as it continued to light the area. I looked around the roof-space; it comprised a wooden vault, with a beam frame that supported the roof. Above the frame, were rough-hewn wooden strips and I could see that they held back a clay surface. From all of this, I would assume the whole structure was built in a hole and was covered over to hide it. This would have been an expensive edifice, and I had never before seen something like this. The clay must keep the moisture from penetrating the vault. However, something must be keeping the air dry down here, as the library was dry, very dry, and warmer than the rest of the maze.

The green mist down below was beginning to thin. More of the light was shining through the mist, and I was so thankful to my goddess that I had the sense to drop the dagger to give me some light to see by. I felt really clever. I had used my gifts to save my life and continue my mission. I waited, probably for about ten minutes in total, before it completely cleared. After this time, I could no longer see any green tint to the light so I decided to swoop down to try the air out. I didn't want to stop and get caught out on the ground.

From the perch, I was able to dive straight down and arc upwards at great speed. As I flew down, I sniffed the air and I found that, although it was still acrid, it wasn't choking. My eyes felt some discomfort as I flew a foot above the ground, but I judged it safe. Landing on the huge desk, I waited for another few minutes and felt that the danger had passed.

I changed back to myself and carefully walked back to the hidden door. I pushed it and the wall opened, slowly and ponderously. Beyond it there was a stairwell, which led downwards in a curve. The walls were rough hewn out of the chalk bedrock and the floor had stone-capped steps of all different heights and widths. Gingerly, I tried out the first step. I put my weight onto the first and, although it felt safe enough, I was still on edge - ready for any eventuality. Reaching into my pack, I took out a piton and my climbing pick. Using these, I wedged the door open with the piton in the frame of the door. I was going to slam a second one in, when I considered the idea that, if this door was open, will the top door open? Although I knew I could get the first one out, would I be able to pull a second one out?

Counting the stairs, I carefully made my way down; there were one hundred and sixty three steps to the end. The stairs ended in a wooden door set into a stone frame. I pushed the door open with the end of the climbing pick. Immediately, the smell of the library was replaced with the smell of vinegar and halted decay.

The room was large, with shelves filled with various pieces of metal and wax. The smell grew more intense as I entered the room. There were several jars of body organs in vinegar and so much glassware, it was like an alchemist's laboratory. There was a bench along one wall covered in notes and different experiments that had dried up, but the most striking thing about this room was the startling blue light coming from the middle of it. The light seemed to be shining from a single point, hanging in space, but I knew this was impossible to achieve. The continual light, or darkness spell that I relied on, used the material that it was cast upon to continue the spell. In the case of my dagger, the material was actually finite and the point of the dagger would eventually be reduced as the material was eaten to light itself. With the metal eaten away, in a hundred or so years my dagger would no longer have a point.

The blue light was striking in its intensity and the colour was sharply defined. It was like looking at the sky on a cloudless day, with the whole sky squeezed into that tiny spot. I moved closer to it and, as I moved towards the light, it felt cold, very cold. I put my hand up to it and I could feel the heat being sucked out of my hand. I blew at it and the breath showed up as mist. The mist seemed to be pulled into the light. It was like seeing the smoke from a fire when it curls up around a chimney; as it approaches the edge of the chimney, the smoke would suddenly change direction and be pulled up it. I had sat for many hours in the main hall, watching the fire as I waited for the right time to go.

A book lay on the floor beside the centre of the light and, upon seeing it, my excitement rose. I reached down for the book, hoping that it was the book I had been searching for. It probably wasn't, but...

Carefully, I opened the front page and watched. As the cover moved, a tiny flicker of a blade traversed across the back edge as it carried its deadly poison. With that danger gone, I read the book's title. In the blue light, I could make out the words in Latin, 'Furacissime De Iniussus'.

I screamed and jumped up in the air! I had found it! I ran around the room screaming and shouting. I danced and sang, skipped and jumped! All of the tensions were relieved and all of my fears evaporated. Mission accomplished, I was going home! Gleefully, I picked up the book, hugged and kissed it - completely oblivious to any danger that it posed.

It was the most beautiful book I had ever seen. The smell of the book was quite different from the rest of the room. To me, at the time, it smelled of a fragrant flower, maybe geraniums, but more likely the smell of the poison on the blade trap. The binding looked to be in purple and the title, "Spontaneous Thievery," exactly matched the contents. The written words within the book had been carefully transcribed in Latin with a brown ink, while the illustrations and gilding looked to be as bright as the first day they had been crafted. I was being so very cautious with this book because of the trap that it contained. Carefully stowing it in my frame pack, I turned to go.

However, something drew me back to the light. Curiosity perhaps! I looked around the room and found that the owner of this laboratory had written notes on pieces of paper, scraps of vellum, etc. Someone had tied them together with string, and I could see from the top sheets that someone, obviously Borrador, had been trying out different ideas about how the gods had accomplished some of their feats. He had amassed copious notes on these religions and was seemingly trying to tie them all together. From the look of the room, I guessed that he had tied them together but had been unlucky to attract the attention of the god that had done this to him. It came to me that the glowing blue light was Borrador, and that it was now the only thing that was left of his cult. What a way to go!

I thought that I would cover over the light, using any of the spare cloths that littered the room. I threw it over the light as I didn't want to go near it, but when the cloth landed onto the light point it was sucked into it. One second the cloth was there, the next it was being pulled in at a fantastic speed. It was gone in a fraction of a second.

Now that was amazing!

It was as if the light was a portal into another place. Puzzled, I tried moving it with a piece of metal and threw it at the light, but this was also sucked into the light. A bit frightened by this, and because I didn't want to disturb it anymore, I left it - alone.

I picked up Borrador's notes before I returned to the library, thinking that they might be useful. I also picked up the Silves books from the library desk, and stowed them in my frame pack. It would be interesting to do some research of my own on the long way home. I could come back and get the rest of the collection later. If I was able to get up to the surface in the next few minutes, I would still have a couple of hours before nightfall. I pulled the piton out of the doorframe, using the climbing pick. This allowed me to shut the door on the secret chamber. I reset the pull handle for the secret door and tried again to pull the lever to let myself out of the library. I heard a familiar and welcome sound as the door swung open, then blackness flooded the library....

Quindecim – Exploro bibliothece

With the door closed to the rest of the world, the room was quiet. In my chest, I felt the warm glow repeated from when I first found the book. My mission was complete, but the final part of it had been disjointed. Now I need to hunt down the book and return it to my Temple. The book should be easy enough to find; I just have to follow the three Detektives back to their home or guard barracks, and they will lead me to it.

The real bonus is Tamzy, and the short conversation we had. My Temple had made contact with me and I felt sure that they would help me recover what is ours. I wondered if Celene will be angry that Tamzy didn't know our Temple? She does know all of the other Temple priestesses around in the area, particularly the Cantebrigia Temple, as it is the closest one to us. I tried to think about the Temple when I was there. I think it had a high priestess called Miranda; if she were still in charge, she would be keen to see me again. I made a big impact on her, indeed I still owe her for releasing me from the College Constables after being caught. What is all of that business about Chipping Walden and Saffron Walden? It sounds like someone is playing silly buggers.

I began to wonder what happened to Penny and Desi. Did they manage to get out and what happened next? I almost willed myself back into the dream to find out what happened. The dream no longer frightened me....

Using the methods I had learned to navigate it, I carefully picked my way through the maze to get back to the real world. It was easy enough to return through, and I quickly found myself back into the cellars. They were a welcome sight, I can tell you! The only thing that I was now worried about was the occasional clash of metal against metal that I could hear reverberating around the cellar. I looked out into the main passageway and found Desidra and Penny going for each other with swords!

"STOP!" I shouted, at the top of my voice. They lowered their swords, grinning at the sight of me, and dropped them while running over to me. I received far too many hugs than I deserved and I was so happy that they were so pleased to see me. Desidra said, "You must be hungry and thirsty after all of that. I am amazed, Merith, that you found your way out so easily."

"Look, what is going on here? I leave you two alone for a few hours and you start fighting? Who is looking out for any one out there? What are you doing?"

They were obviously not worried about anyone coming back to the ruin. Penny explained; "If they do come back, it will be at night. We are safe enough at the moment. Meanwhile, I thought I would teach Desidra a few techniques while we waited."

"And you know this, because?" It was actually what I had assumed anyway, but I wanted her to think about what she was doing. The decision to leave us unguarded was a stupid one, which could have backfired on all of us. I looked at her and saw that she was squirming in her boots. I think she now realised what a mistake this was. I kept the stare for a few moments and then I grinned, "Okay, no harm done! Did someone mention food?

"Yes we did," said Penny. "Desidra here made a delicious soup and we have been sharing that all day. I think there is some still on the fire."

Desidra nodded, her grin reappearing on her face, "We also found some wine to help celebrate. Let's go up and get you fed."

I dropped the frame pack off in the barracks. It should be safer down there.

Tired, but happy to be back with them, we all joined arms and went up the stairs to the kitchens. However, as we approached the top of the stairs, I stopped and said, "Penny, can you just check up top to see if there is anyone up there?" I felt a little paranoid after all the experiences in the maze. I held on to Desidra, as Penny went up.

Desidra looked at me and smiled, "Merith, you are safe now you know. We had only been down there for a few minutes. I'm sure they wouldn't have come back while we weren't looking."

Penny climbed to the top of the stairs and disappeared, we heard her call out our names, and she called down to us, "It's all clear girls! You can come up now."

Hurriedly, I pulled Desidra up the stairs. I wanted to get into the real light of the day before it went and, as I made my way to the kitchens, I could smell the wonderful food that had been prepared there.

Penny said, "I'm going up to the lookout post, before our wise and magnificent leader thinks I'm shirking again."

"Who? You? Penny! Skive off on duty? Never! I would never say it, I might imply it, but not say it!" I smiled, "You are the best friends a woman could ever have."

"Thanks, here eat it before it gets cold." Desidra said, "Tell me, Merith, what was it like down there?"

I took the bowl, nodding with thanks. "Come up top and I'll tell you." Preferring the open top and the view of the surrounds to being confined in the maze, I drew Desi up with me. The maze had been claustrophobic and, although I don't have hang-ups in small confined areas, I could see how a maze could induce this within a child.

Penny was sitting on one of the sides, with a crossbow sat across her lap. There were another seven crossbows up here, all cocked and ready to fire. She smiled, "I am pleased you could join me in the tower room. Mind out for the drapes and tapestries, as they do seem to be getting in the way. Mai maid servant is having her day orff and no-one else seems to have the time to remove them."

"You are so gracious, Lady Penelope, to have invited us to your tower. The decor is a little more discrete than I had assumed. Could one let one check out one's views?" Looking out over the ruins, I said, "I love what you have done with the place. I see you have used the full range of colours. There is light stone and, what is this? More light stone! I must say though, the house looks a little in need of repair work." The girls were chuckling behind me. I needed to lighten the tone and the mood, mostly mine. I was tired and hungry, but I didn't want to bring the whole mood down, so I was so grateful to Penny for starting me off. She is going to be a good member of the group.

I sat down to eat. Both girls looked expectantly at me, smiling as if to say 'Well, get on with it'. I looked at them for a while. Finally, I relented; "Alright, I'll tell the tale, and, yes! I found my book!"

I began telling them what happened down in the maze, skimming over some of the uglier details, as I didn't want them to know that I nearly gave up or that I had panicked at times. I included all of the gory detail of the bodies, and the vision that I had experienced. I told them about the armour and how it had saved my life. Penny wanted to look at the armour. I lifted my robes and in the daylight it looked just like normal chain mail. The links didn't look particularly fine, nor did it gleam at all. It was as if I had been dreaming when I had seen it in the maze. However, it still felt light and very manoeuvrable. Penny asked to try on the armour and I thought, why not? Off came my robes and I un-strapped the armour, I passed the armour to her, but she struggled with it. "Gosh," she complained, "It's heavy!" She tried to put it on, but found that it was too small for her. The straps didn't stretch across, nor did she find it comfortable. Some of the links were snagging her and she was generally uncomfortable. "Just how do you wear that stuff? It is so ill fitting and badly made."

Not understanding what she was talking about, I merely shrugged my shoulders and said "it fits me fine." I took it back and dressed myself again. While I dressed, I carried on with the story. Both were keen to see the library, but Desidra said, "I'd love to see it but there is no way I would want to go down there again. I would never risk getting lost again."

I replied. "Don't worry Desidra, I wouldn't want you to do anything you would not feel comfortable with. If you wanted to go down and try it out, I would hold your hand all the way."

She smiled, but shook her head, and I wasn't going to push it. I did think, though, that she would be a great help in getting all of the books out. After all, three hands are better than two.

I told them about the blue light and what happened to the cloth. "Really?" Penny said. "That is bizarre! I have never heard of any thing like that before. What do you think it was?"

"I don't know, but I thought it might be something caused by the man that had the maze built. It was definitely majickal in nature, and a bit scary. I didn't want to touch it in case…" I paused, not quite knowing what to say. It was a bit of a nameless fear. Although I didn't think I would be sucked in like the cloth had, what if?

"Merith, you must show me after you have rested a bit. We still have nearly an hour of daylight left. After that, I will want to be on full alert."

"The only thing is, Penny, there was this green choking gas that started up when I tried to get into the secret door. I could escape its effects, but I wouldn't be able to help you. I don't want to risk that, so I think we will miss that bit out. However, I would like some help in bringing out some books; I counted over a thousand books in there."

Penny whistled a long low tone. "That's a lot of books and would probably worth a great deal to the right person."

"Yes, but I was going to give most of what we take out to my Temple. They will know what to do with them, and I think Vergoth should also have some of them, if he lives. I don't think we should remove all of the books - some of them would be pointless, unless you are a scholar. I have chosen about sixty that looked interesting. If we could just take those books, I will then bring others back to research the rest of the library. Anyway, what would you want all of those books for? We are going to be rich when we get back!"

"And, to celebrate!" said Desidra. "Let's have some wine." She had brought up a bottle and some mugs, and poured out a full mug for us all. Thudding the mugs into each other, we all saluted, "Friends!" We guzzled the wine, and although it wasn't as good as Petersen's, at least it was refreshing and strong.

I felt happy and secure. The position we held would allow us to view the land around us, but we had work to do. I said to Penny and Desidra, "Right, we need to sort out what we are going to do tonight. We have to defend this place against marauders and anyone else that may come back here. Any suggestions? Penny, you have training in this."

"Umm, well, we need to keep a watch all night, and we will have to take turns, all of us to take a two hour tour of duty."

"I will be able to do at least four hours, I don't need sleep!"

"Ehh! What do you mean, Merith? You don't need sleep?"

"She doesn't, she told me this earlier on." Desidra commented. "She said she meditates to rest. I have been told that an hour of meditation is like four hours of sleep and my dad told me that Silves do this, to sort out their minds. It's like dreaming, but more organised, so it takes less time."

Interesting, she talks about Silves almost with fondness, not hatred. She has really changed and come around to liking my race.

"Okay, Merith! You can take the middle shift, it is the hardest time to stay awake. If I go first at the most dangerous time, then Desidra can be last."

"Okay, Penny, is there anything else you can suggest?"

"Right, all of the crossbows are to be kept loaded, Desidra!"

"Yes."

"You need to get some target practise, take one of the bows and a few bolts and do some firing practise while we are gone, at targets around the ruins. Choose anything but not at the stairs."

"Right boss!" she said, grinning back at Penny

"Merith, when we get back from the library, you need to set out some lanterns so that we can see what is coming out of the forests."

"Okay, I'll find some hooded ones - so I can get rid of the light when I am on duty."

"Umm, yes, and why would you want to do that, Merith?"

"I can see in the dark, as I will show you when we go into the maze. I see heat and I can actually see further using this than you can with the hooded lanterns. I can see people in the edge of the forest that you couldn't see, until they had come half way to you. I will not need the lanterns, but you will."

"Okay, Merith, Finish your soup and let's go to collect the books. What will we need, Merith?"

"Only a frame pack and yourself, I just need another body that is strong enough to carry the books. Let's go and we can talk while we are getting the packs." I hugged Desidra and said to her, "Look after our backs and yourself. If anything comes towards us, assume it is unfriendly and shoot it. If all else fails, grab all the weapons and get to the bottom of the stairs, it will be easier to defend."

Penny hugged Desidra and held her shoulders, whispering, "Don't hold your breath, we will be back."

I accompanied Penny down the stairs and took her to the barracks. I unpacked all of the contents from my frame pack, except for my book and I emptied Neville's pack. As we walked, I explained to her; "Right, Penny, in the maze it is majickally dark. It will seem like you have been cut off from the whole world. When we go in, don't panic about how dark it is. Just hold onto my hand and don't let go! I will be there for you, guiding you through, but, if anything happens to us and we get separated, don't move, just stay where you are! I will come back and find you. If I don't return, find the wall on your left as we go in and the right wall as we leave. This will lead you back. I will count out to you the passages you have to pass, and you should feel them with your hand. It is easy to get lost in there."

"Merith, you don't have to worry about me. I could find my way out of any situation."

"Not this one, the maze actually changes as you go around it."

We entered the cellar that had the maze entrance within, "Gosh it's dark, isn't it?" Penny remarked.

"You haven't seen anything yet!"

"No, Merith, I haven't. It's too dark to see anything."

I held onto her hand as we passed into the dark region. As we entered it, I felt her hand instinctively tighten onto mine. She was frightened. I could feel it in her hand, "Shit! It is so black. It is like your eyes have been removed and a lump of coal has replaced them."

"Put your hand against the wall," I told her as we passed into the maze.

"It's so smooth, isn't it?" Her voice started off loud and she quickly lowered it as the noise echoed. "And so quiet, Merith, like a crypt. I have been in a few crypts and they are always as quiet as this. The procession of the dead, silent as a whisper, you can just hear the sound of their clothes as they walk through - and then the sound of breathing, which is the only sound when they stop. And, the sudden noise when the priest speaks! This is so like that. Even the smell is like a crypt; it smells musty like old death, so damp and earthy but with a metallic hint." I didn't want to tell her that she was actually stepping between the corpses of previous expeditions.

I guided her through to the central part of the maze, "This is the main corridor of the maze. You need to count the passageways off to the right, and this will be the only way out. You need to ensure that you are prepared; this will help you in the maze."

"Okay, gotcha!"

I looked over and could see that she was following my instructions. Her eyes looked so concerned; they were darting around the corridor, desperately searching for something to look at. I don't think she could believe how dark it was. She stopped and said, "Merith, what is that rumbling sound?"

"That is the sound of the maze moving. Each time we pass a passageway, the maze moves around to confuse the explorer. This is the secret to the maze. This is also why so many have become lost and died in the maze. First passageway," I said to signal the count.

"Wide aren't they!"

"They seem to be. All of the passages are five feet wide, just too wide to touch both sides at once. Walking side by side, a pair could explore this maze and save themselves - but it would be difficult for an individual."

"It's lucky for me that I'm with you then. Isn't it?"

"Yes, second passage!"

"Merith?"

"Yes."

"Are you a thief?"

I stopped. I had only been called that by a few guards and usually, it was spat at me as an insult. I let go of her hand. She grabbed my arm and said, "Don't leave me!"

"Let's sit down, for a minute."

I helped her sit down. "I suppose I have a lot of training in that direction. Look Penny, my life and apprenticeship have been difficult for me. Much of what I do and have training in, I cannot tell people about. My Devotion to my goddess insures my silence about it and indeed, everything about my goddess. I have been trained in the same arts as thieves, and we actually do train some of them. But.... No! I would not classify myself as a thief, nor do I think of myself as one. I am a Priestess of Ichmarr and I have been bought by her to serve her. I didn't have any choice when I joined. Now, I fully accept her and am devoted to her. I am blessed by her and have a lot to thank her for."

Mulling this over, she commented; "I have heard of Ichmarr, the goddess of trickery and thieves. I never thought I would be working with one like you. In the 'City' you have a bad reputation, which may be undeserved, but it is still not so good. Tell me, do you really perform ceremonies in the nude dressed in human blood and do you sacrifice young males for their vitality?"

"WHAT!" I cried out in incredulity. "Do you actually think that!"

"No, but I had heard it and just... Look, there are a lot of stories that go about. There was some talk of the city elders closing down the Temples a couple of months ago when I was last there. Apparently, one of the churches was raided and a load of stolen gold, silver and ornaments were found in the rooms. It caused an absolute furore; the women were forced out at sword point, with the Abbess in chains. I didn't hear about what actually happened to them, but you know the penalty for theft."

"Really? Why would they raid the church? We help the poor and needy, and heal the sick and injured."

"Yes, but obviously this is done using the gold and silver taken from the rich."

"I can't say anything about that. However, I know in my church and we would not encourage it. In fact, we usually do make enough to cover costs through donations - the actual church bit pays for itself. The training of young 'Scouts' also helps, so I've been lead to believe. Why would anyone wish to stop us?"

"Hmm, you encourage thievery and general mischief."

"Not so much encourage, Penny, more like.... Well, I suppose we encourage tricks, but not thievery!"

"Yes, yes! But this is not getting the job done is it?"

"Aren't I the one who is supposed to say that?"

I could see her smile in the dark. I knew she had accepted me, but my religion was proving a problem for her.

"Yes," she stood up. "Shall we go, oh wise one?"

I stood up, took her hand and lead her on. I would have to explain a few things to Penny later. I didn't want her to think that I am a bad person. I mean, it wasn't wrong to devote yourself to your goddess; after all, every thing you do in her service and her name is right and just. Isn't it? We do give what we have back to the public, and we help the poorest of society. Why should people want to get rid of us? If we were wrong to do what we do, surely we would have been told this by now and asked to leave the town?

We had arrived and I looked at the wall. Everything looked exactly as I had left it and so I stood on the desk, still left in the position by the door, to open the door. This time, as the door opened, there were no crossbow bolts and no sudden surprises. When the door had closed, I stopped Penny to warn her; "Penny, close your eyes and cover them with your hands."

"Why? This isn't one of the tricks you play on people, is it?"

"No, I just thought you might like to see again. I was going to light a beacon." I watched as she covered her eyes with her hands, and then took my dagger out.

She jumped away from me, "Christ, that's bright! Even through my hands, it's still bright."

"Keep your eyes closed, but take your hands away. It will take a while for your eyes to get used to the light, then I'll lead you down further as your eyes adjust." I guided her down the stairs into the library. She blinked in the light from the dagger, to see what was happening.

"Oh, my god! What an amazing room - look at all of these books and that desk! I have never seen anything like it. Ugh, what's that?" She pointed over to one of the corpses on the ground.

"I believe they are the last followers of the man who built this place. I suspect he was going to do something that would make him like a god, but I don't think he wanted his followers to stop him. When I tried to get into his secret room, where I told you I saw the blue light, I was nearly gassed. I think they all died from it. From the look of them, some were struggling to breathe when they died." I walked carefully over to the corpse I had looked at before, "This one looks like he choked to death."

"What a horrible way to go, Merith! You can't fight it and it doesn't stop."

"Anyway, we have wasted enough time. Grab some books and get started! Only grab the ones on the floor, the rest of these are religious and I think we should leave them for now," I added, as Penny started to step over the books on the floor.

We spent the next ten minutes packing books carefully into our pack. I also I loaded her arms up with another six; at this rate, it will take us two more trips. I put the dagger under my shoulder strap so that it would light our way as we came out of the darkness. I held Penny's arm to guide her out.

On the way back through the darkness, Penny asked, "Do you not get put off by the corpses? Does death not mean anything to you?"

"I suppose I haven't really thought about it. Ichmarr promises an afterlife, full of secrets, and mischief, to be had by all. When you die, you get taken to a place where your status is determined by the things you have done in life and by the extent of your devotions. It is a relaxing place, where we don't have to show our devotions anymore, but where we can plan elaborate tricks and play them out. It is a place of fun and frolicking, in the glow of our goddess. Death doesn't really worry me, nor do corpses. They are only the mortal remains our consciousness leaves behind, after it goes to our goddess."

"Well," she responded. "I have seen corpses before, usually at the end of a long piece of metal. I don't mind that so much. The look on the faces of those poor people gave me the willies! I mean how could anyone do that to their own people? Some people believe that, when you die, you will be judged by your conduct on earth and that, if you have been good, you will be with god. If you are bad, you will be sent to the other place and spend your time in purgatory. My master said to us that this is true; if your fight is good and true and you are protecting your client, your friends or your life then, whatever you do, god will be with you. Any mortal sin is cancelled, and not charged against your name. Thus, everything I do in my job is for my client and not my sin."

"Penny, we are back at the entrance. Close your eyes."

She shut them, but still winced in the sudden light from the dagger. "It's amazing how strong that light is, when your eyes are used to darkness."

"Let's go check on Desidra. I am worried about her."

"Okay!"

I led her to the door. I said to her, "Blink your eyes open now, we are out"....

Sedecim – Ulterior dimicationis

The chair underneath me was hard and cold. I hadn't been sitting here long. There was a strange lack of sound in the room; I could hear breathing of two people, but nothing else. The usual sounds of the healer's hall were gone, to be replaced with... nothing. The light shining into my face must have been what woke me up. I opened my eyes cautiously, blinking in the strong light. I moved to shield my eyes with my arms and found that they were locked to the chair. My feet also appeared to be held to the chair. I looked around the room, but it was all in shadows. In this light, I could make out that the room was about thirty foot by thirty. Closing my eyes again, I could make out the body heat of two others in the room. They were looking at me nervously, as if they were not sure who or what I was.

One of them, a woman, coughed - presumable to get my attention. I realised that both of these people were women, one older than the other. The older one spoke first, "State your real name."

"Merith. Who am I speaking to?"

"We ask the questions."

"Look, if I am going to talk to you, at least tell me what I can call you - to be polite."

"There is no politeness necessary here."

"Why not? There is always a need for politeness. Whenever I deal with people I deal in politeness."

"We ask the questions here!"

"I suppose you need to repeat yourself if you are not going be polite! That is not the way I would play it, Miranda? Tamzin?"

"If that is what you want to call us, then we will agree to this for now."

"Good! So, what is it you girls want to talk about?"

"Who are you?"

"I am Merith, Priestess of Ichmarr."

"Who is Ichmarr?"

"She is the Goddess of deception and trickery."

Tamzin (I recognised her voice), said, "You missed thievery out."

"Sorry, Tamzin, tell me who do you believe in?"

"We ask the questions," said the older one in a stronger voice – the one that I had called Miranda.

"Only asking!"

Tamzin asked, "How do you know the signs?"

"I was taught it by my apprentice master, Alyss, in Infield. She taught me Thieves' Cant when I was just starting out. She also taught me how to open locks and the basic craft of a thief."

Miranda was quick to ask, "So, you are a thief?"

"No, I am a Priestess of Ichmarr, I know about thievery as part of my craft in being a priestess, you know this Tamzin, don't you?"

Miranda said in a doubtful voice, "You told our operative that you operated from the Temple in Saffron Walden. But, what if I were to tell you that the Temple in Saffron Walden was destroyed in fifteen thirty eight?"

"What?" The shock must have been evident on my face. "You are lying! How dare you say these things to me." I felt the tears rolling down my face; my throat tightened, I tensed all of my muscles and just pulled at everything.

"It was burned down by the authorities, as it was seen as a den of thievery. They arrested and imprisoned all they could find within it. But, I have to say, the histories of this are a bit sketchy."

"Histories?" I shrieked, "I was just in it a couple of weeks ago and every one seemed to be happy. They...."

"Merith, it happened in fifteen thirty eight!"

"This year!" I was beginning to get desperate! "Yes... You said! But you talk about it as if it was a long time ago."

"Merith, this is twenty oh six. Nearly five hundred years have passed since then."

The world swam, I just couldn't believe it, "No, it cannot be, I was there only two weeks ago! This is the truth, it is evident all around!" I pulled again at the chair and began to move around, pulling everyway I could.

Tamzin said, "Calm down Merith, you will hurt yourself."

The scream seemed to start from my stomach and just went through my very body. It integrated all of my frustrations and angers into one frightening full bodied animal yell. I thrashed around on the chair and could not stop myself. I felt the metal of the chains bite into my arms, wrists, ankles. There was no way I could believe them.

Tamzin stood up quickly and rushed to my side. Her hands held my head, whilst she looked into my eyes and whispered, "Calm down, Merith! You could be safe here if you tell us the truth." The rush of majick, as it grabbed hold of my emotions, settling them down and caging them in, was evident in this act. Tamzin did it so discreetly, that I wasn't sure I was the only one it was meant to be hidden from. I mouthed to Tamzin, "Who is the other?"

She mouthed back, "Not one of us, M.I.5."

Right, so I am supposed to know what the hell that meant? I assumed that I wasn't to trust her, so I settled down my thoughts. Eventually, I declared firmly, "I will only talk to Tamzin, not her!"

Tamzin looked around and said, "Just as we thought. Would you mind leaving, Miranda? I can handle it from here."

Miranda started to say, "No, I cannot...."

"You WILL go, unless you want to deal with my superiors!" Tamzin's voice lost all of its gentleness and beauty, becoming instead a commanding voice. It spoke into the soul and obviously had its desired effect. Miranda stood up.

As she walked to the door, she said, "I will wait outside. Call if you need me."

"Yes." Tamzin spoke, without turning, and then concentrated on me. The door then closed with a definite thud. "So, Merith, tell me; first of all, how do you intend to prove what you say?"

"What proof do I need? Just give me my dagger back and I can pray for spells like the one you just used!"

"How do you know about them? Only the priestesses know about them!" She looked concerned that I knew some of her secrets, not just the Thieves' Cant, but others.

I smiled, and coughed, "Erm, I think I have told you, I am a priestess of Ichmarr. I can cast six spells from a range of eight."

This time it was her that was taken aback; "Six spells? No one can cast that many, no one knows that many. We only have three that are known, and I have only mastered the one I used earlier!"

"Right, you need to do some more devotions them!" I felt a bit superior now! I could teach this Temple a thing or two. An idea began to form in my mind; "Tamzin, I can teach you all of my majick, if you will help me regain the equipment I lost to the guards."

"We seized all of your things the moment we realised you might be special. Merith, you are genuine, aren't you?"

"How do you mean?"

"You are one of us?" She needed to believe that I was. I could see it in her eyes. I wondered though, what could she see in mine?

"Yes!" I affirmed.

She stood up and walked over to the door. It opened and she spoke to someone just out of sight. I saw a blade being passed to her; it was my blade, my dagger, the one given to me by my apprentice master. She brought it over to me and placed it in my hand, "Can you pray like this? We cannot release you until we have proof, so you will have to do it this way."

Nodding, I said, "I can as long as I have this." I cleared my mind to begin to pray. As I did so, however, the dream intruded once more....

As I opened the cellar door, I could hear Desidra shouting outside. Whatever it was she was saying, it sounded very rude, so we dumped the books and hurried to the top of the stairs. We heard the distinctive 'twip' of a crossbow being fired, and Desidra shouting, "Keep your heads down, boys! I might actually hit you with one of these!"

I reached ground level quickly and stopped to assess the scene. Desidra, crouching low on the raised room we were using as an observation post, was looking over the low wall and aiming at a patch of forest, far off, northwards. However, the low walls around us didn't let me see any further than the house. Penny, crouching low, scurried up the stairs after me and, as she did so, an arrow skimmed off the stair beneath her feet. She took a diving roll into the room, stood up crouching and looked carefully over the side. Sprinting over to join her, I felt something hit my back - but felt nothing penetrate. Upon reaching the top I threw myself into the room, rolled to my feet and surveyed the grounds through one of the gaps in the wall.

Nothing was moving around the house, nor on the open grass, but in the trees I could see the glinting of metal. From this, I guessed there were, maybe, four men in dark clothing. They had weapons drawn and looked ready for anything.

"Penny, can you see them any better than I can?"

"They are in the trees, I can see about four, maybe five, of them."

"They are a little earlier than I thought they would be. They must have left their viewing posts this morning to report back. They would have been quite surprised that they were fired upon when they returned."

"Yes, they bloody were!" Desidra stated. "The first bolt I sent at them whipped between the four of them. They were so shocked that they just reined in their horses and stopped. That gave me an easier shot and I hit one of them on the leg. He provided me with a wonderful display of shock and fury, as the pain hit his brain! I watched them scatter into the trees and, while they have been occasionally firing back with arrows, they can't get a clear shot with us up here. I have fired a few back at them, but I think they are waiting for dark before doing something against us."

"What did they look like?"

"They were dirty, ugly and rough looking. They wore dark cloaks over their clothes and I could see that they were all armed with swords. I think two of them had long bows, but I'm not sure."

"So, you definitely saw no more than four. Anyway, it's getting dark soon and I don't think they will attempt anything before twilight. Let's keep our heads down for the moment. We should sit tight and watch out for them to emerge; then we can take them out when they come. I'll go and set up some lanterns on the outer walls, so that you have a view of the land around the house. What do you think Penny?"

"Yes, good plan! But, what do you think about this idea? I could hide in the rubble of the outer walls and attack them with crossbows as they come in. Hopefully, with surprise, I should be able to take most of them down."

"And what happens if you are on the wrong side, and we are left exposed to their attack? After all, they could move around in the dark and outflank you. Then we would have serious problems."

"Yes, I see that, Merith. However, you can see them in the dark, can't you? You said you could see the heat of them as they came to us?"

"Yes! I actually see them better at night, even a clouded night, than I can in daylight."

"How good are you at shooting the crossbow?"

"Very good, but at the moment they are too far away. However, there would be no way I could hit them at this range - no matter how accurate I can be - the crossbow doesn't have the range."

"How do you like this plan then? We don't set up any lanterns, right? We set up some torches in here, to make us more visible targets, and you go watch them from the nearest side to them. They may stay together. If they do stay in position, as they start to come across when the light is just right, you can then start taking them down when you are happy about the range. Meanwhile we will stay in the tower, making a show for them to think that we are scared of them and their attack. I will be here to deal with them to protect Desidra, and you can always fall back onto this position if you get into trouble."

I had to admit it was a good plan. It allowed for Penny's strength of defence, while allowing us to attack. It gave me the opportunity to use my Darksight to protect us, and possibly win through, without the need for any messy hand-to-hand fighting which would be more dangerous. It also made us look like an easy target; they would be encouraged to stroll in, if they thought it was merely women shooting at them. They would think that we don't know anything about fighting, and would believe that running at us, shouting obscenities, should unsettle us long enough for them to capture or kill us. "Hmm, that sounds like a winning plan, Penny! When do we start?"

"Well, I think you should check up on them, find out where they are and, well, generally do a bit of scouting around for us. Your robes will be perfect for this, as they are already dark and will blend into the environment."

"Okay, well, I will have to take four of the crossbows, loaded and ready to fire. I think I will also need my hand crossbows; they are good for close contact, if I miss with these big beasties." I looked over the edge of the window. Waiting a few seconds, as my eyes adjusted to the growing darkness, I saw that there were several heat sources out there. The four men appeared not to have moved far and I could see the heat of their horses tied up further into the forest. They seemed to be standing in a line near the forest edge, looking over towards us, possibly waiting for the right moment. Two of them looked ready to do something, standing in a fighting stance, maybe ready to fire arrows. Either way, I was definitely sure I could locate them all. I turned to the others, "Right, I can see them all. I will go to the rubble at the edge, watch them as the prepare themselves to attack us and fire on them as they come. You two, keep a close eye out! When I'm gone, set a couple of torches on the approaches to look like you are trying to see better - but do it ineptly, to make it look as if you don't know how to do it. Leave this side free of torches." I pointed towards the men. "It will make it easier for them to sneak up. I'll take care of it from there."

Penny looked at me as if I was patronising her, "Yes. Merith! I do know what to do, it's my plan, remember?"

"I know and I'm sorry. I just wanted to spell it out mostly to myself. I feel like jelly, I'm scared and still a bit unsure of myself."

"If you'd rather...?"

"What? Sit here and wait for them to come to us? No, I think your way is right. I just need to reassure myself. I'll be fine!"

I picked up the crossbows. Fucking hell, I thought, they are heavy! One is okay, but four is much too much. Nonetheless, I slung them over my shoulders and carefully made my way down the stairs. Turning, I waved goodbye to the pair of them and fervently hoped that I will see them again. I made my way through the ruins, darting from one wall to another. Eventually, I was able to see to the forest again. When I looked over, I could see only three of them. One of the bowmen had moved! I looked along the edge; there, he had moved fifty yards around the forest perimeter. He was even further away from me and would be difficult to hit, if I was to shoot from here.

The sun had long gone in and I was able to see very clearly with my Darksight. I bet all those men could see was the light from the tower, and everything else was black. The moon had not risen yet and the stars did not give enough light by which to see anything. I decided to try to get closer to the solitary one. If I could take him out of the situation, it would definitely be in our favour. Leaving two of the crossbows set up in a position where I could get to them quickly, I carefully moved away from the house, staying low and keeping to the shadows. The grass was knee-high, thick and billowing, and I had to move slowly to keep the noise down. Every time I moved my feet on the grass, they sounded like I was honing a dagger on a whetstone!

Moving slowly, and staying low amongst the grass, I managed to get to within twenty yards of the single bowman. I could see the glow of his pipe and smell the sweet, but slightly cloying, aroma of tobacco burning in the bowl. With some trepidation, I lifted one of the two crossbows and took careful aim. I didn't think I would get another chance like this; he was bound to hear or see me, once I pulled the lever. Moreover, the noise would alert him should I miss. I concentrated all of my skill on that one shot. From the shape of the heat source, I could see him looking at the tower. I took aim down the shaft of the bolt, targeting the middle of his chest.

The air was still and the night was silent. I heard the cries of a night bird as it called for its mate. The grass around me quivered, and slowly settled as I relaxed. My mind cleared as I concentrated on the shot. I took in a long breath and held it. Slowly, I began to pull the lever.... I stopped. I was having second thoughts. I didn't really want to kill him, and he hasn't done anything wrong. Or, has he? He could have been involved with what they did..... How stupid I am. He is part of this gang! He is part of what they did.

I pushed these second thoughts to one side and, with grim determination, I began to pull the lever. The crossbow had a much higher draw than I was used to and the bow pushed me back unexpectedly. It took me a moment to refocus on the target. I looked up, just in time to see the puff of heat as the bolt hit him in the neck. His blood must have sprayed out of the wound, producing a gory display! Both of his hands went up to the wound, as he fell to his knees. He cried out in pain and toppled over, on to his side.

Moving swiftly, I picked up the other bow and made my way back. Training my eyes on the patch of forest where the remaining men were located, there were heat sources there - but difficult to see distinctly. I moved as cautiously, but as rapidly, as I dared; I didn't want to alert them to my presence. Halfway across the open ground, I picked up on the fact that they were beginning to move towards the ruins. They were proceeding quite slowly, picking their way through the grass while they discussed what they were going to do when they caught us. "Them bitches won't know what hit them! I'm gonna go in there and hurt them bad."

"Yeah, but you got to catch 'em first."

"Easy, I'll just walk in there and scare the fuck out of them. They'll be so scared of me, that they'll drop their weapons and run like fuck. Specially that Silves girl! I can't wait to see her again - I want to keep her as a pet."

My blood began to boil, as I remembered what they had done to me. My anger was coming back, but this time it was tainted with a fear that something bad might happen again. There was no way that I was going to let that happen!

"You want to keep her strapped to your fucking cock."

"Damn, fucking right!"

I had to be calm and clear. At the speed they were moving, I guessed they would reach the other crossbows at about the same time as me. If I moved any faster, they would be alerted to my presence. I was closing in on them fast. They were coming within range and I could take the lead man out now, but would that make them run forwards or back?

Taking aim, I raised the crossbow up and held my breath. I stared down the shaft of the weapon at the smiling faces, as they bantered about what they would do. My target was the biggest bloke, as they wouldn't be able to carry him off if they ran and certainly wouldn't help him come to me. He was also probably the bully who would do the most damage, if they did get to me.

Behind me, there was a flaring of light. It partially illuminated their faces and I could clearly see the face of Stuart at the back of the group. He was the silent one. What the fuck is he doing here?

They stopped and looked straight at me. Out of panic, I let it go at the big man. As it flew out of the bow, the 'twip' of the bolt sounded so loud. Fortunately, he was obviously unprepared for the attack. He doubled up and fell to his knees as it hit him in the stomach. Immediately, I dropped both crossbows and sprinted towards the place where I had left the other two bows.

The remaining two looked confused as to what to do. "Get her, the fucking devious bitch!" the big man shouted to his friends. They looked at each other and started running towards me.

Just then, the moon started to crest the horizon. I could see it rising through the wood, behind the two men as I looked back at them. It was so bright, that it silhouetted them in its light. The scene was surreal, with the white flesh of the moon surrounding the dark red-heat tones of the two men as they ran towards me. Reaching the ruined outer wall first, I grabbed one of the crossbows; it felt heavy in my hands, but the bolt was held in the runner and the lever was ready to be pulled.

They were closing in fast as I raised the bow. I'd get one shot at them, and then I'd have to deal with the final one by hand to hand. I took aim at the one I didn't recognise, thinking that, although he was the smaller of the two, I should be able to deal with Stuart much more easily. After all, he was an inept thief and I doubted that he would be a better swordsman. I pulled the lever. The tension in the bow was released and the bolt flew straight and true, hitting the bloke in the shoulder. The force of the blow spun him off the ground; he collapsed into a heap and didn't get up.

I dropped the bow and whipped out my holy dagger. The intense white light illuminated the scene so clearly. Stuart's face now betrayed his total surprise, as he could see his opponent for the first time. I didn't think that he had ever envisaged facing someone like me. He was armed with a short sword and had a dagger in his other hand. I smiled at him and, stepping back into the space of the room, I beckoned him forward. The stone floor grated with the sound of his boots, as he carefully stepped across it. He looked in my eyes, and couldn't match my stare.

"So, Stuart, we meet again!"

He was genuinely flabbergasted to hear his name being used. "What? Who are you? How do you know me? What is going on?"

"You may not recognise me, but I was the little novice you were trying to mug back in Chipping Walden. I drank mead and you told me of your plan to break into your parents' business."

"What? How do you know all that? This is a trick!"

"I am a priestess of Ichmarr, but I swear to you this is no trick! I am Alyss, but you may recognise me like this." And, using the hat, I slowly changed my appearance to that of Alyss.

"What? How the...? Alyss? Look, whoever you are, I'm not sure of all this, I haven't um...."

"You were going to say that you are not part of this? And, that you haven't killed anyone yet. This is too much even for you. Are you scared, farm boy? I said you'd be dead in a month; now, it could be in a minute."

"What? Look, Alyss, or whoever you are. Just surrender to me, I have the sword and I'm stronger than any woman. I don't really want to hurt you. If you give it up, we will go easy on you."

I moved towards him. He struck a pose with the weapons, probably as he had been shown in his training; 'Look as if you know what you are doing and the battle is half won.' However, what they never did explain is how to win the other half. I moved in with my dagger and, as he went to clumsily defend himself, I whacked his sword hand with the hilt of the dagger. He released it and cried out in pain. He put his hand under his arm to quench the pain, and looked up at me. In the time he took to do this, I was able to grab his short sword. I put it to his throat and held it there. He gulped and a cloud of steam appeared around his legs. I looked down and could see a puddle gathering around his feet! He was shaking all over.

"Listen, farm boy! You are too clumsy and naïve to be a threat. Now, who has the sword? I actually know how to use it for a change. Look, Stu, I don't want to kill you. Today, I have already been through hell and back - dealing with a whole load of shit that I don't wish to share with the likes of you! I have had people spit on me, slap me and impale me with a crossbow bolt. I have had a really fucking awful day! Please, you are cute. Don't make me kill you, too."

"I... I...only joined them today. I wasn't part of it. They...they told me about it, and how you were so beautiful. They said I'd get a go. But, I didn't want to be part of that scene. They teased me about it, saying I probably couldn't get it up. I wouldn't do that! I couldn't! What would my mum think of me?"

"Then give me your daggers - all of them!" He started to pass me the one he held in his hand, blade first. With my sword, I pointed to the ground, "Drop them there, and be quick!" He dropped the one he was holding and three more. "Step back, now!"

He moved back away from them. He was looking me in the eye, trying to puzzle me out?

As I picked up the daggers, I said to Stuart, "Come with me!" We made our way towards the men lying in pain outside of the ruins. I came to the first one and impaled the sword into his chest, to put him out of his misery. Stuart was outraged, "What are you doing, they are still alive. You can't do that, it's murder!"

"They fucking raped me! And both my friends! They have probably done much worse. They are the lowest sort of scum. What do you expect me to do? Let them go? Let them get more of their mates so they can have a fun time on me again. Think again, farm boy! The only reason you are alive is that I know you couldn't have done this, and that you are innocent of it. "Don't push it!" I managed to pull the sword out of the impaled man's chest and then moved over to the big man, who was managing to drag himself slowly to the forest. He saw us coming and cried out, "Nooo! Have mercy on me!"

"Did you show me any mercy? When I called out, did you say, 'this is wrong guys, stop right now'? No, you fucking didn't. You enjoyed it, didn't you! You were coming back to fuck me, weren't you. In fact, the only reason why you didn't do it last night was that you had to watch the fucking road! You are a fucking rapist bastard and you deserve to die a slow and painful death. However, I will be merciful to you. I will give you a quick out."

He waved his sword at me, "Don't come near me!"

He was too weak to defend himself properly. I tapped aside his weapon and bore down on him, my sword point going between his ribs into his lungs. His face contorted and twisted in pain. Blood came gurgling out of his mouth, in a sound I will want to forget for the rest of my life. His eyes, his evil eyes, stared at me so wide and terrorised. I twisted the blade and pushed it to the side to pull it out. Out of the corner of my eye, I could see Stuart cringing. He was too young and inexperienced for all of this. He threw up.

Standing there, head down, and wiping his mouth, he said, "There is so much blood. Who would have believed that he would have so much in him? It's like an ocean of blood, this pool around him. I feel as if we have been walking on his life all the way up here and, now we stand, with his life soaking our boots."

I stood back, feeling sick in my own stomach. I felt it was over. I could relax and stop for a while. I looked at Stu. He was exactly as I remembered him to be. "You should have been a scholar, talking like that."

Still tearful, but with an angry tone in his voice, he said, "My parents paid for me to be schooled. I hated it! I couldn't stand copying out of a book. What is the point of that?"

"It's better than this, isn't it farm boy! No-one dies from reading and writing do they? Come on, let's get you introduced to the rest of us. I'll turn you loose in the morning. I can't have you wandering around out there all night. You might hurt something."

"You know there is still Garder; he is still out there, ready to cut off your escape."

"Do you mean the other bloke with a bow?"

"Yes."

"Unless he can find a way to breathe metal, he won't worry us tonight."

As we approached the discarded crossbows in the field, I said, "Pick them up, there's a good boy."

"You trust me with these?"

"Why not? You can hardly threaten me with an empty bow. There is another one by the wall. I know that you are young and inexperienced, but then so am I and, if I try to hurt you, I might be able to do it. Oh! And, also the fact that I know you are a thief and I am your priestess, your only way to everlasting peace with Ichmarr."

"Alyss?"

"Yes," he kept on talking, as if to fill the void. He stank of fear and his own pee, but I could feel his terror of the situation he was in beginning to diminish. "Walk as we talk," I told him. "I need to get to my friends, they have to know what has happened."

"Alyss, what is happening? I came out here with Garder; he said there was rich pickings and no danger. I was going to go along with it to get some easy money. Now, everyone is dead and... no offence, but... I'm with a sadistic bitch priest from hell, who has just murdered everyone I knew."

"Well, no offence meant but.... you were stupid enough to team up with a group of murdering rapists who got their jollies from torturing and raping young girls like me! I could have killed you just as easily as the others. Consider yourself lucky you are still alive! That situation may change...."

He stayed silent for the rest of the way. Glancing at him occasionally, I could see that he was thinking - but I didn't know if he was plotting or just scared out of his wits. If I was in his shoes, I would be terrified and, from the smell of him, he definitely was!

We approached the tower, "Hellooo up there," I called. "It's Merith with a prisoner."

"Merith? But you're…"

I let the Alyss appearance drop away from my features. "No, Stu, I'm Merith. I always have been. Alyss is just a disguise that you knew me as. I thought it would be easier for you, if we talked like this."

As I was speaking, a head appeared at the window and I could see it was Penny's. "Cooee! That you, Merith? What's happened? Who's that dishy young feller with you? Bring him up!"

I called up, "All dead, easy targets, no worries! But I had to spare this one." I turned to Stuart, "Let's go, Stu."

He followed me like a lamb, and I guess he didn't have any choice. He didn't have any pressing business anywhere else, and I would chase him down anyway.

Swiftly, I ran up the stairs. From behind me, I could hear the squelching of his shoes as he followed. "Guys, we have a visitor. Don't touch him. He had a little 'accident' before he came here!" I turned to face him and indicated that he should stop at the head of the stairs. "Girls, this is Stuart. He's fallen in with a bad crowd…"

"What, us?" interrupted Desidra.

"And…" I continued, ignoring the interruption. "I have saved him from a fate worse than death."

"Your wrath?" Desidra suggested

"I met him back in Chipping Walden. He is a scout who needs some experience. I thought we might use him, or at least hold onto him until tomorrow - when we can turn him loose."

They both came up to meet him. As they approached, I could see their noses wrinkling and they smartly stepped away. Penny held her nose, "Does he ever wash?"

"As I said, I think he had a little 'accident' when I captured him. He is a little nervous."

"I think, as he is your charge, you should look after him and get him cleaned up a bit," said Desidra, "and… quickly!"

"Actually, Desi, I think you should help him, Penny interjected. I need Merith to stand watch now, we might get others."

She turned to me, "so what happened, Merith?"

I filled her in on the main details, making it seem tougher than it was because I didn't want her to think that I was invincible. I was hardly that, however. I just know a few tricks, and being able to see in the dark is a massive advantage. She listened intently and asked a few questions to fill in the detail. She then asked, "And finally Merith, why didn't you get rid of 'Pisspants' there. He must have been an easy kill. Now we have a loose ballista in our midst that could go off at any time! Are you going soft? Or do you have something else in mind for him?" She grinned a wicked smile.

"Penny, you need to clean your mind out! I didn't kill him because he isn't a threat. He couldn't have been involved with any of what happened to us. He's just an innocent farm boy who wants to play at being a thief. He doesn't know how dangerous it can be. I think tonight was the first night he saw someone die. I could see that it shook him; he was absolutely terrified, so much so he was shaking with fear. I terrified him and I am sorry for that. I didn't want to do it, but, Penny, I heard them talking and the memories came flooding back. I felt so angry, but I also had a fear that it may happen again."

I could feel myself shaking, I reached out and hugged her, while tears broke out on my face again as I sobbed into her shoulder.

She hugged me back, her hand rubbing my back. "You're safe now Merith, It's okay! Shushhh…it's okay! Don't worry, shhuushh."

Gradually I settled down a bit. I pulled away and wiped my eyes and nose. "There I go again, blubbering again! I don't know what is wrong with me."

"It's all right Merith. We had a couple of blubbering sessions of our own, while you were out there. Desi was so concerned about you and whether you were going to return. She feels that she has wronged you so much and she wants to put it right. She is so loyal to you, more than you realise. She told me that she let you into her past, and that you helped her click some things into place that she was confused about. She has been so angry, for so long, with the Silvesi that killed her family, she never thought about why they did it. I think she has forgiven them. Now, she only harbours the fear, as you do, that it may happen again - as, indeed, I do."

"Shall we kill all men to stop this thing from happening again, or is that a bit extreme?"

"Men have their uses and, when the mood takes you, the experience is wonderful. You should try it someday!"

"Maybe, someday. But, at the moment, the experience I have had is still too raw."

Using my hands to shield my eyes from the light and glow from the torches, I looked around the forest edge. There was only the cold forest and the group of horses out there moving around. The moon was now fully up. It was a recent moon – only eight or nine days old and getting larger every night. I scanned the rest of the tree line, and could see no other heat sources than those cooling bodies. Penny began to reload the crossbows; it took all of her strength to pull the string back and reset the lever. "Penny, go and get some sleep, I will watch for the rest of the night. You go and bed down for the night."

She yawned and nodded, "I'll help Desi out, and put them all to bed. Do you think…?"

"Yes, put him in a cell for the night. That should keep us all safe."

"Okay, wake me when it is time for me to watch."

"Look after yourself. Have a good sleep."

"Stay awake!"

"Yes, 'mother'."

Once she had gone, I went around all of the torches and doused them. I closed all of the shutters of the lanterns to remove all of the light. The only light was now coming from the cellars. I climbed up to the highest point of the ruins and sat on the rubble. I surveyed the scene, the forest was quiet and there were small animals moving around in the undergrowth. The moon steadily made its way up through the sky. The breeze was cooling and I held my robes tightly around me. I felt so secure in this position. It's funny that, even though this is the most exposed place in the ruins, it now seemed the safest place. There was a full field of vision, with no obstructions; nothing could sneak up on me without being seen. I scanned the forests time and again. Owls hooted, birds chirped and bats screeched. If anyone ever tells you that the countryside is a quiet peaceful place, they are wrong! Death and mayhem constantly disturb the peace. It was times like this that I rememorize all of those vital spells in my head. I let the memories run down their familiar channels, and the strange images associated with the words and the cryptic messages held within them coursed through my mind.

The dawn chorus sounded marvellous to me. A new day was dawning! It was a fresh day that would herald the return of my Temple's holy book. The holy message this contained would help us for centuries to come, assisting with the development of the Temple and our religion….

Septumdecim – Fallux divinia

The hilt of the dagger was now firm in my hand - the intention to generate spells still lingered there in my mind. I sought out the energy that would drive my spells and I found that it was returning to me - weaker than before, but there nonetheless. I concentrated on summoning up the spells I wanted. As I did so, the feeling of the energy coursing through my mind was blissful. I channelled the energy to awaken two 'Command' spells, one 'Cause Darkness' and a couple of 'Heal' spell, just in case…

Tamzin must still be in the room. I opened my eyes to see that she was reading, or at least trying to read the Furacissime de Iniussus' I called out to her, "Careful of that book, it has a trap!"

"Yes! One of our tekkies died opening it." She said, looking up at me, "Luckily, we recorded the incident and the mechanism was removed. The book seems to be in code and we are trying to decipher it. Is it important?"

"You really have no idea how important that is?"

"No." Slowly she closed the book and I noticed that the blade didn't flick across the edge as it closed. She continued, "So, Merith, show me a spell, go on, I am waiting!"

The grin that spread across my face must have unnerved her, "Do you really want to see some majick?"

She began to look nervous and I mumbled the 'Cause darkness' spell. Everything went pitch black, "Don't worry," she said, "It will be a power cut. You are safe; the generators will kick in soon."

I visualised changing into a mouse, twitchy nose, short feet with small pads and sharp claws. I imagined the short sleek fur covering a small plump body. A smaller stumpy tail than a rat and the small ears set over the face. The familiar ripping noise accompanied the change, Tamzin asked, "What was that noise?"

As quickly as I changed into a mouse I changed back to myself. "That was me coming to get you." I stood up and walked over to Tamzin, whom I could see clearly due to her heat signature. She looked scared; the heat trailing off her face showed fear. I moved behind her, silently on bare feet and loudly said, "Light," whilst simultaneously releasing the Darkness spell.

She stared ahead, "What the…?"

She shuddered as I leaned over her to place the dagger on the desk, "I am a priestess of Ichmarr and am fully vested in the rites and practices. I have met Ichmarr and bear the gift of Ichmarr. Do not underestimate me." I sat down on the vacant seat beside her.

She looked at me, disbelieving what I said; "What do you mean, 'you have met Ichmarr'? We pray to her, but none of us have met her. She is the unseen one that is helping us in every deed or act."

"None of you have ever met her?"

"No."

The notion of this was ridiculous, "Then how can you call yourselves priestesses of Ichmarr, if you haven't passed within?"

"Passed within…what? Look, we can make Magic! This isn't some false god we worship!"

"Yes, I know this as I have met her - all real priestesses have! You have a lot to learn about Ichmarr."

The door flew open and two men in green and brown clothing came rushing in. They waved black metal tubes at me and shouted, "Get down on the floor!"

I blacked out and the world changed….

With the dawn came the need for us to return to my Temple. I went down to the cellars to wake Desi and Penny. They had spent the night huddled together. Unconsciously, Penny's hand lay on Desi's breast. I chuckled at this, then moved it to maintain decency. As I lifted the hand, she became rigid and opened her eyes.

"Oh, it's just you, Merith. I thought…."

I knew the ending to that sentence, and decided not to finish it. "Penny, we have a job to complete."

Desi awoke, with a loud yawn and a stretch. She blinked a few times and said, "What's happening girls? I thought we might have a bit of a lazy sleep in, now that we are going to be rich and famous."

We both looked at her as if she had gone mad. I said to her, "Desi, have you been dreaming again? Have you been listening to the little bard you have in your own head?"

"Nooo! I just think that we can have a bit of fun with all of the silver we have!"

"First, we will have to get it back to Walden," I pointed out.

"Well, shall we hire some other men in the nearest village to help us out?"

"The fewer complications, the better. Eh, Penny?"

Penny looked at me and agreed, by saying, "The fewer people involved the better. But we would look more of an attractive target if we had armed guards. Better to look like we are relatively poor merchants, hoping for a decent cargo. Merith, what did you mean, 'we have a job to complete'?"

"There are hundreds of books in there and I have selected quite a few to take out. We need to grab as many as we can, before we go. Anyway, they would look better as a cargo, wouldn't they?"

"Well, yes, I suppose they would. But, Merith, why don't we just get back to Walden and return with others later to do this?"

"We are here now, so why don't we just grab a few of the important ones?"

"Okay, let's go before I change my mind!"

I looked at Desi and wiped her hair out of her face. She smiled back at me, and I said, "Desi will you be okay to rustle up some breakfast for all of us?"

She smiled and said, "As long as you are not asking me to go into that hole, I will do anything!"

"If you can trust him, Stuart should be able to help you out. Shall I get him out of his cell for you?"

"No, no, Merith. I should be able to handle him - after all, he is only a boy."

She stood up and smoothed down her clothes. Penny picked up her frame pack that she had left the previous night. Desi put her hand on her shoulder and said, "Come back soon." She gave me a wink as she left the room.

Once she had left, Penny looked up from her pack and said, "God, you are a bit of a mother hen!"

"What do you mean?"

"You were fussing over Desidra. I didn't take you as a worrier. I thought that you would only care about yourself, your mission and that was it."

Carefully, I started to unpack all of the books from my frame pack. I left them to the side, to give good clear access through the walkway. "We are friends now, I was just checking to see if she was okay. I would do the same if it was you."

"Yes, I know. You'd worry about both of us."

"Penny, I am not used to working with others. I have found that, every time I had to rely on someone else, I had to be carrying them. I had to check on everything and take all of the important equipment, just in case. I suppose I'm still doing that." I felt uncomfortable about this situation. I put on my frame pack and started going towards the maze.

"Well, I'm sure the girl can look after herself. She does seem to be very capable; a bit too house-wifey and a bit of a soft touch! Apart from that, she's okay." Penny was now struggling awkwardly to put on the pack in the low light.

"You wouldn't say that, if you'd met her like I had. The first time she saw me, she tried to kill me! She was also very scary on the trip to this place; she attacked me several times with a dagger"

"REALLY! I'm sure she had her reasons. Perhaps she didn't like you stealing her purse?" She said it with a smile, and I could tell she was joking. While I was a bit offended by this, I didn't show it.

"No, nothing like that," I responded. "She didn't like my race; her brother and family had been killed by Silves, but they had provoked them. She had a hatred for all Silves and everything to do with Silves. I don't really think I've changed that for her, but I do know that she accepts me."

"So, how do you feel about humans?"

"I dunno. How do you feel about them? Silly question isn't it? It's like asking a fish how it feels about deserts; it's never been in one, so how does it know what it's like! I like and love many humans. I don't see that there is any difference between us. You live a shorter life, but you have more children. We are taller and slimmer, but you are stronger and have greater stamina. You work in teams to succeed, we fail in isolation. We are a dying race; there are fewer of us around. I have seen some of the persecution of my kind. I have been told that we were the first race, yet we have never made an impact on history. We have stayed in the forests, using what we had around us. There is nothing that will mark our passing, except a few books written in a runic language and a few pieces of art no-one understands."

"I think that Silves are beautiful! You are beautiful, Merith."

"Yeah, right. What you see is not necessarily what is there. I see in the mirror someone who is plain and quite different to everyone else. I see a skinny, gaunt, odd-looking, young girl with no tits, and even less brains. My ears are oddly shaped, almost pointed at the top. They would have been much worse if my adopted dad hadn't tried cut them flat when I was a child, to stop the neighbours from looking at me. In the morning, I have to fight with my hair to do something with it and, when I have a bad hair day, watch out! On this trip, I have felt out of place, making mistakes and being laughed at. You see an almost majickal beauty which is, I assure you, artificial."

"That is so sad; you have such a low impression of yourself. I know I'm not a pretty sight, but the first person people would notice in a room would be you. They might notice Desidra, who is with you, but they wouldn't notice me unless I was dripping in gold and jewels."

"Look, we are wasting time. Let's go." The conversation had hit a few raw nerves - and a few, bad, inner-feelings about myself that I didn't want to share with others. I led the way back to the maze and at the entrance I took her arm as we entered the darkness.

I led her back through the maze to the library. The maze was as we had left it. I suppose that I am very paranoid in my nature and, every time I go into anything, I will always check every step and every corner for suspicious differences. We arrived at the door to the library. It felt odd. I couldn't say why, but it was different - it was a feeling that I sometimes get. Normally, I listen to my senses as they have helped me to avoid difficult situations. But, this time, I felt it wasn't that serious.

I stood on the desk and triggered the door to open. It swung open like it had always done. Everything looked quite normal, and I didn't understand why I felt this way. We entered the library, I took my dagger out as the door closed and told Penny to look away and close her eyes. When the door closed, and the darkness spell was cancelled, I immediately noticed there was a blue light coming from down the passageway. I carefully made my way down the stairs, with Penny following me. At the bottom I could see that the stone door to the secret passageway was open and the blue light was shining through the doorway, lighting the library in an eerie light.

"What's that?" Penny asked. "It wasn't like that when we left it fifteen minutes ago."

"I know. Do you think it could have done it by itself?"

"Dunno. What do you think? Should we investigate?"

"Penny, I don't like this. It feels wrong, it feels bad." I felt the hair rising at the back of my neck. The instinct was rising in me to run away, to leave this place and never come back. I began to feel the influence of a majickal charge in my nose; it had to be big, and was rising in intensity. The air was beginning to taste metallic as I breathed in, which was a sure sign of the heavy charge in the air. I looked at Penny, her eyes were very wide, almost hysterical, and her skin had paled so much that she was white as a sheet. She was breathing so quickly, her hand closest to me was twitching, and I could see her whole body shaking.

Reaching out to take her hand, I felt a searing pain in my finger. A blue light arced across from her hand to my finger; it was like a tiny bolt of lightning, stabbing across the gap between our two hands. I made a determined effort to grab her hand, and the pain from the flashes of tiny lightning lanced across my fingers - it was like being stabbed by a thousand nettles. As I grasped her arm, she gasped and looked me square in the eye. She said, "Let go of me child." The voice was unlike any that I had heard before or since; it was certainly not Penny's. It was a masculine voice, gravely and harsh; it had the tone of ages and the weight of a tombstone.

She turned to face me. She grabbed me around the waist in a crushing handhold, picked me up and threw me against the wall. The strength of this was supernatural and I hit the wall with such force, my breath was knocked out of me. I sat dazed, taking in the scene. It was quite surreal; the library was bathed in intense blue light, with the walls and ceiling appearing like the sky on a cloudless day. Penny's face had the appearance of a wrinkled man, grey, spotted and strained. Her own face was still there, but experiencing terrible pain.

She started to move to the door of the laboratory, with stuttered steps - like her body was being controlled by another, who didn't quite have overall control. I thought, if I was able to close the door, perhaps the connection with Penny would be broken - a link that clearly came from Borrador through the blue light. It was, after all, his maze and library and his laboratory that housed this blue light source. He was the one trying to be like god in many respects. I charged towards the door and found that it was propped open by a small bone. It bore the bite marks of a small rodent and looked as if it had been recently gnawed at. I kicked it away and forced the door shut, trapping myself in the room. The door closed with a click, there was a thump on it from the outside, and then silence.

Everything went silent. Even my own body strangely was silent.

The walls had taken on a blue tone, and slowly the shade became darker and even darker blue.

I began to feel a coldness in the air. I couldn't say how it was happening, but it was definitely colder.

The air began to rush past me and through me. The blue became icy and cold, like I had fallen into an icy pond which froze over as I entered. The blue became darker and darker as I fell deeper and deeper into it, until it turned completely black with nothing around me. Void....

The darkness retreated and I focussed my mind on the features. The shape of the room in which I had originally met Ichmarr formed around me and, gradually, all of the details were filled in - books, trinkets, paintings and the dark oak panelling on the walls. Sitting at the desk was my mother, or at least Ichmarr in the likeness of my mother. I stood statuesque, as she stood up gracefully and walked around the desk.

She took my hand and blew warmth into me through it, and, as my body warmed and movement became possible for me, she said to me; "Merith I have a special task for you. Unfortunately, I cannot ask you to do this, I must require it of you. You are the only one who can do this; no other of your kind has gone through what you have and survived the transition. No human can do this task, as no human would be able to live as long as you will. You are unique of your kind - you are a Silves who has been brought up within the human world, your parents abandoning you at such an early age. You will be the last of your kind as they will die out, unable to adapt to the world the humans create. I know that you feel different from them, however you also care about many of them. This gives you a bond that will keep you steady in the future. Many things will have changed in the hundreds of years that will pass, and many things may be strange to you, but I know you will adapt and survive it all."

She continued, "I have tied your life force to a tree in the future; it has not grown yet and until it starts, you have to wait. I will hold you safe until the time is right to start. Merith, you are special. I see a time in the future where your peculiar talents will be necessary and your training essential. You have gathered all of the materials together, to reseed my followers from those who remain. You are the deliverer of my thoughts, the revitaliser of all of the hopes and dreams. You are the little acorn I will plant to create a better place for others to exist. I entrust in you my wisdom and my powers to use and unlock when you see fit. Use them wisely! You will be the prophet that will guide my priestesses back to a path that they have lost. Many years will pass before they sway from the entrusted line and, for many years, they will forget the necessary precepts. Only you will have my gift, my word and my will! You will develop a strong future for me and all that follow on for me. I bind you to this task and know you will do well as you believe in me. Do well, my child….."

The brilliant blue faded, until the room was lit by a single continual light spell. The majick of the future did seem strong to me, but now I also had access to all of the majick of the past. There were four men standing around me and pointing their weapons at me. I looked at them all and said to them, "Sleep." They collapsed into heaps around me, and I turned to face Miranda and Tamzin. Tamzin looked shocked to see me do this and looked about to speak.

Abruptly halting her speech, I stood up and said, simply, "I am Merith. You saw me as I arrived, as a young girl who knew nothing. I am now here and I will change the future."

"The past, present and future is written in that book." I pointed to the 'Furacissime de Iniussus.' "It is the written word of Ichmarr and I will teach you all how to translate the text and use it. I will guide you all along the path that Ichmarr herself has shown me. She has commanded me to revitalise her ailing followers, to bring them back to her and mutually benefit all who stand with us."

To the woman who came from M.I.5 I said, "I called you Miranda mistakenly, as I believed you were a priestess from Cantebrigia, long ago. I see that I was mistaken. I thank you for your stewardship of my Temple. We will need to work together for you fully to realise what we are able to do."

She looked at me sternly, asking, "So what do you offer her majesty's government?"

I smiled back, "Our loyalty, such as it is, but also a multitude of techniques and powers beyond your understanding. I also bring with me the blessings of Ichmarr."

"This is the false god that you people speak of," she said, with all of the arrogance and haughty nature of a believer in another god.

"I do not believe in a false god! I know she exists, like I know the sun will rise and a fool will soon be parted with his money. It is a fact, like the fact that your god exists. I know this, as Ichmarr has spoken of him."

She snorted, "Only the young could believe any of this nonsense! Tamzin, this is your call - what shall we do now?"

Tamzin shrugged her shoulders, advising; "I think we will give her a chance. She obviously knows some extra tricks that we might find useful on necessary missions."

"Okay, Merith, we shall see what you can do. I will be watching you closely from now on." She looked at Tamzin; "Take her to the basic training camp and put her through her paces. She is still a bit young to be used for anything yet."

"Will do! Come on, Merith. Let's go to meet the girls at the training camp." I could see her picking up the book and my dagger, as she said this. She linked arms with me and, as she guided me out of the door. As we walked down the corridor, Tamzin said to me, "Christ girl! You've got some balls standing up to her like that!" She passed my dagger to me hilt first.

"No! I am Ichmarr's girl!" I said back to her, whilst taking the dagger. "Anyway, she wasn't half as scary as Cat - now, she could frighten the life out of anyone!"

She led the way down a series of creamy white walled corridors, whose walls were bare - except for a door every three yards or so on both sides. Occasionally, there would be an open door showing a square room lined with books set around a single desk. The desks were all piled with paper and each had the same funny white stone shape with a glass front. They were lit, majically, with a moving pattern. I began to think these people must just waste so much majick.

We arrived at a different sort of door which had a metal box beside it attached to the wall. She mumbled something like, "Security, I would scan and scramble, but they actually gave me a card!" Tamzin pulled out a square-shaped piece of material, and slid it down a groove in the metal block. I felt the pressure change slightly and the door trilled at us. The noise was like that of birds, just like at the healers but deeper in tone. This was followed by the sound of metal scraping against metal, and the door opened ajar.

Tamzin opened the door further to reveal a darker corridor of stairs, which led downward. The sides of the corridor were of grey stone, the blocks of which must have been assembled by a real crafts-man, as there weren't any discernable cracks or joins. It was almost like as if it had been tunnelled out of the rock itself. I could feel that the air was cooler down here. I jumped when I heard a loud echoing, squealing noise coming from further down. Tamzin must have felt me flinch, because she stopped and turned to face me enquiring, "Are you okay? You look so frightened!"

"What was that noise?

"It was only the noise of the tyres, as a car turned a corner. Haven't you heard that before?"

"No, Tamzin. What's a tyre?"

"Oh, right! You really don't know? Well, it is a type of wheel - like a cart wheel, but made out of rubber. You do know what rubber is, don't you?"

"Yes. Look, Tamzin, I have a lot to learn about at present - just as much, if not more, than I will teach you. I think perhaps we will have to be patient with each other and work together?"

"We shall see! At the moment you are my problem, but when I take you to our training Temple the decision about what to do will be decided by the Temple masters. They may not take so kindly to being told they are not real Priestesses!"

"Where are the rest of my possessions?"

"They are being examined and will be returned to you in due course."

"I need them now!"

"At the moment, Merith, you are hardly in a position to make demands. Yes, I see that what you have to offer could benefit us all. However, we have to trust each other; a little from you and a little from us. I have already shown some trust in you, by returning your holy dagger. Now, show me that you trust me!"

"Alright. Lead on, Tamzy!"

She took the lead once more, and led me down the stairs into a large cave which was filled with the horseless carriages, or 'cars' as Matt had called them. She then rummaged around in her pocket and took out a strange looking key. She pointed it at one of the 'cars', a low red vehicle which looked too small to sit in. I heard a trilling and then metal bolts sliding home. She smiled at me, and said, "Don't you just love the wonders of modern technology."

"Tek-now-logie? What is that, Tamzin? Is it like Majick?"

"No. But I suppose, in some way, yes, it is like the majick you know. Technology is the use of clever ideas and devices to make things work better. For most people nowadays, majick doesn't exist except in made-up books; we know better, but we don't advertise the fact." As she was speaking, she lifted a wide portion of the side of the vehicle up and outwards to reveal a creamy, leather interior. I could see two deep seats; one had a small half-wheel in front of it, while the other featured just a small wooden bar. She indicated for me to go round to the other side, and said, "Jump in, girl."

I walked around to the other side, looking at the vehicle more intently. It had large black rims set onto metal wheels and, at the front it, there were deep round inserts with glass at the back of them. There was a code on a plate at the front, which looked like 55JB 007. I peered at the side of the vehicle, but I couldn't see how to get the door to open and nor could I see into it, as the glass was so dark it obscured the view. The door panel window opened to reveal Tamzin, looking flushed, as she leaned over it from the inside, "Look there! Small red button, press it and the door opens up automatically." She pointed to the back of the door where there was indeed a small red bit sticking out. I pressed it and the door swung open.

I clumsily struggled into the seat, Tamzin helping me to sort out the complicated belts and getting the door closed. Finally, I was in the seat properly! I wondered, 'Why on earth we had to be belted in?' I was just about to ask this of Tamzin, when she pressed a button beside the wheel and my thoughts were shattered by a terrifying noise from behind me. It sounded like a massive beehive that had just been kicked over.

"Sounds a dream, doesn't it!" She shouted over the noise. "This is the latest from Italian styling and German engineering and, boy, does it go fast!"

I knew I was going to regret my next question, but I just had to ask; "How fast?"

"Wait and see!"

As we launched forward, I was glad of the belts holding us in place. The noise was terrifying, but the sight of everything hurtling so quickly towards us was worse! Tamzin barely seemed to be in control of this thing as we screeched, roared and thundered around the maze of grey walls and lines of cars until, eventually, she launched the car into the blazing sunlight. I was temporarily blinded, but a few moments of blinking soon cleared my sight. Tamzin had stopped behind a stationary car and started to fiddle with a box on the dashboard. Suddenly it said, "Right turn, you must go!" in a funny croaky voice. She turned to me and smiled, "I got this voice from a download patch. It's Yoda, from Star Wars!"

"Really, Tamzy! What does that all mean?"

She looked a bit crestfallen, but picked up almost immediately; "There is a lot you will find strange, Merith. Trust me on this one. You will have to open your mind to a lot of new experiences!"

Historical notes from Saffron Walden

Walden has a history dating back to the Mesolithic period, with excavations revealing artefacts from this time. It has evidence of a 'barrow' in Grimsditch wood, as well as a hill fort - the ring hill camp that is thought to be iron-age. It was also a site of Roman occupation and, later, Saxon settlements around Abbey Lane. The town was mentioned in the Doomsday book as Waledana - a town of 122 households and one watermill.

The town title was granted to Geoffrey de Mandeville after the Battle of Hastings in 1066. His grandson later built the castle, still standing at the top of the common, which was finished in 1141. Also around this date, the market was moved from Newport to Walden. The town's centre was settled at this point with the Castle Street, Church Street and Myddleton Place being the network of roads fixed at this time.

At or around the period from the 1230's to 1300, Humphrey de Bohun (who has inherited the town's title) began the building of the Magnum Fossatum - the battle ditches which defined the town for many years. These set the boundaries for future development of the town and the road layout within it.

The real Guild of Our Lady of Pity was an organisation set up in 1400 to provide an almshouse for the succour and sustenance of thirteen of the poor, blind, crooked bedridden and most at need. The guild house was set up by the local church for the good of the area, with a priest in charge of the house and an assistant priest to help in the running. This was established in Park Lane and was used by the author as the setting of the Temple of Ichmarr, "Our Lady of Pity"

Saffron Walden was originally Waledana, as already stated, but this changed over time to Walden. The name Chipping Walden was due to the Market (Chepying) that was moved to Walden - Chipping being the term used for a market. Saffron became a suffix for the town, at or around the late 1500's, before the setting of this book. This was due to it becoming the English centre of cultivation of the saffron crocus, which was used as a dyestuff in the woollen trade and also as a medicine. The cultivation of the crocus and the utilization of saffron developed into big business at this time.

Robert Turner

Printed in the United Kingdom
by Lightning Source UK Ltd.
109989UKS00001B/82-132